GI400984808

LIVING *the* LEGACY

LIVING
the LEGACY

Elisabeth Conway

atmosphere press

© 2024 Elisabeth Conway

Published by Atmosphere Press

Cover design by Ronaldo Alves

No part of this book may be reproduced without permission from the author except in brief quotations and in reviews.

This is a work of fiction. References to real people, events, establishments, organisations, or locales are intended only to provide a sense of authenticity and are used fictitiously. All other characters, and all incidents and dialogue, are drawn from the author's imagination and are not to be construed as real.

Atmospherepress.com

For everyone who lives in or loves
SINGAPORE

Inheritors of the Legacy

LIST OF CHARACTERS

MAIN CHARACTERS

- PIETER STEFFENS Alias: John Sulivan [in Calcutta), Kasim [Anglo-Indian guise in Singapore and Malacca], Stefan [European guise in Singapore]

- DICK – adopted son of Stamford Raffles, artist. Married to SUJANA and father of TOMAS.

- WING YEE – Chinese herbalist and responsible for the new medical clinic.

- VICTOR – Eurasian entrepreneur who enters a business relationship with KASIM/STEFAN.

- EDMUND BEAUMONT – English botanist. Married to CHIN MING and father of CHARLOTTE and WILLIAM.

- CHIN MING – Chinese woman married to EDMUND; mother of CHARLOTTE and WILLIAM. Daughter of LI SOONG HENG

- CHARLOTTE BEAUMONT – daughter of Edmund and Chin Ming.

- ALEXANDER JOHNSTON* – Scottish merchant who arrived in Singapore in 1819. Senior magistrate.

SUPPORTING CAST

- BABA TAN – Peranakan merchant married to Yan Lau and business partner of Wing Yee.

- MADAM HO – Madam, in charge of the most reputable brothel in Singapore.

- PRISONER 710/SANJAY – Gardener employed by Edmund Beaumont.

- TIJAH – A mixed-race girl who comes to Singapore from Malacca.

- MAY LIN– Amah employed by Chin Ming and Edmund Beaumont

- CHOO KENG – Chinese hawker who runs a coffee stall at Boat Quay.

- MUKESH – Indian moneylender, in charge of the desks in Market Street.

- MELATI – One of the Sumatran young women smuggled into Singapore by Victor and Stefan.

- DOUGLAS FERGUSSON – British merchant residing in Calcutta.

- GEORGE COLEMAN* – Irish architect, who built most of the 'colonial' buildings in Singapore.

- ABDULLAH* – Munshi Abdullah, a Malay scholar who wrote a comprehensive eyewitness account of early 19th-century Singapore. [*Hikayat Abdullah*]

- DARMA – Groom employed by Dick and Sujana.

- KIM SENG – Cook employed by Chin Ming and Edmund.

- KENNETH MURCHISON* – Representative of the East India Company, based in Penang.

- FAKINA - Amah employed by Dick and Sujana.

- CHANDA KHAN – Successful Indian merchant who is familiar with the Chetty moneylenders.

- LI SOONG HENG – Chin Ming's father, who returns to Singapore from a visit to his friend Father John [a missionary based in Calcutta]

OTHERS MENTIONED

- STAMFORD RAFFLES*– founder of modern Singapore, who returned to England in 1824 and died at his house in Hendon on 5th July 1826.

- JOHN CRAWFURD* – Scottish physician, and second Resident of Singapore [1823 – 1826].

- WILLIAM FARQUHAR* – First Resident of Singapore, appointed by Raffles in 1819.

- JENAB – Married to Pieter Steffens in Malacca in 1818 and mother of Tijah.

- BOON PENG – Chinese towkay, former business partner of Pieter Steffens

- SMITH – a gangmaster.

NB: An asterisk beside any of the names listed above denotes a real historical figure. What happens to them in this novel is mainly within the author's imagination and not based entirely on fact.

CHAPTER 1
Calcutta, early July, 1830

Pieter Steffens needed a new identity; he wouldn't make the same mistake this time. To achieve his goal, he needed money and a ship that would take him across the Bay of Bengal.

Click. The lock turned easily. The door creaked open and he felt a hand in the small of his back pushing him out into the noonday glare. He felt like an actor, temporarily blinded by the spotlight on an empty stage, exposed in the unpretentious garments issued by the prison. He looked around, but no one was watching. He was all alone on a busy street. He strode away from the gates of the jail determined to implement his plan; to seek revenge for the last seven years. He didn't have long to wait.

Heavily-laden carts jostled against each other along the main highway. It was already hot, and patience was in short supply. Two small carts collided, spilling their loads across the entire road. Cabbages bounced on top of one another, rice poured out of hessian sacks, and bruised mangoes began to turn black. Everything was trampled on as other vehicles tried to navigate their way around the blockage. A cacophony of sounds competed with one another, but nothing was able to move.

Steffens watched with interest for a while, then noxious fumes from overripe vegetables and fly-blown meat began to offend his nostrils. The stink reminded him of the hours spent cleaning prison latrines. He needed to get away. He covered his mouth as his stomach began to heave and he pushed his way through the crowd, knocking into a middle-aged gentleman descending from his carriage. The man lost his balance and fell straight into the gutter. Steffens' instinct was to run; he didn't want any trouble. For a split second, his world came to a halt.

The man in the gutter held up his arm and reluctantly Steffens took it in his hands. The man was European and slightly overweight. His gold fob watch and well-cut garments signified wealth.

'Are you able to stand?' Steffens asked. He checked for broken bones, adjusted his grip, then pulled the stranger into an upright position. He made his excuses for being clumsy as he helped to knock the dust out of the gentleman's coat, straighten his lopsided cravat, and went in search of the bag the man said he'd been carrying.

The two men eyed each other. Steffens wondered what the stranger was thinking. He made his excuses to leave.

'Douglas Fergusson esquire,' the man said. Then, he pursed his lips and Steffens suspected the stranger regretted the hasty introduction. He was already pulling his coat over his chest to conceal the gold watch. This man was well-heeled, a person of influence, maybe he was wondering if the accident had been deliberate.

Steffens took a deep breath; possibly his luck was changing. Just then, he noticed an expensive-looking portmanteau wedged behind the wheel of a cart. He extracted it and handed it to Fergusson.

'Is this, perhaps, the bag you dropped?'

Fergusson seized it, just a moment too quickly. Steffens pretended not to notice but it confirmed his supposition; this man was worth getting to know better.

'I would like to show my appreciation,' Fergusson said. 'How can I reward you?'

Steffens wondered what sort of reward might be on offer. Then he noticed a hint of self-satisfaction in the stranger's eyes, the merest whisper of a smile crossing his lips. Was he merely feigning gratitude to find out something about his rescuer? Steffens' curiosity outweighed his need to get to the docks. He let himself be persuaded to join Fergusson at his club for tiffin.

*****

They climbed into Fergusson's carriage a plush, well-upholstered affair with springs strong enough to cushion any discomfort as they trundled over well-worn tracks in the road. The luxury of the brougham was in direct contrast to Steffens' shabby appearance. It seemed impossible that only an hour ago the prison gates had closed behind him and already he was experiencing the comfort to which he believed he was entitled. When he'd arrived here seven years ago as a criminal, he'd been forced to walk from the harbour to the place of his incarceration. He'd kept his head down and his eyes away from the people and places who would remain on the outside, living their ordinary lives.

Now, he sat up straight in the brougham and cast his eyes around. The names of various merchants appeared on hoardings as they progressed along the street. They were commonplace enough, but to him they represented success, achievement, people who had triumphed. His failures since fleeing the comfort of his family in Java all those years ago tormented him. Now it was time to offset his past mistakes, but in his own mind, there was only one way to ensure success. He must destroy Stamford Raffles.

Maybe he should not have let the temptation of a decent meal lure him away from his goal. He'd spent nearly all his time in prison plotting and scheming about returning to Singapore but he'd always envisaged going there alone and he hadn't given sufficient thought to the story he would tell to anyone he encountered along the way. Fergusson was bound to ask questions. When asked, what name would he use? None of those he'd assumed in the past would do. Whatever name he chose right now would impact upon the person he became when he reached Singapore; he mustn't let that choice jeopardise his plans.

He looked up from his musings to find Fergusson staring straight at him; his head was tilted to one side with his eyebrows raised. The hairs on the back of Steffens' head stood to attention. He guessed a question had been asked of him and Fergusson was awaiting a reply.

'Sorry,' Steffens said. 'I was daydreaming, could you repeat that?'

'I merely said that I hadn't caught your name, sir. I believe your concern for my welfare was so great that we omitted the usual introductions.'

Steffens took a quick glance at Fergusson and then hastily looked away again.

Fergusson was waiting for him to respond, but something about his host's posture alerted Steffens to be cautious. He began to suspect Fergusson was not the benevolent old man he'd first thought him to be.

Steffens cleared his throat. His mind raced, then out of nowhere he heard himself saying, 'Sulivan, John Sulivan.' The name had come to him from a distant memory – a conversation he'd had with a prison inmate.

'Are you related to the Sulivans of Sulivan and De Souza in Madras?'

Steffens cursed himself; he should have taken more time, considered why the name was familiar. Of course, all these merchants knew of one another. 'A cousin,' he said, daring the man sitting opposite to contradict him; 'the black sheep of the family - married locally and was disowned.' He covered his

4

mouth, pressing his lips together to hide a smile. 'Yes, definitely a black sheep,' he said.

'That would account for your swarthy complexion then,' Fergusson said as the brougham drew up outside the Calcutta Club.

Steffens leapt down from the carriage. Facing him was a flight of six stone steps leading to a canopied doorway. A tall Indian, dressed in the uniform of a soldier, was poised ready to fling open the doors for each of the guests and to greet them in the expected manner. Steffens' initial discomfort about his attire surfaced again. 'I feel I'm not appropriately dressed,' he said.

'I admit that I've been wondering about your attire,' Fergusson said with a smile that was hardly visible. 'I assume that you've only lately arrived from Madras? The road was no doubt dusty and opportunities to refresh yourself in short supply. Do not worry, my friend, we get many visitors here who have had similar experiences.'

Steffens stared at the older man. He looked genuine enough, and surely it was worth humouring such an insistent host. A decent meal, a few anecdotes, and if nothing further transpired, he would then be on his way. The moment he made that decision, he let go of all his former lives; from now on, like it or not, he would behave as John Sulivan.

*****

The dining room was filled with men - mainly European – enjoying the delights of the Club's cuisine. The distinctive aromas of cumin, cinnamon, cloves, and other spices filled his nostrils. Shortly after being seated, a platter of mutton kurmah was placed before them. It was followed by other serving dishes containing dhall, brinjal, a strange-looking fish; then came a basket of roti, various sambals, and tomato chutney.

Steffens tried to hide his hunger, taking only a little of each dish that was offered to him by the Indian servant, but once he started to eat, it was difficult to conceal his delight in tasting anything other than the slops he'd become accustomed to in prison.

'Anyone would think you haven't eaten for a week, my boy,' Fergusson said.

Steffens' first reaction was to remonstrate. How dare this man use such a derogatory term to address him? He was a grown man approaching forty, and whether or not he looked smart enough for this place, he was no one's servant. He held his spoon and fork in midair and slowly moved the food in his mouth around before swallowing. He decided it was not in his best interest to challenge his host right now. Instead, he grinned at Douglas Fergusson. 'It is exceedingly good,' he said.

His discomfort grew as he became aware that he was being studied. His dusty clothes could be accounted for, but he began to wonder what the man sitting opposite was really thinking; had he unconsciously given anything away? Was Fergusson already suspicious? What further questions might his host pose, and what answers was he prepared to give? However, he need not have worried. It became obvious that Fergusson liked the sound of his own voice, and during their meal, he entertained his guest with countless stories about life in Calcutta. Steffens nodded every so often and laughed when a response to an amusing anecdote was called for. Nevertheless, he remained alert, all the while feeling he was being tested.

'One of the benefits of success, Mr Sulivan,' Fergusson said, 'is that it enables me to help those less fortunate; someone who has perhaps suffered in some way or another.' His steely-blue eyes stared directly into Steffens' soft, brown gaze, inviting a response. None came. The battle of wills had begun.

'My company has been trading in these parts for three generations and, unlike some of the other agency houses, we continue to go from strength to strength.'

Fergusson prattled on about various trading companies in

Calcutta before focusing on the woes that had befallen a certain John Palmer whose company had recently been declared bankrupt. Steffens was in the act of stifling a yawn when Fergusson mentioned the one name he couldn't ignore; Stamford Raffles. Apparently, Palmer had supported Raffles' plan to establish an educational institution in Singapore. This was of little interest to Steffens; his mind began to drift. As was often the case, he allowed himself to be distracted by loathing and animosity.

' ... after he left Singapore,' Fergusson said. 'Mr Sulivan, am I boring you? Perhaps you are tired after your journey?'

Steffens stared at Fergusson, forgetting he was supposed to answer to his new name.

Fergusson repeated the last piece of information before adding, 'And then, of course, he died less than two years after he returned to England!'

Steffens sat bolt upright. 'What did you say? Raffles isn't in Singapore?

'That's right, Mr. SULIVAN. He went back to Bencoolen before returning to England, but as I said, he died during the summer of twenty-six. News reached here just before Christmas that year I seem to remember. I'm surprised you didn't hear about it yourself.'

'Dead?' Steffens almost whispered. The colour drained from his face. Why hadn't such news spread as far as the prison rumour machine? His plan to return to Singapore to seek revenge for what Raffles had done to him was now thwarted. What was he going to do?

He glanced at Fergusson and cursed himself for making his shock at this news so obvious; his host was bound to wonder why his reaction was so extreme.

'Come and see me at this address in the morning,' was all that Fergusson said. He handed Steffens a piece of paper, making it clear that today's encounter was now over.

Steffens watched Fergusson hurry away from the room. He wasn't sure what to do or where to go. The news of Raffles' death was too much to take in. He rose from the table and somehow found his way to the exit; the uniformed doorman nodded politely as he passed by. The street was almost empty now, most of the populace avoiding the late afternoon humidity. Steffens turned first one way and then the other. He had no idea which direction to take, his mind wouldn't focus. A boy with a cane hoop almost crashed into him and he spun around once more, but he was glad when the boy was able to point him towards the docks. He remained light-headed as he slowly lurched towards one of the oldest ports in India. As his head cleared, he began to ask himself, should he stay to see what Fergusson had to say in the morning or should he cut and run? When he eventually did arrive at the docks, it was only to learn that no ships were due to leave for Singapore for a day or two.

A couple of sailors, already the worse for wear, invited him to join them. He backed away at first, not wanting to squander what little money he had been given by the prison authorities. The two men produced more alcohol; it was fiery and burnt his throat. Sometime later, his companions mysteriously disappeared, and he found himself alone inside one of the many gambling dens along the quay. He hadn't played any form of card game for years and he was not likely to win enough to purchase a passage any further than the mouth of the Hooghly River. He scooped up a flagon of ale as he pushed his way back out onto the quay. He took a deep breath and stretched his arms out wide. A piece of paper fell out of his pocket. He made his way towards one of the oil lamps along the harbour wall and recognised it as the note Fergusson had handed to him earlier. The address had been scribbled in a hurry, but he recognised the location. He decided to go along in the morning; he might as well find out what Fergusson had to say. Finally, the comfort of alcohol, which he had been denied for a long time, provided some solace, enabling him to fall asleep on a hard wooden bench further along the quay.

*****

Steffens arrived at the address at the appointed hour. He looked even more dishevelled than he had done the previous day, but no comment was made.

'You seemed unduly surprised to learn about the death of Stamford Raffles,' Fergusson said. 'Did you know the man well?'

'I met him briefly,' Steffens replied.

'Was that when he was living in Sumatra or Singapore? Or perhaps you came across him here on one of his visits to Lord Hastings?'

'It was in Singapore,' Steffens muttered.

'And am I correct in thinking there may have been some unfinished business between the two of you?' Fergusson added.

Steffens shrugged his shoulders; he knew that he was being examined. What did Douglas Fergusson expect him to say, why was he asking all these questions?

'And you're disappointed that you won't be able to settle matters now the man is dead. The news has obviously upset you, but maybe you could sort things out with his son?'

'His son?'

'I mean the young man Raffles adopted. You must remember him; he chose to call himself Dick because of a story Raffles told him on the way to England. Quite ridiculous when you think about it! He stayed on in Singapore when Raffles and his wife left; he's become quite successful as an artist, I believe.'

Steffens' back stiffened, his knuckles clenched. He controlled his breathing, but his mind was racing. When Raffles interrogated him at the barracks there had been a boy with him, was that who Fergusson was talking about? The boy he remembered was sitting in the corner of the room with a sketchbook. So, he was still in Singapore, he had become successful, he'd benefitted from the patronage of a man Steffens counted

9

as his enemy. With Raffles dead, Steffens knew his options had narrowed. Maybe he would seek out the young man; maybe he could find an alternative way of seeking revenge. He shifted on his seat and became aware of Fergusson's gaze.

The older man cleared his throat. 'If you want to return to Singapore, you might be able to do something for me at the same time. Do you remember, yesterday evening, I said I had a proposition to put to you?'

Steffens nodded. The information about Raffles' adopted son had taken everything else out of his mind. Now he needed to concentrate, to listen to what his host had to say.

'You must be aware of the difficulties that arose after Raffles returned to Singapore. His ideals caused all sorts of problems for those of us with an interest in the opium trade.'

Steffens pasted a smile across his face but said nothing. His body remained stiff, his hands still coiled into tight fists, then a hard expression replaced the false smile.

*****

Fergusson stopped talking; he observed his guest very care-fully. He wondered who this man really was. It was unlikely that he was called Sulivan, having failed to respond to the name several times already. It was feasible that he really was someone with a deeply held grievance, in which case he would fit in with his own plans very nicely. However, there was always the possibility it was a trick. The authorities had recently become more vigilant and had started to check on those they suspected of bending the rules. Could they have sent this man to check on him and his affairs?

'I imagine it's easier now that Raffles has gone?' Steffens said, breaking the silence that hung between them.

'You're right. It started to get better as soon as John Crawfurd took over as Resident, but now Singapore is part of the Straits Settlements it's even better.' Fergusson decided to share his views little by little; he would observe the reactions of his "guest" carefully. It was far more likely that he was a renegade, a criminal even; certainly not a traveller recently arrived from Madras. If at the end of the discussion, he thought Sulivan - or whatever he chose to call himself - was worth the gamble, then he would go ahead with his proposal. If he suspected anything untoward, he would simply walk away.

'I have business interests in Singapore,' Fergusson continued. 'The man who has acted as my agent contracted cholera and died a few months back. I need someone to travel to there on my behalf, to carry a parcel, to make connections, and to seal a contract.'

'You're sending me to Singapore?' Steffens said.

'That is my proposition, but first of all I need to know how fond you are of your current name?'

Steffens felt the heat creeping up the back of his neck; his cheeks burnt and his mouth was dry. Twice now, he'd failed to respond when Fergusson had called him Mr Sulivan. Was the man bluffing, or did he already know that his identity was false?

'I made some enquiries overnight,' Fergusson said, as if he was reading the other man's thoughts. 'I've no idea how long you've been using that particular name, but if as I suspect it is a fairly new persona, I'm hoping you will agree to another name when you reach Singapore.'

'You're assuming I will agree to your proposition,' Steffens said.

'We've already established that you have a need to return to the Settlement and I am willing to pay for your passage. All I want in return is for you to deliver a small package to an Indian gentleman in Market Street.'

'What ...,' Steffens began.

'That's all you need to know for now. If the package arrives safely, you will be paid handsomely – and if you are interested, there may be other work to undertake on my behalf. We can come to an arrangement, and then you'll be told more details about the whole operation.'

'If I choose to agree – and I repeat IF,' Steffens said, 'why do you want me to change my name?'

'The Indian moneylenders in and around Market Street will be your main contacts, they're called Chetties by the local population. You may remember that I commented upon your swarthy skin when we first met. You could easily be mistaken for an Indian – or at least an Anglo-Indian; you'll be able to blend in with the locals easily enough, but it will be easier still if you have an Indian name. Ask for a man called Mukesh; he will decide whether there is further work for you.'

*****

Steffens couldn't believe his good fortune at having his passage paid to the very place he wanted to go. If things turned out well, he'd be able to observe everything going on around him. It could only be a bonus - or was there a catch? What was in the package he was to deliver? How risky was the task he was being given? He was convinced now that Fergusson was no benefactor, that some of his business interests were near the margins of respectability and others were mostly probably entirely illegal. It was clear that rules were still being bent to accommodate the shipping of opium to China, and the British were turning a blind eye to local trade in order to obtain the tea they so desperately wanted. He let a smile creep slowly across his face. He was warming to this man.

'So, are you interested in working for me?' Fergusson said.

*****

Two days later.

Steffens hurriedly untied the parcel Fergusson had handed him only a short while ago; the paper rustled as he rapidly pulled the layers apart.

He seized the garments one by one. First, a broad-shouldered frock coat, with a tightly-clenched waist; it was the colour of soot. He held it high, twirled it around, then buried his nostrils in the clean, agreeable smell of new wool. The ample sleeves, he noticed, would provide a suitable place to conceal a weapon. There was a matching waistcoat with a rolled collar – it pleased him that Fergusson hadn't stinted on quality. Next, he pulled out full-length, light-coloured trousers. Seven years ago, breeches had been the fashion, so these would be something of a novelty.

There were two shirts; both cool, fine cotton. He would have preferred the feel of linen, but that was probably too much to expect, after all, he would only be wearing these garments for the duration of the voyage. Finally, he discovered three identical cravats; white and soft to the touch as he ran them between his fingers. He remembered the cravats he'd left behind in Singapore; colours to match every garment he possessed, all made of silk or the finest cotton lawn. If everything worked out to his satisfaction, it would not be long before he would own many such garments once again.

A layer of paper separated the European clothes from the rest. These were the garments Douglas Fergusson expected him to wear on arrival in Singapore. They were traditional outfits in quiet, reserved colours, chosen deliberately so that he could blend in with the local community. The cotton kurta felt delicate and cool, not unlike the shirts he'd handled earlier; the dark red colour delighted him, but he was less pleased with the pink pyjama trousers. He liked even less the jootis – white, pointed slip-on shoes; believing them to be extremely unmasculine.

Lastly, he pulled out a dark green, silk sherwani, embellished with gold brocade. The bronze-coloured chooridar pants had a sheen to them; both garments were striking and would impress anyone who might care to invite him to dine.

This was more like it, he'd feel good in the sherwani, even if the colour was less flamboyant than he would have chosen for himself. However, Fergusson had instructed him to set it aside, to wait until he was sure he'd been accepted by the Indian money-lenders in Singapore, and not draw attention to himself.

For now, he must be content to don the European clothes and be ready for the voyage. He stepped out of the ill-fitting garments given to him by the prison guard and let them fall to the floor. He was glad to be rid of the coarse fibres, the stale odour; he kicked them all into a corner. He stretched his arms into the folds of one of the shirts and savoured the smooth, white cotton as it fell over his buttocks. It enveloped him; he'd become scrawny during the years in jail and the additional fabric helped to fill the space left around his waist when he pulled on the trousers. When he added the cravat, his neck felt constricted, but he tied it with a flourish. Finally, he donned the frock coat and the boots.

Not much time left now. He neatly folded the other new garments, carefully re-wrapping them in the paper, and tying it together with the string. Then, he picked up the package he was to deliver to Singapore and walked with his head held high towards the quay.

CHAPTER 2
Singapore, 15th August 1830

Dick loosened the reins on his horse and eased him from a steady trot into a more sedate walking pace. The road that led down the hillside was often quiet, but traffic began to increase as soon as he crossed into Flint Street. The horse put back his ears and danced a little jig while they waited for a gang of labourers to pass by. The group was being kept in line by two sepoys; they were no doubt convicts, being escorted from the sheds where they were housed to the beginnings of the new road which would start in Serengoon and then wind its way up the eastern side of Bukit Selegie.

There was a further delay before he could continue his journey; a line of carriages, three landaus, took prominence along the highway. Once the hullaballoo had subsided, Dick headed for the Company Office. He was hoping that the *Indiaman*, which had dropped anchor the previous morning, might have brought a letter from England. There was plenty of time, he reckoned, before he was due to hand over the sketches he'd promised to George Coleman; he had at least another two hours before noon.

He continued along Middle Road at a steady pace, then wound his way through the intervening streets until he reached North Bridge Road. He slowed his pace almost to a halt as he passed by the school. He could just hear a low, repetitive hum, which he presumed was the class demonstrating what they had recently learned. He was glad that one of Raffles' dreams for the Settlement had at last come to fruition but was saddened by the fact that the present building wasn't sturdy enough and would need to be replaced before too long.

When he finally reached the Company Office, the clerk nodded an acknowledgement as he entered. A couple of the younger ones raised their hands to greet him. It all looked very industrious and he didn't want to get anyone into trouble by diverting them from their tasks. There was indeed a letter to collect; he recognised the handwriting immediately and his heart skipped a beat. He stuffed the envelope into his pocket to read later and share whatever news it held with his wife.

The horse nuzzled his shoulder as soon as he returned, blowing warm horse breath into his ear. Dick stroked the animal's neck and offered him a handful of the fodder he'd stowed in one of the saddlebags. As usual, he left the animal with a stable hand before walking over the rickety wooden bridge in the direction of Baba Tan's warehouse.

*****

It was tricky, manoeuvring himself between the coolies, the hawkers, the piled-up crates, and the overflowing baskets. At one point, the heel of his shoe caught the edge of a large fishing net, draped across the quay to dry in the sun. He dragged it along for several yards without noticing before it tightened, causing him to almost lose his balance.

'Stop!' a voice could be heard shouting in Malay. 'Sir, you must stop. You will hurt yourself and ruin my nets.'

Dick hesitated; then he swung round to see what all the fuss was about. By this time, several other fishermen had come to help. They freed the fibres from his shoe and helped him to step away. Dick apologised for the upset and thanked the group who had come to the rescue all in the same breath.

As he strode along the quay, he almost collided with a man stepping onto the wharf from the steps leading up from the river. This time, he found himself apologising to a well-dressed Indian, carrying an old seaman's bag. He assumed the man was newly-arrived as he looked somewhat bemused and made no effort to respond. Dick continued on his way, but something made him feel uncomfortable. He turned, only to see the Indian staring after him. He seemed to be muttering something under his breath but the words were inaudible. There was no doubt, however, about the expression on the man's face; it was distinctly hostile.

Dick was still feeling disturbed when he arrived at Baba Tan's go-down. He had no idea why the Indian – could he have been Anglo-Indian? - had glared at him so accusingly. As far as he knew, he'd never seen the man before. Perhaps he confused me with someone else he thought, as he pushed open the door.

Inside, broad shafts of bright light cascaded down the walls, forming golden pools on the warehouse floor. The shelving on the opposite wall ran from floor to ceiling; it was crammed with bales of silk and cotton - piled high and shielded from direct sunlight. At the far end, he could see his friend checking the contents of a recent shipment from China.

'Welcome, welcome,' Baba Tan said. 'It's good to see you, young man. Do you have time to share some tea?'

'That's what I was hoping you might say,' Dick said. 'I'm always thirsty after riding into town.'

'You did not bring the carriage?'

'No need. I'm here to deliver some drawings to Mr Coleman and I took the opportunity to collect the latest post. Both tasks can be done perfectly well on horseback.'

'In that case, I might be able to persuade you to buy some of this silk, then,' Baba Tan said, drawing out a particularly fine piece of shantung from the bale nearest to his elbow. The colour on the surface of the material appeared to change from deep cobalt to the palest ultramarine as the angle of the light changed.

'Those colours are extraordinary,' Dick said. 'The roll next to the one you're holding reminds me of the garment Sujana was wearing when we first met.'

'This one?' Baba Tan said, pulling out a length of turquoise silk embroidered with tiny, blue hummingbirds. 'Maybe your wife would like to be reminded of that time? You need just enough for the tailor to conjure it into something elegant, maybe a dress, maybe a tunic that could be worn over a long, plain skirt. I have several lengths of silk that would look well with the shantung, and of course, I can offer you a very special price.'

Dick was amused by his old friend's encouragement. It was a beautiful fabric and he knew Sujana would delight in wearing it. He was still dithering when Wing Yee came down the steps from her workroom.

'I thought I hear your voice,' she said.

'Dick has come to share a bowl of tea, but I am trying to convince him to buy some of this new silk for Sujana. He likes this one and I could match it to something simpler for a skirt. What do you think?'

'Why you waste time?' Wing Yee said. She came closer to examine the fabric being considered. 'I think perfect choice. You should buy.'

All three of them started to laugh; these days it was difficult for anyone to escape Wing Yee's powers of persuasion once she had made up her mind. The smile remained on Dick's face. He shrugged his shoulders and agreed to the purchase. He liked being able to buy Sujana an occasional gift and he knew she would look wonderful in whatever she decided to have the shantung made into. Baba Tan carefully cut a generous length of the turquoise fabric from the bale and then selected a slightly darker shade of plain silk to accompany it.

Wing Yee nodded her approval. 'Now you get tea,' she said.

*****

Dick eventually reached the building site where George Coleman was overseeing the various activities being undertaken just short of noon.

'I thought you'd forgotten,' the Irishman shouted above the noise of the workmen.

There were one or two coolies, carrying hods full of earth from one place to another, but most of the men, labouring away in the heat of the midday sun were Indian, another gang of convicts brought to the Settlement for this very purpose.

'Another house?' Dick said. 'Which one of our wealthy merchants has commissioned you this time around?'

'It was for a friend of a friend,' Coleman said. His eyes looked dark and serious; his voice was flat with no hint of his usual Irish lilt. 'I heard the other day that the man has some family issues and has decided to return to England. He's informed me that he won't be needing the house after all.'

'I wouldn't think you'll have any problems finding another buyer. You must have done quite well out of that other great mansion, the one the authorities decided to use as the Court House.'

'I was paid well for building it, that's true, but the revenue for the current lease has nothing to do with me. Besides, that house was already completed for everyone to see. It's the ones that are still on the drawing board I'm concerned about; that's why I'm anxious to have your drawings.'

Dick didn't see the connection. His eyebrows concertinaed; he waited for Coleman to elaborate.

'I can use the drawings to show to some of the other merchants. There are new people arriving all the time and those who intend to stay will eventually need their own home. They could all be potential buyers, but most people find it difficult to make sense of an architectural drawing; they can't envisage what the final structure will look like. These sketches – the houses I've designed for the Browns, the Connells, and for Mr Elliott, will show what is possible. I'm even hoping that certain aspects of those mansions might inspire members of the Armenian community. They're obviously prospering here; I've been asked to design a church for them.'

Dick was amused. 'In that case,' he said, 'you'd better have a good look at what I've done. You need to be sure my sketches meet your needs.'

*****

A few years ago, he'd thought of asking Coleman to take him on as an apprentice and although he'd never followed through with the idea, he had no trouble in seeing how one of the Irishman's plans could result in a gracious building. It had never occurred to him that others might find the concept difficult. 'I'll just wait over there in the shade,' he said.

The men had stopped working for a short, but well-earned break. To give themselves some respite from the scorching heat, most had found a patch of shade where they could rest or take a nap. One of their number had taken himself to the perimeter of the site and Dick wondered if he would try to escape; this would be an ideal time to take flight. But when he thought it through, where would any of these people run to? Singapore's Indian population was comprised of successful merchants, moneylenders, and convicts; it would be easy enough to spot a fugitive. It disturbed Dick whenever he saw the convicts trudging along, chained to one another as they walked to and from the barracks; he thought it unnecessary. The men always looked exhausted. They spent the night in cramped quarters and the daytime, released from their chains, toiling away in the hot sun.

The man who he'd observed was crouching down and scraping away at the soil with his bare hands. By the time Dick reached him, he'd loosened a considerable amount of earth and was carefully extracting a delicate sapling. When he became aware that he was being observed, he lifted the plant and offered it to Dick. 'You take, sahib,' he said. 'This soil not good, you plant in nice garden.'

'What is it?' Dick asked.

'Is called yellow flame tree. When big, many flowers – smell very nice.'

'How do you know this?' Dick said. 'Were you once a gardener?'

'Before ...' the man hesitated. 'In Calcutta ... I work in Botanic Garden. In India, people plant one yellow tree, then one red tree, then one yellow tree, then ...'

Before the erstwhile gardener could finish, George Coleman was standing beside them; he seemed completely oblivious of the conversation that had been taking place. 'These are very good, just what I need,' he said.

'I'm pleased to be of service,' Dick said. 'Let me know if there are any others you require.'

Coleman nodded enthusiastically before returning to supervise the next phase of the building project. The rest period had obviously come to an end, and when Dick looked around, the man he'd been talking to had returned to join the other labourers, leaving the sapling for him to rescue.

*****

The horse snorted and tossed its head as Dick reined it in and turned into the driveway. The last section of the hill always required stamina but more so during the middle of the day when the heat was impossible to avoid. The hooves crunched into gravel, acting as a cue for their elderly retainer to shuffle his way towards them and collect the reins. Darma had been part of the wedding gift to Dick and Sujana from her father. He looked after the horse and kept the carriage spick-and-span. The horse was glistening all over now because of the strenuous climb, but soon the sweat would evaporate and swirls of steam would rise before Darma rubbed him down.

Dick dismounted, thanking the old man, whose fortitude never ceased to amaze him. He carefully removed the sapling from one of the saddlebags and placed it in a patch of shade beside the steps. From the other bag, he withdrew the package containing the silk. He took a deep breath before entering the house, filling his lungs with the sweet fragrance floating across from the frangipani trees, then rushed up the steps, calling his wife's name.

Sujana was waiting on the veranda; she too had heard the approach of the horse and its master. Dick hurried over to embrace her before flopping into the nearest chair.

'Did I see you take a tree out of your saddlebag?'

'It's a sapling, a yellow flame tree apparently.'

Sujana looked quizzical. 'We have quite a lot of trees already.'

'I know,' Dick said, 'but it was rescued by one of the convicts working for Coleman. He gave it to me and asked me to look after it.'

Sujana shook her head from side to side, smiling as she did so. She loved him for his kind and generous nature almost as much as she loved his ability to charm. He still had an innocence about him at times, even though he was now twenty-six years old, a husband, and a father.

'I thought you were just going to collect post and to see Coleman,' she said, trying to sound serious and scolding.

'That was my intention, but I was so parched after the ride, I decided to visit Baba Tan; he always offers the most delicious tea.'

'And I suppose, on the way there, you couldn't resist viewing the latest arrivals in the harbour?'

'Before I left this morning, I noticed one of the smaller ships that the Company commissions – usually in Madras or

Bengal – had dropped anchor. It wasn't there yesterday evening. The lightermen were getting ready to collect the cargo; they told me it had come from Calcutta, but I didn't stop to find out any more.'

'Did you actually collect any mail?' she said. 'I thought I noticed you take a small package from the other saddlebag.'

'I did collect mail; just one letter this time.' He reached into his coat pocket and pulled out a crumpled envelope. 'Oh dear,' he said, 'I should have taken more care, put it into the saddlebag along with the silk.'

'What silk?'

Dick looked at his wife and couldn't help being slightly amused by her youthful enthusiasm. She tried so hard to appear and behave like a respectable married woman, but wisps of her unruly hair had already escaped from the clasp meant to hold it in check, and the flower she usually wore in it was nowhere to be seen. She hastily adjusted her sarong when she realised, he was looking at her. Instead of being tied neatly at her waist, it had slipped around to one side

'Baba Tan had just taken delivery of a new consignment – silk from Shantung. I wasn't going to give it to you straightaway, but he, plus Wing Yee and me, thought you'd look especially beautiful in this.' He handed over the package.

Sujana slowly untied the ribbon. Her hands trembled as she unfolded the layers of paper to reveal the shimmering fabric. 'It's exquisite,' she said as she lifted it up and twirled around the room with it held against her body, 'but you are very naughty, you spoil me,' she said.

'It reminded me of the garment you wore when I was painting the family portrait for your father,' he said, 'the first time I set eyes on you, and fell in love with you.'

Sujana stopped quite still, her cheeks were flushed and not from the exertion of twirling around the veranda. Dick didn't verbalise his affection very often, but when it happened it always made her feel cherished and appreciated. To hide her embarrassment, she asked, 'Should we not see who the letter is from?'

*****

Dick smiled as he opened the envelope and smoothed out the single page of handwriting. These days, he always felt ambivalent, at first, when he received letters from his friends in England. He was glad to hear from them, of course, but part of him always dreaded the receipt of bad news.

'Is it from England?' Sujana asked. Dick returned to the envelope and examined the handwriting carefully.

Dick hesitated. 'It's from Edmund,' he said.

Sujana observed the tension draining away from her husband's face. She knew him well enough to know that he continued to be anxious if he thought an envelope had been addressed by Chin Ming. Generally, Edmund and his wife drafted different sections of the letters they wrote to their friends in Singapore, but it was Edmund who usually addressed the envelope. In truth, only one letter, during the years they had been away, had been scribed entirely by Chin Ming. It had been carefully written and was full of compassion, but nevertheless, the news it contained was like a knife penetrating his heart. It told him that the man who had adopted him all those years ago had died. Stamford Raffles had suffered from debilitating headaches for years. Everyone had hoped returning to a more equable climate would cause them to go away. Instead, they had worsened throughout the summer of 1826. During the night of 5th July, the pain was so intense, it drove him to rise from his bed. The throbbing in his head only got worse as he paced around, causing him to lose consciousness and fall down the stairs. It was the day before his forty-sixth birthday. Chin Ming's letter, which told Dick that Raffles had been suffering from a massive brain tumour, arrived in Singapore five months later.

'What does Edmund have to say? Their new baby must be about six months old now; he was born only a couple of months after our Tomas. And Charlotte, how old is Charlotte?'

'She was born in August, so she'll just have had her third birthday,' Dick said, making himself more comfortable in the chair as he spoke.

The letter from England was much shorter than usual; just the one sheet of paper with a hasty note scribbled by Chin Ming at the very end. Dick skimmed through it quickly.

'They're coming home!' he almost shouted when he'd finished reading. 'Edmund promised to bring her back to Singapore, but it's been so long, I thought it would never happen. This letter was written at the end of May, shortly before they planned to leave. They might even arrive on the next ship.'

There was great excitement that evening. Dick couldn't wait to introduce Sujana to Chin Ming and Edmund; he thought it would be wonderful for their children to be able to play together. He had told his wife so much about them during the time they had spent in England, but she couldn't help being a little concerned about meeting someone who had been such an important figure in her husband's life before she knew him.

For once, Dick was totally unaware of Sujana's qualms. Once the excitement of the news had settled, his thoughts returned to the man who had glared at him so alarmingly earlier in the day. He told himself that it must have been a mistake, he was sure he had never seen the man before in his life. Nevertheless, he remained haunted by the feeling of animosity the man had transmitted.

CHAPTER 3
Singapore, September 1830

Pieter Steffens had been back in Singapore for exactly one month. Not that he was using his own name, of course; nor was he any longer trying to think of himself as John Sulivan. The moment he'd stepped off the vessel that had brought him here from Calcutta, he had assumed yet another persona. Following a conversation with one of the deck-hands he'd chosen the name Kasim; apparently, it meant *controller of anger.* Keeping his temper under control had been a hard-won lesson during his time in prison, so the new name seemed particularly appropriate, given the circumstances.

He'd been put to the test very early on. He'd narrowly missed crashing into someone as he'd stepped onto the quay. His first inclination had been to curse out loud, but the shock of recognition had stopped him just in time. The young man had apologised, the tone of his skin and his tightly-curled hair had given him away; it had to be Raffles' adopted son. Kasim had glared after him before stepping away. He'd been glad of the subdued garments Douglas Fergusson had insisted upon. He remembered how he'd continued to detest the pink trousers and white, pointed shoes, but the dark red kurta he liked well enough, and such garments had since proved to help him blend in with the Indian community

No one else had paid him any attention that day, and he

knew Fergusson had advised him wisely. He'd asked for directions to Market Street, although he could remember the way well enough, and then sought out the man he'd been told to contact.

He'd handed over the package discreetly, still not knowing what it contained. Mukesh, as the man was simply known, had examined the package carefully and Kasim was relieved he'd overcome the temptation to see for himself what was inside. Mukesh had disappeared behind a flimsy curtain; Kasim had observed his silhouette, holding aloft something between his thumb and index finger. It caught the light for a moment only; there was a flash of deep red and then it was gone. Mukesh returned a few minutes later with a money bag containing fifty silver dollars.

'You come tomorrow,' Mukesh had said. 'I show you where to sit, what to do.'

As he'd walked away with his newly-acquired wealth, Kasim remembered smiling to himself. I must have passed the test – whatever the test was – he'd told himself. The role he'd been given provided a base from which to observe all the goings-on, listen to the gossip, learn about certain people and their habits. Fergusson's last instructions told him that he would be required to receive messages, meet the shipments sent from Calcutta and redistribute the goods amongst the vessels belonging to country traders in the port-to-port business. It all seemed easy enough and he'd hoped it would provide a cover for his own personal agenda.

*****

The establishments in Market Street were mostly one-man firms with several people sharing one shophouse. He'd quickly assumed the role of a manager in one of the money-lending

firms; it entitled him to occupy a seat on a raised wooden platform with his own safe and small box for keeping records.
The task he'd been given was simple enough, but already he
was bored. One month of the same routine: arriving at Market
Street in time to occupy his seat and being available to lend
money to anyone who was in need. His small safe and a box
for keeping records of the borrowers had been inherited from
his predecessor. People came and went. Some were quite open
about their transactions because they were confident of their
ability to pay back the loan; others were more furtive, embarrassed, ashamed. These were often Chinese labourers who
inevitably owed money in the gambling dens; they were poor
creatures with garments that hung limply off their scraggy
shoulders and had wisps of hair escaping from their queues.
Those with dark brown hands, he'd been told, worked on the
gambier plantation, the dark colour being the result of spending hours boiling the plants in water for use in tanning hides.

His fellow moneylenders, with whom he shared the shophouse, had accepted Kasim without question. His name was
never doubted, neither was his background. He was there
to represent the interests of Mr Fergusson in Calcutta; that
was all that was necessary. He despised these people, he
loathed being trapped within this Tamil community, but for
the moment, he had no choice. At least he could escape each
night. The money he'd received from Mukesh was more than
enough to purchase a small *prahu* from a Bugis trader a few
days after his arrival. It was now anchored west of the river
near to Telok Blangah. It provided him anonymity as well as a
place to sleep, but his increasing restlessness was leading him
to think that before too long he would need to take it out into
the harbour. He wanted to see what other activities he could
engage in beyond the shoreline.

*****

14th September 1830

Today was the day when Kasim was due to hand over another package. This time, it was to be delivered to the captain of a ship due to depart for Calcutta on the evening tide. It contained payment for the various shipments he'd arranged on Fergusson's behalf; opium from Bengal, arriving on ships that remained well out in the harbour, then transferred to local trading vessels in Singapore for the remaining part of the journey to Guangzhou. The money was buried within a layer of sand, on top of which were small, colourful pieces of rock. The customs declaration on the outside of the box simply stated that it contained decorative stones for ornamental gardens. For the first time since coming here, he began to resent his continued involvement with Fergusson; a man who benefitted from the risks others took on his behalf. Kasim thought it might soon be time to become less accommodating.

Before securing the box, he slipped in the letter that he'd already drafted to Douglas Fergusson. It contained a brief report of his activities, and the contacts he'd made. With gritted teeth, he concluded with the phrase, *Your obedient servant*, before signing his new name.

*****

The following day, there were fewer customers than normal wanting to borrow money or extend their loan. The seat that Kasim occupied amongst the other moneylenders gave him ample opportunity to observe and listen to the people who frequented the area. He was already aware of confidences that the people disclosing such information might regret him hearing. However, this environment had its limitations; he needed to investigate other possibilities around the harbour to find out who was doing what and for whom. He needed to widen his circle of contacts, to know who he could trust. He slipped down from his high stool, gathered the tools of his newly acquired trade, and walked away from Market Street in the direction of Boat Quay.

During the seven years he'd been away, Singapore had become, unmistakably, an Asian city. The quayside was crowded with natives from all parts of India. Vast numbers of Chinese labourers pulled and pushed huge chests, cases, and cartons from the warehouses lining the wharf before loading them into the bumboats that would take them out into the harbour. There, they were loaded onto the vessels upon which they would continue their journey to the Coromandel coast.

Kasim watched the activity carefully, scrutinising every action, noting the contents of the cargoes and the names displayed above the warehouses. The aromatic fragrance of cloves pervaded the atmosphere, almost obliterating any hint of sweat from the coolies or stench from the river.

'Can I help you, my friend?' a tall Eurasian man asked. 'You look as if you're new to these parts.'

'Fairly new,' Kasim replied. The response suited his purpose well enough. The last thing he wanted was to say anything that might lead someone to make a connection with the man he'd been during his previous years in the Settlement.

'Perhaps you will join me for some coffee? That stall over there in front of the warehouse. Choo Keng serves an excellent local brew.'

The man introduced himself merely as Victor. Having ordered coffee, he went on to tell Kasim about the many industrial enterprises he might encounter in the Settlement, the difference between the people living in the brick-built houses in the main streets and those in the humble dwellings made of wood and palm-frond thatch on the outskirts of the town. He was about to embark on a description of the ships and their cargoes when, much to Kasim's relief, the coffee arrived.

Victor made no attempt to ask Kasim about himself. He made a point of explaining, however, that although Singapore was becoming the hub for produce from around the region – rice, pepper, gambier – the most important product that passed through the harbour was opium.

Kasim wondered who this man calling himself Victor really was. Could it have been a chance meeting, or had Douglas Fergusson sent the man to test his loyalty? That was ridiculous, of course; he'd only decided to take the afternoon off at the last minute. But maybe one of the other moneylenders had some means of sending a message to Victor. Perhaps they had been waiting for an opportunity to test him from the moment he arrived.

'I was under the impression that Singapore looked down on the opium business, that it was, in fact illegal?'

'You've been listening to romantic stories about that fool Stamford Raffles,' Victor said. 'He did try to stamp it out during the time he spent here; he had the most enormous row with my uncle about it. No one was allowed to be involved with the trade, and for a few years everything went very quiet.'

'But you're saying things are different now?' Kasim said.

'It accounts for the major part of the East India Company's revenue. It's still officially illegal, of course, but they get round it by issuing licences to Chinese businessmen. The opium trade not only fills the coffers of the Company's administrators, my friend, it also enriches the Asian entrepreneurs too.'

'I see,' Kasim said. He still had no idea whether this was a chance encounter, but if it turned out to be the case, then he believed this man might be very useful to him. It seemed that Victor also bore some sort of grudge towards Raffles - the man who had quarrelled with his uncle - and that was something Kasim had every intention of exploiting. He would seek Victor out again. If nothing else, such an acquaintance might provide him with an opportunity to wear the dark green silk sherwani embellished with gold brocade

*****

From that day on, Kasim made a habit of finishing his work early whenever an opportunity arose, if trade was slow, if there was no expectation of a message from Fergusson, or no package to deliver. Some days he sought out Victor at Choo Keng's coffee stall, but most of the time, he took his boat out from its mooring and navigated his way at a leisurely pace between the myriad ships in harbour.

He gazed at the brightly painted Chinese junks with their eyes marked on the bows to guide their path. He cast his own eyes over their decks to observe crowds of settlers eager for a first glimpse of their new home, more young men to add to the already male-dominated world of the Settlement. If the ships had any women on board, they would most probably be join-ing all the others who had been smuggled into Singapore to work in the brothels.

The sight of a magnificent *Indiamen* reminded Kasim once again of Raffles and how he'd tried to wipe out pros-titution in the Settlement as well as gambling, slavery, and the opium trade. Some chance of that, he thought to himself. Plying backwards and forwards between all this hive of activ-ity there were also local craft like his own; vessels that had come from Arabia, Sumatra, Siam, and Malacca. His skills at manoeuvring his *prahu* improved with each outing and soon he hoped to venture as far as Malacca himself.

*****

Singapore, 27th September 1830

Sujana gently wiped Tomas's mouth, rearranged his shawl, and lifted him onto her shoulder. When she looked up, she became aware of her husband standing quite still on the veranda of their house. There was something about his pos-ture she recognised; the rigid back, the tense shoulders. His eyes, she knew, would be fixed on the multitude of ships in the harbour. She rose from her seat and walked towards him.

'Chin Ming is probably just as nervous about meeting you again as you are about meeting her,' Sujana said as she approached.

Dick turned. His brow was creased and his lips pressed firmly together. 'How do you always know what I'm thinking?' he said.

'Because I'm your wife. Because I've lived with you long enough to recognise your state of mind; what makes you happy, what makes you sad.'

'I am happy; it's just that ...,'

'It's just that you haven't seen each other in over four years and so much has changed in all our lives during that time. Remember, you and I had only just met when she and Edmund left, to get married in England.'

'I was painting your family portrait. I remember telling Wing Yee about you and she never stopped teasing me. I think she knew I'd fallen in love with you even before I did.'

'It still took another two years before you plucked up enough courage to ask my father's permission for us to marry. By then, Chin Ming had given birth to a daughter and now she has a son too; we have our own dear Tomas. We are bound to have changed after all that has happened, but the bond you formed with her – and with Wing Yee – after you rescued them from that awful Dutchman, that will always be strong.'

Dick nodded. A smile crossed his lips.

'You've always said you think of Chin Ming like a sister; even brothers and sisters get worried when they haven't seen each other in a while, but there is something deep down that always overcomes the initial hesitation. Believe me, I always tied myself in knots when any of my brothers returned home, despite being happy to see them.'

'You're right; I'm probably worrying over nothing.'

Sujana touched Dick's shoulder and then stroked his arm. She was aware that not only would it be the first time Chin

Ming and Dick had met since they had each married and started their own families, more importantly, it was the first time they would see each other knowing that the man who had been such an inspiration to them both was dead. Sujana was wise enough, however, to know that Stamford Raffles would remain an important figure in both their lives. She was also wise enough to keep this thought to herself.

'Look,' Sujana said, pointing in the direction of Government Hill, 'the flag has been raised; that confirms the arrival of the *Castle Huntly* - such an odd name for a ship! How long before they're ready to bring the passengers ashore?'

'I'm not sure. I don't remember seeing this ship before. I've no idea how big it is, how many passengers they are carrying, or how many will disembark. When Edmund first came here with his brother, they were amongst the last to come ashore. It was sheer luck that I was still at the quay sketching. Normally, I would have packed up my materials long before they arrived.'

'But you would have met them eventually. You told me they brought letters for you from England.'

'Yes, but ordinarily they would be delivered to the Company office. We might only have met in passing. They might have returned to their ship instead of staying with Alexander Johnston and ...'

'But you DID meet them, you DID go with them to China, and think of all the things that happened as a result. It was all inevitable. And now, you and I will go down to the quay to meet Chin Ming, Edmund, and their children.' She handed baby Tomas to him, straightened her sarong, then looped her arm through his, and smiled. 'Come, we must hurry,' she said. 'You wouldn't want them to arrive at the quay and find no one there to welcome them home.'

Dick and Sujana left Tomas in the care of their *amah*. When they arrived at the quay, Wing Yee and Baba Tan greeted them with a familiarity developed over many years of close friendship.

'Have any of the passengers disembarked yet?' Dick asked. 'It took longer to get here than I'd anticipated; the horse was reluctant to be harnessed and the road was busier than usual.'

'We've seen no one,' Baba Tan said, 'and we've been here for nearly an hour.'

'Not want to miss them,' Wing Yee said. She knew they had arrived at the quay far too early, but a mixture of excitement and pent-up anxiety had overtaken reason. The idea of seeing Chin Ming again after a separation of four years was making all of them feel nervous.

'Perhaps we should wait over there,' Baba Tan said, pointing towards the nearest shophouse. 'We can enjoy some coffee while we wait.'

Sujana heaved a sigh of relief. 'What a good idea,' she said as she led her husband towards the round, marble-topped tables. 'We'll be able to see everything from there just as easily.'

*****

Edmund picked up his daughter and pointed towards the shore. 'This is going to be our new home,' he said. 'It's a very special place because it's where your mama and I first met.'

The little girl gazed at the long line of houses that stood to attention along the coastline. The bright sunlight on the white facades made her screw up her eyes and nestle her face into her father's shoulder; she sucked one end of her forget-me-not blue sash. She fidgeted to be put down and watched as some of the other passengers queued to join the bumboats bobbing up and down around the side of their ship. Her mother was still below with baby William. Chin Ming had said she'd prefer to wait until the others had disembarked before they left the ship. Edmund had readily agreed. He knew their friends would be at the quay to welcome them home and he didn't want the reunion to be spoiled by having to jostle amongst groups of coolies, new arrivals, and any temporary visitors to the Settlement.

It was almost an hour later before Chin Ming appeared on deck; she was carrying William in her arms. A gentle breeze rippled through the skirt of her pale-green gown, causing the butterflies embroidered around the hem to look as if they were taking flight. It was a pretty, muslin dress, but Edmund said he'd be glad when she returned to the attractive tunics and *quipaos* she was used to wearing in the Orient. It had been her own decision to wear European fashions during their time in England because she wanted to fit in and not draw attention to herself, but he was pleased he'd managed to convince her not to cover her lustrous, dark hair with one of the silly lace caps favoured by European women. As she walked towards him now, a smile that was for him alone lit up her whole face and her eyes shone with happiness.

✶✶✶✶✶

Edmund, Chin Ming, and the two children finally left the *Castle Huntly* behind. They sat in the stern of a bumboat surrounded by most of their luggage. Only two more crates had yet to be unloaded and would follow on later. The oarsman made good progress, steering the small craft in between countless other vessels vying for position in the busy harbour. Once they turned into the mouth of the Singapore River, it became much more obvious to see how the Settlement had grown in the last four years. On the south bank of Boat Quay, they admired the row of well-established masonry warehouses, each with its own flight of steps built to enable ships to offload cargo at high and low tide. On the opposite bank, there stood several impressive government buildings and a two-story merchant house.

Chin Ming pointed to the mast immediately next to the house built by Raffles on top of the Bukit Larangan.

'I'm glad some things are still the same,' she said. 'The flag is flying, announcing our arrival; they'll know we are here.'

Edmund remembered his first visit here, on his way to China to collect specimens of plants for the Physic Garden in Oxford. He was almost as excited today as he was back then but now he had a different reason to be happy. He was returning with his family, fulfilling a promise he'd made to Chin Ming when he persuaded her to marry him. They were coming home.

CHAPTER 4
27th September 1830

When Kasim had told Mukesh he'd decided to take the whole day off, the only reaction he received was a mere shrug of his shoulders. He'd given Mukesh no explanation and hadn't bothered to add that he found the business of moneylending both tedious and tiring.

He now lay on his bunk, thinking about the lazy days of his youth back home in Java when he did exactly as he pleased and had people waiting on him hand and foot. He listened to the rhythmical splish-splash of the waves against the side of his boat. The huge red disc that had ballooned over the horizon at dawn was already climbing steadily through the cloudless expanse above him; its reflected light inching gradually towards him across the water. He could have stayed there all day, apart from the tantalising aromas of freshly made roti, sizzling omelettes, and steaming coffee that drifted across from the nearby hawker stalls to tease his taste buds.

An hour later, Kasim had washed, dressed, enjoyed a leisurely breakfast, listened to the local gossip, and was back on board his boat. There was great excitement amongst the stallholders that morning; some were talking about the *Castle Huntly*, newly arrived from England and others were chattering about the latest consignment of convicts who had come on an overcrowded vessel from Calcutta. Today might provide an opportunity to spot another means of supporting himself so that he could return to the lifestyle he thought he deserved.

*****

He pulled the gangplank back on board, hoisted the mainsail and used a boat hook to push away from the jetty. As soon as the wind filled the mainsail, and the boat began to move, he set the foresail and headed eastward.

He proceeded to the mouth of the river, lowered the mainsail, and then guided the craft to a point along the wharf where he could tie up easily. Watching the activity from this viewpoint, instead of seeing it from his usual quayside position, was quite strange; everything looked distorted, the noises louder, the stench stronger. He almost lost his balance when the boat began to rock from side to side. Someone on the wharf pointed back towards the mouth of the river; the first of the bumboats, bringing cargo from the *Castle Huntly,* was making its way steadily towards him.

'You must move,' the lighterman shouted in Malay. 'This place is reserved for offloading cargo!'

Kasim paid no attention; it amused him to pretend not to understand. After all, the Indian merchants with whom he now associated spoke either Urdu, Hindi, or broken English; why should anyone expect anything different from him? None of the people he'd known when he lived here before were around to reveal he could converse in Malay very well indeed.

'Move, you move now!' The lighterman insisted. Others joined in; they waved their arms and pointed towards several other bumboats approaching from the harbour.

Kasim shrugged; he'd had his fun, but now it was time to quit. It took a while to manoeuvre his boat away from the wharf, and he had to use the oars to guide it between the tightly packed vessels. Having moved past the first of the bumboats, he was then blocking the passage of the others. The shouting match continued; the lightermen got more and more annoyed. He found their frustration entertaining for a while, but then he decided he'd better hurry in case they turned on him. He raised the mainsail and steered the boat in the direction of the open water.

The squabble with the lightermen and the upheaval it caused had distracted him; he was not paying enough attention and a sudden gust of wind propelled the *prahu* forward, straight into the path of an approaching bumboat. He only just managed to narrowly avoid the bulk of the approaching vessel; it had been a narrow escape. It would have been a disaster to damage the *prahu*, it was his home as well as a means of transport. He must be more careful.

An outburst in Malay from the oarsman in the nearby vessel, exploded across the water, but Kasim just waved to him and laughed. It was then that he noticed the passengers: an Englishman holding a little girl in a muslin dress with a bright blue sash and a woman carrying a baby. The woman was wearing European clothes, but there was no bonnet; she wore her hair long and uncovered. It had a lustrous blue sheen when she turned; only Chinese women had hair like that. He took a sharp intake of breath. Their eyes met for an instant only; there was the briefest hint of recollection, then the wind caught his sail again and carried the *prahu* away out into the harbour.

*****

Two of the other boats carrying passengers from the *Castle Huntly* hovered further upstream; they had not yet found a space to tie up and offload. Edmund shielded his eyes from the noonday glare, hoping to see some sign of their friends, but the quay was too crowded and they were still too far away to recognise anyone.

Their oarsman nudged his way forward; he shouted to

someone on another boat, but all he got by way of response was a shrug of the man's shoulders. There seemed to be nothing for it but to sit and wait their turn. He stowed the oars just as Charlotte slipped from Edmund's grasp and jumped up and down. The oarsman turned around and glared at the child when the boat rocked from side to side. 'I'm sorry,' Edmund said, 'it's been a long journey and she is restless.' He wasn't sure whether he'd been understood, but the oarsman nodded his head and took Charlotte's hand. Then, he lifted her high above his head so that she had a better view of the busy river and its traffic. He pointed to the quay and the crowd eagerly awaiting the arrival of cargo or visitors. The child giggled.

'Please be careful,' Chin Ming called out, trying not to panic. Edmund wrapped his arms around her and William who had fallen asleep on his mother's shoulder. He hoped to reassure her and assuage the alarm they both instinctively felt. Moments later, they were distracted by a commotion just ahead; a Malay *prahu* passed dangerously close to their bumboat, forcing its way past them. Charlotte squealed as the oarsman handed her back to her father; he shouted what could only be an angry tirade in Malay. Chin Ming stared after the vessel, but she was more concerned about the children than an ill-mannered boat handler. The children were exhausted; Charlotte overexcited and William unable to stay awake for more than a few minutes.

The congestion in the river was beginning to clear and the other bumboats had already tied up; their passengers had begun to disembark.

'I think it was that Malay boat causing the holdup,' Edmund said as they approached. the quay. 'Maybe Dick or Baba Tan will be able to tell us more.'

*****

Their oarsman helped them offload their luggage but was anxious to be gone; he needed to make up for lost time, return to the other ships in the harbour, and collect his next cargo to bring ashore.

There was hardly any room to move on the crowded quay. Edmund searched for any sign of Dick, and Chin Ming held the children close. They were busy checking their luggage when something tugged at Chin Ming's sleeve. She turned slowly, being careful not to knock William's head, and found herself looking directly into Wing Yee's eyes. Wing Yee looked hesitant, Chin Ming bit her lip; she felt awkward and overjoyed at the same time. Wing Yee held her arms out, ready to enfold her friend. Both women burst into tears.

The others hurried across from the coffee-stall and Baba Tan came forward to shake Edmund's hand; Dick was close behind. Their self-conscious and clumsy greeting was vanquished as soon as Dick introduced Edmund to Sujana. He looked very pleased with himself and Edmund could understand why, she was willowy, elegant, and had the most endearing smile.

Baba Tan searched the crowd for any sign of Chin Ming's father. 'Li Soong Heng is not with you,' he said. 'I hope he is not unwell?'

'Soong Heng is in excellent health,' Edmund said. 'He sailed with us as far as Calcutta, but during the time we spent there, he visited his old friend Father John. Whilst Soon Heng's been in England, he's enjoyed conversations with my father and various dinner-party guests, but I think he really missed the sort of philosophical discussions he used to have with Father John. After only a few hours together, Soong Heng decided he would like to stay on in Calcutta for a while. I think he might remain there for several months.'

'Say hello to others,' Wing Yee whispered as she and Chin Ming dabbed their eyes dry. She had learned to speak Malay in the years they'd been apart, but opportunities to practise her English had not presented themselves too often; her command of the language remained limited.

Chin Ming apologised and turned to greet the rest of her friends. Edmund was engaged in conversation with a woman she'd never seen before; Baba Tan and Wing Yee joined them. Standing all alone, crossing his arms and rubbing his hands up to his shoulders and back again, was Dick. She took a step towards him. He opened his mouth to speak, but no words would come out.

She hadn't thought about the awkwardness of this moment. They'd exchanged letters during the last four years, they'd kept each other informed about what was happening in their lives, but she never considered how she would feel, how to react when they met once again. Her life in England had been so very different. Soon after they arrived, she and Edmund had married, and the following August, Charlotte was born. She'd been kept busy, and she was extremely happy, but she'd found no female friend to replace Wing Yee and no one to challenge her when need be, as Dick had done. She realised now how much she had missed them both.

'Am I still allowed to tease you?' she said, 'now that you are a successful artist and a respectable married man?'

He coughed. 'I was a successful artist when you left!'

She laughed. 'And already captivated by a certain Javanese beauty, if my memory is correct. Wing Yee teased you so much on that last evening.'

'Sujana's father had commissioned me to paint a family portrait.'

'That's right – but you refused to admit you'd become infatuated with his eldest daughter.'

'I was no more reluctant to divulge how I felt than you - to admit that you'd fallen in love with Edmund.'

Now they were both laughing; the ice had been broken and their friendship could be resumed. It began by Dick introducing Chin Ming to Sujana. He need not have worried about their first encounter; Sujana welcomed Chin Ming with warmth and sincerity, making everything easy by talking about the children.

Right on cue, Charlotte decided it was her turn to be introduced.

'My name is Charlotte Beaumont,' she said slowly and carefully, looking at each of the strangers in turn. 'That's my brother, Will-yam,' she added, pointing to the bundle Edmund now held in his arms, 'but he's a boy and he's always asleep.' Edmund and Chin Ming exchanged glances; Charlotte's opinion of her brother was well-known to them.

'I also have a Chinese name; would you like to know what it is?'

Everyone gave their attention to the small, serious-looking replica of Chin Ming; they smiled and all agreed that they would like that very much.

Charlotte pressed her lips together and frowned. 'What is my Chinese name, mama?' Chin Ming crouched down so that her eyes gazed directly at the beautiful face of her charming daughter; she held Charlotte's hands in her own and smiled. 'Your Chinese name is Ming ....'

'Ming Yue,' the child said, beaming back at her mother.

'That's correct – and can you remember what it means?'

Charlotte bit her lower lip and her eyes moved to the left and then the right before looking up to see her father pointing to the sky and drawing a circle with his finger in the air. She grinned. 'It means Bright Moon,' she said.

*****

Dick had arranged for the Beaumont family to stay with their old friend Alexander Johnston until they had found a house of their own. It was the only dwelling large enough to accommodate two additional adults and their children without causing a major upheaval. Alexander had lived alone since Dick moved out, following his marriage to Sujana two years ago. It was the house that Edmund had stayed in with his brother James on their first visit to Singapore; it was also the place to provide refuge for Soong Heng after being rescued by Father John in Sumatra. Alexander was always glad to offer hospitality to his many visitors, even more so when it provided an excuse for a party.

Dick gave a coin to one of the young boys playing hop-scotch further along the quay and told him to deliver a note to Alexander Johnston's warehouse. In no time at all, the distinctive sound of horse's hooves on cobblestones rang out on the far side of the bridge; the carriage in which the Beaumont's would travel to Beach Road was approaching.

Edmund made sure his wife and daughter were safely aboard before handing the baby to Chin Ming and then climbing aboard himself. Baba Tan supervised the loading of their luggage, packing some around their feet, and ordering the rest to be conveyed in a handcart. 'You are to rest today,' Dick said, 'but we will see you tomorrow evening. Alexander has arranged a celebratory dinner to welcome you home. Just the eight of us. I can't wait; we have so much to catch up on.'

Dick, Sujana, Baba Tan, and Wing Yee remained on the quay until the carriage was out of sight. No one noticed the tall Anglo-Indian merchant who had alighted from his *prahu* further downstream and had walked back to take a closer look at the reunion of a group of close friends; people who he was sure he recognised. And if he was right, they were the people with whom he intended to eventually reacquaint himself.

*****

The image of the woman's face troubled Kasim. It couldn't be, surely not? How old would she be now? The bitch, who had befriended the young women he remembered, had insisted she was too young, too inexperienced, but that was over seven years ago. If it was her, what was she doing in that boat; was

45

she married to that Englishman or just his whore? He was curious to find out. He guided the *prahu* back towards the edge of the harbour wall, found a place to tie up, and leapt back onto the quay.

Kasim dodged in and out of the fishermen mending their nets at the edge of the harbour. He quickened his pace once he reached the far end of Boat Quay, but not so fast that he would attract undue attention. The strong shadows cast by the warehouses made it impossible to get a clear view of the area where passengers took their first steps onto Singapore soil until he was almost on top of it.

The earlier arrivals had already found coolies to handle their luggage and were beginning to move away, but there was one group - quite a few people in fact – so totally absorbed in greeting each other that they had no idea they were being watched. He counted at least half a dozen adults, possibly a baby and a child; a little girl wearing a blue sash. He fell back into the shadows of the nearest godown but in a position where his view was unrestricted. This was a scene worth observing.

There was a Peranakan merchant standing slightly apart from the rest; he thought he recognised him, but couldn't remember his name. It was of no consequence; the focus of his attention was on the two Chinese women and a dark-skinned young man. If he was correct in his assumptions, he had unfinished business with all three of them.

The two women disentangled themselves from an embrace. The one he'd seen in the bumboat turned to speak to the others, more greetings, this time including the Peranakan merchant. The other woman turned in his direction, taking time to wipe her eyes dry before rejoining the others. He was positive now; she was the one who had spat in his face, she was the one he'd left tied to a chair whilst he chased after the younger one. She didn't look as haughty as he remembered, actually she looked rather handsome, very self-assured. Both women, in fact, looked confident, successful, all the things he was no longer; both vastly different to the women he'd abducted all those years ago. He'd done it to get his own back on his dead business partner, and it had led to his ruin. This time, he wouldn't let his attention be diverted by the thought of seducing either woman. He would find another way to exert his power over them.

A carriage arrived on the far side of the bridge. The family from the bumboat climbed aboard; the others packed various items of luggage around them and then they were gone, heading in the direction of Beach Road. The four remaining people returned to the wharf, enabling him to get a better view. They included the dark-skinned young man. Even though his view was only partial, Kasim was sure he was the same young man he'd almost collided with when he first returned here. He willed him to turn around, to dispel any last doubt. He strained to hear any small snippet of conversation, but the area around him was crowded; the disharmony caused by coolies yelling to each other, crashing crates, and unloading cargo was ear-splitting.

The two men shook hands, then the merchant and the Chinese bitch moved away in the direction of Market Street. The other two joined hands and started to walk in his direction; Kasim took a step further back into the shadows but not before he'd gained a clear-enough view of the young man's face. It was unmistakable. Even after seven years and growing into maturity, it was the face of the Papuan boy who Raffles had adopted and called his son.

The bile he could taste in his mouth was as bitter as his hatred. The three people who he held responsible for his arrest and removal to India had prospered well in his absence, it seemed. He stared straight ahead; his eyes cold, hard, unforgiving. He ground the heel of his shoes into some foolhardy ants that crossed his path. Right at that moment, he was finding it difficult to live up to the meaning of his new name.

As he began to walk back towards his *prahu*, his mood soured even further. How dare they be so fortunate, he thought. Two were mere women and the other the half-caste child of a peasant, whereas he'd been born into a family with status, a family whose wealth and reputation had been built up over several generations. The reason, of course, was that they'd all received the patronage of the man he'd come to loathe – Stamford Raffles. Well, if he had anything to do with it, they were going to live to regret their association with him.

His breathing became more regular; his pace increased along with his thoughts. 'I'll make them suffer for the way I've been treated,' he whispered to himself. 'I'll crush all three of them. I don't know how, but I'll begin by finding out where they all live, who they visit, how they fill their days. I'll observe them, immersed in their self-satisfied comfort. I'll make sure they suspect nothing, then I'll take my revenge. I will destroy them in the same way that Raffles destroyed me!'

CHAPTER 5
Singapore, 1st October 1830

There was very little time between putting the children to bed and when the guests were due to arrive. Chin Ming changed into her favourite red silk tunic, brushed her hair, and tip-toed towards the door of the bedroom ready to join the others. She turned to take one last look at Charlotte and William and smiled to find them fast asleep already. She swallowed hard; they were perfect, but they looked so vulnerable. She knew she would do anything to protect them.

Dick had arranged to meet the party from Baba Tan's house on the north side of the bridge so that the two house-holds would arrive together. It was a tight squeeze in the car-riage; Sujana eased herself out first, followed by Wing Yee, Baba Tan, and his wife, Yan Lau. Dick jumped down from the 'driving seat' and handed the reins to Alexander's groom.

Edmund and Alexander were deep in conversation when the guests entered the drawing room; they continued talking, not noticing the arrival of their visitors for several minutes. 'I happen to know of a property on Bukit Selegie that's just become available for rent,' Alexander said.

'What's that?' Dick asked. 'Did I hear you mention Bukit Selegie?'

'Alexander says there's a vacant property quite near to you that we might want to look at,' Edmund said, addressing

49

his old friend. 'How would you feel about having us as close neighbours?'

'Really?' Dick replied, 'I've not heard of anything; which house are you meaning? If it's true, I can't think of anything better. And I know Sujana will be pleased; she wants all the children to get on well together.'

'It's the house owned by Teddy Wilson,' Alexander said. 'He's been posted to Penang for a couple of years. I met him earlier today. His wife isn't too pleased about the move, but it's a promotion for him; he's only just decided to accept it.'

'Who's accepting what?' Chin Ming said. She'd been engrossed in conversation with Wing Yee until now, but having picked up the odd word from the three men, she decided it was time to pay attention.

Edmund explained about the possibility of renting a house on Bukit Selegie not far from Dick and Sujana. 'That would be perfect,' she said. 'When can we go to look at it?'

*****

A small gong sounded, a signal from the cook that their meal was about to be served. After taking their seats, the conversation continued at a brisk pace. Edmund told the others about the time he and Chin Ming had visited Sophia following Raffles' death and how she had subsequently decided to rent out their house in Hendon. She was planning to spend some time travelling in Europe.

Dick said very little. His shoulders slumped and there was a faraway look in his eyes. Sujana, who was sitting next to him, took his hand in hers beneath the tablecloth and gently squeezed it. He turned to her and smiled.

Edmund was aware that some discomfort had arisen amongst them all. It was bound to be awkward talking about Raffles for the first time, acknowledging his death, but he had every intention of keeping his name alive in other ways. 'How

50

are you getting on with the Spice Garden?' he asked Wing Yee, hoping to add some cheer.

'No more,' she said.

Edmund wasn't sure what that meant; he waited for her to continue.

'Spice Garden close last year. No money. No person in charge.' Wing Yee sighed heavily and shrugged her shoulders.

'I can't believe it,' Edmund said. 'That's such a waste; the garden had so much potential and Raffles had very high hopes for it. What has happened to all the plants? Has the land just been abandoned? Surely, they're not planning to build on that part of the hill?' he asked, his voice full of alarm.

'All Wing Yee's cuttings and seedlings have been moved,' Baba Tan said. 'My new home has a large courtyard garden and there is ample space for the herbs she uses in her medicines.'

'That's good news,' Edmund said, 'but what about the nutmeg and the cloves? Those trees must be quite large now, I can't believe the garden has been laid to ruin. The idea of an experimental garden was an important part of Raffles' plans for the Settlement.'

'It's not only the spice garden that's fallen out of favour,' Alexander Johnston said. 'Now we find ourselves being administered from Penang. It's often difficult to communicate with the powers that be. I'm afraid it's become impossible to get them interested in the majority of the ideas Raffles had for the place.'

'But the new warehouses, the new streets, they were all in his Town Plan,' Edmund said. 'What is it that you're not telling us?'

'Oh yes, the shops, houses, and godowns are developing apace,' Alexander continued. 'Especially the godowns - the more warehouses the better. Most of the merchants are eager to invest in anything they see as potential for making a profit. Most of them are recent arrivals; they're not concerned with the schemes Raffles had to improve the lives of local people. We all know he was an idealist, of course, and some of his ideas were not feasible. Sorry Dick, but it's true. The bureaucrats who represent the East India Company – as well as most of the new arrivals - are not interested in ethics. In fact, I'm sad to say that their morals are at times highly questionable.' He glanced at Dick for approval before venturing to say anything further. 'Such ideals as Raffles held are not profitable, you see, and I'm afraid the administration is only interested in profit these days,' Johnston said.

'But surely, the Company has always been like that,' Edmund said. 'I remember Raffles telling me he'd had difficulty in persuading them to support his recommendation to establish a Settlement here in the first place. But they couldn't have been more wrong, could they? Merchants flocked here then and continue to do so, even if their motives are somewhat dubious. There must be something else.' Deep furrows developed on his brow as he looked at his host and awaited an explanation.

'There have been a few rows, I believe,' Johnston said 'The power lies in Penang, where the Governor resides. Any spare energy has been focused on Malacca because of local land disputes. Singapore gets very little attention and even less opportunity to develop anything other than the East India trade.'

'Singapore is considered to be an upstart Settlement by some of the people who have worked out East for most of their lives, and they're envious of our rapid development,' Baba Tan said. 'Malacca has been a European settlement for nearly two hundred years, remember, and even Penang has now been a British settlement for over fifty years.'

'And because those places are believed to have better facilities than Singapore,' Alexander said, 'people coming out from England prefer to be posted there. Teddy Wilson's wife might be reluctant to relocate at present, but I'd wager she won't want to come back here in two years' time.'

'But that's so short-sighted,' Edmund said. 'The location of Singapore is so much better for the trade routes between India and China. That's why Raffles recommended it in the first place. Surely the Company bureaucrats know that?'

Baba Tan's wife whispered something in Malay to Wing Yee, across the table. Wing Yee shrugged her shoulders and turned her head slowly from side to side.

'Enough gentlemen,' Johnston said, noticing the inter-change. 'This is not a subject for the dinner table and the ladies are getting restless. I hope the meal is to your liking?' He couldn't remember on any of the previous occasions they had shared a celebratory meal when the conversation had not included the quality of the food being served.

Chin Ming bit her lip. How dare these men decide what women could and couldn't discuss or be interested in. She knew Alexander hadn't meant to be unkind, but there were a million questions buzzing around inside her head. When she looked up again, she realised everyone was waiting for her to respond to Alexander's question. She took a deep breath.

'It is as delicious as always,' she said. 'I can't tell you how much I've missed *beef rendang* and *ayam kalio*.'

'Our English beef stew and chicken casserole just didn't impress you, did it my dear?' Edmund said.

Everyone laughed. The mood had been lightened. For the most part, the meal continued at a leisurely pace. Dick was unusually quiet, but only Sujana seemed to notice. Wing Yee was encouraged by Baba Tan to tell the others about their plans to open a clinic.

'So many people here now,' she said. 'Many ailments. Some get hurt, some infected. Only men come to buy medicine; often they not know what is the matter with wife or concubine. We need place for men and women to talk about illness; place for us to see them and ask many question.'

'I'm having something purpose built in Amoy Street,' Baba

Tan said. 'It's only small, but that's all we need at the beginning. If we are successful, then we can always move to a larger space. I hope we can encourage people to see that some illnesses might be prevented, as well as healing wounds and calming fevers.'

Everyone began to ask questions all at once. Even Dick hadn't heard the latest proposals for the clinic and he let himself become as engrossed as the rest of them in finding out more.

'So, you see,' he said, 'we do have some good news to tell you. Raffles would have been overjoyed to hear about the clinic and the progress Wing Yee has made with developing all her medicines.'

'And don't forget about the school,' Alexander said. 'We all know how much you wanted the small children you taught to progress, Chin Ming. Well, Raffles' idea for a Singapore Institution has at last become a reality. It's not completed, but Lieutenant Jackson has designed a building which is good enough for the time being. We should take you along to Bras Basah Road to inspect it.'

'Is Abdullah involved? Does he still teach the younger children or is he sharing his knowledge with older pupils now?' Chin Ming asked.

'He still provides advice and support to the two young men who now teach the younger children and he's also involved with the older pupils at the Institution. But the exciting news about Abdullah is that he's started to write a book.'

'You mean ...,' she said.

'Yes,' Alexander replied. 'He's writing his story, just as your father told him he should.'

Chin Ming smiled. She remembered that occasion. They'd all gathered at the tiny, fledgling school; they were waiting for Wing Yee to arrive. Her father was expecting to ask her friends to persuade her that she was being foolish in rejecting Edmund's initial proposal of marriage. The air had been as heavy with the sweet fragrance of frangipani back then as it was now. It was a useful reminder that her life might have been very different; it made her appreciate the fact that things had turned out the way that they had.

'And even better,' Alexander added, 'Instead of writing the usual romanticised chronicle, Abdullah is writing an eyewitness account of Singapore, beginning with the early years of this century. But not just a historical record either. He's writing an autobiography, filled with his personal observations, and it will include some of his poetry. I've seen a little of what he's already written; it's full of wit, but he's also managed to capture the transitory nature of the Settlement.'

'What do you mean?' the others asked.

'Well, he seems able to show the passage of time as a series of changes between a traditional world and a modern world; between Malacca and Singapore; between different peoples, their languages, and beliefs. It's quite extraordinary.'

'So, does that mean he's in favour of all the changes that have occurred, including recent developments?' Dick asked. He'd heard that Abdullah had started to write a book but hadn't paid much attention to what it was about until now.

'I get the impression that whilst he's definitely an advocate of many of the developments brought to the region by Europeans,' Alexander said, taking his time to continue and looking directly at Dick, 'Abdullah, like some others of us around this table, also feels great regret at the endlessly changing present we live in.'

Whilst Chin Ming was delighted to hear about the school and the plans for a clinic, the concerns which had arisen just before they began to discuss the meal, resurfaced. She was disturbed to learn that the Settlement had not entirely been allowed to develop in the way that Raffles had intended. She needed to know more, but now was not the time to pursue such a discussion. She would store up her questions for another occasion.

*****

Two days after the dinner party, Chin Ming and Edmund left the children in the care of Wing Yee and arrived on Selegie Hill to view the house they'd been told about. Alexander's groom helped them to climb down from the carriage, then he took up the reins and turned back in the direction of the town.

The house was larger than she was expecting it to be, but it looked welcoming from the outside. It was typically made of wood, standing squarely on fat wooden posts. On the wide veranda, large ceramic pots containing bougainvillea in colours ranging from orange to deep purple adorned the entrance; their foliage spilled over the edge of the platform and cascaded to the earth below. The steeply sloping roof provided ample shade and, beyond all that, was a well-established garden which would please Edmund. The faint but very distinctive fragrance of jasmine floated all around.

Chin Ming's heart began to race and every fibre of her body began to tingle. The house was perfect, but could they afford it? Edmund's father had been so good to them in England, rearranging the vicarage to accommodate their needs, but she wanted so much to have a place they could call their own.

'Alexander tells me that he's at liberty to negotiate the rent,' Edmund said as if he was reading her thoughts, 'and he thinks the Wilsons will be glad to have someone he knows and can recommend to take it on. He also says, if we can say that we'll take it for the entire time they'll be away, that will be another point in our favour.'

'Two years? Will it take that long for you to write your book? How long will your funding last?'

'Ever the practical one, my love. The university will only want to publish a thoroughly researched manuscript. The advance I've received will cover our expenses for at least twelve months and if, in addition, I can send them some new plant specimens they will pay handsomely, I'm sure.'

'But won't that mean you will have to go away from here for several months?' She frowned. 'Are you thinking of returning to China?'

'No. I have no contacts there now. I think that would not be wise.'

'I could come with you – as your translator!'

'And what would happen to the children? They're far too young to be taken on such an expedition. Besides, I don't like the sound of some of the disturbances that have been happening around the Pearl River. The emperor is determined to quash the opium trade and the Company employees remain as arrogant as ever. Things could flare up at any moment and I wouldn't want to get caught in the middle. No, I was thinking of visiting Malacca or maybe even Penang. Raffles told me he acquired much of his early material from the countryside surrounding Malacca.'

'Then I could definitely come with you,' Chin Ming said. 'I might not want to trek through the jungle, but the children and I would be there to welcome you home at night.'

Edmund laughed. He loved his wife's capacity for thinking of alternatives and her desire to share everything with each other.

'That sounds wonderful,' he said. 'But in the meantime, I think we can confidently say we can afford to take on Wilson's house. Shall we take a closer look?'

Chin Ming danced a little jig, then she took Edmund's hand and they climbed the steps together. Just over an hour later, Dick turned into the drive of Wilson's house. He found Chin Ming and Edmund sitting on the veranda deep in conversation. He coughed as he approached the wooden steps.

'Where did you appear from?' Edmund asked.

'I told you we live very close by. Have you decided? Are we to be neighbours?'

Chin Ming and Edmund eyed each other carefully, each trying to ascertain what the other was thinking. Their eyes gave everything away: a matching smile settled on their lips, then they turned towards Dick and nodded.

He held his arms out wide as he quickened his pace and moved closer. He embraced them both, making loud, whooping sounds. 'Come,' he said, 'let's go and tell Sujana the good news.'

*****

Five days after seeing the house for the first time, the Beaumont family were preparing to move into it. As Edmund had anticipated, there had been no issues regarding the rent; Alexander assured them that the Wilsons would be delighted with the arrangement. He'd drawn up a formal agreement for the signatures of both parties and informed Edmund they would be able to move within a few days.

Their crates were loaded onto Johnston's carriage and Dick sent his own, smaller vehicle to convey the family from Beach Road to Selegie Hill. Charlotte was very excited and had to be persuaded to sit down more than once. When they reached the house, the three-year-old trotted off to explore the garden on her own before anyone noticed. Chin Ming directed Dick and Edmund to various parts of the house as they moved the luggage from the vehicles to their allotted rooms. Sujana arrived, carrying Tomas in something that looked very much like a sling tied to her back. In her hands, she carefully balanced a tray full of cooling drinks.

'Where are the children?' she said as she placed the tray on a small bamboo table.

'William is asleep in his basket,' Chin Ming said. 'That child could sleep through an earthquake, I'm sure.'

'But what about Charlotte?' Sujana said. 'Where has she got to?'

58

CHAPTER 6
Singapore, 8th - 9th October 1830

Chin Ming rushed to the edge of the veranda but there was no sign of Charlotte. She almost fell down the steps into the garden, catching the hem of her tunic in her haste. 'Charlotte!' she called, when she regained her balance, looking first to the right and then to the left. 'Charlotte ... Charlotte, where are you?' she shouted, her voice rising and beads of sweat developing on her forehead. The only response was the distinctive warning screech of a mynah bird, but it too was well out of sight.

The blood drained from her face. 'Why didn't I pay more attention? Why did I let myself be distracted, focusing on which boxes went to each room?' she almost whispered to herself as her gaze drifted from one flowerbed to another. The last time she'd seen Charlotte was when the little girl jumped down from the carriage; where on earth could she have got to?

Edmund and Dick stepped onto the veranda, pleased that the last of the luggage was now securely placed inside the house. It had been warm work and the sight of the cooling drinks brought along by Sujana was most welcome. Their self-gratification crumbled, however, the moment they heard about Charlotte.

'She'll not be too far away,' Edmund said, trying to comfort his wife as he encouraged her to move into the shade. 'You know what she's like, always eager to explore and make new friends. It's not the first time she has supposedly vanished. I'm beginning to think my daughter is destined to join a group of travelling players or possibly join the circus.'

'Please don't joke, Edmund,' Chin Ming said, her gaze flitting across the veranda, around the garden, and back again.

'What should we do, where should we start to look for her?' Sujana said. Her eyes turned to Dick; she silently implored him to come up with a solution.

'You stay here with Chin Ming,' he said. 'If Charlotte gets bored with whatever is occupying her and comes looking for her mother, she needs to be able to find you.'

Edmund embraced Chin Ming, trying to reassure her without showing his own unease. 'Dick's right,' he said, 'you two stay here. I'm sure she wouldn't have strayed as far as the road, and Sujana would have seen her if she's taken that route.'

Dick immediately took charge of the situation. 'We'll look further along the hillside in the other direction just to be sure and then we'll search the grounds,' he said. He told Edmund to search the formal garden in front of the house whilst he surveyed the road. He ran along the uneven track, investigating every possible hiding place, only giving up when all possibilities had been checked. He returned to explore the rear part of the grounds, an area that was overgrown and unkempt.

The drinks remained on the tray, untouched. Despite Sujana's encouragement to sit, Chin Ming couldn't settle and insisted on searching every room in the house When she returned to the veranda, Sujana patted the cushions next to her. 'We'll be able to see any sign of activity from here,' she said. 'Please sit beside me so that we can keep watch together.'

*****

For the next hour, Edmund explored every path, checked the shadows created by the larger shrubs, and rummaged in the shed at the rear of the property, in search of his daughter.

Dick crawled through and between ancient roots, the lower branches of a tembusu tree, and evil-looking vines intent on winding themselves around him. It was an area that had not yet been reclaimed from the original jungle flora, full of traps, tendrils, and other examples of vigorous growth that had encompassed the hillside for centuries. The air was musty and overpowering.

He was in the process of disentangling himself from a particularly pernicious creeper when something looking like a dark, shiny rope dropped at his feet. He froze. It was about four feet long and arranged itself into several concentric circles only a yard or so away from him. He'd encountered snakes before and had learned to be extremely cautious. He kept very still. On closer scrutiny, he recognised it as a rat snake, non-venomous and posing no threat to humans. He assumed the sound of the undergrowth snapping and lianas being pulled away had disturbed its daytime slumber; maybe even causing it to fall out of the tree. Would it now start foraging for small rodents or return to a tree cavity to seek its prey later? Seconds later, it uncurled, resembling a black, glossy cord, and slithered away amongst the tree roots.

Dick shuddered. How many other snakes might there be here? What if Charlotte had encountered something more dangerous? If she'd found her way to this part of the garden, she could easily have tripped or fallen; maybe she was lying somewhere hurt, unconscious, or just frightened. He began to call her name.

'Charlotte, can you hear me? It's Dick, your new uncle. You're not in any trouble, can you shout out if you can hear me?'

No response. He called again, this time a little louder. Then again. 'Charlotte ..., Ming Yue ...' He used her Chinese name alongside her English one, hoping that would encourage her to respond but still no reply. He was reluctant to give up but finally emerged from the dense vegetation and moved onto the main path closer to the house. He was covered in broken twigs and assorted foliage. Edmund came from the opposite direction; both men looked wretched. How could they return to Chin Ming and tell her they had failed to find the little girl?

Dick rubbed the back of his neck, letting out short breaths as he tried to gain control. He watched Edmund run trembling hands through his hair before steadying them, prayer-like, over his mouth. When his eyes lifted to meet Dick's, they were full of panic and despair.

A bird screeched as it dived after its prey and was gone; there was only the occasional rustle of dry leaves. Minutes passed, then, something changed.

'Did you hear that?' Dick said.

They both strained their ears to pick up the slightest murmur. Could it be the muffled sound of someone sobbing, or was it their imagination? Then they heard it again, floating through the air; it was indistinct, feeble even, a sort of whimpering but signifying distress all the same. Where was it coming from?

Dick pointed in the direction of the house. Then he whispered, 'Underneath, I think.' He signalled to Edmund that he would go ahead. There was no time to ask any questions. Dick had already begun to quicken his pace.

The sound came and went, it wasn't audible all the time; perhaps they had imagined it after all, maybe they were clinging to a false hope. Dick leant against one of the posts supporting the house, trying to control his breathing. It was difficult to keep his hands from shaking and his palms were clammy. His imagination was beginning to take over his innermost thoughts. Was it Charlotte they could hear? had she been bitten by something more dangerous than a rat snake? Was she bleeding? He was worried that his fear would soon become apparent to Edmund.

'Listen,' Edmund said, 'there it is again.' Between the gulps of silence, there was intermittent whimpering followed by the occasional sniff and small soft sounds of someone uttering indistinguishable words.

Dick dropped to his knees and crawled towards the source of the sound. Edmund followed close behind; he struggled to breathe, all too aware of his pounding heart. He uttered a silent prayer to himself: *Keep her safe. I'll do anything to make sure she doesn't get lost or wander off again ... but please keep her safe.*

Charlotte was kneeling with her small legs tucked underneath a dress, which, earlier in the day, had been pale-pink muslin. Now, she was covered in debris and the pretty dress had turned it into a limp, brown rag. One of her shoes was missing, the other festooned with rotting leaves. She rocked herself backwards and forwards, not noticing the arrival of either her father or Dick. She wiped a grubby hand, wetted with tears, across her eyes, making her face look more like a tiger's than a child's. She was a patchwork of colours ranging from honey to yam with hints of papaya.

'Charlotte ...,' Edmund said.

'Papa!' she squealed as he scooped her into his arms. A collection of dry leaves cascaded from her hair, but more obstinate varieties still clung to her clothing.

'We thought we'd lost you,' he said, trying not to frighten her. 'We thought you were just looking at the flowers in the garden. What made you come here?'

'A bird, I heard it singing; it was so pretty.'

'Did something happen to the bird, Charlotte?' Dick said.

She nodded very slowly, and the tears resurfaced. She buried her head in Edmund's shoulder and couldn't be consoled.

Dick started to cast his eyes around to see if he could discover what had caused such upset for the little girl. About three strides away from them, he found the answer. Caught in a rat trap and quite dead was a straw-headed bulbul bird. He let out a huge breath and uttered his silent gratitude there was no evidence of snakes, poisonous or otherwise.

No wonder Charlotte had been attracted to it. This species, with its yellow-orange crown and a profusion of brown, white, and olive feathers covering the rest of its body was well-known for its singing ability.

Edmund spoke softly to his daughter, stroking her tangled hair, brushing away the surplus debris. Now, he decided was not the time to admonish.

Dick beamed at them both, bringing a shaky hand to his forehead. 'I'll run ahead,' he said, 'Chin Ming needs to hear the good news as quickly as possible. You two take your time.'

*****

Out in the sunshine, Dick hurried from the chaos of the back garden to the more ordered plot at the front. As he rounded the corner of the house, Chin Ming turned towards him. He waved.

She couldn't see the expression on his face, the glare of the sun prevented that. Surely, he wouldn't wave so furiously if there was anything wrong, but on the other hand, perhaps it was a warning of some sort. She gripped Sujana's arm; both women remained fixed to the spot.

Dick leapt up the six wooden steps in two athletic movements. He was grinning now. 'All is well,' he said. 'We found her underneath the house. She was attracted to a songbird, but I'm afraid it didn't end well for the feathered creature. Charlotte was understandably upset. I think the Wilsons laid some rat traps down there.'

Chin Ming gasped. 'How many are there? I didn't realise that rats are still a problem in Singapore.'

'This house hasn't been empty for long, but to be safe, I think the whole area should be checked for vermin. I came across a snake when I was searching through the undergrowth at the back of the house. I'll have a word with Alexander to see if we can get a gang of coolies up here to search for any other traps and to secure the ground beneath the house.'

Just then, Edmund appeared. He was almost as dishevelled as his daughter. She'd stopped crying and had fallen asleep on his shoulder. When he reached the others, he laid Charlotte down on a bench. She curled into a ball, put her thumb into her mouth, and carried on sleeping. He put his arms around his wife and held her close.

Chin Ming's head was full of jumbled thoughts. She stroked the soft, perfect skin on her sleeping daughter's leg, then lifted her matted hair to check for any hidden signs of injury. She felt weak and light-headed and was glad Edmund was standing close by. Tears welled up behind her eyelids. 'We really do need to make her understand that she can't just wander off on her own,' she said.

'She's always been inquisitive,' Edmund said. 'I've always rather liked the fact that she is so interested in everything. It's her natural curiosity that leads her to ask so many questions, and I like the fact that she is so fond of animals.'

'That was all well and good,' said Chin Ming, 'when we were at your father's vicarage. The garden was completely fenced in; it wasn't so dangerous.'

'True, and I will make it less hazardous here. I promise I will make it easier to keep an eye on her.'

'But this is such a large area with so much of it left wild, I don't know how you're going to manage it. Dick told me about the rat trap – and he said he'd seen a snake today, there might be others.'

'Then we'll get some help,' Edmund said. 'I already have an idea.'

Chin Ming looked exhausted; she couldn't begin to think what he had in mind.

'We'll get the area under the house fenced in and we'll get the land at the back of the house cleared.'

'What about the dead bird?' she said.

'Don't worry,' Dick, who had been listening to their concerns, said. 'I'll deal with that. Do you have a small box you could let me use? I'll release the bird and get rid of the trap, then I'll lay the bird carefully in the box. Tomorrow, we can all give it a proper funeral and Charlotte can see where it's buried.'

'We'll talk to her in the morning,' Chin Ming said. 'There's no point in waking her now.' She lifted her daughter from the bench and carried her into the house and laid her on her bed. She was still dirty, but that was the least of Chin Ming's worries.

*****

Later that evening, when Dick and Sujana had returned to their own home, Edmund and Chin Ming sat on their veranda delighting in the sounds and fragrances of the night. There had been a light shower earlier in the evening, cleansing the air and cooling the temperature. The sleeping town below them was bathed in moonlight and stars shone above their heads. Edmund moved nearer and held his wife's hands.

'We've waited over four years for this moment,' he said, 'our first moment alone, looking at the tropical sky, hearing the crickets chirping away, feeling warmth on our skin even though it's quite late and ....'

'I've missed the sweet scent of frangipani,' Chin Ming added, smiling. 'Do you remember the night before we left for England? We stood in Alexander's garden and discussed whether or not the moon would look the same when we reached England.'

'How could I possibly forget?' Edmund said. 'I was so terrified that you would be unhappy in England, that you'd loathe the long, cold winters ...'

'But you promised that we would return here one day, and

here we are. Besides, England wasn't all that bad; the countryside is beautiful, especially in spring. It was good to see the place where you were born, where you studied, and the people who, on the whole, were kind, but I am glad to be back here. This is my special place.'

Edmund nodded. 'Time to retire, I think,' he said. He took a lamp in one hand and wrapped his other arm around Chin Ming's shoulders. They walked through the open door together. 'It's a bit of a novelty,' he said, 'having our very own front door and closing it each night.'

*****

After breakfast a few days later, Edmund and Chin Ming sat with Charlotte between them. They explained, carefully, that now they were no longer living in England they all had to learn new things and be wary of some things that might be dangerous.

'What sort of things?' Charlotte wanted to know.

They told her that not all the animals who lived in Singapore liked having people around and sometimes got upset about having their space disturbed.

'What is up - set?' Charlotte said.

'Well,' Edmund began, 'if an animal has lived here for a while – long before we arrived - it might not want to share its favourite spot; it may not be friendly and might even hurt you.'

'Something hurt the pretty bird.'

Neither of them mentioned the rat trap specifically, but they did their best to allude to a range of reasons why they all needed to be very careful. They told her it was important that she didn't wander off on her own because how would they know where to find her if she got into difficulty?

'But Papa and Uncle Dick found me the other day,' she said.

Chin Ming and Edmund exchanged glances. They didn't

want to frighten her, but it was important that she understood not to stray too far away from them.

'What if I fence off a special part of the garden for you to play in?' Edmund said. 'I will teach you the names of all the new plants we discover and we'll look out for anything you should avoid.'

'My very own garden?' Charlotte said, obviously pleased with the idea.

'Yes, it will be a place where you will be safe, where you can play, dig the ground, do anything you like really,' Edmund said.

'But you mustn't go anywhere else without Mama and Papa; you mustn't talk to strangers, do you understand?' Chin Ming said, anxious that Charlotte was so besotted with the idea of her own garden that she hadn't paid enough attention to the other messages they had tried to convey.

'Like that man?' the little girl asked, pointing towards the entrance to their drive.

Edmund and Chin Ming swung around to stare at an empty driveway.

'Who did you see, darling?' she said.

'Just a man,' Charlotte replied. 'He's gone now.'

CHAPTER 7
Singapore, 9th October

It was almost a fortnight since Kasim had witnessed the reunion of Dick and his friends. The arrival of several vessels in addition to the *Castle Huntly* and a convict ship had resulted in a great deal of activity in and around Market Street. Another Chinese junk had delivered a fresh consignment of labourers, and the first thing they wanted to do was acquaint themselves with the moneylenders. They already owed money to the gangmasters for their passage and whatever they earned on the gambier plantation was unlikely to lighten that debt for some considerable time. Hence, Kasim's days were fully occupied and his quest to locate the exact whereabouts of his adversaries had not been possible.

The advantage of this situation, however, was that it gave him time to think. In the brief moments between dealing with his customers, he scrutinised the comings and goings in Market Street with a more critical eye, he listened more astutely to unguarded conversations, and he did not allow himself to be distracted by superfluous exchanges.

Towards the end of the sixth day, a chance encounter made his diligence worthwhile. He was busy tidying his desk and preparing to lock his cashbox when he heard someone call out a familiar name. The Peranakan merchant he'd seen at the quay a few days ago was hurrying along Market Street, waving a bright red handkerchief to attract the attention of a young man a little way ahead of him.

'Master Dick,' he heard the man call out. Kasim's muscles tightened, he listened more intently, and kept watch from his position, half-hidden behind his desk. The merchant increased his pace as he continued along the road and shouted louder; the young man – Dick - stopped in his tracks and turned around.

'Baba Tan,' he said, 'what's all the excitement about?' They became engrossed in an animated conversation almost immediately, but Kasim could no longer catch what was being discussed. No matter, both their names were now familiar; names that resonated from before. They both had an association with Stamford Raffles; a relationship he would soon make sure they regretted.

Kasim slipped down from his stool, stuffed his belongings into a canvas bag, and left the shophouse behind. Long shadows provided him with ample cover, and soon he was within earshot of the pair.

'Yes, it's all agreed,' Dick said. 'Alexander drew up the contract on behalf of the Wilsons. Chin Ming and Edmund moved into the house yesterday.'

'So, they are your neighbours?' Baba Tan said.

'Indeed. I can't quite believe how fortunate it is for a house on Bukit Selegie to become vacant just at the right moment.'

Kasim pressed himself against the pillar of the shophouse where he was hiding. There was no sign of the owner, but the place was stacked high with sacks of pepper, star anise, and cloves. The heady aromas began to tickle Kasim's nostrils and he covered his face with the sleeve of his kurta to dull the sound of a sneeze.

'You were not aware that the Wilsons had moved to Penang then?' Baba Tan said.

'To be honest, we hardly knew them,' Dick replied. 'They socialised with others who worked for the Company, I believe. We saw very little of them.'

'Then I consider their move to Penang to be auspicious,' Baba Tan continued. 'It was their destiny to travel north and your good fortune to be able to welcome your friends ....'

The two men began to walk away in the direction of High Street. Kasim's opportunity to eavesdrop was at an end, but he had all the information he required, at least for the time being.

✻✻✻✻✻

After all the flurry of activity during the last few days, every-thing settled down again. The occasional customer called in to pay back a portion of their debt, but that apart, the only activities to occupy Kasim involved the usual routine – counting coins, checking lists, noting down the names of outstanding loans. None of the people passing by on Market Street inter-ested him in the way that Baba Tan and Dick had.

'Do you know anyone who lives on Bukit Selegie?' Kasim said to a fellow moneylender. 'I heard someone mention it the other day, and I wondered what sort of houses had been built there.'

The man shrugged his shoulders. 'Cannot tell much,' he said in halting English. 'Not for us *Chetties*, you understand. I hear that land belong to Colonel Farquhar, but many year now since he leave Singapore. Maybe the Company take it over? Sorry, no idea.'

The phrase 'not for us' stabbed at the core of Kasim's pride. How dare the man assume the dwellings on Bukit Selegie were too good for the likes of him. He muttered under his breath ... cursing himself for having to dress like an Indian, reviling himself for having to live alongside people he despised. Once again, his loathing and his jealousy came bubbling to the sur-face. The name Farquhar, however, rang bells in Kasim's head. This was the man who had been appointed the first Resident and left in charge of the Settlement when Raffles went back to Bencoolen. It was the man with whom Raffles had quarrelled

71

when he returned to the Settlement a few years later; the man Victor had claimed as his uncle. If he had an opportunity to get away this afternoon, he must seek out his new friend.

*****

It was almost 4 o'clock. when Kasim eventually located him. Victor was seated on his usual stool at the coffee stall in front of Choo Keng's warehouse. Kasim quickened his pace as he crossed the road and waved. Victor looked pleased to see him.

'Haven't seen you for a few days,' Victor said. 'I was beginning to think you'd left town.'

Kasim ignored the remark and sat down on the stool opposite his friend. 'One of my work colleagues told me that your uncle owned land on Bukit Selegie,' he said. 'Has it been passed down to you or perhaps another member of the family?'

Victor narrowed his eyes and clenched his jaw. His left foot started to tap, tap, tap the ground, joined shortly afterwards by the fingers of his right hand which drummed the tabletop.

'My apologies,' Kasim said, 'I didn't mean to upset you.' He studied Victor's face, secretly amused that he'd managed to cause such a revealing response.

'I have to confess,' Victor said, his cheeks now the colour of his favourite chilli peppers, 'that William Farquhar isn't exactly my uncle.'

I'd worked that our for myself, Kasim thought, but remained silent.

'My mother was the sister of Farquhar's common-law wife. He brought the whole family here when he moved from Malacca; we all lived in the Malay kampong. He, my aunt, and their six children had a large house. My mother and I lived separately, but we had a good life.'

'So, did Farquhar intend to build on the land he purchased around Bukit Selegie, or was he content to remain in the kampong?'

'The latter, I imagine,' Victor said. 'We knew nothing about that purchase until long after he'd left Singapore.'

'Did your aunt not want to accompany him?'

'She had no choice in the matter. It was never even considered. He was angry because Raffles dismissed him as Resident and took over the responsibility of running everything himself until John Crawfurd arrived. Farquhar kicked up quite a stink but was forced to leave at the end of '23. My aunt stayed in the kampong for a while, but eventually, she decided to return to Malacca; Farquhar had left her with no means of support, you see.'

'No wonder you hold a grudge,' Kasim said.

'Wouldn't you? My father was also European, but I never knew him. It seems to me that it's far too easy for European men to come out East, make enough money to have a decent life, then, when it suits them, return to the comfort of Britain. I've been told that Farquhar now has a wife in Scotland and has produced yet more children. The ones he left behind here are quite forgotten.'

Kasim thought about his own background; his experience was entirely different to that of Victor, but they still had a great deal in common. His own father had enjoyed local women all across the Pacific, but he'd always returned to Batavia and his family. The young Pieter Steffens had enjoyed the best of everything – until the British arrived. He'd managed to escape in a local fishing boat long before Raffles took charge, but that didn't stop him holding Raffles responsible for ruining his life. That's what he had in common with Victor - the bitterness, the envy, the hatred. He intended to exploit this friendship to its limits; it might well help him achieve his retribution.

They spent the evening together at one of the illegal liquor houses. Alcohol loosened Victor's tongue even further, and by the time they fell out onto the pavement, Kasim had not only discovered that Dick's wife was the daughter of a wealthy Javanese merchant, but the house they lived in had been given to them as a wedding present. Further along the ridge, was a house owned by a man called Wilson; Victor had heard that it was about to be rented out, he knew not to whom. The name Wilson rang a bell in Kasim's head; this must be the house being referred in the conversation he'd overheard a few days ago. How convenient to have all his adversaries clustered so close together.

*****

The whole of the following day was taken up with overseeing the transfer of one of Fergusson's shipments to local trading vessels. It required Kasim to travel out into the harbour, check that the opium had not been tampered with, and then wait for the country traders to arrive. There were four or five such men he'd come to rely upon. They arrived, loaded their consignment from the starboard side of the Indian vessels, and then went on their way. It was a slow business. It had to look casual and not draw any undue attention. By the time the last vessel had departed, the sun was already low in the sky and it was far too late when he returned to shore to think about embarking upon a stroll in the direction of Bukit Selegie.

When he stepped onto Boat Quay, he looked to see if Victor was anywhere around, but the stool at his usual hawker stall was empty. Kasim decided to stretch his legs. Perhaps he would have something to eat before he returned to his *prahu* for the evening. He hadn't eaten since early morning and now he felt ravenous. He hurried towards the end of the wharf, anxious to get to the curry house at the end of Market Street, but his progress was thwarted by the sudden appearance of a gang of workmen.

Over the last few years, the convict workforce brought in from India had increased tenfold. As a result of their labours, there was an expansion in the number of government buildings and warehouses as well as many more roads being constructed. At the end of each day, gangs of convict labourers

74

were escorted back to the sheds in which they were housed. One of these gangs was now being forced across North Bridge Road. The policeman who accompanied them lifted his hand to prevent anyone else in the vicinity travelling any further until the convicts had been moved on.

Kasim crossed his arms and fidgeted with the cuffs of his kurta before letting out several loud exasperated breaths. He needed no reminder that he'd been a prisoner himself not so long ago. His noisy agitation, though, resulted in one of their number turning to stare at him. The man stopped walking, frowned, then he laughed. It was a nervous sort of laugh – short, high pitched, and tense. The policeman prodded him with a wooden baton and told him to hurry.

'What was that about?' the man walking alongside convict number 7-1-0 asked.

'I think I recognised that man,' he replied. 'Someone from Calcutta. Someone who cause me great misery.'

*****

The next morning, Kasim's curiosity got the better of him. He called in to tell Mukesh that he had an urgent appointment but would be back at his desk in the afternoon. He turned towards the river, keeping his head down whilst weaving his way between the people crossing Monkey Bridge. Then, he hurried along North Bridge Road until he reached the junction with Selegie Road.

Initially, the walk was pleasant enough; the only people around were gardeners cutting down foliage, sweeping drives, or piling up fallen branches. A couple in a pony and trap passed by and turned into one of the driveways. He was beginning to feel hot and he regretted not stopping for a cooling drink before he embarked upon his exploration. The road at present was flat but he could already see the point where it started to climb; he needed to take it slowly and keep in the shade.

Kasim reached the point where the road levelled out again nearly an hour later. He'd been careful to disappear into wooded areas whenever he heard an approaching carriage. There had been three altogether and he hadn't recognised any of the occupants, but he couldn't risk anyone stopping to enquire about his purpose. He passed the entrance to a driveway with the name Curtiss on the gatepost; the next one identified the owners as Hamilton and across from them the family was called Brown. None of these names matched the people he was seeking. Had he misunderstood what he'd overheard? Did they not live on Selegie Hill after all? He could see no other houses, but something compelled him to continue walking. The heat from the sun and the exertion of climbing the hill began to take its toll; he cursed himself for failing to bring something to protect his head, something to quench his thirst.

Further along the road, he was beginning to wonder if there were any more houses or whether he'd missed a turning that led to another part of the hill where he would find who he was looking for. He rounded a particularly sharp bend and thought he saw another pair of gateposts just beyond a casuarina tree, but maybe it was wishful thinking, the effect of the sun? He was passing a high hibiscus hedge when he heard some voices; they were too far away to distinguish what was being said, but he was sure now that the gateposts were real and beyond them lay the inhabitants of a dwelling. He continued further along the road.

'Are ... planning ... Ming and Ed ... this morn...?' On the other side of the hedge Kasim picked up the bare bones of a conversation – hardly more than a whisper, but it was enough to alert him, to stop him in his tracks. The voice he'd heard was light and pleasant, a woman; she spoke clearly and in English with only a slight accent. It was like something he'd heard before – years ago - but he couldn't remember where.

'I thought I'd take the carriage and offer to take Edmund

into town. He might want to make arrangements for transferring money, sending letters or reports back to Oxford.'

This time it was a male voice, strong, confident, self-assured. He couldn't be positive, of course, but he would be willing to gamble that it was the voice of the young man known as Dick – Raffles' adopted son. He couldn't afford to check out his assumption, couldn't risk being seen skulking outside on the road but if he was right it meant the Chinese woman and her husband would not be far away.

He hurried on, oblivious now of the increasing heat. A short distance away there was indeed another house; it had a short, sweeping driveway with a formal garden laid out in front of a substantial wooden dwelling. The sun was high now and the shadows were strong. It was easy to slip into the dark patches to examine the scene more closely.

Kasim noted the empty veranda, the seats with their plumped-up cushions, and a wooden toy precariously balanced on the edge of the steps leading down to the drive. He thought this might indicate that the house was occupied, but there was no sign of life. He was on the point of giving up his vigil when the door onto the veranda opened. The Englishman he'd seen in the bumboat stepped out, followed by the Chinese woman who held hands with the little girl. Today, she was wearing a pale-green dress, but there was no sign of the blue sash.

The two adults sat with the little girl between them. First, one of them spoke to her, then the other; he wondered if she was in trouble. She was obviously a bright little thing, not sitting passively to await correction but asking questions, wanting answers. Kasim couldn't hear a word of what passed between them but became mesmerised by the interchange. At one point the man stood up and pointed to the unkempt garden at the side of the property. The little girl joined him. She jumped up and down and squealed. The woman called them back to join her and the earnest conversation seemed to continue.

The sun had moved higher in the sky and taken with it the cloak of shadows enveloping Kasim. He wasn't aware of his exposure until he saw the little girl pointing in his direction. He leapt into the undergrowth, tearing the sleeve of his kurta as he did so. He was quietly cursing himself for being so careless when he heard the unmistakable sound of a horse and carriage approaching. He remained in his hiding place until the vehicle had swept past him and pulled up in front of the house.

As soon as it was safe to do so, he hurried further along the road. Eventually, it gave way to swathes of nibong palm and beyond them to the beginning of a new road being cut into the hillside from the east. He had no option but to take this route. He daren't risk being overtaken on the other road and especially by the carriage that he presumed had come to collect Chin Ming's husband and take him into town.

CHAPTER 8
Singapore, early November 1830

Edmund and Chin Ming had been back in Singapore for nearly six weeks when he remembered it would soon be their fourth wedding anniversary. Whilst in England, they had enjoyed quiet celebrations at the vicarage with his father and his brother, James. But now that they had settled into their own home, he wanted something else, something more significant. He went in search of his wife.

'You're looking very pleased with yourself,' Chin Ming said when he found her. She was sitting in her favourite chair on the veranda, writing a letter to her father.

'I thought it would be enjoyable to invite all our friends to dinner on the anniversary of our marriage next week. It would enable us to make up for the fact that they couldn't be present at the actual event,' Edmund said.

Chin Ming needed no persuading. Since moving into the house, they had acquired a cook called Kim Seng and an *amah* named May Lin. The children would be well cared for during the evening, and Kim Seng would delight in the challenge of feeding several more people.

'I'll write the invitations straightaway,' she said. 'And we must include Abdullah.'

*****

17th November 1830

It was only a short distance between their two houses, so Dick and Sujana decided to go on foot to Chin Ming and Edmund's party. They walked close together, holding hands; Dick held an oil lamp aloft in his free hand to illuminate their path. Sujana carried a large bouquet of flowers, which she had cut from the garden earlier in the evening. The perfume from the sprays of jasmine kept them company along the way, drifting all around in the brief, tropical twilight.

The other guests arrived in two carriages; Alexander and Abdullah in one, then Baba Tan, Yan Lau, and Wing Yee in the other. They both pulled up in front of the house only minutes after the arrival of Dick and Sujana.

Conversation during the evening became increasingly animated. They discussed the food, as usual – complimenting Kim Seng on his abilities. There was much admiration of the garments chosen by each of the four women and the usual jokes concerning the formal attire chosen by most of the men. Abdullah, it seemed was the only one sensible enough to choose an outfit that was both elegant and suitable for the warm, tropical evening.

When everyone's appetite was replete, most of the group continued to chatter but Chin Ming stood up and lightly tapped her spoon on the table. The conversation continued to buzz for a while, so she repeated the action a little louder than before, now feeling more self-assured. A hush descended upon them like a shower of rain; everyone turned to face her.

'I have a proposition for you all,' she said.

'Ah, you've devised a game to entertain us,' Alexander replied, hoping it wouldn't be too complicated.

'No, this is something more serious,' she said. 'Since Edmund and I have been back here, we've made it our business to visit the Singapore Institution, the remains of the Spice Garden, and the place where the new clinic will be built. We've spent time at Boat Quay, admiring the new warehouses as well as the mansions being built for the wealthy merchants further along the Esplanade.'

Except for Edmund, the expression on everyone's face was one of pride; they waited for her to resume, to say how wonderful it all was.

'In order to find an *amah* to look after our children,' she continued, 'we had to deal with a fairly unsavoury character, one who had connections with Madam Ho at the brothel.'

Sujana gulped in a mouthful of air. 'You should have asked me,' she said, 'my father would have helped you to find...'

'That's kind,' Chin Ming said, 'but I'm glad I've found out about these unsavoury dealings. I was under the impression that bringing women into the Settlement for that sort of purpose was illegal.'

'It is,' Alexander said, 'as is the trade in guns and other odious endeavours, but it is all very difficult to control. Our police force is painfully small and the Bugis traders are particularly good at smuggling anything and everything.'

'But I'm sure you'll agree with me that this is exactly the sort of thing that would have caused Raffles so much grief.'

Each of the guests nodded. They said nothing as it was clear that she had more to say.

'If we simply stand by and ignore all these practices, then surely, we are condoning them. If we want to honour the name of Stamford Raffles and the values he held, then I think we should try to expose anything illegal and find ways to have them stopped.' She lowered herself gracefully back onto her chair and waited.

Edmund smiled to himself, she was just like her father, always intent on justice without thinking of any personal danger it might bring. He was secretly proud of his wife for speaking up, for challenging the group of friends; for saying out loud what he'd been thinking about himself but letting it continue to rumble around in his head rather than vocalise his thoughts.

Alexander opened his mouth to speak.

'I'm sorry, Alexander,' Chin Ming interrupted. 'I know you think such matters are not suitable for the dinner table. If we were not amongst friends I would, of course, agree. But just look around this table, each of us has been touched by knowing Stamford Raffles. He laid the foundation for something very special on this island and we can't let that be destroyed by a group of selfish bureaucrats.' The colour of her cheeks rivalled the setting sun, but it was the intensity in her blazing eyes that compelled everyone around the table to take notice.

'He save my life,' Wing Yee was the first to speak. 'He say I should use knowledge to make medicine; he gave me courage to live new life.'

'You make me feel ashamed,' Dick said. 'I owe him everything. When he left Singapore, I promised I would make sure his name was kept alive, but I've let other things get in the way. Raffles saved me from slavery; without him I might even be dead. Everything you've said is true, Chin Ming, we need to find some way of challenging all the corruption, identify those who bend the rules to suit themselves, and build a future for our children that they will be proud to be part of.'

Instead of feeling the usual embarrassment when he made an impassioned speech, Dick felt taller than he was half an hour ago, his lungs expanded, and he took several deep, measured breaths.

Each of the others added their own recollections of meeting and working with Raffles, especially during the last few months he'd spent in Singapore. Abdullah, who until now had remained silent throughout the discussions, reminded them of the day when Raffles departed for Sumatra and the accolades he'd received from all the people who had turned out to see him off.

'I hope that's going to be included in your book,' Baba Tan said.

'It's already there,' Abdullah said.

Dick grinned. 'Chin Ming is right,' he said. 'But it's getting late and we can't solve anything tonight. What matters is the fact that the idea has been planted, the spark ignited. Why don't we all meet in the next few days - to share our thoughts, identify what we can achieve, and make a plan?'

'You're welcome to use the boardroom at Johnston & Co.,' Alexander said. 'I'll make sure it's in a fit state by the end of the week.'

For a short while, the atmosphere around the table began to buzz again. Now it possessed a different pitch, a different pace. It reverberated with excitement, but after another ten minutes, their energy flagged and it was time for everyone to depart. Dick and Sujana gladly accepted a lift in Alexander's landau, even though it was only a short distance to their home. Baba Tan's carriage followed close behind. Edmund and Chin Ming stood on the veranda holding hands, neither of them spoke; they simply enjoyed the pleasure of touching and standing close together. A soft, melodic chorus from the crickets arose from the garden.

They were so wrapped up in their own happiness that they failed to notice the door between the drawing room and the veranda slowly opening. As it closed again, the hinge that needed oiling alerted them to the presence of Charlotte approaching them from behind.

'We can see you, young lady,' Chin Ming said.

'I wanted to say goodnight to all the nice people,' Charlotte said, hoping to convince her parents that her motives for leaving her bed and creeping out onto the veranda were entirely innocent.

'Well, I'm afraid you have missed them. They were all very tired and have gone home to their beds, which is where you should be.'

'But ...'

'No buts, Charlotte. It's very late and time for all of us to retire. Take my hand and I'll take you back to your room, and if you're good I'll read one short story.'

'We'll tell you all about the meal and what our guests were wearing in the morning,' Edmund added. He picked up a lamp to guide their path; he followed behind his wife and daughter and made sure the door was firmly closed behind him.

*****

For the next two months, Chin Ming and Edmund concentrated on settling into their new home and making sure their children were safe. Chin Ming visited the tailor who had made many garments for her in the past. She took Charlotte along to be measured for a wardrobe more practical than the pretty dresses she'd worn in England. The little girl loved the collection of tunic and matching trousers though she remained attached to the blue sash she was so fond of. She was rarely seen without it draped around her shoulders, tied around her waist, or simply being dragged along behind her.

Edmund spent each morning clearing the part of the garden that eventually became Charlotte's own plot. When the day arrived for her to be taken there for the first time, she was so excited that she couldn't eat breakfast. Chin Ming insisted that she should at least eat some fruit. Edmund took her hand and led her to the plot and showed her what to do. His garden implements were much too big for her, but Charlotte managed to charm Kim Seng into giving her a small bowl from the kitchen that could be used as a bucket and a spoon that worked very well for digging.

She began work straightaway, but first, she placed her favourite rag doll made of a piece of folded sacking in the garden cart. The doll was given instructions to watch very carefully while Charlotte prepared to plant her first precious seeds.

*****

Having established a small area of the garden for his daughter, Edmund then began to concentrate on the remainder of the untamed area. This was a far greater challenge, but it was only when Alexander Johnston asked him how the project was progressing that he admitted he was struggling.

'It's taking far too much of my time, I'm afraid,' he said. 'The ground is very dry and most of the plant roots go down deep; they are stubborn to remove. I've neglected my writing, which I can't afford to do because I must send some sample material – or at least a detailed outline – back to Oxford on the next ship.'

'You need someone to help with clearing the land,' Alexander replied. 'It's far too big a task to complete on your own.'

'That would be wonderful, but where do I find such a person? I wouldn't be able to pay very much.'

'I have an idea. You've seen the gangs of convicts working on the roads and on the building sites?'

Edmund nodded.

'Well, those that are well-behaved are given a certain amount of freedom. They're even encouraged to look for ways of making some money for themselves, doing other work once their labouring has finished for the day. Would you like me to make some enquiries?'

*****

A week after the conversation with Alexander, Edmund was faced with a possible solution to his dilemma. It was Dick who came up with the suggestion.

'Alexander told me you're looking for someone to help with clearing the garden,' he said. 'I'm not surprised it's getting too much for you, it's a huge area and I know I wouldn't want to do it. Well, I may have a solution.'

Edmund looked interested. 'Tell me more,' he said.

'I've been doing some work for George Coleman – you

85

know, the architect,' he said. 'Just some sketches for some of the houses he's been asked to build – that sort of thing. He has several of the convicts working for him and one of them is an experienced gardener.'

'What's this man like? Is he trustworthy? I'd need to know it was safe to have him around in case Chin Ming or one of the children come across him.'

'He's one of the labourers who is allowed to do other work if that's what you mean. I first met him a few months ago, but I try to chat to him whenever I visit the building site. I saw him again a couple of days ago and it's pretty clear he's just had a run of bad luck. He used to work in the botanical gardens in Calcutta. In fact, he worked for Nathaniel Wallich, the man who came here to advise Raffles about the Spice Garden.'

'So how did your contact end up in prison?'

'It's a long story. Something to do with his brother who got into debt. I'm not sure of the details, but it would be easy enough to ask Coleman what he's like as a worker. It might even be possible to talk to someone else he's done any work for. What do you think?'

'It certainly sounds as if the idea is worth exploring,' Edmund said. 'Can you introduce me to Coleman?'

*****

Two weeks later, prisoner 710 began to spend his evenings clearing the rough ground at the side of the Wilson property. It took him almost ten days before he was able to tell Edmund that the task was complete and the soil was ready for planting. He sought out his employer, expecting to be paid what was due to him, and then dismissed.

'I'm told you used to work in a botanic garden,' Edmund said.

'That is correct, sahib. In Calcutta - I work with plants for many years. This is work I like very much.'

'Would you like to work with plants again? Would you like to help me develop an experimental garden here in Singapore?'

'Sahib, that would give me great joy.'

Edmund told prisoner 710 about the demise of the Spice Garden and his own plans to build on the ideas started by Raffles. 'Not the nutmeg or cloves,' he said, 'we could never produce enough to be economically viable, but I want to propagate some of the local flora, to experiment with hybrid versions, that sort of thing.'

The convict's eyes lit up. He grinned at Edmund and nodded furiously.

'We can't go on calling you prisoner 710 though,' Edmund said. 'What is your real name – the one you were known by before ....'

'My name is Sanjay, sahib.' He seemed to grow in height as he said his name and continued to grin, revealing a mouth full of chipped teeth.

'That's a good, strong name, Sanjay. What does it mean?'

'It means triumphant, sahib.'

'How appropriate. I have every intention of triumphing - succeeding – with this project, Sanjay, and I would very much welcome your assistance in helping me to achieve it.'

CHAPTER 9
Singapore, February 1831

Between the end of October and the beginning of February, Kasim spent much of his spare time tracking down and trailing after the people living on Selegie Hill, those he now considered to be his adversaries. He mainly used the newly cut back road, keeping well out of sight, but even so, there was still a need to be vigilant and keep himself hidden. The more obsessed he became, the more restless he was spending his days amongst the moneylenders. He needed to find some way of revoking his obligation to Douglas Fergusson and discover another scheme that would provide him with sufficient funds. Finally, during one of their regular coffee-shop encounters, Victor provided him with a possible solution.

'I'm planning a trip to Malacca very soon,' he said, 'why don't you come with me?'

'And what would I do once we got there?'

'I can introduce you to some of my acquaintances, my business partners. I've a feeling you're getting restless on your high stool in Market Street. I can show you some more interesting ways of making a living.'

Kasim wondered what Victor had in mind. Maybe a change of scene would do him good, provide some better opportunities, enable him to sort out the jumble of information he'd gleaned about the bitch and her friends, make it possible to plan their demise.

'You'd get a better choice of women too,' Victor added. 'There are many more brothels in Malacca, my friend.'

Kasim had avoided Madam Ho's establishment since arriving in Singapore; there was a possibility she would remember him from before, remember the trouble that arose following the death of his business partner, Boon Peng. Instead, he'd frequented one or two of the brothels that had opened their doors more recently but he'd found the women there too compliant; he liked the challenge of feistier specimens.

He might well join Victor in the delights that Malacca had to offer, but if he could lose his friend for an hour or two, the prospect of re-acquainting himself with a certain young beauty was far more inviting. Jenab was by far the best woman he'd ever had.

*****

Neither Victor nor Kasim had any reason to remain in Singapore for the imminent local festivals. This year, the Chinese community would commence their celebrations for Lunar New Year on the same day the Muslims began the fasting month of Ramadan. When Victor discovered a Bugis trader would be departing from the Settlement on the evening of 12th February, he hurried to find Kasim and they seized the opportunity to get away quickly.

A few days later, Kasim sat on deck as the vessel approached the old drawbridge on the Malacca River. They waited whilst several pedestrians and a man riding his horse crossed from one side to the other. The quay was exactly as Kasim remembered it with its closely-packed buildings in the Dutch style, even though the town had been handed over to the British in exchange for Bencoolen almost seven years ago. He spotted a couple of soldiers keeping a careful watch on the goings-on. A large crowd had gathered under two ancient trees, but they seemed peaceful enough; some simply exchanging information, others obviously bartering. He supposed them to be mainly European by their dress – light-coloured trousers, brown or black jackets, and all with matching ochre-coloured hats. The only dark-skinned people he could readily see were a few Indians – all wearing turbans. He wished, straightaway, that he could shed his kurta which he continued to think of as dull and unsophisticated. He would have preferred to walk onto the wharf wearing the fine, European clothes he had hidden in his travelling bag but he wasn't yet ready to share that much of his history with Victor.

*****

Victor, who had no idea that Kasim had lived in Malacca for almost a year before coming to Singapore, had arranged for them both to stay with his relatives. His aunt had hollow cheeks and had obviously suffered since being abandoned by William Farquhar. She was welcoming enough but kept herself to herself. He introduced Kasim to his cousins and to some of his business acquaintances. He was given a guided tour of the town. He feigned interest when it was called for and decided there was little point in revealing he had seen it all before.

At the beginning of the second week, Victor announced that he had some business to deal with which would occupy most of the day. Kasim was curious to know why he wasn't invited along on this occasion but chose not to comment. He assured Victor he would enjoy exploring on his own and agreed to meet his friend outside the Stadthuys at dusk.

The moment Victor left for his appointment, Kasim reached amongst the clothes he'd brought with him and, from the bottom of his bag, pulled out the trousers and shirt that belonged to his European self. He rolled them into a bundle and covered it with a towel. If any of Victor's cousins asked, he would say that he intended to take a swim in the river. He left the kampong around mid-morning when everyone was busy, and instead of taking the direct route into town, he turned in the direction of Bukit China, skirting around the back of the hill and entering the graveyard at a place that took him past several old *Keramat*. Beyond these sacred Muslim graves, the surface became uneven; it was scattered with the remains of a Portuguese fortress that the Dutch destroyed in the 1600s. The ground was full of hollows, which provided the perfect cover for Kasim's plan. He jumped into one of them, almost hidden by vines and long grasses, and removed his kurta and baggy white trousers, replacing them with his more sedate European garb.

When he reached the summit of the hill, he stopped to get his bearings. On a nearby hill, he could see St John's Fort glowing white in the noonday sun and the patchwork of red-tiled roofs in the oldest part of the town. Memories of the drunken orgies he enjoyed there came flooding back. If Boon Peng's business proposition hadn't been so enticing, he would never have joined him in Singapore. But nostalgia was certainly something he never indulged in, and when his intended destination came into focus on the other side of the river, it was simply lust combined with the thrill of manly vigour and dominance that consumed him.

He wondered if Jenab was still living in the kampong, whether she might provide a pleasant interlude, whether he would have to use his considerable powers of persuasion; he hurried on.

He headed towards St Peter's Church. It resembled a church he'd seen in Macau, but that was a memory best forgotten. He turned into Jalan Bunga Raya, then crossed the river at the footbridge. He could already hear the familiar call of the Imam from the Tranquerah Mosque right next door to his destination.

✶✶✶✶✶

A group of young boys, playing with a rattan ball, kicked up dust all around themselves and didn't notice him until he was almost level with them. Curiosity overcame their interest in the game; they saw very few European guests, so this man was a novelty. One of them was bold enough to touch his sleeve; the others giggled and prepared to run away if reprimanded.

'I've come to see Jenab,' Kasim said in perfect Malay. 'Is she here?'

None of the boys seemed to understand. It was well over twelve years since he'd last visited and he guessed that they were not even born at the time.

'Take me to the village elder.'

The boys jostled for position, each wanting to be the one who led the way.

'I will take you,' said a short, stocky youth, hitching up his sarong.

'No, it should be me,' another member of the group shouted, 'he is my grandfather.'

The noise they made attracted the attention of two women who sat on a veranda weaving lengths of cloth. They stared at him. One nudged the other and then looked away, the other one continued to stare. The gaze of several other women followed the little band along the path that led to their destination.

The elderly Malay chief was seated on his balcony; he had been observing the visitor for some time, and it had done nothing to sweeten his mood. This was a man from the past; he hadn't liked him then, but now he had every reason to hate him.

'YOU!' he shouted in Malay when Kasim was nearly at the top of the steps. 'The *orang puteh*, the Dutchman who promised my daughter the earth and then disappeared.'

'I made no promises. And I had business to deal with in Singapore,' Kasim said with no hint of remorse.

The old man ranted for a long time. He stood with his chin

held high, his nostrils flaring, and his complexion deepening until it almost matched his maroon sarong. Kasim flinched. He could feel the waves of hatred and his muscles tightened. He clutched his chest to protect himself in case the headman hit out at him. Soon he was to learn the reason for the outburst.

'You did indeed leave. When you failed to return, I knew I had been correct to distrust you, but it was too late. I have never forgiven you for abandoning your young wife – my daughter, leaving her pregnant.'

Wife! It seemed there had been a marriage ceremony, but he had no recollection of it. Had he been drunk or perhaps he'd smoked too much opium? According to the irate man standing before him, there had been a great deal of opposition to the marriage. Jenab had eventually persuaded her father, saying that she loved the European trader and had even suggested he would become a Muslim. Reluctantly, the chief had given in, and special arrangements had been made.

Steffens, or Kasim as he now called himself, was lost for words. It was partly the shock of finding he had a wife and child, but more so the contempt, the disgust, and the animosity that surrounded him. After a long silence he began to panic; he needed to get out of here.

The old man planted his legs wide apart as if blocking the way, his lips narrowed and his cold, steely eyes glared at Kasim.

'Go!' the old man bellowed. 'There's nothing for you here. My only daughter - you have no idea what anguish her death brought to our family. I blame you and you alone for everything that happened both to the mother and her child!'

For the briefest of moments, Kasim remained fixed to the spot. Jenab was dead? The child was dead? He was relieved he wasn't going to be asked for money to raise a brat that might or might not be his, but a small part of him regretted not being able to lie with Jenab again. He longed to get away from these people, but the old man continued to stare at him, his body remaining completely rigid. Kasim's heart was racing. He wanted to run, but his legs felt weak and incapable of moving.

Would the village elders be summoned? Would they decide to punish him for the misdemeanours they'd decided he'd committed. Would they be upset because when he'd chosen to reappear, it was during the fasting month? It was all too ridiculous, and he wasn't going to hang around to find out. He spun around, hurried down the steps, and fled across the kampong in the direction from which he had arrived.

The children had disappeared, gone back to their game, he presumed. He'd almost reached the road when one of the women he'd seen earlier emerged from the shadows. She was not unattractive, but there was something about her demeanour that warned him to stay away from her.

'I was Jenab's friend,' the woman said in Malay. 'I know all about you. I am not like her, I am not easily flattered by men, you will not be able to seduce me. You should go quickly before Maeena discovers you are here; she is Jenab's younger sister and she hates you even more than everyone else.'

*****

For the first time in his life, Kasim felt bewildered; his usual swagger and self-assurance fell from his shoulders like water plummeting over a cascade. He'd had a narrow escape. He walked in a haze along the road that led away from the kampong. It was only when he almost crashed into a bullock cart just before he turned into the main road that he came to his senses. He glanced quickly behind to make sure that he was not being followed and then turned into the street that led to the bridge across the river. As he approached the town square, his breathing steadied. He told himself there was nothing to worry about. He certainly didn't believe there had been an actual marriage, so no one could hold him responsible, and

Jenab's father had made it clear that both mother and child had died, so what was there to worry about? It must be the shock that had made him panic; that and the hostility he'd encountered. He was relieved to have got away from the kampong without any real threat of vengeance; he was glad it was over. Soon he'd be leaving Malacca behind him, that would be the end of it.

He found himself facing the bold, terracotta edifice of Christ Church on the left of the square; the church built to commemorate the centenary of Dutch occupation. Its straight lines and its bright red walls calmed him, reminding him of his family and happier days – before he lost everything. Victor was not expecting him for another half hour, he decided to take a closer look.

He was surprised to find the interior had not changed much under the current British administration: the hand-made wooden pews, the brass lectern, and the pulpit dating back to 1773 were all still in place. Still, his loathing for the British resurfaced, replacing the composure the building had instilled in him initially; this, in turn, sparked his hatred of Raffles. He had yet to decide how he was going to execute any form of revenge – to punish the three friends in Singapore but punish them he would.

Someone else entered the church and he realised it must be getting late. He needed to change out of his European clothes before he met Victor. It was only then that he became aware of the fact that in his haste to get away from the kampong, away from the woman who declared herself to be one of Jenab's friends, he'd left behind the bundle containing his kurta and the other garments he'd been wearing earlier in the day.

*****

Kasim stood inside the church porch until he saw Victor arrive at the Stadthuys. He waited for several minutes, but there was nothing for it; he'd have to brazen it out, make up a story that he hoped his friend would believe. He strolled across the square. Victor shaded his eyes from the last of the afternoon light, his gaze swept straight past Kasim and on to the streets that led into the square. Kasim tapped him on the shoulder.

'Good afternoon,' he said.

Victor looked him up and down. Deep furrows formed across his forehead, his eyes narrowed to thin lines, and his bottom lip curled downwards. The voice he recognised, or thought he did, but the person standing beside him was a stranger.

'I've had enough of being treated as second-rate,' Kasim said. 'I thought I'd get myself some European clothes to see if that made a difference to the way I'm treated.'

Victor started to laugh. He pointed at Kasim's trousers, then flicked the collar of his shirt; he walked all around to get a better look at this new image from all angles, then he continued to laugh. It was some time before he was able to speak without the mirth bubbling up all over again.

'You've certainly got some nerve,' he managed to say once he'd settled down. 'But I must admit, the tailor you found has done a good job. I might have to go there myself.'

Kasim grinned. 'It was a small place in one of the back streets, I'm not sure I'd be able to find it again.'

Victor's frown returned, then he shrugged his shoulders. 'I see you want to keep your bright ideas to yourself. Well, let's go home and see what the rest of the family think of you.'

Victor's family were initially amused by the transformation in their visitor, but as the days passed by, it went unnoticed. Kasim, however, now had a dilemma; before they returned to Singapore, he would need to visit one of the Indian tailors to replenish what had become his usual apparel in Market Street.

*****

The two men made the return journey in another local trading vessel. They arrived back in Singapore to find the familiar harbour packed tight with vessels from Europe, Arabia, India, and the Spice Islands; it was as busy and as colourful as ever.

'I might grumble about the place,' Victor said, 'but I've really missed it. I wouldn't be at all surprised if the British don't shift the administration from Penang to here sometime soon. The trading opportunities are far greater here than either George Town or Malacca.' When he turned to see what Kasim had to say, he noticed that he had reverted to wearing a pale-green kurta, and matching trousers.

'What happened to the belief you'd be treated better in European clothing?' he said.

'I can't afford to break away from Mukesh and the moneylenders right now. I need to stay with them for a few more months before setting up on my own and I don't feel like explaining the change of garb to any of them.' He didn't mention his connection with Douglas Fergusson nor the fact he'd been cheating on the man of late. His exit from Market Street would need to be carefully handled.

Victor shrugged his shoulders. 'It's up to you, my friend, but remember, I have contacts all over the region. I've introduced you to some of my acquaintances, my business partners in Malacca, I can introduce you to more. When impatience replaces reason, let me know. There are many more ways of making a living.' Half an hour later, they both stepped onto Boat Quay. They shook hands and parted company. 'Remember,' Victor said as he made straight for Choo Keng's coffee stall, 'if you wear European clothing when we visit the brothel, you're sure to get a better-quality whore!' He guffawed, pleased with his little jest, but Kasim continued on to Market Street.

97

CHAPTER 10
Early March 1831

It was only a few weeks since Sanjay had begun to clear the land at the side of the house, but already good progress had been made. Edmund had helped occasionally, but he'd spent most of the time getting on with the first draft of his book. Now, he'd reached the stage when he needed to do some additional research. He had it in mind to undertake a visit to Malacca – to explore the surrounding countryside and to collect some of the local plants. He would study their habitats closely, make notes, and with any luck, he would be able to send some specimens back to England to generate some extra income. He'd hoped to persuade Dick to accompany him, maintaining that it would be like the days they'd spent together in China. So far, his powers of persuasion had not been successful and Dick remained undecided.

Chin Ming was determined to accompany her husband. Each evening, after supper, she talked to Edmund about the arrangements but she made no mention of the fact that she had not been feeling herself. She was much more tired than usual and first thing in the morning she often felt queasy.

Edmund discussed his plans with Sanjay and told him he would bring back some plants that they could propagate in the newly-prepared plot.

'I wish it possible to work here all time,' Sanjay said.

'I would like that too,' Edmund said. 'When you have been

here for a while –maybe when I return from Malacca, I could talk to Mr Johnston to see if such a move might be possible. I would hope the authorities might at least consider such an idea, especially if they were to see the results of your labour.'

*****

A few days before the Beaumonts were due to depart for Malacca, Baba Tan's carriage pulled onto their drive. Wing Yee stepped down, waving Baba Tan on his way before she moved towards stairs leading onto the veranda. There was no sign of the family, but she thought she could hear the baby crying from somewhere within the house. She pushed the door into the drawing room open and called out. May Lin appeared, carrying William who was still sobbing; she was rubbing his knee.

'He fell over,' May Lin said in Malay. 'He's not really hurt, just a little bit upset.'

'Is Madam Beaumont at home?' Wing Yee said.

May Lin nodded. 'In her bedroom, resting. Master is in garden with Char-lotte.'

Wing Yee was astonished to learn that Chin Ming was taking it easy; it was most unlike her. She told May Lin that she would go to find her. May Lin nodded and took William outside to distract him.

'Hello,' Wing Yee called out as she pushed the bedroom door open. 'What wrong?' Chin Ming was sitting on the side of the bed, paler than usual and looking tired. Her hair was tied back and she was in the process of wiping her mouth with a damp cloth. Wing Yee hurried to her side. 'How long you feel like this?' she asked.

'I'll be alright in a minute,' Chin Ming said. 'I'm not sure what's the matter, maybe something I ate, but it won't go away. I've felt nauseous every morning for the last week. I've even stopped eating breakfast, but it doesn't make any difference.'

'I think you need some of my ginger tea,' Wing Yee said. 'It is very good for pregnant ladies.'

'Pregnant! I can't be pregnant. William is only twelve months old, and besides, I must be ready to travel to Malacca in a few days. Is there nothing else you can give me to stop the vomiting?'

'Edmund not notice you unwell?'

'I told him to have breakfast without me so that he could get on with preparing for the trip. I didn't want him to be concerned.'

'So, you not suspect new baby?' Wing Yee reverted to Cantonese, to be sure that she was getting all the facts from her friend. 'Did you not experience sickness when you were expecting Charlotte and William?'

'No. Nothing at all. Both pregnancies were easy; I was very lucky.'

'There's no reason why this pregnancy won't be easy either,' Wing Yee said, 'once we deal with the nausea. However, I don't think it would be wise for you to accompany Edmund on his travels.'

'But I must go. I know what he's like. He'll worry about me being here on my own and want to postpone his trip. It's important that he goes soon; some of the plants he's hoping to find will be at their best at this time of year. I don't want to be the reason for him delaying this opportunity.'

Wing Yee smiled to herself; she did know what Edmund was like – the kindest of men who would concern himself about leaving his wife alone. She asked her friend a few more questions to ascertain her diagnosis, but each response she received merely confirmed that she was correct. 'What if I came to live with you while Edmund goes on his travels? It would be like old times – when we stayed with Raffles and Sophia on Bukit Larangan. You can help me make some decisions about the new clinic, and we can discuss how to make sure the women who need medicines are able to receive them.'

Chin Ming looked better already. The colour had returned to her cheeks and the nausea had eased. When Edmund learned the news, he was delighted.

'How wonderful to have one of our children born in Singapore,' he said but then he began to think about the implications. Wing Yee repeated her offer to stay in the house during his absence.

'I am so grateful, Wing Yee. I know the two of you will enjoy spending time together, but how will you manage? We don't have a carriage and it's a long trek down the hill on foot to your workshop?'

'Not go every day. I ask to go with Dick when necessary,' Wing Yee reassured him.

He was thankful to Wing Yee for her suggestion. With another baby on the way, they would need more money and the expedition would give him a chance to collect plants that English nurseries would welcome. He knew they would be happy to pay handsomely for the opportunity of enhancing their displays.

Edmund left Singapore half way through March, alone. He'd been incapable of persuading Dick to accompany him on this occasion, and to some extent, he was pleased that his friend was unable to join him. He knew Wing Yee would look after Chin Ming, but the fact remained there were two women, May Lin, and his two children all alone in the house. It was comforting to know that Dick was on hand to keep an eye on everyone.

On the day of Edmund's departure, Dick drove the whole Beaumont family, together with Sujana, down to Boat Quay. Wing Yee and Baba Tan joined them there. Everyone waved one last time as the country trader taking Edmund to Malacca steered the *prahu* out of the river into open waters.

*****

Kasim had led Mukesh to believe that his visit to Malacca concerned some business he was carrying out for Douglas Fergusson. Mukesh's mood when Kasim returned to his stool in Market Street indicated that he had discovered this was not the case. By the afternoon, Mukesh had made it clear that the work that had piled up during Kasim's absence must be dealt with immediately; there should be no more excuses to finish early or stroll in halfway through the morning.

Kasim remained silent. His mouth twisted into a sour expression and his eyes narrowed into a scowl and he turned away from any further rebuke. Inside, there was a pounding sensation in his ears and adrenaline rushed through his body. How dare this man, an Indian, a moneylender, presume to criticise him. Until he'd been forced to leave behind all the luxury of his upbringing in Batavia, Pieter Steffens had Indian servants to wait on him, to provide him with whatever he wanted. He'd been a young man of twenty when he left – after the British had arrived. Stamford Raffles had become the Lieutenant Governor – and it was Stamford Raffles he blamed for his change of circumstance – and the reason for the many names he'd adopted along the way. His hatred for the man had hung over him like the sword of Damocles for years; he'd dragged his bitterness around with him and let it ruin his life.

He was still intent on destroying the people who had been patronised by Raffles but he needed money to establish himself and that couldn't be achieved in his current position. The sooner he joined forces with Victor and got away from the confines of this place, the better.

*****

Despite his intentions, Kasim found himself forced to continue working in Market Street for the next few weeks. Victor was nowhere to be found and Mukesh was insistent that contracts needed to be completed. The harbour was busier than usual at this time of year with ships from China, Sumatra, and the Spice Islands anxious to complete their trade and get on their way. In a couple of weeks, the northerly and northeasterly winds would be replaced with light sea breezes and the route to India and beyond would stagnate. This meant that he was fully occupied supervising the transfer of Fergusson's cargoes between ships carrying the Company flag and local trading vessels. There was no time at the end of the day to trek up Bukit Selegie to keep an eye on the two families he had chosen to target. Neither was there any sign of the woman he always referred to as 'the bitch.' He hadn't discovered where she lived; he knew nothing of her whereabouts or what she did with herself. Hot afternoons had been extremely common since his return, which often led to a thunderstorm. When he returned to the quay in the early evening, often soaked to the skin, all he wanted was to return to his boat and collapse onto the bunk.

By the end of the month, the need to spend time traversing the harbour had ceased and all the outstanding business Mukesh had harangued him about was dealt with. Kasim hoped that April would bring more luck than the last few weeks had shown him. He needed to grasp any opportunity to improve his prospects that presented itself and, above all, to seek his revenge. This evening, as soon as he finished work, he would try his best to find Victor, even if it meant tracking him down in the Malay village.

*****

Victor sat cross-legged on the veranda of his house with his hands clasped in a prayer-like position. His index fingers pointed upwards to rest on his lips. He'd been listening to Kasim's ranting for a good half hour without making any comment, but now it was time to intervene.

'It's the things that you are not telling me that I am most interested in,' he said, gazing directly into Kasim's eyes.

'What do you mean? When we arrived back from Malacca you urged me to leave Market Street. The last thing you said when we parted on the quay was to come to you when impatience overcame reason; well, that time has come. I want you to introduce me to some of your business contacts, I want my life to be ...'

'More interesting?' Victor offered. 'If I am to involve you in my business, then I need to know who you really are; I have no intention of being cheated by another European.'

'But,' Kasim began ...

'My friend, I am very much aware that you are not what you seem. I doubt whether you are even half Indian, let alone a full-blooded Hindu merchant or Tamil trader. I wasn't convinced by any of the stories you contrived during our visit to Malacca and when we met at the Stadthuys I noticed you were able to read the inscriptions in the wall left by the Dutch. I watched you closely during those last few days.'

There was a long silence. Kasim's head was spinning. He needed Victor. He must get away from the limitations of working with the moneylenders; the entire situation was holding him back. There was nothing for it; he would have to take a risk.

'Well ...,' he began. For the next couple of hours, he gave Victor an edited version of his life, revealing only those episodes that suited his purpose. Getting Victor to relate to parts of the story that showed he, too, had been treated unfairly by representatives of the East Indian Company was paramount. It provided a common bond, and once achieved, they had a shared enemy and a mutual need for retribution.

By the end of the evening, Victor knew for certain that his new friend was Dutch by birth and he'd lived in China for several years. However, Kasim managed not to disclose his family name, the name he'd had when growing up in Java; neither did he tell his new business partner he'd spent some time in Malacca, had married a local woman, and had fathered a child.

He was also careful not to reveal what had brought him to Singapore. Victor remained ignorant about his true motivation and hadn't the slightest inkling of what Kasim was planning in order to settle his grievance.

*****

Later that week, the desire to take another look at the people he'd identified as targets for retaliation took Kasim to the top of Bukit Selegie once more. He chose the back road leading up the slope from Serengoon, hoping to avoid being noticed. When he reached the place where he'd observed the Chinese woman and her family, he paused. There was no one sitting on the veranda, but he could hear childish squeals from the side of the garden. It was impossible to see whether anyone else was present or if she was playing on her own. He leapt over the ditch that lay between himself and the perimeter fence and crept around in the direction of the excited shrieks.

The paling was broken in several places, making it easy at those points to get a clear view inside the compound. The first fracture revealed nothing more than a carefully-tended plot with some plants that had been recently watered. The second rupture exposed a similar space. He could now hear a child talking, and when he reached the point where the barrier had collapsed altogether, he could see an adult –probably a man, but partly concealed by a low bush - kneeling beside a little girl. Her head was protected from the sun by a small coolie hat, but her dark hair had escaped and was hanging loosely down her back. She was dressed in a leaf-green tunic with matching trousers; the familiar blue sash was tied around her waist. Both had their backs towards Kasim.

He couldn't understand how the man could put up with this child prattling on. He disliked children intensely; demanding, selfish creatures. No, he was glad that he'd never got sucked into all that and relieved that he'd got away from

Malacca all those years ago and come to Singapore with Boon Peng. Nothing now remained from that time and no one need know anything about it.

'Look!' he heard the child call in her recognisably high-pitched manner.

Kasim strained to see if the object she was offering to the man was anything of consequence; he imagined it was something she'd found while digging around in the soil. The man turned as he held it up to the light. It appeared to be a piece of coloured glass, most likely of no importance, whereas, the man - he was most definitely of interest. He was Indian.

This was not the child's father, the man he'd seen on the day of their arrival at Boat Quay. Neither was he the adopted son of Stamford Raffles. He must, however, be someone who the parents were happy to have looking after their child.

Kasim crouched down on his haunches which provided a more comfortable position for observation. He supposed the man must be one of the convicts allowed to take on extra work for himself. If this was the case, the hours he would be able to spend here would be restricted to the end of each day when his work on one of the construction sites was finished. This made it simple to deduce the times when he was likely to be found here.

He continued to watch the pair. There was still no sign of the child's parents, which meant they must indeed trust the Indian with their child. The brat, in turn, showed no fear of this man; she even seemed to be enjoying his company. That could be very useful, very useful indeed.

*****

Three days later, Victor came looking for him in Market Street, explaining that if Kasim was to join forces with him in his next business venture, then he needed to quit his current position immediately. Victor was leaving for Sumatra in a couple of days and it was essential that they travel there together.

Kasim led Victor outside onto the pavement so their conversation could not be overheard. Of course, he wanted to join him, of course, he wanted to get away from the boredom of Market Street, but there were other things to consider. He needed to keep an eye on the brat with the blue sash and he wanted to pursue the Chinese bitch; he required time to cover his tracks. He didn't want Mukesh or Fergusson making a fuss when they discovered he'd been cheating on the last few transactions he'd undertaken on behalf of the Calcutta merchant.

'Give me the rest of the day to sort everything out,' he said. 'When exactly are you leaving?'

'On the morning tide, the day after tomorrow. Be at the quay before first light if you intend to join me,' Victor said. 'A chance like this might not come your way again,' he added as he strolled away in the direction of the river.

When Kasim returned; Mukesh was studiously tidying his own work area, giving the impression that he was oblivious of the encounter that had just taken place. Kasim busied himself with moving papers from one place to another and pretending to complete his record of the day's transactions. Victor's proposal was tempting, but he wished there was more time to prepare.

He looked up from his musings to find Mukesh standing directly in front of his desk.

'Douglas Fergusson has sent message.'

Kasim raised his head higher and straightened his back. He stared into the eyes of the other man. Had Mukesh been able to read his thoughts? He kept his gaze steady, intent on giving nothing away.

'He will arrive on next ship from Calcutta. He has new job for you.'

Kasim nodded. A wan smile fluttered on his lips. That's it. Time to go before Fergusson arrives. I won't let him or any of these pathetic moneylenders hold me back. I deserve better, and that's what Victor is offering me. It looks as if I will have to wait a while longer to seek revenge on the Bukit Selegie households – and the Chinese bitch. While I'm away, I'll have more time to plan, to wait for the perfect moment but I do not intend to wait forever.

CHAPTER 11
Early April 1831

Wing Yee decided not to venture down the hill during the first week Edmund was away. Instead, she kept Chin Ming company and made endless cups of ginger tea to ease the sickness her friend was experiencing until the middle of each morning. Halfway through the second week, the nausea eased and Chin Ming became restless. She persuaded Wing Yee she was perfectly able to undertake a visit into town and it was time for them to check what progress was being made on the new clinic.

When Dick and Sujana came to visit that evening, Chin Ming asked if it might be possible for him to drive them down the hill the following day.

'Haven't you arranged another visit with Mr Coleman for tomorrow?' Sujana said. 'If you took the carriage, you could collect our friends on the way. I might even join you all if that would be acceptable.'

'An outing,' Chin Ming said. 'How delightful. I've been feeling like a caged bird for the last few weeks and it's even worse with Edmund away from home.'

Wing Yee coughed.

'Please don't be upset,' Chin Ming said, 'it's lovely to have your company – and a constant supply of tea. I don't mean to be ungrateful. The view from the house is magnificent, the children entertain me with their funny little games, but I'm just not used to being cooped up for so long.'

'I'll collect you around mid-morning and deliver you to Baba Tan's warehouse,' Dick said. 'You can all inspect the plans he has for the clinic – and no doubt you'll then bombard him with questions. If it's ready for inspection, I'm sure he'll be happy to show you the new building and you can tell me all about it when I return from my meeting with George Coleman.'

*****

The two women were glad to see Sujana sitting beside Dick when the carriage swept into the drive. Chin Ming waved to the children who had arranged themselves around May Lin's ankles with no intention of letting her go too. For a moment, she felt guilty about leaving them but she knew they were in safe hands and would soon be absorbed in one of the *amah's* distracting games.

Chin Ming lifted her hair away from her shoulders with both hands, allowing the breeze to weave its way through her waist-length, tresses. She looked more like an eighteen-year-old than a mother of two in her late twenties. The other two women both smiled. They admired Chin Ming's effortless vitality and endless enthusiasm.

Dick brought the carriage to a halt and tethered the horse just in time to help the three women step out onto the cobbled pavement. Wing Yee marched ahead of the other two on her way to the bridge into what was for her familiar territory. Sujana waved goodbye to her husband as he headed off towards the building site and then followed close behind. When they reached the far side of the bridge Chin Ming lingered just long enough to fill her lungs with the distinctive blend of sweet and sour odours she associated with the wharf. A light breeze scurried between the buildings, lifting anything in its path that was not tied down. One of the coolies grabbed at the rim of his conical hat just in time to prevent it becoming airborne.

Baba Tan was nowhere to be seen when she caught up with the others. 'Perhaps in workshop,' Wing Yee said. 'Stay here, I go look. No need to climb stairs if he not there,' she added by way of an order to Chin Ming. 'You show Sujana pretty silk, she not come here often before.'

A few minutes later, she could be seen at the top of the flight of stairs directly outside the entrance to the room where she prepared her herbal remedies; she invited the other two to join her. 'Baba Tan here, he tell you about clinic.'

'No, I will come to you ladies,' Baba Tan said, having now joined Wing Yee on the landing. 'I can bring the plans down to show you and then, if you would like, we can walk over to view the new premises.'

*****

The drawings, which covered several sheets of paper, were interesting enough, but all three of the women wanted to inspect the structure that would soon become the new medical hall. Baba Tan led them along the full length of Market Street before turning into Cross Street.

'Before the fire happened last year, we would have been able to take the shortcut down Philip Street,' Baba Tan told them, 'but it is too risky, I wouldn't want any of you to trip over the damage that still remains.'

They turned into Telok Ayer Street, merely to take a nostalgic glance at the house that Chin Ming and Wing Yee had once shared with Baba Tan and his family. Just beyond the house, a small lane led them straight into Amoy Street. The two-storey building looked solid and dependable even in its still unfinished state. The floor had been laid, the window frames installed, and a group of labourers were now busy adding a coat of paint to the walls.

Wing Yee led Sujana through to one of the side rooms which, she explained, would give any woman who came to the clinic some privacy. Chin Ming wandered in the direction of the workmen, interested to know how soon it would be before the building was ready to open its doors. One of the men, who had been standing on top of a ladder to complete the upper section of the wall, reversed back down the steps, not realising anyone was close by. They narrowly avoided a collision.

'Madam Beaumont,' the man said, apologising for his clumsiness.

It took a while for Chin Ming to realise it was Sanjay. She had never seen him anywhere other than in their garden and had almost forgotten that he was still required to fulfil his obligation as a convict labourer. 'If I'd known you were working on this building, I would have asked you all about it,' she said. 'It is a project that is close to my heart.'

'Sorry, sorry madam,' Sanjay said.

'No need to be sorry,' she said. 'It is I who should apologise; first, I nearly bump into you and then I say something to upset you. Forgive me for causing any problems. Baba Tan brought me here with two of my friends to show us all what good progress you are making.'

'Clinic ready very soon,' Sanjay said. 'It is very good thing; many people get sick.'

'It's the women I'm particularly concerned about,' Chin Ming said. 'I think some husbands are not good at looking after them.'

Sanjay nodded. He looked around to see if his fellow workers had noticed he was talking to one of the visitors. 'Is true,' he said, lowering his voice. 'Especially women with no husband. Many from China come all time, some now come from Sumatra and other islands.'

Chin Ming took a sharp intake of breath and her hands flew to cover her mouth. Her stomach felt heavy and it was nothing to do with being pregnant. Sanjay had just confirmed what she had struggled to believe was still happening and to what extent. True, she'd known that May Lin had worked for Madam Ho before she and Edmund engaged her, but she had never questioned how her children's *amah* arrived in Singapore.

'Well, we must do something about that,' she said. 'Something to make their lives more tolerable.' She didn't want to make a fuss in front of the workmen, but she would certainly make it her business to find out more. It was something that made her very uneasy.

Wing Yee, Sujana, and Baba Tan returned from their tour of the adjacent rooms. They were deep in conversation and didn't notice her flushed cheeks or her downcast expression.

*****

That evening, Chin Ming confronted Wing Yee; she told her what Sanjay had said. 'There must be something we can do.'

'Women already here. Need to stop bad men bringing more.'

'I really thought things would be different now. When you and I first arrived in Singapore, there was only Madam Ho and the place on the gambier plantation, but it seems to me there are many more such establishments now, especially in Chinatown.'

'Madam Ho still has place in Cross Street. She make lot of money.'

'That's the problem, too many people make money from *pelacurs*; everyone apart from the women themselves, it seems. They have no say in the matter; is there nothing we can do?'

'I think you talk to May Lin.'

'And we should talk to Dick,' Chin Ming said. 'We should persuade him to talk to Kenneth Murchison.'

Wing Yee frowned.

'The Resident Councillor, based in Penang. He's the man who has the authority to do something, and he's due to visit Singapore next month. Maybe Dick and Edmund could go together?'

'When Edmund return?'

'He said he would be away for six weeks, so not for a while I'm afraid.'

'You talk to May Lin tomorrow. Then we speak to Dick.'

*****

It took almost the whole morning before Chin Ming could convince May Lin she wasn't in any trouble. Eventually, the girl's story was like so many she had heard before; a poverty-stricken family who felt compelled to sell at least one child to an establishment such as the one that belonged to Madam Ho. Indeed, Wing Yee had suffered a similar fate herself as a young girl. A mother who needed to provide a dowry for her younger, prettier child had taken the sixteen-year-old Wing Yee to one of the more reputable brothels in Guangzhou. It had only been Wing Yee's ability to create herbal remedies, passed on by her father, that had saved her.

The story Sanjay had told Chin Ming was verified by May Lin. Most of the women being smuggled into Singapore these days were from Sumatra with only a few coming directly from China. May Lin knew no details, but she had heard rumours about a group of local merchants who regularly travelled to Sumatra, Java, and even to some of the smaller Spice Islands with the intention of purchasing a few young girls. No more than six ever came at a time, apparently; that made it easier to transfer them from the local trading vessels to lighters that could navigate the rivers further along the coast and secretly bring them ashore.

When Chin Ming shared this information with her friend, Wing Yee came up with an idea. 'You, me, we cannot fight the men; cannot even fight Madam Ho. We should make friend with her.'

Chin Ming was horrified. 'What ever do you mean?'

'She want clean women for men. Too many to check by herself; also need examine often – make sure men not pass on disease, make sure women not pregnant. I go talk to her, tell her about new clinic, say we look after women for her.'

'I'm not sure,' Chin Ming said, 'and surely she'll never agree?'

'She greedy woman, she get more money when can promise girls very clean. Also, she lazy woman; we do work for her. She pay us well.'

'Pay us? But that will mean we'd be accepting money made from prostitution; the very thing we're trying to stop!'

'You never stop,' Wing Yee said, 'but we can help women. Maybe you teach them; they have better life if they speak English.'

Chin Ming threw her arms around her friend and held her close. She was still uncomfortable about taking what she considered to be tainted money, but maybe it was the only way. If Madam Ho went along with the idea, they might at least be able to help some of the women who were trapped into a wretched and demeaning existence. 'We must still speak to Dick,' she said. 'I'm sure we can persuade him to talk to Kenneth Murchison.'

*****

Chin Ming was waiting on the veranda when Dick arrived the following morning. Wing Yee was still gathering her belongings.

'Do we have the pleasure of your company again today?' Dick said, with a broad grin on his face.

She shook her head. 'No, not today, but I need to talk to

you.' She patted the cushion beside her, giving a clear indication that she meant to have the conversation straightaway. He was hardly settled before she revealed the essence of her discussions with May Lin and Sanjay, and before he had time to respond, she told him about Wing Yee's proposal.

'But you can't do that,' Dick said. 'It could be dangerous. If Madam Ho discovers what you really have in mind, she could turn nasty. Besides, there are others – people with influence who have the authorities eating out of their hands ...'

'May I remind you of the conversation we had not too long ago when you agreed we needed to find some way to challenge all the corruption that has crept into the Settlement. We made a pledge to change things, but as usual, we've all let other things get in the way. I think you should arrange to have a meeting with Kenneth Murchison when he next visits.'

'Why me? I have no influence with anyone. Besides, I'm not sure what Sujana would think. You and I both have children now; I wouldn't want to do anything that jeopardised their future.'

'It's their future I'm thinking about!' Chin Ming almost shouted. Her cheeks had developed a warm glow and her eyes looked like burnished, black sapphires. 'You are still the adopted son of Stamford Raffles, people respect you. Please, Dick, if we truly value what that man did for us, go and speak to Murchison. Tell him what's going on here.'

*****

It wasn't until the middle of April that Murchison prised himself away from the comfort of Penang. The local newspaper had announced his visit – the date of his arrival and, only five days later, his subsequent departure. It was to be a short visit.

Dick rode his horse down the hill immediately after breakfast. He took the route along Middle Road and then along Bencoolen Street. The town was relatively quiet at this hour apart from the laundrymen, the water carriers, and the lines of labourers being escorted to some building site or other. He reached the road that snaked its way up what was now called Government Hill, but which he still referred to as Bukit Larangan. Murchison would be lodging in the house on the peak – a revamped version of the home built for Raffles over ten years ago.

He led the horse around the side of the house into the shade and tethered it to a small Angsana tree. There was little sign of any activity, but he decided to investigate anyway. The front section of the house had now become the Government Office; the place from where all the important Company business was conducted. Dick could hear signs of activity beyond the closed door. He knocked.

'Come!' a disembodied voice shouted in response.

A couple of clerks scribbled away in a corner, not lifting their heads from their task. The light was poor and the room was stuffy. Dick felt sorry for them. An officious-looking man in some sort of uniform glared at him. 'What do you want?' he barked.

'I would like to talk to Mr Murchison,' he said.

'That will not be possible,' the man replied.

'I know he arrived yesterday evening,' Dick said. 'I waited until this morning because I thought he might be tired after his journey but I was hoping he might be refreshed by now. Will it be possible to make an appointment for later today?'

'He has engagements for the whole day.'

'Then might I make an appointment for another day?'

'You must realise, young man, the Resident Councillor is very busy. He has court cases to attend to, correspondence to deal with, applications to consider ...'

'I realise all of that,' Dick said. 'I also realise he spends very little time in Singapore. What I need to discuss with him is of extreme importance, it will not wait until he comes this way again.'

The man blinked; he couldn't believe what he was hearing. Such insolence – and from a native too! He was at a loss for words.

Dick tried again. 'I know Murchison has a lot to deal with but I am sure he will want to hear what I have to say. He's here for another four days, I believe; surely, you could fit me in sometime during that time?'

Neither Dick nor the obnoxious secretary had noticed the door opening.

'What's all this rumpus?'

Kenneth Murchison glanced from one to the other, awaiting an explanation. He looked hot and flustered but otherwise harmless.

'I was hoping to speak to you, sir,' Dick said quickly, 'but I understand you are busy all day today. We were just discussing any other possibilities when I might speak with you during your visit to Singapore.'

'What is it that you need to discuss with me, young man?'

'Sir, I am the adopted son of Stamford Raffles. I have become aware of a number of illegal happenings in the Settlement which I think you need to know about.'

Dick never mentioned his connection to Raffles; he made a point of not doing so, but Chin Ming had made it clear that such a reminder might make a difference. He was beginning to agree with her; this might now be the only way of getting people like Murchison to take any notice of what he had to say.

'Eleven o'clock sharp. I will see you immediately before I leave.' Murchison glared at the secretary. 'Give him an appointment for Thursday morning.'

⋆⋆⋆⋆⋆

Three days later, Dick knocked and pushed open the door without waiting for a reply. The secretary rolled his eyes heavenwards and sighed noisily. 'You're back then.'

'Of course, I'm back,' Dick said, ignoring the contemptuous attitude of the gatekeeper. 'I was promised an appointment at eleven o'clock this morning – and here I am, exactly on time.'

The man pulled out his pocket watch, sniffed, and pointed to a chair. 'I will let Mr Murchison know you're here.'

He was kept waiting another fifteen minutes, but determined to keep calm, he made no comment. When he was finally admitted to the inner sanctum, he found Murchison stuffing papers into a leather bag. 'Say what you have to say, young man, and be quick about it. I have a passage booked on a boat that leaves in a couple of hours.'

Dick held his hands behind his back, gripping his own wrists so as not to reveal his annoyance about the way he was being treated. He had a small opportunity to speak his mind, and he wasn't going to jeopardise his chances of being heard by complaining.

'Sir, I realise your demanding schedule doesn't permit you to visit Singapore as often as you might like and that is why I feel it my duty to bring something to your attention.'

Murchison stopped what he was doing and turned to face his visitor. The youth was clever, no doubt about that; no direct criticism had been levied, but it was quite clear that he thought too little attention was being paid to the Settlement. 'Go on,' he said.

Dick quickly outlined the problem. He began by pointing out the increase in the number of brothels in and around the town. He went on, noting the fact that women continued to be smuggled into the Settlement, forced to work in illegal establishments, and kept in overcrowded, unhealthy conditions.

Murchison looked perplexed. 'What proof do you have?'

'One of my friends now employs one of the women who used to work at the place in Cross Street; she has told us about groups of women arriving from Sumatra. They always arrive after dark, spend a short time at Cross Street, then they often disappear. She thinks they are taken to the gambier plantation or perhaps to some of the newer establishments around town.'

'She thinks but she doesn't know for certain?'

'She was in no position to be sure but she isn't the only one who is aware of this activity. My friend's gardener has also spoken about the boats arriving from Sumatra. I wouldn't be surprised if they weren't the same gangs that bring in the opium, guns, and other contraband. It's all getting out of hand, and something needs to be done.'

'And you're expecting me to do something, based on such flimsy information, hearsay in fact. Prostitution isn't something that is unique to Singapore, young man. It's as old as the hills and wherever you have a population dominated by men far from home you will never stamp it out. I imagine you've inherited your idealism from the man who adopted you, but you need to face reality ...'

'But it's against the law,' Dick interrupted before the dressing-down went any further. 'And besides,' he continued, 'Singapore has developed a reputation as a trading hub for the whole region. Would the Company want to see their prospects jeopardised, which is what will happen if the lawbreakers see an opening for more dangerous activities?'

'You are too clever for your own good!' Murchison snapped. 'And I'm running out of time. There is nothing I can do until you can come back to me with some real evidence, some definite proof of malpractice. I bid you good morning.'

*****

Dick wasn't looking forward to telling Chin Ming and Wing Yee that he'd been unsuccessful in making his case to Murchison. Neither was he pleased with himself for having failed to convince the man that something needed to be done. He decided to visit Alexander Johnston and ask for his advice. When Raffles left Singapore, he'd asked his best friend to take care of Dick and Johnston had been more than pleased to take on the role of guardian. During the time Dick had lived with Alexander, they had become close friends, and even though Dick was now married with his own home and family, it was to Alexander that he always turned when he needed advice.

'What you've told me comes as no surprise,' Alexander said. 'There's been so much change in recent years and the Company are loath to put any money into supporting a decent judiciary. From what I hear, Murchison is more interested in geology than in administration; he finds rocks less irksome than people. Let me think about what you've told me; I'll talk to some of the magistrates – the ones that I trust – and we'll see what can be done.'

*****

Chin Ming tried her best not to reveal her frustration when Dick reported back on his meeting. She didn't want him to feel that she blamed him in any way.

When they were alone, she sat down with Wing Yee to discuss what might be done through their work at the clinic. The building was now finished and Baba Tan had told everyone it would be ready to open its doors at the end of the month. Edmund was expected back in Singapore around then, so Chin Ming thought that now was an ideal time for them to make their plans. She'd still prefer to avoid Madam Ho's ill-gotten money, but it seemed there was no other way.

'I'll visit Madam Ho this week,' Wing Yee said, speaking in Cantonese again to make sure nothing she wanted to say was omitted. 'It might take a while before she'll agree to our idea.'

'But I thought you said she would be happy for her charges to come to the clinic, that there are too many for her to cope with now?'

'She said that but did she mean it? She may think she will lose face; she might not want to pay for our services.'

'Oh, I do hope you can convince her. But we'll need to get

121

the women to come to the clinic on a regular basis.'

'What are you thinking about?'

'If they are to believe their lives can improve, maybe meeting May Lin will help; she can tell them about escaping the clutches of Madam Ho and working with a family, earning her own money. Once Edmund has returned, I will ask him to look after the children.'

'It's a good idea,' said Wing Yee, 'but May Lin might not want to come. She might be afraid to return there; you said she told you Madam Ho wasn't kind to her. Anyway, what will happen if Edmund decides to stay longer in Malacca?'

'I will discuss the idea with May Lin,' Chin Ming said, 'but I think she'll want to help. I'll tell her what we have in mind and make sure she understands one of us will always be with her.'

'What about Edmund?'

'I'm sure he will be back soon, but if he is delayed, then I'll ask Sujana if she could take care of Charlotte and William. It need only be on one, possibly two occasions.'

*****

Chin Ming was disappointed there was still no news from Edmund or any sign of his return when the clinic opened on 25th April. She spent the morning following instructions from Wing Yee and making lists of the medications they had transferred from her workshop. Just before she returned home to help May Lin with the children, one of the towkays from along Boat Quay bustled in through the door. He demanded to speak to Baba Tan, refusing to discuss his situation with a mere woman.

'Baba Tan will be here later,' Chin Ming told him, 'but all he will do is ask my friend here to suggest some suitable medication. It is Wing Yee who is the herbalist, it is she who mixes the lotions and prepares the salves. If you tell her what is wrong, she will be able to help you now. If you won't talk to her, then you must wait until the end of the afternoon.'

The towkay, who was not used to such forthright language from a woman, scowled, uttered several mouthfuls of abuse, and strode off in the direction of the quay.

Wing Yee giggled. 'You speak to him like man, he not like.'

'He might not like it,' Chin Ming said, 'but I bet he'll be back later and he'll see for himself that you are the expert and he could have saved himself a good deal of time if he'd listened to what I said.'

Both women were still smiling when Madam Ho walked in. All Chin Ming's self-assurance dissipated immediately. Even after all these years, the sight of the person who had stripped away her sense of dignity, made her feel embarrassed and ashamed when she first arrived in Singapore sent a shiver down her spine. It was unlikely that Madam Ho had any recollection of the event, of course. Establishing whether a new arrival was a virgin or not was an everyday occurrence for her. If she remembered anything it would probably be her annoyance that Chin Ming was not destined for the brothel.

'I've come to discuss your proposition,' she said to Wing Yee in Cantonese. 'I've just heard that another boatload of women will be arriving from Sumatra shortly. Are you still willing to examine them?'

CHAPTER 12
Late April 1831

Tijah had always known she was different from the other children in the kampong. It wasn't just that her mother was dead and she lived with her aunt. The family never spoke about either of her parents, and when three years ago she had asked her grandfather, he told her that after her mother died his heart had died too. He told her to never mention it again.

Being an obedient child, she had not dared to ask any more questions. However, her curiosity had been rekindled a few weeks ago. She'd returned from the padi fields with her aunt to find everyone in the kampong talking in hushed tones about a European who had arrived that afternoon only to be sent packing by her grandfather. It had taken all the young girl's persuasiveness to coax her aunt into admitting the man who had visited was indeed Tijah's father. More questions followed. The thirteen-year-old was determined to make sense of what she heard, but her aunt refused to say anything more apart from the fact that he'd gone scurrying back to the place he'd come from - Singapore.

Tijah was angry that her relatives had prevented her from meeting the man. She'd always known her father was European; she now knew he lived in Singapore. She believed she had a right to make up her own mind about him, and the only way to do that, it seemed, was to follow him. She'd heard people talk about the settlement at the tip of the peninsula. It was much smaller than Malacca, so it shouldn't be too hard to locate him. Her problem, of course, was how to get herself there.

This morning, she had told her aunt she felt unwell and excused herself from their daily routine in the padi fields. Her aunt had forgotten to mention this to anyone else. When the kampong was quiet in the middle of the morning, Tijah hid a few of her cherished possessions in a bundle of clothing and slipped into the shadows of the coconut trees. She crossed the river and eventually found her way to the quay and that's when her plan hit a brick wall. She had no money, she was a young girl on her own, she had no means of travelling beyond this point.

*****

Edmund was exhausted after four weeks travelling amongst the hills and valleys inland from Malacca. He'd been lucky to find a couple of Malay guides who were willing to accompany him. One of them was the nephew of a man who remembered a collecting expedition that Raffles had instigated when he spent some time in the area almost two decades ago.

Their first exploratory trip had taken them along the coast to visit mangrove swamps where Edmund discovered a perfect habitat for insects, reptiles, and small mammals amongst the tree trunks, aerial roots, and sediment. He saw sponges, barnacles, and algae amongst the roots that hung over the water and filled his nostrils with the musty aroma of damp earth. In the forest, he saw small invertebrates but none of the plants that he was seeking. He put the misunderstanding down to his rudimentary command of Malay and made a greater effort to explain himself. Once the confusion had been overcome, the expedition proceeded with spectacular success.

The group returned to Malacca with tree ferns, bamboos,

lilies, numerous types of pitcher plant, several different begonias, and something Edmund had never seen before that had laurel-like leaves and clusters of small white flowers with a scent that reminded him of jasmine. The guides informed him the leaves were useful for thatching roofs. In the forest margins, they found a climbing plant with small, bluish-green flowers and in the swamps, they came across orchids. Edmund's favourite was a specimen known locally as kinta weed. It had no perfume at all but was a delightful orchid-like flower with white petals decorated with fine, purple stripes in the shape of a fan, which stopped abruptly just short of the petal's frilly edge.

*****

The day after returning to Malacca, Edmund heard about an Indian trading vessel that would be leaving for Singapore in the next couple of days. The captain was at first reluctant to take him on board, especially as he would also have to find space for the crates containing Edmund's precious collection. In the end, the gift of a corky coral tree with its showy, orange flowers had proved irresistible to the otherwise hard-nosed skipper.

Edmund had twenty-four hours to find a carpenter to make the cases he needed to protect the plants. Most of them were straightforward as the specimens were small and several could fit snuggly together in one container. The crate designed for the tree ferns was enormous compared with the others, but it was decided no lid was necessary and the fronds would do just as well left open to the elements. The smaller cases arrived first and the guides helped Edmund place the begonias, the lilies, and the pitcher plants safely inside. He begged a barrel full of cork from one of the nearby merchants and spread this liberally between each of the specimens. By the time this task was completed to Edmund's satisfaction, the two larger crates had been delivered. The bamboos fitted tightly together in the first and then two young tree ferns were packed into the base of the other. When the job was complete, they pushed all eight cases against a nearby wall to await loading onto the ship later in the day. To express his thanks for their help, Edmund invited the two guides to join him for a meal at one of the many stalls surrounding the harbour. Neither Edmund nor the guides noticed a small girl dressed in sarong kebaya huddled in the shadows.

*****

From her hiding place, Tijah watched three men busily engaged in transferring a collection of plants into several containers; two of them were Malay and the third was most likely European. They finished their work by lowering the larger plants – she didn't know their name – into much bigger crates; one was tightly packed, the other looked more spacious with a profusion of green foliage protruding from the top. When they had finished, all three walked away in the direction of the market stalls. Tijah had heard them conversing in Malay; they had agreed to return when the plants had been loaded onto the ship. The European occasionally spoke another language which she assumed was English, and although she didn't understand what he said, she did recognise the word Singapore. From the way he spoke, she worked out that was where the vessel was heading. He was European like her father and he was going where she wanted to go – where she hoped to find her father. Perhaps this man could help her? All she needed to do was hide inside the largest crate and wait until they were safely on their way.

*****

127

To Edmund's delight, a strong breeze filled the sails as soon as the ship was clear of the harbour. The strong wind continued to push them along at a steady pace, bringing with it a light shower nearly every evening. Members of the crew welcomed these cloudbursts because they left everything feeling clean and refreshed. Edmund, too, was pleased; the rain would reach the roots of the bamboo and the tree ferns, preventing them from drying out during the voyage. His pleasure increased when the winds continued to be favourable, enabling him to complete his homeward journey in just under a week.

When they reached Singapore, the smaller crates fitted into one bumboat, but the larger one came ashore with Edmund in a second vessel. As usual, several coolies appeared within seconds of them arriving at the quay, but it took Edmund nearly half an hour before he could find enough men who were willing to load his crates onto their handcarts and then push them up the winding slope to his home. They needed two small wagons to accommodate all but the largest crate. The one with green foliage waving in the breeze was tipped onto its side before being consigned to the third vehicle which lined up behind the others ready to begin the long haul to the top of Bukit Selegie.

They were off-loaded nearly an hour later. Chin Ming was so excited to see her husband back home that she forgot to offer the hot and sweaty labourers any refreshment. Fortunately, Kim Seng had heard all the commotion of their arrival and produced a tray of cooling drinks almost immediately. The men lolled against their carts; their bodies glistened as they consumed the refreshments, and lopsided grins spread from ear to ear when Edmund handed each of them a bonus payment shortly before they returned to the harbour.

'I should take the smaller crates apart,' Edmund said as soon as all the excitement had died down. 'It will give the plants a chance to enjoy something other than salt in the air.

The larger specimens benefitted from the occasional shower, but the smaller ones haven't seen daylight for a while. I'll be sending some of them back to England eventually but I've also brought some to plant here.'

'Why not wait for Sanjay to arrive,' Chin Ming said. 'He'll be able to help you.'

'That won't be for another three or four hours. I think I'd like to get them into the shade, at least. I've brought some ginger plants for Wing Yee; I hope she'll like them.'

'She will be extremely happy, I'm sure. I think I must have depleted her stock considerably with all the ginger tea she made for me after you left.'

'But you're feeling well now?' Edmund asked, taking his wife's hand and squeezing it affectionately.

'Never better,' she said.

There was something about his wife's demeanour that was different, but he couldn't decide exactly what. Her body had changed shape, it was now obvious she was pregnant, but there was something else, something he couldn't put his finger on. Was it simply the fact that she was no longer constantly nauseous and had more energy than before; he thought not. It was almost as if she had a secret, but he knew his wife was incapable of keeping her enthusiasm to herself. Maybe he was imagining things.

'Now, if you're not going to wait for Sanjay, why don't you begin on the crates,' Chin Ming said, interrupting his thoughts. 'Best to get them out of the way before Charlotte and William arrive. They've gone to play with young Tomas; Sujana collected them just after breakfast.'

Edmund began with the smaller boxes, carefully lifting each specimen out in turn and inspecting it closely. None of them seemed to have suffered from their adventure at sea. He left the largest box on its side, planning to pull the two tree ferns out and then stand them upright. The first one came easily enough, but the second one wouldn't budge.

'I need something to use to lever the panels apart,' he said, disappearing in the direction of the garden shed. When he returned, Chin Ming was standing beside the wooden case. 'I hope you haven't been trying to open it,' Edmund said.

'I thought I heard a noise, a faint sort of groaning,' Chin Ming said. 'And there's a strange sort of odour. Are you sure you haven't got an animal trapped inside there?'

Edmund sniffed. He detected an earthy, slightly acidic odour but nothing more than would be expected from plants that had been sitting in very damp soil for several days. Then, he listened, but couldn't hear a thing. He thought his wife's imagination, together with her sense of smell, might have intensified along with her belly. Nevertheless, he was careful when he prised the wooden panels apart. A scrap of fabric, tied together with some raffia landed at his feet. He handed it to Chin Ming.

'I don't care what you say,' she said, 'this cloth smells odd. A bit like the compost you make to put on your garden.'

'That's probably exactly what it is,' Edmund said. 'I made sure there was sufficient soil around the roots when I boxed-up the plants. Any foliage that dropped during the voyage, plus the rainwater, might easily cause some decomposition.'

She sighed; he probably knew best. Inside the material, she found a small brooch, some coloured beads, and a piece of embroidery. Edmund had no idea how the strange assortment had ended up in one of his crates. He wondered what other treasures he might find. His shadow fell across the contents of the box, blocking out all the light. It wasn't until he began to move the second fern that he saw the body.

Chin Ming gasped; her fingers flew to her parted lips as she stepped back from the container. 'Who is she? How did she get there? Is she breathing?'

The girl was motionless. Edmund put his hand near her mouth and could just detect the warmth of her breath. He bent down and carefully lifted her out of the crate and car-

ried her up the steps and onto the veranda. Chin Ming hurried
inside to find something for her to drink and some water to
bathe her face. When she returned, the girl's eyes were fluttering, she was passing in and out of consciousness.

'Has she been inside that thing since you left Malacca?'
she asked. 'How could she possibly survive without food or
water?'

'I have no idea,' Edmund said, 'but maybe the showers as
well as my tree ferns helped her to survive. The main point is
that she is still alive. I think we'd better send for Wing Yee to
make sure she stays that way.'

*****

It took almost three days before Tree Fern girl, as they took
to calling her, recovered enough to tell them her name. Wing
Yee and Chin Ming had taken turns to sit with her, bathe her
face and hands, and speak soothing words whenever she
became agitated. Sometimes, they both remained in the room
all through the night. One would lift her into a position that
enabled the other to part her lips and encourage her to swallow some of the tea that Wing Yee had prepared. The concoctions would vary according to the time of day and whether her
body was hot or cold. Wing Yee was insistent that the yin and
yang needed to be in balance; only then would her *qi* – her
vital energy – be restored. It was during these times that they
spoke quietly in Cantonese, reminding each other of their own
journey to Singapore almost ten years ago.

'I'll never forget the day the bosun threw open the door
and pushed you into the cabin I shared with Shu Fang.'

'You looked so angry, I was terrified of you,' Chin Ming
said.

'It was the shock, that's all. Do you remember the storm
when the ship was blown off course and Shu Fang was constantly sick, vomiting up the last traces of opium in her body?

131

That's when I really got to know you, that's when I knew we would become close friends.'

'We were lucky to have each other – especially after Boon Peng died and that horrible Dutchman locked us in his house along the Rochor River. We never did find out what happened to Shu Fang.'

'Wasn't there a rumour that she'd been taken out to the gambier plantation? Raffles tried to find her after the Dutchman was taken into custody, but there was no trace. I suspect the temptation to take opium again became too much; it would have helped her to obliterate all the bad things that had happened. She could easily have been in some sort of intoxicated state when Raffles looked for her, but there is always the possibility that she didn't survive long enough for that to happen.'

'We must ensure that nothing like that happens to Tree-Fern girl. She looks so very young, even younger than I was when we arrived here.'

CHAPTER 13
Early May 1831

'You haven't told Edmund anything about our plans for the clinic yet, have you?' Wing Yee said. She was sure she was correct in her assumption, and if so, it was better to continue in Cantonese to avoid causing any awkwardness should Edmund suddenly return from his work in the garden.

'He knows that the clinic is open and I've been there to help you a few times.'

'Yes, but you haven't told him about our arrangement with Madam Ho. Why not?'

'It wasn't deliberate – at least not at first. I'll need to explain all the details, and there's been no opportunity, that's all. You know how he worries about me. I need time to tell him about our concerns, about Dick's visit to Murchison, and our need to collect solid evidence before Murchison will do anything,' Chin Ming said. 'I've hardly seen Edmund since he returned; most of my time is spent here in the sick room.' She didn't tell Wing Yee that another reason for avoiding a conversation with her husband was that she still had reservations about accepting Madam Ho's money. And if she couldn't wholly convince herself on the matter, how on earth was she going to justify it to Edmund?

'Has Dick said anything to Sujana?' Wing Yee said.

'I'm not sure. I think he may have said something the day

he visited Murchison but I suspect he hasn't filled in all the details.'

*****

When Tijah finally opened her eyes, she couldn't remember very much apart from her name. She had a pounding headache and she felt weak. Her vision was blurred, but as soon as she realised there were figures - she wasn't sure how many or even whether they were men or women – sitting close to where she lay, she tried to move. What was she doing here? Why was she being watched? Who were these people?

It was Chin Ming who noticed the first movement. She shifted closer to the bed and took one of the girl's hands in her own; they were cool and clammy.

'You are safe,' she said in English.

Tijah didn't understand. She started to tremble and tried to withdraw her hand but it was held firmly and she hadn't the strength to resist. Chin Ming loosened her hold, turning to Wing Yee for guidance.

'*Jangan takut, anda selamat,*' Wing Yee said in Malay, hoping to reassure the girl that she was safe and had no need to worry.

During the years Chin Ming had spent in England, Dick had continued to teach the local language to Wing Yee and she was now almost as fluent as someone who had been born here. 'We will look after you. I am Wing Yee, this my friend, Chin Ming. What is your name?'

Tijah turned away from the two women and curled up in a ball. She was desperately trying to remember how she might have arrived in this house that certainly wasn't the one in which she had spent most of her life, but the strands of memory that drifted in and out of her consciousness were obliterated by waves of nausea, sapping all her strength.

The next time she opened her eyes, there was a third shape

gradually coming into focus. It was a man, probably about the same age as the two women, but his skin was darker than theirs and his hair was tightly curled. The three of them were talking in low whispers. She tried to keep still, but somewhere from within, a low whimper escaped from her lips.

Dick turned around immediately. He also spoke to Tijah in Malay, trying to reassure her and make her understand that they were trying to help. It was Wing Yee who sat on the bed this time, gently stroking Tijah's hands as Dick talked and told her their names and that they wanted to look after her. He pointed to Chin Ming to explain that it was this lady's husband who had discovered her, that she had been found in one of the wooden crates he had brought to Singapore from Malacca. Chin Ming moved closer. In her hand, she held a scrap of batik cloth. She unfolded it slowly and lifted each of the items it contained so that the girl could see them clearly. 'These are yours,' she said. 'We have kept them safe for you.'

The hint of a small smile fluttered across Tijah's lips. The image of the boxes piled up along the wharf back home came into sharp focus and then disappeared as quickly as it had materialised. Similar episodes when she was lucid for a while and then relapsed into a state of confusion continued for another week. But each day, there was a small amount of progress; a desire to touch either the brooch or the piece of embroidery she had brought with her, an increased interest in her surroundings, and less crying out in her sleep.

Tijah was encouraged to drink coconut water laced with juice from limes and pomegranates. If she began to feel faint, they insisted she sip water mixed with a small spoonful of salt. Wing Yee introduced a potion containing feverfew for her headaches and ginseng to improve her general well-being. She began to eat small amounts of plain boiled rice and chicken, some broth, and slices of pineapple. They decided to ask no more questions until she was stronger and ready to trust them with her story.

With each new day, Tijah looked stronger. Her speech was still occasionally slurred, and when she was encouraged to get out of bed and walk around the room with Wing Yee on one side and Chin Ming on the other, she sometimes felt dizzy, but her skin was no longer flaky and the headaches had almost disappeared. The major problem now was communication. Chin Ming only used Malay when she went to the market, which wasn't often since this pregnancy had upset her equilibrium. She was rusty not having used it for four years. Wing Yee was more than competent, but she had no reason to practise every day as most of the people she encountered at the clinic spoke either Cantonese or English. It was when Dick visited that they were able to begin the process of finding out a little more information about their guest, but what brought her to Singapore remained a mystery.

'She is thirteen years old; her name is Tijah,' Dick said. He reverted to English to relay the information Tijah had shared with him. 'And she was born in a kampong on the outskirts of Malacca.'

Dick continued to chat with Tijah each time he visited, but she avoided giving any details about her former life apart from describing daily life in the kampong. She shied away from anything that might cause her hosts to ask what she was doing on the quayside in Malacca or why she had risked her life by hiding inside a crate filled with plants.

*****

At the end of the first week, following Tijah's arrival, Charlotte had been found at the foot of her bed, standing on tiptoe, and staring at their emaciated guest. 'Why is she still in bed?' she asked her mother as Chin Ming returned to her vigil with a bowl of fresh water to bathe the girl's face.

'She is not very well, darling. She needs a lot of rest, so we need to be very quiet. Can you do that for me?'

'When will she be able to play?'

'That depends on how quickly she gets better,' Chin Ming said. 'Would you like to help me wash her face?'

Charlotte shook her head from side to side. She wasn't too keen on having her own face washed, let alone wash someone else. She had once tried to wash her baby brother, but it had ended abruptly when she had poured cold water over his head. He had screamed, and she had been well and truly told off. She wasn't going to risk that again.

Edmund came to the rescue when he arrived to tell Chin Ming that he was about to go into the garden.

'Can I come to help, Papa?' Charlotte said, rushing over to him and flinging her arms tightly around his legs with no intention of letting go. He led her outside and soon she was busy watering her seedlings. That task completed, she placed her blue sash between her teeth and started to canter around the limits of her plot. This was a game she'd recently devised to inspect the boundary of 'her' garden.

When Edmund emerged from his shed to observe this ritual, he couldn't help smiling to himself. He was pleased that he'd created this safe place for his daughter, an area in which she was free to play and do whatever she wanted.

*****

During this time, whilst Chin Ming and Wing Yee occupied themselves with restoring Tijah to full health, Edmund had already begun to busy himself in the garden. The plants he intended for onward passage to England had been selected based on them being healthy enough to survive the long sea voyage. They were now firmly ensconced in a variety of wooden barrels, which he'd been able to purchase from one of the importers of Chinese porcelain along Boat Quay. It had taken only a couple of days for him to make sure they would be well-nourished in a protective environment. They had now been returned to the wharf ready for transfer to the next *Indiaman* heading for London or to one of the ports along the coast of Devon and Cornwall. Even the most delicate specimens should be safe.

The remainder of the collection had already been allocated a place in the newly-prepared plot at the side of the house. He'd given two of the sturdier specimens to his daughter and helped her place them in her own small plot. His plan now was to spend part of each day developing his experimental garden even further. His original intention had included heading outside as soon after breakfast as possible so that he could begin work before the heat made it too uncomfortable. Sometimes, he managed to slip out ahead of Charlotte who much preferred to be in the garden than stay inside with May Lin and William. Edmund always hoped to make sufficient progress before Charlotte's arrival, but she was never very far behind.

She always told him she had come to help, but her presence made progress slower than he would have liked. He loved the fact that his three-year-old daughter enjoyed working alongside him and he decided it was more important to indulge the little girl, who was missing her mother's attention, at least until Chin Ming was able to spend less time in the sick room. William, however, was so well cared for by May Lin that he seemed not to notice his mother was occupied elsewhere.

Towards the end of the morning, Edmund took hold of Charlotte's hand and led her inside where May Lin was always waiting with a glass of coconut water for each of them. Refreshed and feeling cooler, Charlotte was led away – often reluctantly – to join in games with her young brother; Edmund then retired to his study to work on the next section of his book.

Frequently, as the afternoon light softened and crept nearer to evening, Charlotte would wake up from her nap and wander through the house to find her father. Her main desire was to make sure he hadn't returned to the garden without her. A slight draught from the window that Edmund always kept open alerted him to her presence; the appearance of a small section of shiny, blue fabric fluttering in the doorway drawing her to his attention. No matter how quietly Charlotte waited, it was the blue sash she always trailed around that gave her away. Typically, he would let her stay. He handed her a picture book and placed her on a cushion in the corner of the room. Usually, when he looked up half an hour or so later, she had curled up on the cushion and was fast asleep. Most days, Edmund continued working in his study until the early evening when May Lin came looking for Charlotte to feed her, bathe her, and put her to bed. Then, he knew it was time for him to stop scribbling and try to persuade his wife to take a break from the sick room.

*****

As soon as Tijah became stronger, Wing Yee suggested it might help her recovery if she could meet someone nearer her own age. It was Dick who came up with the idea of introducing her to Fakina, the young girl who had been brought to Singapore from Java by a friend of the family to help Sujana look after Tomas. Fakina was thought to be about sixteen years old and she spoke Malay. It was evident after only their second meeting that the two girls got along well together. When Dick asked Tijah if she would like to come and live with Fakina all the time, she nodded excitedly. The smile on her lips took only seconds to reach her eyes.

Chin Ming protested at first, thinking that she should be able to provide a home for Tijah as it was Edmund who had brought her to Singapore. Wing Yee told her that Dick and Sujana were just as capable of looking after her, if not more so. She pointed out that Chin Ming was now in the fifth month of her pregnancy, that everyone in Dick's household spoke Malay fluently, and that Tijah and Fakina would be good company for each other. Chin Ming had to agree with her friend's forth-right assessment of the situation. If she was honest, this preg-nancy was more tiring than the other two had been, she had less energy these days and needed to rest from the heat almost every afternoon.

'You should not feel bad,' Wing Yee said. 'When you were pregnant with Charlotte and William, you could relax in a cool climate and you had all Edmund's relatives to fuss over you. Now, you have hot and sticky weather, two energetic young-sters demanding attention, and me telling you what to do all the time. No wonder you're exhausted.'

*****

It was just two days later when Tijah made the move to Dick and Sujana's house. As well as the personal treasures she had brought with her in the scrap of batik fabric, her possessions consisted of those that had been given to her since she arrived in Singapore; some brightly-coloured sarongs each with a matching *kabaya*, two pairs of slippers and some undergar-ments. Chin Ming was anxious to present her with a parting gift, but struggled to know what to choose. At thirteen, she thought Tijah was too old for a toy and too young for anything overly ornate by way of jewellery. In the end, she settled for a slim, silver bangle that she found hidden in her box of trea-sures. She'd purchased it in the bazaar in Calcutta along with two other pieces when their ship had docked there last year. This one had a simple leaf design etched around its outer sur-face. When she had shown it to Edmund, they both agreed that it was the perfect gift for Tree Fern girl.

Although it was only a short distance between the two houses, Chin Ming knew she didn't have the energy to walk there and back again, so it was decided that Wing Yee would accompany Tijah to her new home. Both women waited on the veranda for Tijah to return from the garden where she had been saying goodbye to Edmund and Charlotte. The temperature was still pleasant and Wing Yee wanted to start out before the heat became too intense, but there was still no sign of Tijah. Just as Wing Yee thought she should go to investigate, Charlotte came running around the corner of the house in an agitated state. Chin Ming flopped down onto a nearby sofa, ready to console her daughter.

'Mama, mama,' she shouted at the top of her voice. 'You said Tijah could play with me when she was better. If she goes to live with uncle and auntie, she will play with Tomas; she won't be able to play with me!'

Chin Ming pressed her lips together in an effort not to laugh. 'Tijah won't be too far away and I'm sure she will often come to see us. Having a visitor to play with will be very special, won't it, and I know you will make her welcome.'

Charlotte frowned. She wasn't entirely convinced by her mother's response.

'Besides,' Chin Ming added, noting the furrowed brow, 'very soon, you will have a baby brother or sister to play with.'

'Can it be a sister? Not another brother,' Charlotte sighed.

'I can't make any promises,' Chin Ming said, taking her daughter's hands in her own. 'But whether it is a girl or a boy, I will need you to help me look after the new baby. Being a big sister is a very important job.'

Charlotte screwed up her face, considering this idea; finally, she nodded her agreement and then allowed a toothy smile to light up her face.

When Chin Ming looked up, Tijah and Edmund had arrived. Edmund had been listening in on the conversation between his wife and daughter and a knowing grin spread across his face. Tijah wore only a slight smile and her gaze was unfocused. Chin Ming wondered if her health was fully restored.

'Are you feeling unwell, Tijah? You're looking pale,' she managed to say in Malay.

'I am very well, thanks to you and Wing Yee,' Tijah replied.

'But something is upsetting you,' Chin Ming said.

'I am very happy to live with Fakina but I am not happy to leave here. You have been so good to me.'

Chin Ming patted the seat beside her, inviting Tijah to sit. 'Look at me,' she said, 'you will only be a short distance along the road –as I've just explained to Charlotte. You are welcome to come here whenever you want. In Dick and Sujana's house, you will have someone to talk to who is much nearer your own age, someone who speaks Malay better than me and much better than my husband.' She forced herself to smile as she was talking, trying to convince herself as well as the girl sitting next to her that it made good sense and all would be well.

A wan smile spread across Tijah's face, but her eyes filled with tears.

'Take this,' Chin Ming said, removing the bangle from her pocket and slipping it onto Tijah's wrist. 'It's just a small gift to help you remember the time you've spent with us. The leaf design will remind you of the plants that you hid amongst on your way to Singapore.'

'I will never forget your kindness – or the plants,' Tijah said, attempting to throw her arms around Chin Ming but being prevented from getting too close by her growing belly.

Everyone began to laugh. Wing Yee took Tijah's hand and led her in the direction of her new home.

CHAPTER 14
Singapore, late May 1831

Some leaves on the papaya tree that grew close to the house tapped on the shutters. Edmund looked up from his desk. A light breeze was frolicking amongst the foliage. It brought with it the scent of damp earth from an earlier shower, a scattering of petals, and an opportunity to reflect. His book was beginning to take shape. Nearly all the notes he'd made about his trip to Malacca had been incorporated into the draft manuscript, but watching the plants outside his window as they swayed in the warm air reminded him that it would be much improved with Dick's illustrations. That, however, would have to wait until they were better established. Dick had promised to complete as many sketches as Edmund wanted once the shrubs, saplings, and cuttings had matured.

As usual, he continued to work in his study until the early evening when Sanjay arrived. He always looked forward to discussing the next phase of their project with the Indian gardener and agreeing on a strategy. He still found it difficult to believe that the man had committed a crime serious enough to justify his current lack of liberty. His work and his attitude were impeccable, and he never complained about Charlotte's constant chatter. Whatever he had done to upset the authorities in Calcutta, Edmund was convinced that his gardener was completely harmless.

On the occasions when he'd been able to talk to Sanjay

without Charlotte tagging along, he'd discovered small pieces of information about the circumstances of Sanjay's imprisonment, and hints had been made about Sanjay's brother. However, there was nothing tangible, nothing to explain why the brother had eventually been transported to Australia. Edmund believed that one day Sanjay would confide in him - tell him the whole story. But for now, he would have to content himself with the pleasure of sharing his ideas with a fellow enthusiast; a man who could also see the potential of the patch of dry earth beside the house. Edmund intended to transform the area into an experimental garden; something to replace Raffles' Spice Garden which was now neglected and choked with weeds. It would be the beginning of a great botanical garden; worthy of the ambitions Raffles had dreamt of for the Settlement.

Edmund pushed his chair away from the desk, ready to tidy his papers and clean his pens when he became aware of someone tapping on the door.

'Come in,' he said, wondering who might have called to see him at this hour. The door opened slowly, revealing Sanjay who was hovering in the space between the hallway and the study. He shuffled his feet, moving forwards hesitantly when Edmund beckoned him to come in.

'What is it, Sanjay? You usually meet me in the garden. Is there a problem?'

'Sorry, sorry, sahib,' Sanjay replied. 'I have letter for you. Mr Johnston call me to office. He say, give you letter straightaway, not wait in garden as usual.'

'That's most intriguing, Sanjay. Do you know what the letter contains?'

'Not really, sahib, but I have much hope.'

Edmund was puzzled. He'd quite forgotten the conversation he'd had with Alexander before leaving for his trip to Malacca. He sliced open the envelope with a tiny *kris* given to him by Chin Ming at Christmastime. Its small, twisted handle and sharp blade made it perfect as a letter opener. There was only one sheet of paper inside the envelope; he quickly scanned Alexander's elaborate copperplate handwriting, then grinned.

'Sit,' Edmund said to Sanjay, waving his hand in the direction of a nearby chair. 'Please sit down while I read the letter through again; I will take it slowly this time to make sure I've not misunderstood what it says.' He screwed up his eyes and focused on the elaborately written script. He didn't notice that Sanjay had lowered himself cross-legged onto the floor instead of taking a seat as he had intended.

'Your hope is fully justified,' Edmund said when he looked up from the note. 'It's very good news. It has been decided that you have worked on building sites for long enough. My friend Wing Yee has spoken up for you. She invited one of the magistrates to visit the garden and view your handiwork whilst I was away. I must admit I was unaware of this and....'

Edmund continued to explain what had happened. His enthusiasm failed to consider that he was talking too much, too quickly and including far too much detail; he still hadn't noticed the gardener was sitting on the floor. Sanjay thought he understood what was being said but hadn't grasped every single detail.

'If I not work on road building, sahib, am I allowed to work in garden?'

'Yes, yes! Oh, I'm so sorry, Sanjay, I got carried away. Please get up, take a seat in the chair. You can work with me in the garden all the time from now on. We can really begin to make some progress at last – but first, we need to find a place for you to live. We'll build something for you in the garden itself, how about that?'

*****

With Tijah now firmly established in Dick's household and in no need of constant medical attention, Wing Yee decided it was time to return to the clinic. She planned to spend a little of each day there, building up the hours she spent away from Chin Ming gradually but continuing to return each evening, at least until the baby was born. Her plan did not quite work out as intended. On the second day, she found Madam Ho pacing about in the street, waiting for her arrival. The owner of the most eminent brothel in the town was impatient, not pleased to have been kept waiting. She was anxious to talk to Wing Yee in private. The women she had mentioned when they last met would be arriving the following week. She seemed nervous when questioned further, especially when Wing Yee asked her how many women to expect. When she returned to Bukit Selegie later in the day, Wing Yee told Chin Ming about the encounter and Madam Ho's uneasy behaviour.

'Perhaps she is getting cold feet because she knows the whole set up is illegal,' Chin Ming said. 'Ought we to think again about getting involved?'

'She – what is English phrase - hard as spike,' Wing Yee said.

'Hard as nails,' Chin Ming said, smiling. She had to agree that the old crone was unlikely to worry about anything illegal at this stage of her life; it had never concerned her before. 'From what Dick has told us, I hardly think the authorities are much concerned about the practice of prostitution but I still think we should find out as soon as possible whether these women have chosen to come here or have been forced to make the journey from Sumatra by someone else.'

'Not easy to find out. I see women only one time. They not want to speak to stranger; need to get trust.'

'Perhaps you could ask to see one or two of them a second time. I'm sure Madam Ho will agree if she thinks there might be a problem.'

'What sort of problem,' Wing Yee said, reverting to Cantonese again. 'What do you have in mind?'

'I'm not sure. After such a voyage, I imagine at least one of them might be suffering from sickness or something else that might provide you with a reason to see them again. Madam Ho will want to be sure each one of the women is healthy before she puts them to work.'

'It's a good idea, but I'm still not sure I'll have enough time to find out what we need to know,' Wing Yee said.

'What if I bring May Lin down to the clinic? When the women find out that she was caught up in an unsavoury life-style herself, they might be interested to learn how she was able to get away.'

'That depends on whether or not they have come here by choice,' Wing Yee said.

'I agree, but do you really think that is very likely? I suspect it's the fact that Madam Ho knows the women have been coerced into coming here that is making her tetchy. We've already agreed that it's impossible to stamp out prostitution, but if we can prove that these young women – and others like them – are being forced to leave their homes against their will, then it's a start, and the authorities will have to take some notice.'

*****

One evening towards the end of the month, Chin Ming asked May Lin to join her on the veranda. One of the hinges on the door needed oiling; it squeaked to announce her arrival. The girl tiptoed across the wooden boards of the veranda, still warm from the late afternoon sun. She bit her bottom lip and avoided Chin Ming's steady gaze.

'You're not in any trouble, May Lin,' Chin Ming said. 'I just wanted to share an idea with you, to ask for your advice.'

May Lin looked puzzled. She couldn't think what use her opinion could possibly be to someone as self-assured as her young mistress. They spoke in Cantonese as May Lin's use of English comprised only basic phrases, plus an unusual collection of unrelated words. Chin Ming began by asking her about her life in China before she came to Singapore. It seemed that she was yet another female from a poverty-stricken family who had been sold in order to regain face. Chin Ming poured out some pineapple juice and offered it to May Lin before she asked anything about the life she had led in the brothel.

'When did you learn to speak English?' Chin Ming asked.

'One gentleman, who became a regular visitor, taught me a few words,' May Lin said. 'I asked him to teach me more and he seemed pleased. He invented a game. He used objects in the room, but when I was able to memorise them all, he began to bring in small gifts so that we could discuss them and he would teach me new words – paper, soft, tasty, things like that.'

It appeared that the man had visited the brothel every few months when his ship was in port. May Lin's lessons had continued until last September. There had been no sign of him since. When May Lin had asked Madam Ho what had happened to him, all she received by way of an answer was a slap across her face. Madam Ho had continued to show her displeasure whenever May Lin came across her after that. Now Chin Ming understood how May Lin had come by such a curious vocabulary. She promised herself that she would continue with the girl's education. She was obviously a quick learner.

'She said I was no longer attractive and she wanted to get rid of me,' May Lin said. 'She was very glad when you and your friend came along to ask if she had anyone suitable to look after small children. I think she was only interested in how much you would pay her, but she was glad to let me go.'

Chin Ming spent the next hour telling May Lin about Wing Yee's clinic and their ambitions to provide medicines that would help women. They continued to speak in Cantonese as Chin Ming was anxious for May Lin to completely understand what she was saying. 'We want women to be able to come to the clinic themselves, to feel comfortable to do so. Wing Yee has remedies for bruises, for sprains, for headaches. She can help a woman who doesn't want to become pregnant, she can make lotions and creams that ease aches and pains.'

'This is good,' May Lin said, 'but I think most husbands, even men with many concubines, will not allow such a thing to happen. They will want to do what they have always done – visit an apothecary themselves and ask for what they think is needed.'

'You're right,' Chin Ming said, 'but things need to change and it's not only married women and concubines that concern us. There are many more men living in Singapore than women. As you know, many amuse themselves in the brothels – either in the town or in the gambier plantation - and they care nothing for the women they come across. All that concerns them is their own enjoyment and hoping they don't catch any nasty disease.'

May Lin started to fidget; she looked down at her feet. She knew that in some ways she had been lucky to have worked at Madam Ho's establishment, which had a good reputation. When she looked up, Chin Ming was still talking, saying something about men repaying debts, sending money back to China, gambling, and seeking solace in the brothels. But when Chin Ming started to talk about men taking local wives and them not being treated well, May Lin's attention sharpened.

Her eyes grew large. She knew someone from the brothel who had gone to live as a concubine of one of the local merchants. All the other girls had been envious at the time, but perhaps she wasn't so lucky, after all.

'They often become ill,' Chin Ming said, 'but we cannot make them better if we do not see them, find out what is wrong. Somehow, we need to convince the men that their women will live longer and give more pleasure if they have good health.'

May Lin wondered how her young mistress had acquired all this knowledge; surely, she hadn't once worked in the brothel herself? 'But I still don't understand why you ask to speak with me, ask for my advice.'

'I'm coming to that,' Chin Ming said. 'Madam Ho is expecting a group of women from Sumatra to arrive any day now. She has asked my friend Wing Yee to examine them.'

May Lin folded her arms across her own body as her posture stiffened and her muscles became rigid. She remembered only too well how she had been treated when she first arrived in the Settlement. She shuddered. She would never forget the pain and indignity she, too, had endured when undergoing such a close inspection herself. She remembered too, over-hearing Madam Ho boast about the women and girls she was able to offer to the men from the ships – and to certain well-established local merchants. 'But, madam, I don't understand why your friend would do this horrible thing for Madam Ho.'

'Wing Yee will not hurt them. We think they're being brought here illegally,' Chin Ming replied.

'What is illegal, I don't understand?'

'Many of the women who end up in the brothels are there because their family has sold them to a man who is paid by someone else to bring them here. That is not good, but it is something that has been happening for a long, long time.'

'That is what happened to me,' May Lin said. 'My family had no choice, they were starving.'

'In some cases, there is not even an exchange of money. There are many young girls who are snatched from their village and forced onto a boat before their family realise what is happening.'

May Lin covered her face with trembling fingers; she'd heard some of the older women talking about these things, but she had always wanted to believe that such cruelty did not actually exist.

'The authorities will do nothing to stop this awful practice unless we can prove it is taking place,' Chin Ming continued. 'I'm sorry if I've shocked you, May Lin. Wing Yee and I are hoping we can do something to make a difference, but we need your help.'

May Lin let her hands slip back into her lap. She kept her eyes cast down and waited for Chin Ming to say more. She was terrified that her new mistress might be about to send her back to that awful existence.

'Wing Yee will find a reason for some of the women to return to the clinic for a second, maybe even a third visit. That will enable us to gain their trust.'

May Lin nodded, but she was still not sure how she fitted into their plan. She waited for an explanation.

'Their journey from Sumatra will take a long time – the villages the women are likely to come from are a long way from Singapore. It is likely that one or two of them might have developed cuts, bruises, or minor ailments during the voyage. Such things will provide Wing Yee with a reason to ask them to return to the clinic.'

'What will you say to them when they come back?'

'We'll begin by telling them about things they might be able to do other than be forced to work in the brothel; that's where you come in.'

A frown crept across May Lin's wide forehead. What would happen if all the women in the brothels wanted to have jobs like her own? Would there be enough families wanting help with their children to go around? Perhaps other women would be better than her ...

'If we can arrange this, I'd like you to come and meet them. We are hoping you might be able to talk to them – to tell what it is like to live with a family. If they heard it from you, then maybe they might begin to believe that their own life could be better,' Chin Ming said with a smile that generated encouragement.

May Lin nodded slowly. She wanted to help her lovely young mistress but she couldn't see how it would be possible. 'Do they speak Cantonese?' she asked. 'I only know a few words in Malay, I think we won't be able to understand each other.'

Chin Ming couldn't believe she'd made such an obvious mistake. May Lin spoke Cantonese and some English, the Sumatran women spoke a language similar to Malay; of course, they wouldn't understand one another. She needed to think again.

CHAPTER 15
29th May 1831

The return journey from Sumatra had been fraught from the very start. The six women crouching in the hold had been sick for almost the entire passage. None of them had chosen to be here, none of them had been to sea before and none of them had the faintest idea about where they were bound. The circumstances of their backgrounds were what they had in common, though they had met only three weeks ago. Each one was young, attractive, and vulnerable. Their families had all suffered under the Dutch regime. They had been forced to grow coffee and pepper for the voracious European markets, but the farmers in their villages had been given very little by way of recompense. Many had reached a point where they could no longer support their entire family. They had no means of providing a dowry for their eligible daughters, and the payment offered by the European gentlemen, on this occasion, had been too great a temptation to resist. Promises had been made to their parents or to the headman of their village to provide a better life for these burdensome young women.

Each of the girls had been surprised to find herself one of a group of six. They came from different villages and the elders had told them a great future lay ahead. The hold of the ship was dark and damp, a musty smell pervaded the air.

When the ship began to move, each of the girls held on to whatever she could to steady herself. When they felt able to do so, they squatted against the side of the ship with their arms held tightly around their knees. No one said a word for several hours. Finally, the eldest one asked the question that was on everyone's lips, 'Does anyone know where we are going?'

No one had an answer. They exchanged names, but that was all. For most of the journey, one or more of them was sick – either because of the unsavoury scraps they were given for food, the pitching and tossing of the vessel, or from unadulterated fear.

*****

Victor had insisted Kasim reverted to his European persona the moment they arrived in Palembang towards the end of April. They had spent a couple of days exchanging news with some of Victor's contacts and then proceeded further south, finally turning north again along the west coast to Bencoolen. It had given Kasim a great deal of pleasure to learn that the place from which their cargo was to be gathered was the very same place where Stamford Raffles had resided during his years as Lieutenant Governor.

The trousers, shirt, and jacket he'd worn when he'd left Calcutta had come in useful. Whilst in Palembang, other sets of trousers and jackets had been skilfully sewn by a local tailor, together with half a dozen cool linen shirts. Kasim had enjoyed haggling in his native language and Victor made it clear that his proficiency in Dutch was one of the main reasons he had been brought along.

'You can't go on using your Indian name either,' Victor had said. 'You no longer look the part and my business associates will not be impressed by anyone other than a full-blooded Dutchman.'

Initially, Kasim had been reluctant to reveal his actual name, but neither was he happy to revert to one of the many pseudonyms he'd adopted over the years. When pressed, he'd opted to be called Stefan but chose not to reveal whether it was a familiar or family name.

*****

They dropped anchor in the calm waters of Singapore's harbour at the end of a sweltering afternoon in late May, but no attempt was made to go ashore. Victor had made it quite clear they needed to wait under the cover of darkness. The low moan of women's voices irritated Kasim – now to be known as Stefan - but Victor seemed oblivious to the sound and disappeared below.

The road which led from the town along the shoreline to Kampong Glam was clearly visible from where they were anchored. Stefan gazed at the villas facing the sea, large, handsome buildings fronted by green verandas and venetian blinds. His nostrils twitched and his mouth twisted into a sour expression. He had just as much right to be living in one of these grand mansions as any of the merchants from England, France, or America. One day soon, he vowed he would purchase such a villa for himself.

Later, a pitch-black mantle engulfed all the vessels anchored nearby. Stefan stared into the inky night with all his senses heightened. He didn't have long to wait before he recognised the unquestionable squeal of oars against rowlocks in need of a spot of oil. He peered into the shadows but still he could see nothing.

'I need you to help me,' Victor said, tapping him on the shoulder.

They went below together. Each of the women had a rag stuffed into her mouth and her hands tied behind her back. They lolled against each other, indicating that whatever the rags had been soaked in had reduced them to a soporific state. It was only now that Stefan realised the annoying sound of their whimpering had ceased some time ago.

They carried one woman at a time onto the deck. Crouched in each of the three clumsy-looking sampans now positioned alongside was a Malay boatman wearing only a sarong tied around his waist and a large, conical-shaped hat, hiding his face. These boats did not belong to the smarter craft plying between the harbour and the Singapore River; these were the illicit vessels available for hire by those engaged in illegal conduct. Between them, Victor and Stefan lowered two women into each of the three boats, taking care not to wake them or attract undue attention. Stefan almost dropped the last woman. Her hair had fallen away from her face, revealing a youthful, unblemished skin, full lips, and long, dark lashes that fluttered in a most enticing manner. This was exactly the sort of woman he enjoyed – young, graceful, eager to please, he imagined – someone who he could dominate and control. Maybe he would make a point of finding out where this one ended up; he would enjoy breaking her in.

As the unwieldy contingent made its way towards the shore, no one said a word. They travelled to a spot just east of the kampong where the water was shallow and the boats could easily be dragged onto the sand. Some figures emerged from the shadows to help carry the listless, immobile bodies from the sampans to a dilapidated house on the outskirts of the village.

At first light, a horse and cart arrived. The same figures who had emerged from the gloom the previous evening helped to propel the women from the dwelling to the wagon. The effect of the sedative Victor had used was beginning to wear off, but none of the women were able to walk without assistance. They were forced to lie down, close to one another, and then a sheet, stinking of fish, was thrown on top of them. Victor climbed aboard to take up the reins and Stefan was instructed to stay with the women to make sure they kept quiet. His instinct was to protest. The noxious fumes irritated his nostrils, and he was affronted by being assigned to the rear of the wagon. On the other hand, he was inconspicuous in this position, no one would recognise him or wonder what he was doing there. He pulled his hat down over his eyes and held a red-spotted handkerchief to his nose. They arrived at Madam Ho's establishment nearly an hour later.

*****

As soon as the last of the women had been handed over, Victor pulled on the reins and steered the horse away from the confines of Cross Street. Stefan chose to remain in the wagon rather than join his business partner up front. Neither of them spoke until they reached the kampong.

'There's an empty house next to mine if you want somewhere to stay while we're in Singapore,' Victor said.

Stefan needed no persuading. He could hardly return to his *prahu* wearing European clothing and, besides, he needed to claim his share of the fee Victor would collect later in the day. The house had obviously been unoccupied for some time; the air was musty and a layer of dust covered the few items of furniture that had been left by the previous occupant. Victor told him to settle in, saying that he intended to rest until the middle of the afternoon, then he would collect payment for the merchandise.

As soon as he was alone, Stefan opened all the shutters to allow air to flow through the place; he shook the mats and began to move the furniture around. He took his kurta and baggy trousers from his bag and laid them carefully at the bottom of a chest of drawers. His European clothes were essential to his current role, but his Indian disguise would be necessary whenever he visited Bukit Selegie – which is somewhere he intended to go at the earliest opportunity. He needed to know what had been happening to the two families who lived there during his absence. He wanted to see whether the convict was still around, entertaining the brat as he worked away in the garden.

*****

Victor returned to the kampong later that evening with a substantial amount of money; he handed a purse containing Stefan's share to him and then suggested they spend the evening amusing themselves. 'We should try one of the new brothels,' he said. 'It wouldn't be wise to give Madam Ho our custom!'

*****

30th May 1831

The following morning, Madam Ho sent a message to Wing Yee asking her to come to Cross Street. No mention was made about the purpose of the visit, but it was obvious to Wing Yee that the women from Sumatra had arrived. She had always assumed the women would be brought to her at the clinic and she was uncomfortable about being asked to visit the brothel. She doubted that Madam Ho knew or even cared that Baba Tan had built the clinic, neither had she ever mentioned Chin Ming's involvement. Maybe it was better to keep it that way. She considered the risk in going there alone, but what harm could be done? The instruction merely confirmed in Wing Yee's head the clandestine nature of the arrangement. Madam Ho did not want these women to be seen on the street. She decided to conform to the request. How else could she discover whether the women had been coerced into coming here? She selected various herbs, tinctures, and salves and placed them in her basket ready for Madam Ho to inspect, should it be necessary. Finally, she wrote a note that only Chin Ming would understand – just as a precaution.

As soon as Wing Yee lifted her hand to knock on Madam Ho's bright red door, it mysteriously opened. The proprietor was waiting in the shadows. She beckoned Wing Yee to follow her to a room at the rear of the building. It was empty apart from a long, narrow table and a chair that had seen better days left abandoned in the far corner. Madam Ho told her to expect six women; they would be brought into the room one at a time, and she should be as quick as possible. The door closed, leaving Wing Yee alone; there was no opportunity to object. She had only just finished unpacking her basket and arranging everything she needed on the forlorn-looking chair when the door reopened. A Chinese woman, one of the established members of the house, stepped into the room holding onto the sleeve of someone whose reluctance to follow was obvious.

Wing Yee moved towards the pair. 'I won't hurt you,' Wing Yee said in Malay, hoping the girl would understand. The girl looked away. The woman pushed her further into the room. The girl stumbled, but Wing Yee caught her before she could fall to the floor.

'I think it's better if you wait outside,' she said to the woman in Cantonese.

'Madam Ho won't like that.'

'Madam Ho won't like it if I take all morning to examine these girls. It will take less time if I can help them relax; they are unlikely to do that if they have an audience.'

The woman made a snorting noise and tossed her head. 'I will be on the other side of the door,' she said.

As soon as she was gone, Wing Yee led the girl to the table. 'I need you to sit here,' she said, reverting to Malay.

'Tell me something about yourself,' Wing Yee said.

The girl looked up. 'My name is Melati,' she said.

Wing Yee hoped the girl understood what she was saying – she wasn't sure. 'All I need to know is whether you are a virgin.'

'Of course,' the girl almost screamed. 'In my village, there is great shame for a woman to know a man before marriage. Why does the fierce-looking lady want to know that? Who is she?'

Wing Yee didn't know where to start. These were obviously village girls with very little experience of life, let alone knowing about the world of corruption and greed of which they were about to become an intricate part.

'I'm not accusing you of anything, Melati,' Wing Yee said, trying to calm the girl down. 'I am a herbalist. Madam Ho has asked me to ensure all six of you are virgins and have no infection. She expects me to do a physical examination, but I see no need to do so; I can tell her that all is well.'

'Infection? Do you mean an illness we caught on our way here?'

'No, I didn't mean that, but no matter. Have any of you become unwell since you left Sumatra?'

'The sea was very rough at times. We were all sick. Two of the girls cut themselves badly when they fell. The deck was always soaked when we were allowed to go out there. There was a lot of blood, which was not properly cleaned, and now the wounds are swollen and festering.'

When Wing Yee said she thought that was convenient, Melati was shocked. Then, she listened while Wing Yee explained the plan to bring as many of them as possible to her clinic. 'We haven't much time, the woman outside the door will want to know what is taking so long. I'm going to ask her to let you stay. I'll tell her I need you to reassure the others and help them to relax.'

She had just finished speaking when the door was flung open. As predicted, an explanation of the slow progress was demanded. Wing Yee refused to be intimidated.

'I understood I'd come here to examine several women,' she said, reverting again to Cantonese, 'but this one is only a young girl. She was scared, but I've managed to calm her down. If you want me to work quicker, then let this one stay. She can help me to pacify the others.'

'I don't know,' the woman said. 'Madam Ho might not ...'

'Madam Ho will certainly not like it if I need to take as long with the other five young ladies as I've spent with this one. There is no point in frightening them, they will not be able to – entertain – if they are scared to death.'

'Very well, but please be quick.'

*****

During the time she spent with the other arrivals, Wing Yee was able to ascertain that none of them had any experience of a sexual nature. She told them about her plan to contrive a reason for them to come to her clinic and her hope that she might be able to help them further. Two of the girls had cuts and bruises, which proved advantageous; a legitimate reason to consult Wing Yee on another occasion. One girl had tried to clean her own wound but only succeeded in making it worse. Another one had a deep lesion that had not even started to heal and was oozing pus. Wing Yee placed her belongings back in the basket while the last girl, accompanied by Melati, was led away. Smears of blood from one of the injured arms had seeped onto the cloth that covered the table, providing a fortunate assumption that internal examinations had taken place. Madam Ho's eyes were drawn to the mark the moment she entered the room.

'Are they all as innocent as promised? I trust there are no problems?'

'They are all pure and virtuous,' Wing Yee said. 'However, ...'

'However, what? What have you found wrong with them? I hope I haven't paid good money for a bunch of problems. Maybe I shouldn't have trusted you – examined them myself after all!'

'Two of them fell and hurt themselves during a bad storm at sea; they both cut their arms quite badly and the wounds have not healed. In fact, they have become severely infected. Bring them to my clinic and I will be able to treat them. Once the wounds begin to heal all will be well.'

'Why can't you treat them here?'

'Because the space you have is not good for treatment. Because I never expected to come here in the first place. I agreed to conduct your basic examinations, and that's what I've done today, but the space is not suitable and I will need time to see which herbs work best with each of the girls. If you don't have time to bring them yourself, I would be happy to collect them. Shall we say tomorrow morning?' Had she been too forthright? Madam Ho might tell her to go, to cancel their arrangement. She was a woman who was not used to being challenged. Wing Yee regretted her sudden hastiness; she might never be able to find out about the people involved in the smuggling business.

'I never imagined the day I'd be asking for help from the concubine of that rogue Boon Peng,' Madam Ho said. 'I'm getting old. There are too many new places opening in Chinatown. But my place is still well-known, it still has a good reputation. Men pay more for that. I'm not sure I trust you but I can't afford to let things slide. I need you to help.'

Wing Yee kept calm and said nothing. She waited for Madam Ho to finish.

'It must be early,' the older woman said. 'I don't want them to be seen on the street once the town becomes busy.'

'Have them ready at nine o'clock,' Wing Yee said. She picked up her basket and departed before Madam Ho could contradict her. Once outside, she hurried away, startled by her own temerity.

*****

The tropical climate did not help with the healing process; since the girls had arrived in Singapore the humidity had soared and their wounds continued to weep. Wing Yee cleaned the broken skin, used a salve that would help the healing process, then she wrapped each of the wounds in bandages to keep them clean. This meant the women would need to return to the clinic every few days; the bandages needed to be changed and the healing process regularly checked. She wanted to give these women as much time away from the brothel as possible. The girls had grown up speaking Minangkabau, a local language like Malay, but they could converse with Wing Yee easily enough. It soon became clear Melati had made sure the other five girls had gained some understanding of the discussions that had taken place at the brothel so they were all very happy to visit Wing Yee at the clinic.

'I could do so much more for them if I had someone working alongside me,' Wing Yee said to Chin Ming on one of her visits to the clinic. 'Obviously, not May Lin, but why don't we ask Tijah to help?'

'She is nearer their age, and she'll be able to speak to them in a familiar language,' Chin Ming said, 'but is she strong enough?'

'She's stronger than she looks,' Wing Yee replied, 'and she's always anxious to learn. I think we should try anything that will protect these women from the grasp of Madam Ho.'

Both Chin Ming and Wing Yee knew that if Tijah had not succeeded in hiding amongst Edmund's plants, then she might very well have ended up in the brothel herself when she reached Singapore. During the short time they had spent together, Wing Yee also suspected that Tijah was only too aware of what fate might have held for her. She would be an excellent advocate for their scheme.

'I'll ask Dick,' Wing Yee said. 'I'll invite him to bring her to the clinic for a visit and if she likes it, we can then suggest she might like to help me.'

*****

Dick talked to Tijah regarding the proposed visit. Part of him was reluctant about her becoming involved in what Chin Ming and Wing Yee were about to do, but he was careful not to let his feelings show. He admired his friends for coming up with the idea; attempting to provide the women in Madam Ho's clutches with something better. But at the same time, he was concerned that the whole idea could be dangerous. Now that they were thinking of involving Tijah, maybe he should mention it to Edmund. Perhaps together they could persuade these headstrong women to at least be cautious, especially now that Chin Ming was two-thirds of the way through her pregnancy.

On the morning of the visit, Dick collected Wing Yee in his carriage. Tijah was seated beside him, obviously eager to visit Baba Tan's warehouse and be shown the workroom where Wing Yee prepared all her medicines. She had always been interested in healing and had spent many hours listening to the older women in the kampong talk about a miraculous potion called *jamu*. Sometimes, when Tijah went to the padi fields with her aunt she would see one of those women leaving the kampong with a bamboo basket containing bottles of *jamu* tied to her back. Tijah had often longed to accompany the woman, knowing she was heading off towards the town to meet people who came to purchase the bottles of golden liquid; she had wanted to know what lay beyond the village for a long, long time.

It took only half an hour to drive down the hill and another fifteen minutes to walk across the bridge after leaving the horse and carriage in its usual place. Now, standing at the entrance to Wing Yee's workroom, Tijah was overwhelmed with the sight of so many herbs in one place; they hung in bunches to be dried and the air was filled with intoxicating aromas. She couldn't name many of them, but perhaps Wing Yee would teach her to distinguish one from another. The older woman watched Tijah enjoying the sensation before welcoming her to the workshop and giving her a conducted tour. She was delighted that her visitor seemed to enjoy the considerable variety of aromas as much as she did herself.

'Now you've seen where I make all the medicines, would you like to visit the clinic? I can show you how we help people to recover from various upsets.'

Dick coughed. He wasn't at all sure how many details Tijah needed to be told. He wanted to protect her.

'Oh, yes, please,' she said, completely unaware of his concerns.

A few minutes later, Dick and Wing Yee walked along the quay with Tijah moving between them with increased energy. She chatted continuously, asking one question after another until they reached Amoy Street. Three of the Sumatran girls from the brothel had already been escorted through the quiet, early morning streets to the clinic. They were attempting to talk to Chin Ming when Wing Yee and Tijah arrived. Dick said he would return after concluding some business in town. He offered to collect Tijah at the end of the morning.

One of the visitors awaiting their arrival was Melati, the first of the Sumatran girls Wing Yee had spoken to. No one knew how she was managing it but she had continued to come to Amoy Street on a regular basis. She was introduced to Tijah and the two of them retreated into a corner whilst Wing Yee dressed the cuts and sores on the arms of her other patients.

*****

Several visits later, Melati said that she would like to learn English and so would some of the other women and girls at the brothel. This was encouraging news, but when Wing Yee reported the conversation to Chin Ming that evening her friend remained unsure about Madam Ho's reaction. 'How would you persuade her to support such a notion?' she said.

165

'Remember she is only interested in making money,' Wing Yee replied. 'We should tell her that more men will visit her establishment if some of the women can speak English. The crews of the *Indiamen* are unlikely to understand Cantonese or Malay. I think she will like the idea of European customers; they will pay more than the Chinese, more even than the Arab merchants.'

'Do you really think that will work?' Chin Ming asked.

'I know she is worried about competition from some of the newer establishments and this would give her an advantage. It's all very well getting regular trade from the poor devils who work on the gambier plantations and the crews from the country traders in the harbour, but I think she'll like the idea of entertaining some of the *Ang Mohs* who are missing their wives.'

They continued to talk until the oil in the lamps ran low and insects were no longer attracted to their radiance. Edmund came out onto the veranda to suggest it was time to retire.

'I will go along to see Madam Ho in the morning,' Wing Yee said. 'I'm sure she won't be able to resist the idea of increased revenue.'

'Madam Ho?' Edmund said. 'What's all this about? Is there something you need to tell me?'

Both women looked shamefaced, but Wing Yee excused herself. She decided she ought to leave Chin Ming alone to explain the details of their plan to Edmund.

CHAPTER 16
Thursday 9th June 1831

Dick was gathering some papers together when Sujana entered his studio, she was carrying Tomas in her arms.

'Are you planning to go into town today?' she asked. 'I hadn't realised.'

'I've been tossing and turning all night,' he said. 'I need to see Alexander.'

'What's wrong?'

'Nothing for you to worry about, but I've been putting off what needs to be done for too long. It's time for action, I can't sit around here any longer hoping that it will all sort itself out.'

'Hoping what will sort itself out? I don't understand.'

'I'll explain everything this evening when, hopefully, I'll have something of consequence to share with you. I'm going to drop Tijah off at the clinic. It seems her enthusiasm to learn about herbal remedies and urge to help Wing Yee has not waned one little bit.'

Sujana held her son close; a strange feeling crept over her as she waved them off and she couldn't help fretting. She wondered what had disturbed her husband's sleep so much that he felt it necessary to seek out Alexander Johnston as a matter of urgency. What was on his mind that he couldn't tell her right now? Was he trying to protect her from something – or somebody? Whatever it was Dick planned to do today, she felt it was about to change their lives forever.

*****

Before reaching Monkey Bridge, Dick drove around the corner into a side street and found a space where he could leave the horse and carriage for a few hours. He gave a coin to one of the boys playing in the gutter, asking him to hold the reins and look after the animal while he was away. He helped Tijah climb down and then they began the short walk. It was a pleasant morning with a satisfying breeze coming off the water. They reached the clinic in no time at all.

'I wasn't expecting visitors,' Wing Yee said as soon as they walked through the door.

'Tijah tells me she loves being here. She wants to help. I think she would like to learn more from you and maybe even work alongside you. How would you feel about that?'

'I feel much honour,' Wing Yee said. 'Can stay all day. If not too tired, we walk back together later.'

'I have the carriage. I plan to be in town for most of the day, so I will call in and take you both home. It's quite a trek up the hill and I'm sure you'll both be weary by then.'

'What are you doing that will take so long? Has someone asked you to do one of your family portraits for them?' Wing Yee said, reverting to Malay.

'No, I'm going to see Alexander, and if our conversation works out as I'm hoping it will, then I will be fully occupied until late afternoon.'

Wing Yee was curious. It was unlike Dick to be evasive and unlike her not to be able to get him to share his plans. She tilted her head to one side and raised her eyebrows, but he ignored her silent questioning. Instead, he interrogated her about the women she had been dealing with since the clinic opened –, in particular, those who had recently arrived from Sumatra. She was still no wiser when he left ten minutes later.

*****

He was slightly amused by Wing Yee's reaction; it wasn't always that easy to sidestep her determined interrogations. He was still thinking about their conversation when he turned the corner and narrowly avoided two stevedores engaged in a horrifying brawl. Their fists whooshed towards each other; pummelling, clouting, thumping. Blood poured down their faces, they tore at each other's clothing and hurled abuse in loud, unrecognisable language. No one, including Dick, attempted to intervene.

Unlike the small crowd that had gathered to watch, he had no interest in such violence. He couldn't imagine any circumstance in which he would feel it necessary to attack another human being.

It was already the middle of the morning when he reached the firm of Johnston & Co. He found Alexander immersed in a pile of paperwork and looking frustrated. The door into the office was wide open, but he made a point of knocking before he entered.

'Come in, come in,' Alexander said, looking up. 'What a pleasant surprise. Are you just passing by or did you need to speak to me about something?'

'The latter,' Dick said.

'You're looking very serious, is there a problem?'

'Nothing new, but I can't hang around any longer. Do you recall my disappointment when I returned from speaking to Kenneth Murchison?'

'I do. And I remember promising to think about it. I'm sorry I haven't had time to get back to you, things have been a bit hectic around here of late. One of my business partners has gone on leave and I'm having to take on additional work.'

'Not to worry,' Dick said. 'All I want to ask is if I could use one of the rooms here as an office. I intend to gather as much evidence as possible about these law-breakers so that when Murchison returns, I can present him with the facts.'

'Of course, you can have an office here – and I will help

whenever I can, but what's brought on this sense of urgency?'

'Do you know what the date is today?'

Johnston scratched the back of his neck and looked at his desk to consult his calendar before replying. 'It's the ninth of June,' he said, still not sure why Dick had asked the question.

'Exactly,' Dick said. 'It's eight years today since Raffles left Singapore for the last time. He wouldn't have put up with all this shilly-shallying; he wouldn't have let these people get away with bending the rules to suit their own selfish ends. He would have found a way to challenge them. I promised him I would ensure that his name stayed alive here; what better way than to uphold his values and rid the place of all the corruption?'

A smile crept across Alexander's face. 'You sound just like him,' he said. 'And everything you've said, everything you want to achieve is very laudable, but it's going to be a tough fight. There are systems in place that conveniently hide the dishonesty, the exploitation, and injustice. The people who make a lot of money from all of that will do anything to protect their profits and their cosy lifestyle.'

'I know all of that but I must try. I've already made a start by asking questions about a group of women who have been brought here from Sumatra, against their will, I think.'

'You know what would help your cause enormously?' Alexander said.

'What do you have in mind?'

'You should become a magistrate. You can do all the research you want – and I applaud that, but until you have some authority, the powers that be can continue to turn a blind eye. If you sit on the bench and have some of the felons appearing before you, that's when you can ensure they get their just deserts.'

*****

Dick spent the remainder of the morning rearranging the space in the room he'd been allocated as his office. There was a window that overlooked the road leading to the quay. He pulled the desk into a position where he could observe all the comings and goings as well as have the maximum amount of natural daylight at his disposal. Alexander arrived with a pile of paper, notebooks, a collection of pens, and a pot of ink. Finally, two of the clerks came carrying a lockable cupboard and an empty bookcase. It had taken precisely two hours to create a workplace; somewhere apart from his painting studio and his family, a place from where he was determined to achieve the goal he had set himself.

*****

Towards the end of the afternoon, he said goodbye to Alexander and walked towards Amoy Street. He collected Wing Yee and Tijah. They retrieved the carriage, hitched it to the horse and drove back home at a leisurely pace. The intensity of working alongside Wing Yee had obviously sapped all Tijah's energy, but she would never admit it. Nevertheless, he was glad to see her cheeks glowing, and for the first time since arriving in Singapore, she looked extremely happy. Afternoon turned into early evening, but it was still warm, and the regular clip clop of the horse's hooves against the surface of the road was soporific; she fell asleep against Wing Yee's shoulder as soon as they began the gentle climb up the hillside.

'I can walk from your house,' Wing Yee said. 'It's a pity to wake her unnecessarily.'

Dick protested, but she assured him the walk would do her good; the clinic had been busy and she had been inside the building all day long. The horse whinnied to announce their arrival home as soon as they turned into the drive, arousing Tijah from her slumber. She thanked Wing Yee for letting her help and asked if she might come again.

'If you want, I will train you to become a herbalist,' Wing Yee said in Malay.

'Well, that's praise indeed,' said Dick. 'You must have made a good impression, she doesn't often tolerate people anywhere near her when she's working.'

Wing Yee scoffed as she walked away from them, back towards the road.

Tijah's cheeks looked flushed, but a smile brightened her whole face. '*Terima kasih*,' she called after Wing Yee's retreating figure. 'Thank you, thank you.'

'I will call for you in the morning,' Wing Yee said as she waved goodbye.

*****

It was cooler now and the daylight was beginning to fade. Wing Yee strolled along the road, occasionally glancing out towards the fading images of ships in the harbour but mainly intent on breathing in the cool, early evening air heavy with the scent of frangipani. She closed her eyes and stood completely still, relishing the pleasure of having Tijah working alongside her. She was looking forward to training the girl who had shown such enthusiasm and interest in learning the names of the herbs and their different qualities. It would be a delight. She might even teach her how to recognise certain ailments, then she would show her how to make various medicines. Not having children of her own had never bothered her, but now she realised what pleasure there was to be gained in being able to pass on her skills and knowledge to someone else, someone who was so eager to learn.

She quickened her pace as she approached the house, hoping that either Edmund or Chin Ming would be waiting for her. The drive was empty, but she could hear a scuffling sound in the undergrowth; she hoped it wasn't a snake. It was only a short distance to the house now, and she focused on the oil lamps, already lit, and placed along the edge of the veranda. She heard a whooshing sound not far away, maybe a bat flying low. Then something swept past her right arm; she flicked her sleeve and spun round to see what she thought might be a human figure disappearing into the shadows. It seemed to take the shape of someone wearing garments like those worn by the convicts, but she was sure it wasn't Sanjay; he would have spoken to her, apologised in his usual polite manner. As she searched the darkness, she could feel her heart thumping against her ribs. When her gaze reached the side of the house, she spotted Sanjay emerging from the gloom. He was some distance away, walking towards her with his gardening tools in his hand. Perhaps it was an animal that had briefly touched her, but she thought not. More likely, it was her imagination playing tricks in the half-light.

✶✶✶✶✶

'Well?' Sujana said as soon as Dick stepped inside the house. Tijah had already excused herself to go in search of Fakina, so Dick and Sujana had the veranda to themselves. 'You promised to tell me why you rushed out to see Alexander this morning, whatever it is that's been troubling you, and why it's taken all day to sort it out.'

Dick took a deep breath as he flopped onto the nearest sofa. 'Eight years ago, you were still living with your family in Java,' he said, 'so you won't know why today's date is so significant.'

'I'm listening,' Sujana said. His grave expression conveyed his mood, so she sat down beside him and waited patiently. She continued to listen to him for the next half hour.

He stood up again and told her about the day Raffles left and the promise he'd made. He told her about the dreams that had tormented him the previous evening and his concerns regarding the corruption that had been allowed to develop. He told her about his concern for Wing Yee and Chin Ming and the danger they might be putting themselves in if they continued to help the women from Madam Ho's establishment. He spoke about his conversation with Alexander and his decision to gather information involving all the wrongdoings, and, finally, he shared with her Alexander's suggestion that he become a magistrate.

At first, Sujana sat perfectly still, unable to move, unable to say anything. What her husband had told her served to reinforce the strange feeling that had enveloped her earlier in the day. Then she noticed the way he stood with his chin held high, his shoulders back, and his chest thrust out. He was determined to carry out his mission, there was no doubt about that, and she was proud of him. The light from the oil lamps was reflected in her eyes, making them sparkle. Since the birth of their son, she had noticed Dick's natural enthusiasm turn inwards, almost as if he thought the only important thing in life was to protect his family, but listening to him now, she recognised the fire and passion that attracted him to her in the first place. She loved him more than ever as he rejoined her on the sofa and continued to tell her about his ideas, his hopes, and his ambitions.

*****

Dick was finishing his breakfast when Sujana walked into the room. She was still sleepy but could tell from his demeanour that her husband was bursting with pent-up energy.

'What are you planning to do today?' she asked, yawning.

'I'm going to walk along the road to see if the Beaumonts are awake. I want to tell Chin Ming and Edmund what I have in mind. I talked to Wing Yee yesterday about the women she has been treating, but Chin Ming might have something to add.'

'Are you going to mention your concern for their safety?

Do you think you ought to say something to Edmund?'

'I will certainly try, but you know how headstrong Chin Ming is.'

'I do, but she is pregnant, surely she wouldn't do anything to jeopardise the baby.'

'Perhaps I'll talk to Wing Yee and Edmund first. Between us, I'm sure we can persuade her to be careful.'

'How much have you told Tijah? You said the last group of girls to arrive at Madam Ho's are quite young. They might feel more comfortable talking to her about things that they can't tell Wing Yee.'

'You thought that too? She's a few years younger than them, but I think that's what Wing Yee hopes will happen. On the other hand, how much does she understand about the sort of establishment run by Madam Ho? She's only just got over the trauma of her journey here, I wouldn't want to frighten her.'

'She's tougher than she looks, you know. Besides, Wing Yee has already spoken to her. She's perfectly aware that she could easily have ended up in a place like that herself. Possibly, that's part of the reason why she's so eager to help Wing Yee at the clinic.'

*****

After breakfast the following day, Chin Ming and Edmund were sitting on their veranda. Edmund was cradling William, who was sleeping peacefully. They were enjoying some moments together before Charlotte arrived to disturb their calm.

'I can't get over how heavy he's becoming,' Edmund marvelled.

'He's sixteen months old now. He's no longer a baby.'

At that moment, May Lin arrived to collect William and take him to the nursery. As she returned inside the house, Edmund couldn't help being pleased that his wife had some help with the children, especially as this latest pregnancy was causing her to feel exhausted most of the time.

When Dick arrived a short while later, he saw them enjoying some moments together. They were holding hands and Edmund was gazing affectionately at the bump that would soon be his third child. As soon as he noticed their visitor, he stood up, letting go of Chin Ming's hand.

'You're an early bird,' he said.

Chin Ming remained seated. With only another three months before the new baby was due and finding the heat difficult to cope with, she was trying to take things slowly. She offered Dick some pineapple juice.

'This time next year, I'm planning that we'll be able to offer you juice from our own crop,' Edmund said, standing tall with a gleam in his eye.

'This time next year, I'm hoping we'll see quite a lot of changes,' Dick said, 'most importantly, having made some significant progress towards the things we talked about at your dinner party.'

'Has something happened?' Chin Ming said. 'What have you heard?'

Dick looked from Chin Ming to Edmund, unaware that the couple had talked hard and long about the various illegal goings-on that had corrupted the Settlement during the time they had been away in England. Edmund had expressed his concern for his wife's involvement in Wing's Yee's scheme and she had promised to be careful.

'It's fine,' Chin Ming said. 'Edmund knows about the trafficking and what Wing Yee is planning. Now, tell us about your meeting with Alexander.'

Dick nodded. He divulged everything he and Alexander had discussed the previous day, then he shared his plan to accumulate enough evidence to convince Murchison that something should be done about the level of corruption in and around the Settlement. He told them about the office he'd set up at Johnston & Co., and Alexander's suggestions that he should become a magistrate.

'He still needs to recommend me to the other magistrates, of course, but if he can get them to support me, I'll start to read up on the law and learn about the procedures straight away. I wasn't sure, when he first suggested it,' Dick added, 'but the more I think about it, the more interested I become.'

'Of course, it makes sense,' Chin Ming said. 'It's all very well to be guided by a few Europeans who have some knowledge and experience of taking responsibility, but most of Singapore's population are Peranakan or Chinese. And the Malays, – people who were here long before most of the Europeans came.'

Edmund coughed, raising his eyebrows as he looked at Chin Ming. 'I hope I will be allowed to stay,' he said, grinning at his wife.

'And others,' she added, looking embarrassed, 'who have chosen to adopt this place as their home.'

'And don't forget the Indian population,' Dick joined in. 'There are several Indian merchants running businesses in town. The successful ones have houses along the Plain and others will be moving to Serengoon before long,' He couldn't help being amused as he continued to join Edmund in baiting Chin Ming.

She grinned; she knew she was being teased but she was almost as enthusiastic about the prospect as Dick was himself. She wanted to make sure he knew he had her support.

'Our destiny,' she continued, suddenly looking very serious, 'shouldn't be dependent on people who will most likely return to the other side of the world one day. We need people like you; people with integrity, energy, and determination.'

*****

Chin Ming's words echoed in Dick's ears as he hurried back home. He intended to write them down when he reached the office; they would inspire him if ever he became dispirited, which was bound to happen at times, bearing in mind the enormous task he had set himself. Nevertheless, he couldn't wait to get started.

CHAPTER 17
June 1831

Stefan had been living in the house allocated to him by Victor for over a fortnight. The six women had been delivered to Madam Ho and a sum of money handed over. He was relieved that Victor had been happy to carry out that part of the transaction alone; it was still possible that Madam Ho would recognise him from his connection with a young woman called Shu Fang eight years ago. She'd been brought from China and her purchase had been arranged by Boon Peng, his business partner at the time. He remembered seeing her for the first time when Madam Ho handed her over to him. She'd had delicate features, glossy hair, but sad eyes. Initially, he'd been pleased with his purchase, but then he discovered her *lily feet*, and very soon the constant tok, tok-tok of her tiny shoes on the wooden boards of his house had driven him to distraction. After only a few days, in a terrible rage, full of foul language about being duped, he'd returned Shu Fang to Madam Ho. By then, the girl's face, covered in cuts and bruises, was no longer delicate. It was unlikely that a woman like Madam Ho had forgotten the exchange.

He couldn't remember how many times he had now changed his name to suit his circumstances, and he was beginning to feel irritated by having to live a double life once again. Here, in the kampong, he was Stefan, a name that no one questioned. He and Victor continued to visit the harbour on a regular basis, discussing potential business transactions at Choo Keng's coffee stall. Sometimes they were joined by another of Victor's associates who usually had a proposition to put to them. The hustle and bustle of the quay went on all around them, but it was easy to ignore the noise and the chaos as soon as they became absorbed in discussing the many lucrative proposals being made available to them. Both men believed the venue was harmless enough that no one paid them much attention. They assumed anyone who did notice their presence would ignore them, supposing them to be respectable Europeans engaged in a business transaction, merely because of the clothes they wore.

*****

Since their return, Stefan had donned his kurta and baggy trousers whenever an opportunity arose, sneaking out of the kampong at a time of day when everyone was occupied with family business. He always chose subdued colours so that he would not stand out or be remembered. On these occasions, he thought of himself as Kasim again, but he made sure he kept himself well away from Market Street. Even after four months, he wasn't going to risk bumping into Mukesh or any of the other moneylenders; even worse was the possibility that Douglas Fergusson might still be in Singapore. He had no intention of becoming involved in an argument with someone like him now that he'd found a less arduous and more lucrative way to make money; far better than anything Fergusson had offered.

It was only a short distance from the kampong to the Serengoon River. He generally took this route nowadays, following the new road to the top of Bukit Selegie and hiding in the ditch beside the Beaumonts' house. Arriving during the early evening was in many ways a disadvantage because the brat had been put to bed. Studying the way she walked, ran, or

180

jumped around the garden, seeing her play with her toys, or digging her own patch of soil, listening to her chat to the convict – all these things had helped him to decide what he would do when the opportunity arose.

On the other hand, with the garden empty, he could risk positioning himself within its perimeter and observe the adults sitting on the balcony. This evening, two things surprised him; he made a mental note. The younger Chinese woman was obviously pregnant. This he found satisfying. It meant she would be slow to give chase when he was ready to put his plan into practice. The second factor he found irritating; the Chinese bitch was nearly always present. Did this mean she now shared this house with her friends? She would be more difficult to deter, but he would, if necessary, get rid of her.

*****

Last week, Kasim stayed in his hideout for longer than usual. It was an unusually dark night, due to the large amount of cloud which frequently obscured the moon. It provided good cover for him, and the oil lamps on the veranda illuminated the young couple perfectly, but he found it difficult to hear any details of their conversation. He noticed the Chinese bitch was nowhere to be seen. He'd wondered about edging forward to listen more intently but decided it wasn't worth the risk of being caught. With no more to be gained that night, he finally decided to return to the kampong. Cloud cover now obscured the moon completely, and for a few seconds, he found himself disorientated by the gulf of pitch-black night. He stumbled along the path, but at the junction with the road, he almost bumped into something. It felt like the edge of some cotton fabric. What would something like that be doing floating past him? Then he'd realised it must have been the bitch; her sarong or a skirt of some sort. He'd forgotten her absence from the cosy family group on the balcony until that moment. Now was not the time to confront her. He fled into the darkness.

*****

When he wasn't keeping vigil on Bukit Selegie, Kasim occupied much of the time by returning to his *prahu*. It was still anchored at Telok Blangah and he was reluctant to let it go, at least until he had dealt with the brat. He needed to ensure it would be seaworthy at short notice. His practice was to arrive under cover of darkness, then cast off at first light. He was now adept at manoeuvring his way between all the other craft in the harbour, often venturing all along the coast in both directions. Sometimes he explored the myriad tiny islands that lay offshore, looking for a hideout should it ever be needed.

Some mornings, he would deliberately sail parallel to the section of beach that enabled him to observe his neighbours in the kampong. It amused him to watch them begin their daily duties from the safe distance of his *prahu*. One day he noticed Victor emerging from a house that wasn't his own, but this was information he decided to keep to himself for the time being. One day, it might prove useful.

*****

'It's not good enough,' Victor said on one occasion when Kasim crept back to the kampong late in the afternoon. He was not happy about the frequent disappearances. 'You vanish sometimes for a couple of days, and most of the time I have no idea where you go or what you are doing.'

'You are not my keeper.'

'Of course not, but I thought you were committed to our business venture,' Victor said. 'If I'm to plan another expedition I need to know you'll be around to join me. I need to know you are serious.'

Kasim had mentally transformed himself back into Stefan once again; he tossed his head back, grinned, and walked confidently towards his friend. 'Well, I'm here now. Of course, I'm serious about our little business arrangement. What is it you have in mind this time?'

An hour later. Stefan had replaced his kurta with a simple sarong. It was cool and comfortable and enabled him to fit in with all the other inhabitants whilst he was lounging around the kampong. Even Victor, who had insisted they continue their discussion once he had changed, preferred this attire when he was away from town.

'One of my contacts has offered us a considerable fee if we can leave for Sumatra the day after tomorrow,' Victor said. 'I thought we might use your *prahu* this time?'

Stefan's mouth fell open.

'You thought I didn't know about your boat, didn't you?' Victor said. 'You don't think I'd allow myself to get involved in a business arrangement without checking on who I'm dealing with, do you?'

Stefan remained fixed to the spot; he held his nerve, replacing the initial incredulous stare with a look of disdain. He said nothing.

'You'd be surprised what I've found out about you,' Victor said. 'Don't look so horrified, my friend, the important thing is that you are not averse to bending the rules. Now, what do you say to taking your vessel for a short voyage?'

Stefan shrugged his shoulders. 'I can't go that far. I'm not even sure that I'm competent enough to navigate those waters around the southern tip of Sumatra.'

'We're only going on a short journey, just across the water to the east coast of Sumatra to a place called Selat Panjang.'

'Why there?'

'Because, my friend, the town is a trading centre. It's full of Chinese as well as Malays. Your countrymen have a considerable interest in the place, but our concern is to do with the traffic in human goods from China, not sugar or spices, if you understand me.'

A grin spread across Stefan's face. 'How many passengers?' he said.

'The usual number,' Victor said. 'If you think we can accommodate them in your *prahu* that would mean we get to keep the whole of the fee being offered.'

'Women of that sort are unlikely to complain about lack of space. I'm sure we can fit them in,' Stefan said. 'When do we finalise the deal?'

'First thing in the morning,' Victor said. 'Be ready to visit Choo Keng for coffee around mid-morning. I suggest you wear your finest silk shirt and that crimson cravat you're so fond of if you want to impress our associate.'

*****

Precisely one week after first setting up his office, Dick sat at his desk gazing out of the window. He'd spent most of that time talking to the people he trusted; merchants who owned warehouses along the quay, fishermen, stallholders in the market, and, of course, Wing Yee. He'd made copious notes on the comings and goings around the harbour and coded them according to whether it was fact or hearsay. So far, he had very little evidence that could be used to support the case he intended to put together.

Ever since the Governor of the Straits Settlements closed the courts and dismissed the judicial establishment twelve months ago, there had been legal chaos. Merchants in Penang, Malacca, and Singapore had appealed to the British Parliament, and in January, the titles of Governor and Resident Councillor had been revived, but the power now lay in Penang. No new Recorder had been appointed, so trying offenders and passing judgment was left to the quarterly visits of the Resident Councillor Kenneth Murchison. He had paid them a brief visit in April but was expected again in another six weeks. Dick intended to have something tangible by then.

Integrity, Energy, Determination – he'd written Chin Ming's words on a piece of card and attached it to the wall beside his desk. He began to doodle on his notepad, capturing the scene below, the whole length of Boat Quay. Drawing was a distraction, but it also enabled him to reflect upon the small pieces of information he had been able to gather. He concentrated on the people rather than the crates of cargo that surrounded them, using bold strokes to capture the intense activity of the coolies scurrying from place to place. He noticed Baba Tan strolling leisurely along the wharf, carrying a small box with what looked like a collection of small twigs and leaves poking out of the top. No doubt he was on his way to visit Wing Yee at the clinic –maybe delivering the latest consignment of herbs, roots, and pieces of bark. His assumption was upheld when he saw his friend turn in the direction of Amoy Street where the clinic was located.

Dick scanned the scene again, looking for anyone else he might add to his drawing, but today it seemed there were no other merchants to be seen, either standing around giving orders or negotiating a bargain. Then, further along the quay, he noticed a trio of men seated outside Choo Keng's coffee stall. They reminded him of the tableaux he associated with Chinese opera, each of them perfectly still with their back towards him. Moments later, they became excited, bursting into life, just like the theatrical scenes of his imagination. He couldn't help smiling but wondered what had ignited their change of mood.

He tried to sketch their outlines, but as they became more and more involved in animated discussion, it was difficult to capture sufficient detail. Dick wondered whether an argument was about to begin; he watched them closely, but no further clues became obvious. One of them stood up. Was it his imagination or did the fellow have a substantial moustache? Before Dick had a chance to pick up his spyglass, the man shook hands with the other two and hurried away. He disappeared down one of the small alleys leading from the wharf, leaving the other two gazing after him.

Now, it seemed some dispute was happening between the remaining pair. One of them stood and pointed in the direction of Telok Blangah whilst mouthing inaudible words, then he gestured towards the Malay kampong, finally, he put both hands on his hips and stared out to sea. The other man, who had a slim build and was quite a bit taller than his companion, stood up too. He put one arm around the other fellow's shoulders whilst extending his other hand and sweeping it from right to left, but Dick had no idea what the gesture was intended to convey.

Dick did not recognise either of the men, but his curiosity had been roused. He couldn't help wondering who they were, why he'd never seen them before, and what they had been talking about. He got up from his desk and decided to go for a stroll. At the last minute, he returned to pick up his sketchbook.

It took no time at all for Dick to reach Choo Keng's coffee stall, but when he arrived the table he'd been watching was empty and the two men were nowhere to be seen.

Choo Keng shuffled towards him, wiping his hands on his sarong as he did so. Both the sarong and his oversized, off-white singlet had seen better days. 'You want coffee?' he asked in Malay.

Dick's first instinct was to decline; there was no longer anything of interest here, but something made him hesitate. '*Kopi O Kosong,*' he said, placing himself at the same table that had been occupied by the two Europeans.

A few minutes later, Choo Keng appeared again. The dark black liquid slopped over the top of the cup into the ample saucer as he made his way towards Dick. He placed it on the table with no apology; his own preference being to pour the coffee into the saucer to cool quickly and to slurp at leisure through his few remaining teeth. Dick chose not to do that, but he had to admit the coffee was good, thick and strong – just the way he liked it. When it was finished, he handed over a few coins to Choo Keng. 'Wonderful,' he said.

Choo Keng nodded. He knew his coffee was the best along this part of the quay, but it was good to be appreciated.

'The men who were here earlier,' Dick began, 'they also enjoy your coffee?'

'Two come many times.' Choo Keng had seen this young man around the town on numerous occasions. He knew who he was, but had never spoken to him before. He wondered what his interest was in his previous customers. He'd never thought of them as noteworthy. The pair who frequented his stall most often sometimes stayed for a long time but, much to his annoyance, only ever drank one cup of coffee each.

Dick flipped his sketchbook open. 'These men?' he said, just to be sure there was no confusion. 'I sketched them from my office, but I was at the other end of the quay and couldn't capture much detail. He pointed to the darker lines, emphasising the facial hair on one of the figures. Maybe you recognise them?'

Choo Keng nodded.

'You say they come here often. What do they talk about?'

'They speak quietly, they speak English; I not understand,' Choo Keng said.

'Are there usually two or three men?' Dick asked. He wasn't sure why he was asking all these questions. It was just a strange feeling he had about two men who no one seemed to know anything about.

'You draw me?'

This wasn't the response Dick had expected. He wasn't sure whether Choo Keng was asking to have his likeness made or checking to see if Dick had already included him in his drawing. He hoped it was the former as he knew some older members of the Chinese population were superstitious about having their image captured, believing it took away their souls.

He decided to take a risk. 'I'd be glad to draw you, sir, possibly standing with a cup of your delicious coffee in your hand.'

Choo Keng grinned. This reply was obviously sufficient to encourage him to share a little more information.

'Mostly just two men come,' he said, 'sometimes one other person for short time like today.' He sighed heavily. 'That's all I know, except...'

Dick raised an eyebrow and waited for Choo Keng to continue, wondering what else might be revealed.

'The tall man, he come to my stall for many years; usually alone. Then, few months ago an Indian – a moneylender from Market Street, I think - join him. That man come a few times at beginning of year; now he come no more.'

'That's interesting,' Dick said, sitting up straight. His mind began to race. Perhaps I should ask around amongst the moneylenders, he thought. Perhaps Baba Tan might have some contacts there.

Choo Keng began to speak again. 'Last few weeks, only Europeans come; sometime two men, sometimes three. One man wear bright red scarf!' The weight of his disapproval matched the height of his raised eyebrows.

'When they leave, man on own hurries towards Chinatown, the other two leave together, they always go in opposite direction, they walk towards Monkey Bridge.'

CHAPTER 18
Mid-June 1831

It took almost six weeks before Tijah felt confident enough to divulge her secrets; to make known her history and the reason why she had hidden inside one of Edmund's crates.

She had been helping Wing Yee at the clinic in one way or another from the first time she had visited. Now, she was familiar with the names of nearly all the herbs Wing Yee used and was becoming adept at applying a poultice and cleaning wounds; she was eager to learn more.

'You're very good at this,' Wing Yee told her one day. 'Have you ever done anything like it before?' They conversed in Malay most of the time as Tijah knew no Cantonese and was only just beginning to acquire a few words in English.

'In my village, I watched the older women. They make a drink from herbs; it helps to prevent people getting sick.'

'What do they call this drink? Do you know how to make it?'

'They call it *jamu*. It's the colour of sunshine, but I'm sorry I don't know how it's made; I was never allowed to help. I always had to work with my aunt in the padi fields.'

Wing Yee decided to push the conversation a bit further. She was itching to know what had brought this thirteen-year-old to the Settlement. She'd shown no awareness of the brothels in town, let alone an interest in joining any of the women who resided there. Why had she come here? Why had she come alone? What was it she was seeking?

'Your aunt?' Wing Yee said. 'You didn't stay behind to help your mother?'

Tijah lowered her eyes before whispering, 'My mother died when I was born. My aunt has looked after me since I was a baby.'

'What about your father?' Wing Yee said, regretting the question almost as soon as it left her lips. The girl was beginning to speak freely, she hoped her forthright questioning wouldn't cause her to clam up again.

Tijah swallowed hard. She hadn't told anyone about her reason for coming to Singapore; she hadn't spoken about any member of her family since she arrived here. Chin Ming and Edmund, Dick, and Sujana, they had all been so good to her, welcoming her into their lives. Wing Yee had nursed her back to health and now she was letting her help at the clinic. Before today, none of them had asked any difficult questions, but perhaps she should begin to tell them her story. How else would she be able to find her father?

'My father ... , he is European, he left the kampong after marrying my mother and never returned. That's all I have ever been told. But you see, I believe he did come back and quite recently, but my grandfather sent him away. I like to think he had come to look for me.'

Wing Yee stopped grinding a concoction of herbs and put the pestle aside. She took Tijah's hands in her own and led her to a chair in the corner of the room. She knelt in front of her and stroked her hands. 'Is that what brought you here?' she said. 'Did someone tell you your father was in Singapore?'

For the whole time Tijah was telling her story, Wing Yee's thoughts kept returning to the time she had first met Chin Ming, another young woman who had come to Singapore in search of a lost father. Was history repeating itself?

'... my grandfather, he refused to say anything about the day a visitor arrived, but I heard odd phrases being muttered by some of the women in the village. I didn't understand at first, but my aunt finally told me the truth,' Tijah clenched her fists as her voice reduced to nothing more than a murmur.

'You said your father came back to the village recently. When was that, exactly?'

'About halfway through Ramadan,' Tijah said. 'But I didn't know anything about it at the time. A friend of my aunt's made a comment when I was helping her with the preparations for Eid al Fitr – the celebration we have at the end of Ramadan. Even then it took a while before I was able to discover any details.'

Wing Yee wondered if the girl's grandfather had actually driven the stranger away or asked him to leave because guests were not welcome during the fasting month? However, she thought it was more likely that he had fled when he discovered he had a daughter. Surely any father who cared would have wanted to see her. It sounded to Wing Yee as if this man wanted nothing to do with her. And why had he left his young wife in the first place? Why had it taken so many years before he returned? If he did live in Singapore as Tijah believed, what had taken him back to Malacca a couple of months ago? Wing Yee frowned and twisted her lips to one side as she tried to make sense of such a complicated puzzle.

'You are thirteen,' she said after a little while, 'which means your parents must have married just before Raffles arrived in Singapore. During those initial years, quite a few people came here from Malacca. My friend Baba Tan was one of the early settlers. If your father was amongst that group of people, Baba Tan might be able to tell us something that will help.'

The effort of revealing her story had exhausted Tijah, but she was glad she had now shared her hopes as well as her anxieties with Wing Yee. She allowed a smile to spread from her lips to her eyes.

*****

Later that evening, Wing Yee began to relay Tijah's story to Chin Ming. She told her about the mysterious visitor to the kampong, the man who Tijah believed might be her missing father. She answered Chin Ming's many questions about the rest of Tijah's family and her grandfather's determination to shield her from the man who had married and abandoned his daughter.

'What makes her think the visitor had come looking for her?' Chin Ming said.

'She gathered snippets of information by listening to the women who had been her mother's friends, but most of all, I think that's what she wants to believe.'

Wing Yee and Chin Ming exchanged glances.

A shiver travelled down Chin Ming's spine, causing her to flinch. These days, she hardly ever thought about the search she had undertaken for her own father, but Tijah's story rekindled some of the agony she had experienced. Chin Ming's story was entirely different, of course. Her father had been abducted. She'd had months to plan how she would search for him, and even then, it had taken two years before he was discovered. Their reunion was joyful and full of happiness, but like Wing Yee, she doubted whether a man who had shown no interest in his family for so long would be quite so delighted to see his daughter.

✳✳✳✳✳

The following morning, as soon as she had consumed a bowl of *nasi lemak* hastily followed by a glass of green tea, Wing Yee hurried along the road to Dick and Sujana's house She wanted to get to the house before Dick instructed Darma to bring round the horse and carriage. Since Dick had set up office in Mr Johnston's warehouse, Wing Yee and Tijah had benefitted from a ride into town each day, instead of having to walk down the hill to the clinic.

'I was expecting to collect you from the Beaumonts in about half an hour,' Dick said as Wing Yee joined him on their veranda. 'Are you not going to the clinic today? Tijah will be disappointed.'

'Clinic, yes, yes,' Wing Yee said. 'Where is Tijah now?'

'I imagine she's with Fakina. They've become great friends and she enjoys helping Fakina with Tomas first thing in the morning. Is something wrong? Have you changed your mind about letting her work alongside you at the clinic?'

'She great help. I teach her all about medicines; she learn fast. No, she tell me about her life before she come here. I think you should know these things, but first, I make sure she happy to tell.'

'Why don't you go through to the nursery? I'm sure that's where you'll find her. You can have a quiet word without involving me. If she agrees to your suggestion, then I'll be here, ready to listen to her story. If not, then you can come back by yourself and there will be no embarrassment.'

Wing Yee nodded and disappeared behind the screen which partitioned the veranda from the drawing room and prevented unwelcome insects from entering the house. Dick was relieved to learn that Tijah had confided in someone. Both he and Sujana had been concerned about their young guest, conscious of the fact that there must be something she was not telling them, secrets that she was keeping locked up inside herself.

When Wing Yee reappeared, both Tijah and Fakina could be seen hovering in the shadows. 'I've told Tijah that I talked to Chin Ming last night,' she said in Malay, wanting the girl to understand their conversation. 'She is happy for you and Sujana to know her story too, but she is shy and embarrassed. She has asked me to tell you what I told Chin Ming.'

'Can we wait for Sujana to join us?' Dick said. 'I think it's important that we hear this tale together.'

Fakina was dispatched to find Sujana and to ask the cook

to bring some cold drinks. Sujana arrived, holding Tomas in her arms. She raised her eyebrows when Dick asked her to sit beside him; she had no idea what all the mystery was about. The drinks were handed round and Wing Yee seated herself opposite her hosts. Tijah crept nearer to Wing Yee and lowered herself to the floor, sitting as close to her confidant as possible; Fakina curled up on the other side of Wing Yee, reaching across to hold Tijah's hand. Wing Yee told the story slowly, inviting Tijah to interject or correct her if any of the information was wrong, but Tijah fixed her gaze on a line of ants marching across the wooden floorboards in a determined fashion and said nothing at all.

'You poor child,' Sujana said as soon as Wing Yee finished. She handed Tomas to Dick and hurried over to Tijah, putting her arm around her shoulders as she knelt beside her 'It was a very brave thing to attempt but also terrifying. It shows that you have determination and courage. We'll do everything we can to help, won't we?' she said, her voice trembling as she looked across at Dick.

Dick stroked his son's head. Instantly, he thought of Chin Ming's quest to find her father, and just as the others who made the same connection had done, he also knew instinctively that this would be a very different kind of search and perhaps not end well.

$$*\,*\,*\,*\,*$$

In his pursuit of the men involved in smuggling, Dick spent the next week visiting every single merchant who owned a warehouse along Boat Quay. Initially, he engaged them in everyday conversation, showing a casual interest in any product that was easily visible and asking how well their business was doing. He always carried his sketchbook with him as this had given him numerous opportunities in the past to observe his surroundings unobtrusively. Nowadays, he also discovered that someone who sat innocently sketching the scene spread out before him was able to tune in to conversations that might otherwise be private. When he returned to his office, he recorded every conversation as far as he could remember it and identified questions for those merchants he wanted to revisit. By the end of the month, he had identified six people whose activity was worthy of further investigation.

*****

Dick had become sentimental over the years and on the anniversary of Raffles' birth - 6th July - he reiterated his resolve. He must get to the bottom of the clandestine arrangements that resulted in smuggling women into the Settlement. The previous evening, he'd watched a violent storm out at sea. It hadn't made landfall, but its outer margins had washed clean the streets and now everything smelt fresh; a good day to begin. First, he would visit Choo Keng; the coffee was always good and he could check to see if there was any news. After that, he resolved to visit Baba Tan.

'No sign of my regulars,' Choo Keng told him. 'They away over three week now.'

'Maybe they have gone travelling again. Did they mention anything the last time you saw them? Did you hear them talking about their plans? Have you heard any rumours about their destination?' Dick asked.

'Too many question,' Choo Keng said, looking very flustered. 'Me not hear what men say,' he added as he wiped clean the table nearest to where Dick was sitting.

Dick opened his mouth to ask another question but stopped as soon as he noticed Choo Keng's change of expression. The Chinaman stood perfectly still. His eyes seemed to grow to twice their size as he stared at the figure of a European man of medium height striding in their direction. Choo Keng glanced briefly at Dick and nodded his head with great vigour.

Then, he turned to busy himself elsewhere, polishing the marble-topped tables and tidying the stools. The new customer seated himself at a table adjacent to where Dick was seated. Choo Keng hurried inside to produce more coffee. When he returned, he was careful not to look in Dick's direction and he avoided any further conversation. His actions told Dick everything he wanted to know; this man was the third member of the clandestine trio.

Dick stirred his coffee and sipped it slowly; he could wait all morning, if necessary. His sketchbook, once again, provided the perfect cover. He'd drawn so many harbour scenes over the years that he could probably reproduce the whole vista blindfolded. He sketched a rough outline of two lighters tied up in parallel, close to the quay. A rope held them together, and a young man sat cross-legged on the bow of the second boat. It was a scene to which he could quickly return should the man at the nearby table become aware of his attention. The man sat at an angle that enabled Dick to capture him in silhouette, showing an ample moustache, ruddy cheeks, and balding head.

A little while later, the other man scraped back his chair, threw some coins onto the table, and began to walk away. There was no doubt about it, he was the same man who Dick had seen with the other two men; the generous growth of dark brown hair above the stranger's upper lip made him very distinctive. Dick closed his sketchbook, rose from his chair without a sound, and followed at a discreet distance.

The man strolled further along Boat Quay in the direction of Baba Tan's warehouse. Dick offered up a silent prayer; he didn't want his friend to suddenly appear and engage him in conversation. Thankfully, there was no sign of any activity on that part of the wharf. The man hurried along Philip Street. Even now, there remained a lingering odour that reminded him of the destructive fire that had raged there last year.

At the junction with Church Street, the stranger briefly

looked around before diving into a narrow alleyway. Dick slipped into the shadows the moment the man stopped and kept perfectly still until he was sure it was safe to move. The alley was dark and stank of urine. He had no idea which way the man would turn at the other end. He ran, once he felt it was safe to do so, nearly stumbling over obscure piles of detritus along the way. He emerged into bright sunlight and covered his eyes as he looked from left to right. He was just in time to see the man approaching a well-known, bright red door. He stepped over the threshold, and although it was gloomy inside, Dick was certain that the person who greeted him was no less a person than Madam Ho herself.

Dick stopped in his tracks. He could hardly go any further, but he was desperate to know who this man was and why he was visiting Madam Ho at this time of day. He was still searching his brain for ideas while he wandered back along Cross Street. At the junction with Amoy Street, he wondered about visiting the clinic. He was halfway across the road when Wing Yee came hurrying in his direction. They almost collided with each other.

'Where you go?' she said.

'I could ask you the same question,' Dick said. 'You seem to be in a hurry.'

'Madam Ho, she send for me.'

'I didn't realise the two of you had become friends.'

Wing Yee snorted and began to protest when she saw the grin on Dick's face. 'You tease me,' she said. 'You know we not friends. I get her to send women from brothel to me. I ask them many question about how they get to Singapore. One woman tell me more young girls arrive soon.'

'I'm sorry I made a joke. The conversations you and Chin Ming have had with the women who came last time gave me some good leads. You might be able to help me again now.'

'What you mean?'

'I've been following a man who makes me very suspicious.

I think he might have something to do with the smuggling business. He went inside Madam Ho's front door a short while ago and I'm sure he's still there. Do you think you could find out who he is and what he's doing there? If she's expecting you, she won't think it unusual if you ask a few questions.'

Wing Yee grinned. 'I hurry. I try find out more about man and if more women arrive soon. We talk tonight.' She rushed along the street without a backwards glance. Dick watched until she was safely inside Madam Ho's famous emporium.

*****

Dick decided there was nothing further he could do until he met with Wing Yee later. He turned on his heel and made his way back to his office to make some notes on the morning's activity.

He leapt up the stairs to his office two at a time and it was not until he reached the top that he heard Alexander calling his name from the lobby below.

'I've got something to tell you,' Alexander said, a broad smile spreading across his face.

'Could it wait a few minutes?' Dick said. 'I need to write a few notes – something I discovered this morning, and I don't want to forget anything or leave anything out.'

'Just come down to see me when you're ready, there's no hurry.'

Dick found a clean sheet of paper and began to scribble. He made a note of the time the man had arrived at Choo Keng's stall and the time he left. He estimated it had taken about ten minutes for the man to reach Cross Street and enter the brothel. He opened his sketchbook and examined the drawing he'd made of the man's side view. Now he made a note about the colour of the clothes he'd been wearing – a tawny frock coat, warm brown trousers with a strong yellowish tone and hints of green. His boots were long and black with no adornments. At the bottom of his page of notes, he recorded everything he could remember from what Choo Keng had told him about the previous time when the man had met up with two other Europeans, neither of whom – according to Choo Keng - had now been seen for almost a month.

Once he was satisfied, he gathered the papers together and placed them with his other notebooks in a drawer inside the desk. He turned the key, put it in his pocket, and made his way downstairs.

*****

When Dick pushed open the door to his private office, Alexander Johnston was sitting with his feet up on his desk, arms folded across his chest, and eyes closed. He jumped at the sound made by a hinge badly in need of a little oil.

'Take a seat,' he said to Dick. 'I've finished all I need to do today and the warm air was making me drowsy. Would you like some tea?'

Dick hadn't eaten anything since breakfast, neither had he stopped to drink anything since leaving Choo Keng's coffee stall; he'd been unaware of his mounting thirst until now.

'That would be most welcome,' he said, 'and do you by any chance have any biscuits? I missed lunch and I'm feeling rather hungry.'

'I don't even keep ship's biscuits here anymore,' Alexander said. 'Too great a temptation for vermin, but I can send out for something. What would you like, sweet or savoury? I can recommend the vegetable *bao* from a stall just over the road or I can get some of the best *kueh* you've ever tasted from another place further along the quay.'

'Sujana won't be pleased if I haven't any appetite left for supper, but something light would be wonderful. Won't you join me?'

Alexander called out to one of the clerks and asked him to

purchase a couple of vegetable *bao* from across the street. 'And when you return, could you please make some tea for us?'

Dick flopped into the nearest chair. He hadn't realised how much of his energy had been sapped until that moment. 'What is it you wanted to tell me?' he said.

'I had a meeting with the other magistrates this morning,' Alexander replied, giving nothing away by the expression on his face.

Dick's first reaction was to tilt his head to one side. His attention for the last few weeks had been entirely focused on his desire to expose the men who were smuggling young women into the Settlement; he'd completely forgotten about Alexander's suggestion. Alexander interpreted his reaction as a question, wanting to know the outcome of the meeting.

'They all agree with me. You have one hundred per cent support from every single one of them; they are eager to welcome you to the magisterial team.'

Dick's mouth fell open. He was unable to utter a single word for several seconds. 'Well, that's something I did not expect to hear,' he said.

'I don't know why you're so surprised. You're an artist which means you are good at observing people. I also know you're a good listener. The fact that you are a member of Stamford Raffles' family gives you added credibility. I'm not sure why we haven't thought of it before. Everyone thinks it's an excellent idea, so now we can start to plan.'

Dick swallowed hard. He was pleased. Of course, he was pleased and a perfect thing to be told on Raffles' birthday. However, would he have time to read all the required documents, would he have time to sit in on however many sessions of the court to observe procedure, would he have time to learn how the law operates in practice?

'You're looking worried,' Alexander said. 'I thought you would be pleased. I'll be your mentor, so you can ask me about anything that gives you cause for concern.'

'Oh, I am pleased,' Dick said. 'It's just that I think I'm beginning to get somewhere with accumulating evidence. This morning, I followed a man who I have my doubts about. He ended up at the brothel run by Madam Ho.'

'A bit early in the day I would have thought?' Alexander said.

'Quite. So, what was he doing there? Not long after I saw him enter, I bumped into Wing Yee. She'd received a note from Madam Ho and she thinks that means another group of women might be due to arrive very soon. She agreed to find out anything she could about the stranger.'

'That all sounds very positive, and you should certainly continue to explore that idea as a possibility, but it doesn't mean we can't begin to look at some of the things you'll need to know as a magistrate as well. We don't have to rush anything; we can make it work at whatever pace suits you best.'

'Thank you,' Dick said. 'Thank you for your understanding and thank you for believing in me.'

'It's no more than Raffles would have done,' Johnston replied.

CHAPTER 19
A Week Later

After riding out a ferocious storm on their return from Sumatra, far more violent than the rough seas they had experienced before, both Victor and Stefan were glad to be back in Singapore. One of the women in this latest consignment had caused them problems from the moment she had been handed over to them. Slightly older than the others, she had been extremely vocal about the way she was being treated. During the storm, she had somehow hoisted herself onto the deck, after which she simply disappeared. Neither Victor nor Stefan knew for certain what had happened. Did she jump or was her frail body swept overboard and engulfed by the sea? Afterwards, Victor announced in an authoritative and deafening voice that a giant wave had swept her away instantly. This was the story both he and Stefan agreed to tell anyone who asked awkward questions.

With only Stefan to steer the boat and Victor to take care of the women, those few hours had been a living nightmare. It had tested their strength, endurance, and Stefan's seamanship to the bitter limits. They told themselves they were lucky no serious damage had been done to either the boat or themselves.

Nothing further was said during the rest of the voyage. Victor hardly spoke to Stefan, and for once, Stefan nursed his antagonism quietly. Victor barked orders to the five remaining women but they stayed in a semi-conscious state and gave no trouble. This made their transfer to shore easier than on the previous occasion when Stefan and Victor had returned from the west coast of Sumatra. As before, the women waited in a house on the edge of the kampong during the night and were taken by cart to Madam Ho in the early hours of the following morning.

✳✳✳✳✳

Later that day, Stefan went with Victor to meet the man who acted as agent for the supply of women to the brothels. On the two previous occasions when the deal was being set up, the man was always on time; today he was late. As usual, Victor and Stefan sipped coffee from Choo Keng's thick earthenware cups, casually looking around to make sure no one was close enough to overhear their conversation. Their focus had settled on a lighterman slowly climbing the sodden steps from the river to the wharf when a fist punched the table, spilling thick, sooty coffee over the surface and onto Stefan's trousers.

'Only five!' the man bellowed. 'I specifically said six, can neither of you count?'

Stefan leapt to his feet, scrutinised their surroundings, and fixed his eyes on the man, silently imploring him to lower his voice. 'Hush!' he whispered as he returned to his seat.

A row ensued between the three of them with Victor and the man yelling at each other in English interspersed with an occasional phrase in Malay. The trio attracted a group of coolies who closed in on the scene, amused by the distraction and glad to have a break away from their usual drudgery. Stefan stood up again, bidding the other two to calm down.

'We have an audience,' he said. 'They look as if they're expecting you to entertain them with a fight,' he added, then in a quieter tone, 'Surely, we don't want to draw any more attention to ourselves?'

203

Victor and the other man glared at each other. 'Tell him about the storm, for God's sake,' Stefan said. 'We didn't lose a portion of the cargo on purpose. A fee was agreed and that is what is due to us, we need to be paid!'

Victor understood what Stefan was implying. He did his best to describe the storm, the ferocity of the waves, and the problems they had keeping the cargo secure. 'She managed to climb out of one of the rear hatches while I was tying down those at the bow,' he said. 'It was imperative to deal with those first, we needed to keep the water out.'

Stefan winced when he heard the word SHE. They never referred to the women as anything other than cargo, it was safer that way. He cast his eyes all around to make sure that no one was listening, but even the coolies had lost interest and drifted back to their tasks.

'There was no way I could help,' he said, 'I needed to remain at the helm, otherwise, we might have capsized; then there would be no cargo at all for you!'

'I don't care about you or the storm,' the man spat the words back to them. 'It was your decision to sail with a minimal crew, it was your greed that caused you to cut corners, to use your own boat rather than employ experienced sailors. I will pay for five and five only!' He slammed a money bag down on the table, still wet from the splattered coffee, then he turned on his heel and strode away towards Commercial Square.

Victor slumped down on his stool; he knew there was nothing more to be done. Stefan on the other hand was seething. He ranted first about the way the man had behaved, the stain left on his trousers by the splattered coffee, and, finally, about their loss of income.

'There is no point in arguing,' Victor said. 'We understood that the fee being offered was for the assignment. Our friend who has just left approached the problem from a different point of view. In his mind, he was offering a fee for each piece of the cargo; we only delivered five bodies and hence the total we receive is less than we expected.'

Stefan opened his mouth to continue his own line of reasoning, but Victor held up his hand to prevent further discussion. 'I know it's infuriating to have our fee reduced, but we still have a considerable sum to fuel our enjoyment. Let's get away from here before anyone wants to know what the quarrel was about,' he said. 'I think a night of pleasure is called for.'

They rose from the table, briefly glancing all around, but the coolies had long ago disappeared and no one else appeared to be taking much notice. All apart from one person, and neither Victor nor Stefan had thought of glancing as far as the warehouse belonging to Johnston and Co. They hadn't the slightest idea they were being observed from an upper window at the far end of the quay.

*****

Since the terrible storm he'd observed out at sea over a week ago, there had been no rain at all. The atmosphere in Dick's office was oppressive, and he kept losing his concentration. He'd not managed to gain any new information about the two men who had, until a few weeks ago, been seen at Choo Keng's coffee stall. No one around the quay could tell him where they could be found, let alone the reason why they came and went. All the other snippets of news he'd gathered from his various contacts amounted to nothing of any significance; he'd come to a halt and was beginning to run out of ideas.

He'd decided to spend the afternoon reading through some legal papers Alexander had given him as part of the preparation for his magisterial duties. He found the language unnecessarily protracted and the content dull; he was finding it increasingly difficult to stop his chin falling forwards onto his chest and his eyelids from closing. After continuing this battle for almost an hour, he only just managed to prevent his head banging onto the desk. He sat bolt upright, squeezed his eyes tight shut, and opened them again. He heaved his shoulders up and down several times. A mosquito buzzed past his right ear; he jumped up to avoid it feasting on his bare arm.

He paced around the room several times before reaching up to the window and pushing it open to allow in more air. When he straightened, he let his gaze travel along the quay for any sign of activity. He thought it was unlikely in this heat; anyone with any sense would be taking advantage of any area of shade they could find. At first, he thought his eyes were playing tricks; he rubbed them with his fists, then looked out again. There was no mistaking it this time. There were two, no three men at Choo Keng's coffee stall. One of them stood tall over the others; he was waving his arms around. Could it be the man he'd sketched only a few days ago? Dick couldn't see their facial expressions, but something was awry. He concluded there was some sort of argument going on. He continued to watch, absolutely transfixed.

The spell was broken when the man who had been gesticulating threw something onto the table and marched away towards Commercial Square. Dick thought he caught sight of a moustache when he turned, but that might have been wishful thinking. Dick focused on the other two; he was almost sure they were the same men he'd seen before, the pair that he'd asked Choo Keng about. They hadn't been seen for well over a month. Where had they been? What were they doing back in their usual position on the quay? How did the third man fit in? Whilst he was considering various possibilities, both men rose from their chairs, they glanced all around before making a move, and then in no time at all, they hurried off towards Monkey Bridge.

Dick grabbed his bag and made for the stairs, he scuttled down them as fast as he could and threw open the outside door. The heat hit him like a heavy, damp blanket, making him swallow hard and steady his pace. He walked as fast as the steamy afternoon would allow towards Choo Keng.

'Men just leave,' Choo Keng said as soon as he saw Dick. 'Make much mess,' he continued, shaking his head from side to side and pointing to the dried-up streaks of coffee on the table.

'I noticed them from the window in Mr Johnston's warehouse,' Dick said. 'Had they been here long? Was the third man the one who came when I was here last week? Did you hear any of what they said? Did they argue?'

'Always too many question!' Choo Keng said, still shaking his head.

'My apologies,' said Dick. He sat at a table adjacent to the one that had been occupied by the group who had aroused his suspicions. 'I'll start again. Did you hear anything of what those three men discussed?'

Choo Keng scrubbed the other table clean with water from the river and a brush that had seen better days. 'Lot of shouting,' he eventually said. 'Some quarrel about money.'

'I saw the shorter man place something on the table before he left,' Dick said. 'Could that have been the money they were arguing about?'

'Man say he only pay for five, not six,' Choo Keng added. He picked up his bucket and returned to the back of his stall. Either he hadn't heard any further details or he wasn't prepared to discuss the matter any further. Dick thought the first option was most likely as they would not have wanted anyone to overhear the details of their business transaction. What Choo Keng had told him was a good start. It indicated a payment was being made for something underhand and the numbers mentioned could easily refer to the number of women they had smuggled into the Settlement. Wing Yee might be able to provide the answer to that conundrum if she was invited back to the brothel. If Madam Ho required her to conduct further examination, it meant that more women had arrived at her establishment. On her first attempt to discover the identity of the mysterious man, Madam Ho would not tell Wing Yee his name, but she had muttered something about a business arrangement. If only Wing Yee could find out more about him it might prove to be invaluable. Dick was sure the stranger was the master of ceremonies in this illegal scheme.

*****

It was well into the evening before Victor and Stefan arrived at the brothel in an alley leading off Hokkien Street. Most of the women who worked there had been in Singapore for two or three years, so on entering Victor asked for his favourite; her name was Lan Fen. The Madam, in charge of this property asked Stefan whether he too had a favourite, but as he made it a rule to remain indifferent towards these women, who he thought had little worth other than to entertain, he shook his head. His philosophy when paying for the pleasure of a night with one of these whores was to register no interest in them as people. Then he could indulge his desires and treat them as he felt fit. For a fleeting moment, he thought about the girl he'd lusted after when they'd offloaded the first half dozen Sumatran beauties but dismissed the idea straightaway. No complications was his rule. Victor suggested he might enjoy a woman called Li Ling as he knew her to be someone who was pretty and eager to please.

*****

It was almost time for breakfast the following day when Victor and Stefan bumped into each other again. They had consumed copious amounts of alcohol during the night and their gaits were unsteady, to say the least; both had stale breath. Neither had washed and they emerged onto the street looking weary and unkempt. There were few passers-by at that hour, and most took no notice as they had seen many others emerge from that establishment in a similar state. One older man held his hand over his nose and crossed to the other side of the street.

'I think some *roti* – and probably some eggs- is what's called for,' said Victor.

'And coffee, I need some good, strong local coffee,' Stefan added.

'Follow me, my friend,' Victor said. 'I know the very place. And afterwards, you can accompany me to see Madam Ho. I want to know where she plans to send our latest delivery; there's one of the five I have my eye on.'

*****

Madam Ho had summoned Wing Yee first thing. Being beckoned in such a manner had irritated her considerably and even now she was left feeling more than a little annoyed. The woman seemed to assume that whenever she snapped her fingers, Wing Yee would come running. If it wasn't for the fact that she and Chin Ming had at last begun to develop a relationship with some of the women now residing at the establishment in Cross Street, she would have refused to comply. She was, however, reluctant to take Tijah with her to Cross Street, so she had left her at the clinic with instructions not to admit anyone until she returned.

This time, there were only five women to see. As on the previous occasion, she had tried to calm each one in turn and to explain that she would try to help them. She told them to speak to someone who had also only recently arrived in Singapore. Her name was Melati.

Wing Yee made her excuses to leave, instructing Madam Ho to send all five to the clinic for further examination the following day. As always, Madam Ho insisted on referring to them as women, but Wing Yee knew already they could be not much older than Tijah, certainly no older than Fakina. Once again, they were young girls snatched from their villages in Sumatra; they were like all the others she had spoken to.

She slammed the bright red door behind her and almost bumped into a man as he approached the entrance. Typical, Wing Yee thought, men like that don't even see women like me. He could have knocked me over, but it wouldn't matter because all that concerns him is getting what he wants. As she hurried away, muttering to herself, she began to wonder what he was doing visiting Madam Ho at this hour of the morning. He wasn't the one with the whiskers she'd seen on a previous visit - the man Dick had asked her to find out about. Nevertheless, she wondered if this one might also be involved with smuggling the women.

*****

Stefan had hung back when Victor turned into Cross Street. He was still unsure about confronting Madam Ho and didn't want to risk being recognised. When they parted, he told Victor he intended to replace some trousers that had been ruined during the storm and order a new shirt from a nearby tailor. Stefan watched his friend quicken his pace and head off in the opposite direction. Instead of continuing on his way, he hesitated; he thought it might be amusing to watch, to note how long Victor spent with the ageing proprietor, to observe his mood when he left the emporium.

He swatted an insect on the back of his sweaty neck, wondering whether it would be better to return to the kampong to freshen up – to dowse himself with cooling liquid from the water tank before flopping onto his bed to rest. When he glanced back towards the place where Victor had disappeared, he saw a woman emerging from the famous red door; his friend must have missed colliding with her by a very narrow margin. He wondered why Madam Ho was allowing one of her charges to leave the premises unchaperoned and so early in the morning. As she came closer, there was something about the woman that was vaguely familiar; something about the way she carried herself, even the way she walked. He strained his eyes to get a better look and immediately the muscles in his legs tightened, rendering him immobile. His instinct was to run, to hide, to make sure she didn't see him. It was the bitch, there was no doubt about it.

She hurried past him on the other side of the road, she seemed intent on getting to her destination quickly and looked neither right nor left. He wondered what she had been doing at Madam Ho's; surely, she wasn't working there? He began to follow; he couldn't stop himself. He knew where she lived and he knew she worked somewhere in the town, making potions out of weeds and the like; he needed to tie the ends of her story together.

Stefan briefly wondered if he ought to leave a message for Victor, but it was soon dismissed. He hadn't said that he would wait, hadn't said he would meet his friend back at the kampong, hadn't said anything at all really. Good god, he thought, the bitch can certainly move quickly; she was disappearing down a side street, he needed to hurry. He barged into two young boys struggling with a load far too heavy for them. He swore in Dutch and carried on, leaving the youngsters to retrieve cabbages, yams, and the remains of a bag of rice that had scattered all over the road.

He was hot and sweating profusely when he emerged from the lane into Amoy Street. He caught a glimpse of a green tunic worn by a woman with lustrous black hair held together by some sort of stick. It was a back view, but it was the bitch – no doubt about it; he quickened his pace. She crossed the road without a second glance, heading straight towards a wooden door intricately carved with leaves and flowers. The door opened as she approached. Stefan retreated into the shadows of a doorway.

The bitch was greeted by a young girl; could it be her

daughter? He gazed in the direction of the youngster, unable to take his eyes off her. She too looked vaguely familiar, but how could she be – especially if she was related to the bitch.

He gasped, then covered his mouth to prevent any sound escaping and attracting attention. He wanted to get away, but his muscles had tightened again and he could hardly breathe. Surely, it couldn't be? How old was the girl? She must be more than seven or eight. He counted quickly. He realised that it was, in fact, over nine years since he'd forced himself on the bitch, taken her, thinking he was merely warming up before having the other one. No, he convinced himself, the girl was older than nine; there was no way that she could be his daughter.

CHAPTER 20
13th July

Tijah had seen the man. She was glad that Wing Yee had not left her alone for too long, especially now she'd seen him looking at her. There was something uncanny in the way he stared at her, something haunting, something unsettling. She fiddled with the bangle around on her wrist, twisting it first one way and then the other.

'What's wrong?' Wing Yee said. 'You have an expression on your face just like the one that you wore when you discovered two strange women sitting at the side of your bed.'

'There was a man ...' Tijah said, 'I thought he was following you. He made me feel uncomfortable ...'

'Where?' Wing Yee turned on her heel and scanned the whole street. It was busy with coolies, water-carriers, merchants hurrying to and fro, but there was no one she recognised.

'He's gone,' Tijah said. 'I can't see him now. Perhaps it was my imagination. I was feeling lonely and wondering how long it might be before you returned.'

'I'm sorry,' Wing Yee said. 'Madam Ho was not in a good mood today. I was hoping to talk to her about the English lessons, but that will have to wait. There was a man who I bumped into as I was leaving Cross Street but I can't think he would follow me here. Was the person you saw European?'

'I'm not sure. He was dressed in European clothes, but he

was not pale like Edmund and Mr Johnston.'

'It could be the same person, but I hope not. I think the man I saw has something to do with the women who are brought here from Sumatra. Melati will possibly be able to tell us more. She can ask the new arrivals when they come here tomorrow. I've told Madam Ho I want Melati to accompany them.'

*****

That evening, Wing Yee remained silent for most of the journey back to the house. Tijah chatted incessantly, covering the silence. She was overjoyed about the things she had learned, working alongside Wing Yee, and couldn't wait to tell Fakina about her day. They reached Dick's house first and as soon as Tijah had alighted, she ran in to find her friend. Wing Yee asked Dick if she could speak to him in private. Wing Yee and Dick remained in the carriage. He turned towards her to be more comfortable and to be sure he heard whatever it was she had to say.

'Don't look so alarmed,' Wing Yee said in Malay. 'It's probably nothing at all, but since you and Edmund made it clear that you have some reservations about the work Chin Ming and I are trying to do with the Sumatran women, I thought I ought to tell you about the man I saw this morning.'

'What man? Where? Was someone foul-mouthed or disrespectful towards you?'

Wing Yee told him about the figure who came hurrying into Madam Ho's emporium as she was leaving. 'Later, when I returned to the clinic, Tijah spotted a man who she thought had been following me. They could be the same person,' she said, 'but it's unlikely. If it was the same person, he couldn't have spent very long with Madam Ho.'

'Was the man you bumped into today the same one you saw at Madam Ho's last time - the one you asked her about?'

'Definitely not same man,' Wing Yee said, reverting to

English. 'Last time, man was leaving when I arrive. He have fat face, very red cheeks, lots of – what you call them – whiskers. This one tall, quite good-looking, but he has hands like farmer.'

'What on earth does that mean?' Dick said.

'He wear nice clothes, but he has big, strong hands. I notice when he push past me.'

Dick was puzzled. It must be more than a coincidence that these men visited Madam Ho shortly after the arrival of a new group of women. Could it be that the one with the moustache was the person who ran the business, and the second was one of the pair who did the dirty work, collecting the women from their villages and bringing them to Singapore? He was now convinced that he had stumbled upon the existence of an organised gang. But how to collect sufficient evidence, hard facts that he could present to Kenneth Murchison at the end of August, was a different matter entirely.

Dick took a deep breath. 'What makes you think the man you observed and the one Tijah noticed are not the same person?'

'I ask Tijah to describe man she saw. She said he had European clothes. She notice some red cloth around his neck, then she see colour of his skin. It quite dark, not like any other Englishmen she know.'

'And the man you caught sight of wasn't dressed like that?'

'The one I see today at Madam Ho's, he definitely tall and he dress like European, but no red scarf around his neck.'

Dick remained quiet for what seemed like an eternity. When he looked up, his expression was grave. 'I think the men you've seen at Madam Ho's must be involved in the smuggling business; I believe there are at least three of them mixed up in the scheme. Two of them regularly meet at Choo Keng's coffee stall; he's told me all he knows about them. He doesn't like them; he says they are demanding and discourteous. And from the snippets of their conversation he's overheard, I'm almost certain they're connected with something underhand. They come and go. They haven't been seen anywhere near the quay for the last few weeks, but yesterday afternoon, they returned. I happened to be gazing out of the office window and I saw them quite clearly, but this time there was another man with them.'

'You think same men as ones I see at Cross Street?'

'I think there is someone who does the organising and the other two work for him. The reason they occasionally vanish and then reappear is linked to the arrival of the women from Sumatra.'

'They ones who bring women here?'

'The frequency of their visits to Choo Keng's is significant. They are absent for weeks at a time, but their reappearance always coincides with the arrival of a new group of women at Madam Ho's emporium. It seems too great a coincidence to ignore; there must be a connection.'

'What you see from office?'

'The three of them seemed to be engaged in some sort of argument. Two were seated, the third man stood over them waving his arms around. I saw him thump the table and then he left. That's when I thought the other two looked familiar. I left the office as quickly as I could and hurried to the coffee stall, hoping to confront them.'

Wing Yee's eyes widened. She remained silent, unable to find the right words. A stony expression was the only outward sign of how she was feeling inside. Her English was still too limited to pose the questions that she needed to ask. She reverted to Malay.

'So, you think that two of the men who argued are the same ones I saw at Madam Ho's? What about the third man, who is he?'

Dick suggested they should continue their conversation on the veranda where they would be more comfortable. Darma, who had been waiting patiently in the shade, asked if he should lead the horse and carriage away. Dick agreed that the animal should be given a drink but told Darma he would need the carriage later to take Wing Yee home.

He joined Wing Yee on the veranda and continued with his story. He told her as much as he knew.

'What are you going to do?'

'I don't know what I can do at present. I have nothing substantial to back up my suspicions ...'

'Then you'd better find something,' Wing Yee said, 'and quick time. No more young girls, it needs to stop.'

'Of course, it does,' Dick said, 'but it won't be easy. The latest consignment of women has already been handed over to Madam Ho – you said so yourself – so we need to find out if any more women are expected soon. Catching the men in the act of handing over the women to Madam Ho would be indisputable, you see.'

'In-dis-pute ..., what that mean?' Wing Yee asked, with her eyebrows raised. 'You use many long words since you decide to be a magistrate! I not understand.'

Dick couldn't help laughing; Wing Yee could always be relied upon to be the sensible one, not letting him get away with anything. 'It means we need evidence that is clear-cut, it would prove they are breaking the law, and no one will be able to say otherwise.'

'I know something else that is certain,' Wing Yee said.

'And what is that?' said Dick, still smiling.

'We shouldn't tell Chin Ming what we know. She will want to get involved and that will not be good for her or the new baby.'

'You're right, of course,' said Dick, 'but that might be easier said than done. You know what she's like.'

'Perhaps you should talk to Edmund. I can distract Chin Ming. He will understand, he will want to make sure that she doesn't take unnecessary risks.'

'I'm sure he'll agree with us, and if he doesn't, I'll tell him about Raffles and Sophia.'

This time, Wing Yee was totally baffled, she hadn't any idea what Dick was talking about.

'When they left here, Sophia was five months pregnant. The baby was due in October but was born early, in September. Not long afterwards, Sophia developed a dreadful fever. Others suffered from the same illness, including Flora, the baby. I think Sophia must have been worse than anyone else and she couldn't look after the baby. Flora died at the end of November.'

'Why didn't I know that?' Wing Yee exclaimed.

'It's a few years ago now and it was a long time before I found out; Raffles eventually told me in one of his letters. But you're right, we must warn Edmund about what we know and we must make sure that no one tells Chin Ming.'

****

The following morning when Dick stopped his carriage in front of the Beaumonts' house, he tied the reins to a post and told Tijah he needed to have a word with Edmund. He suggested she should go inside to find Wing Yee and they both wait for him on the veranda. 'I won't be long,' he said, as he went in search of his friend. He'd given it a lot of thought overnight, wondering how he could have a private conversation with Edmund without Chin Ming wanting to know what was going on.

'How's the book going?' he asked when he eventually tracked Edmund down amongst a cluster of young papaya trees.

'Actually, it's all coming together well now. It was difficult to concentrate when I first returned from Malacca, there was so much else going on. But now we don't have to worry about Tijah, I'm spending the afternoons writing and not having to constantly entertain Charlotte.'

'I didn't realise there was a problem,' Dick said.

'Not a problem. I love my daughter and she can be very entertaining, but all the while Chin Ming was in the sick room with Tijah, Charlotte was unsettled. She's too young to explain what had happened, we just told her that Tijah was unwell, but she didn't understand. She wanted to know when our guest would be well enough to play with her, when her mother would not be too tired to tell her a story at bedtime.'

'But she's less anxious now?'

'Chin Ming has persuaded her that she will have a very important role when the new baby is born, being the big sister to two younger siblings.' A huge grin spread across Edmund's face. 'I just hope she doesn't turn into a little tyrant.'

They both started to laugh at this idea, and right on cue, Charlotte trotted along the path towards them with a small trowel in one hand and the familiar blue sash trailing along behind her. 'Hello, Papa,' she said, 'can I show Uncle Dick the flowers in my garden?'

After they had both inspected the bright orange shrub she was so proud of and praised her efforts, Edmund had given her the task of making a small channel in the soil for planting seeds. He hoped that would keep her occupied while he continued his conversation with Dick.

'I was editing the first few chapters the other day,' Edmund said, 'and began to make some notes about the illustrations when you're able to work on them.'

'That's why I've come to see you,' Dick said. 'I've had some ideas about that too. Would you be able to come to the office this afternoon? We could give it some serious thought.'

'The office you've set up in Alexander's warehouse, not your studio?' Edmund said.

'I'll be taking Wing Yee and Tijah into town as usual, so I'll be in the office anyway. Is that a problem, would you rather not leave Chin Ming?'

'I could come down about mid-afternoon if that suits you?

Chin Ming usually takes a nap then and May Lin will be here if she needs anything; Sanjay will be here too, of course.'

*****

Dick spent the first hour of their meeting listening to Edmund and making suggestions about the illustrations that would enhance his manuscript. He promised to produce a few sketches by the end of the week and then they could decide how to proceed.

'Actually, discussing the illustrations for the book was an excuse to get you here this afternoon,' Dick admitted.

Edmund looked up from the pages he'd been sifting. 'Why the mystery?' he said.

Dick began by telling Edmund about the men he suspected of smuggling the women into the Settlement. He outlined everything he knew about them and the near encounters that two of them had had with Wing Yee. 'We had a long talk yesterday evening,' he said. 'Wing Yee has told me about both the men she encountered at Madam Ho's, but what Choo Keng has overheard when the men visit the coffee shop is vague and muddled. Not everything makes sense.'

'I thought you said you'd sketched one of the men,' Edmund said.

'I managed a rough sketch of the person who visited the coffee shop when I was there and another of the three of them together – done from here. So, you see, I haven't much detail. The only positive thing is that the person in the first drawing had a moustache and Wing Yee says one of the men she saw at the clinic had whiskers!' He rifled through a pile of papers, then pulled open a drawer. 'Ah, here they are,' he said, 'here's the moustache, but it's hardly any use for identification.'

'But the notes you made might be useful,' Edmund said. 'You've described the colour of their garments in great detail ...'

'We can't go around following everyone who wears a tawny frock coat, long black boots, or colourful cravats. We'd be pursuing most of the European population if we did.'

'So, what are you suggesting?' Edmund said.

'I don't have a precise plan right now,' Dick said, 'but Wing Yee and I have discussed various possibilities. We wanted you to be aware of the situation, that's all. We both agree it's in Chin Ming's best interests not to be told about any of this for the time being.'

Edmund burst out laughing. 'You seriously think I can keep something like this from my wife?'

'Think about it,' Dick said. 'You know what's she's like; she'll want to confront Madam Ho or anyone else she thinks might provide us with some answers. She's about to have another baby, do you really want to jeopardise her health or that of the baby?'

The colour drained from Edmund's face and his heart began to race. 'You really think it's that serious?'

'I believe it could be,' Dick said. 'These men, whoever they are, have gone to a great deal of effort to bring the women here, to deliver them to Madam Ho in secret, and are, no doubt, being well recompensed for their trouble.'

They continued to discuss the situation for another hour. Dick shared some of his plans with Edmund but was careful not to go into any great detail so that his friend would not feel even more uncomfortable about not sharing the things he had learned with his wife.

'I've got an idea,' Edmund said, rubbing the side of his neck as he continued to sort out his thoughts.

Dick waited. He knew he was asking a lot of his friend and he hoped he'd managed to convince him of the logic behind his proposal to keep Chin Ming in the dark for the time being. He hoped Edmund was not about to suggest otherwise.

'I think you should talk to Sanjay,' Edmund said. 'Since he's been living with us and working for me full time, he's begun to talk to me more. There is something about his past that I've still not got to the bottom of, but he's mentioned seeing someone walking around town that he recognised – someone who was in the prison in Calcutta.'

'I would have thought that most of the convict gangs comprised men who had come from Calcutta. It's inevitable he would recognise some of them.'

'The man he told me about wasn't working on a building site or digging a road. He wasn't here as a prisoner. He was crossing North Bridge Road, heading in the direction of Market Street.'

CHAPTER 21
15th July 1831

The following morning, Dick hurried along the road, back towards the Beaumonts' house. He'd slept badly again, considering how he might proceed. The only evidence of corruption he'd been able to establish was flimsy. He hoped that Edmund had been successful in persuading Sanjay to talk to him.

When he reached the house, there was no sign of movement; perhaps the household was still asleep? He decided to sit quietly on the veranda and wait for some signs of activity. The outlook from this house was entirely different from the one he enjoyed at his own home, even though they were so close together. The road between them wound around the eastern side of the hill just far enough to provide a view of the new waterway that had been dug to irrigate the padi fields north of the mangrove swamp. His concentration was such that he didn't notice the door from the drawing room open to reveal Edmund, fully dressed and looking cheerful.

'I've had a word with Sanjay,' he said, 'and he's happy to talk to you.'

'You made me jump,' Dick said, 'I was daydreaming. The view from here has a strange appeal, I'd like to paint it one day.'

'We'd love that, but I think you have enough to do at present. Sanjay has asked me to sit in when you talk to him, I hope you don't mind.'

'Of course not. I'd be glad of your company and any thoughts you want to add. Where is he?'

'I suggested we meet near the garden shed. No one will overhear us there, and if Chin Ming wants to know what we're doing, we can say we're telling Sanjay about the illustrations for the book.'

'You're becoming devious.'

'No, it's the people you might be dealing with who are devious, and in the light of our conversation about them, I don't want Chin Ming getting upset. As you reminded me yesterday, it's important to make sure she doesn't get involved with the baby being due in a couple of months.'

*****

During their conversation, Sanjay told Dick about the man he'd seen several months ago, a man that he'd recognised from the jail in Calcutta.

'It was early morning, sahib. Each day, escort take convicts to place they work. This man, he making to wait on pavement while we cross road. He not happy. If he not make such big noise, I not look to see who make trouble. But, sahib, this man he good at making trouble.'

'I imagine the number of people you came across in the jail was considerable, but you obviously remember this one very well, Sanjay. Do you mind telling me why? What happened there that made him stand out?'

Sanjay lowered his eyes and fidgeted with the hem of his kurta. He swallowed hard and then looked towards Edmund for reassurance. Edmund nodded and moved from where he was sitting to be closer to Sanjay.

'No need to worry, Sanjay, you can speak freely to my friend,' Edmund said in a voice that he hoped would be encouraging. 'No one is going to criticise you or pass judgment; we are eager to hear what you have to say.'

'It about my brother,' he said, waiting for a reaction, but both Dick and Edmund remained silent.

'This man cheat my brother,' he added.

Little by little, Sanjay told them about his younger brother's addiction to opium. Prakash was born with no hearing or ability to speak. All his life, Sanjay had tried to protect his sibling, but Prakash was often bullied and eventually he fell in with a bad crowd. Prakash was the one who took the blame when his so-called friends got involved in stealing. They had all run away, and because Prakash couldn't speak up, the authorities had arrested him and put him in prison. 'I take some plants from Botanic Garden where I work. I make sure they see me. I get arrested and put in jail,' Sanjay told them. 'This way I can join Prakash and – what is it you say – keep in my eye?'

'Keep an eye on him,' Edmund said. 'That was a very generous thing to do, Sanjay,' Edmund said, then straightaway rephrased his comment to accommodate Sanjay's limited use of English. 'You did a good thing. I'm sure your brother was glad you were there to look after him.'

'Alas, I too late,' Sanjay said.

'What do you mean?' Dick said. 'I thought your arrest happened shortly after Prakash had received his sentence.'

'My employer, he speak for me. He say I good worker and they make mistake; he try save me from jail. I tell him NO, he wrong, I am bad man. But still I not find Prakash.'

'But you did find him in the end?' Dick said.

'No, sahib. That man – the one I see here in street - he do bad things in prison. Prison Governor say he must go on ship to Aus-tral – ya.'

Neither Edmund nor Dick could believe their ears. They didn't want to interrupt in case Sanjay lost his nerve, but waiting for him to reveal the details of his story was almost more than they could bear. Eventually, Sanjay told them everything he knew.

It had taken months before he could get any of the other

prisoners to tell him what had happened to his brother. The man he had recognised shortly after arriving in Singapore had persuaded Prakash to swap places with him. How it had happened and why no one seemed to know. None of the authorities had seemed to notice, nothing had ever come to light. The man had a reputation within the prison for being able to obtain goods with which he could bribe the jailors, sell to other inmates at an exorbitant rate, or simply indulge his own selfish existence. Everyone knew the man was a bully, but they were all too afraid of him to complain.

'And did you ever know his name?' Dick said.

'He have strange name. Some say Dutch, but I not know,' Sanjay said. 'His name was Pee-ter, Pee-ter Stef-fens.'

'What did you say?' Dick said, giving Edmund a sidelong glance. Sanjay repeated the name and Dick gasped; an incredulous stare settled on his face. He felt as if he'd been punched in the stomach.

Edmund broke the silence. He thanked Sanjay for talking to them and suggested he return to watering the newly planted saplings. Edmund waited until they were alone before he dared look at Dick.

'Pieter Steffens. PIETER STEFFENS! Here!' Dick shrieked. 'I can't believe it. What about Chin Ming? What about Wing Yee? Do you think he knows they are still here in Singapore?'

Edmund opened his mouth to speak, but Dick's mind was racing and he gave his friend no opportunity to respond.

'If Sanjay is correct, if it was indeed Pieter Steffens who he saw that day, then we all need to be extremely cautious. He was dangerous in the past and I have no doubt that he hasn't changed in the slightest.' Dick did a quick mental calculation; it was over eight years since Raffles had arrested him and sent him to trial in Calcutta. They'd received news about his eventual imprisonment there but had given no thought as to what would happen when he had served his sentence. Had they even known that he was supposed to be transported to

Australia? Dick couldn't remember.

'What are you going to do?' Edmund said, cutting through the silence with a crack in his voice that failed to hide his concern.

'I think I should tell Alexander,' Dick said, 'and the sooner the better. He had just been appointed Chief Magistrate when Raffles set up the investigation into Steffens' various crimes and he was part of the group who conducted the interrogation.'

'Am I right in thinking it was Alexander who accompanied Steffens to the trial in Calcutta?' Edmund said. 'I seem to remember Chin Ming telling me all about that. You stood with her and Wing Yee and watched the ship depart from the top of Bukit Larangan, is that correct?'

'Yes,' said Dick, 'I'd forgotten but you're right. They didn't want to watch, but I encouraged them to do so. I thought they ought to witness his departure from their lives.'

'And now he's back,' Edmund said. 'Dick, please don't say anything to Chin Ming yet. I don't want her to worry. The memory of that man is the last thing she needs right now.'

'Of course, I won't say anything,' Dick said. 'I won't mention it to Wing Yee either – not until I must. I think she never really got over what Steffens did to her; she appears to be confident and cheery on the surface, but deep down ...'

'We'd better get back,' Edmund said. 'She'll be expecting you to take her and Tijah to the clinic. I wouldn't be surprised if she was already waiting on the veranda for you. What shall we say when she sees us appear from the garden?'

'We can tell the truth – or part of it at least. Don't forget, we agreed to say, if she asks, that I needed to talk to you and Sanjay about the illustrations for your book.'

'You seem to have everything worked out,' Edmund said. 'Better make a move before the women start asking awkward questions. And you're right, we should try to behave normally, as far as we can, at least for the time being.'

*****

Dick dropped his two passengers close to Monkey Bridge about half an hour later. He tugged at the reins and turned the horse in the direction of High Street. As far as Wing Yee and Tijah were concerned, he was heading towards his office in Alexander Johnston's warehouse and everything was perfectly normal.

He knocked on Alexander's door, but there was no reply. He pushed the door open, but there was no sign of activity. He hurried into the clerk's office and made enquiries. He was informed that Mr Johnston had attended a function last night and was not expected until the middle of the morning. The head clerk asked if there was anything that he could help with, but Dick shook his head and promised to return later.

He spent the next couple of hours making notes. He jotted down every single aspect of his conversation with Sanjay so that he would be ready when Alexander asked his usual probing questions. The notes were extensive and he'd covered several pages when a blast of warm air announced the door to his office opening; in the doorway stood the tall, slim figure of Alexander Johnston.

'Lim Chee said you were looking for me. Do you have a problem? Some of the clauses in that last pile of legal papers I left for you can be quite confusing. They're not exactly written in the most accessible way.'

'I do have something I need to discuss with you, but it's not about those papers. I'm afraid I haven't had time to look at them yet. Do you recollect the man who caused so much trouble for Raffles, Chin Ming, and Wing Yee? You accompanied him to Calcutta; his name Pieter Steffens?'

'I'll never forget him, or that journey. Why do you ask?'

'I think he's back in Singapore.'

Johnston steadied himself, holding onto the doorpost. 'Bloody man! Damn his eyes!' Johnston spat out the words as he moved to a chair beside Dick's desk. He sat bolt upright and repeated his curse. Dick had never heard him swear before.

'Are you sure? Have you seen him?'

'I think I may have done. Until this morning, everything was very muddled. I'd heard about two men who met at Choo Keng's coffee stall. Choo Keng himself confirmed this and told me another man occasionally joined them. Their comings and goings seemed to coincide with the dates when new groups of women arrived at Madam Ho's emporium.'

Dick continued to tell Alexander all that he knew about the mysterious trio and the connection he thought they had with the young women from Sumatra.

'But what makes you think one of those men is Pieter Steffens? Don't forget, in order to prove any link between the men and Madam Ho, you're going to need some firm evidence.'

'Well, that's why I need to talk to you,' Dick said. 'Edmund suggested that I speak to Sanjay. He's the so-called convict who is helping Edmund develop his experimental garden.'

Alexander looked puzzled. He remembered the quietly-spoken Indian from the time he'd spent convincing the authorities that his talents would be better spent in an occupation other than building roads but he failed to see the connection.

'Sanjay and Edmund talk about different plants and share ideas. Quite recently, Sanjay told Edmund about his background, why he had gone to prison, and ....'

'I'm sorry Dick, I still don't understand how this all relates to the man you think is Pieter Steffens,' Alexander said, his brow becoming more and more creased by the second.

Dick apologised and then focused on the essential information it was vital for Alexander to hear. In the hour that followed, Alexander interrogated Dick as thoroughly as if he was standing in the witness box himself. Occasionally, Dick consulted his notes to be sure of dates, times, and anything else he could think of that would help to substantiate what he was saying.

'You've done a good job,' Alexander said. 'Sanjay will make an excellent witness if he's willing to testify. Unfortunately, all we know right now is that the man we sent to Calcutta eight years ago is back in Singapore. In order to prove that he is up to his old tricks, that he is involved in anything illegal, we need substantive proof. I think you should visit Baba Tan. The position of his warehouse enables him to pick up all sorts of information, snippets that may not have made much sense at the time, but in the light of what we now know might add up to something useful.'

CHAPTER 22
14th July 1831

Stefan woke later than normal. The after-effect of a night at the brothel in Hokkien Street and copious amounts of alcohol, followed by the shock of seeing that young girl with the bitch had addled his brain. His dreams last night had been haunted by that scene; playing and replaying from different angles. He had tossed and turned until he eventually sank into a deep, exhausted state and now he emerged feeling fuzzy-headed and confused.

He heard Victor call his name. He struggled out of bed and pulled the sarong, which had parted company with him during the night, around his middle.

'We agreed to have breakfast together,' Victor said suddenly standing before him. 'There is much to discuss about our next trip. Pull yourself together, man. I'll be waiting for you on my veranda.'

Stefan walked slowly into the adjacent room where a substantial stone water tank was housed. He removed the lid and lowered a large wooden ladle into the cool liquid. He closed his eyes and poured the rainwater over his head, then he continued the action until his whole body was soaked and all his nerve endings had been kicked back into life. A frenetic mosquito just escaped being squashed as he pulled a towel from a hook on the back of the door; he wound the fabric around his damp, glistening flesh. He rubbed himself down quickly, donned a fresh sarong, and slipped his feet into a pair of raffia sandals. He arrived at Victor's house just as the coffee was being poured.

'We're going to Java,' Victor said, looking pleased with himself.

Stefan almost choked on the slice of papaya he'd begun to consume. He coughed, stared hard at Victor, and said, 'Since when?'

'My associate summoned me yesterday afternoon,' Victor said, 'There was a note waiting for me when I was leaving Madam Ho.'

'Does that mean he's no longer feeling short-changed? Has his mood improved? Might he think about paying out the additional money owing to us after all?'

'Not a chance,' Victor said. 'He says this is an opportunity to redeem ourselves.'

'Damned cheek!' Stefan said, glaring at Victor.

'I think his bad mood was about more than the missing item of cargo. He tells me someone's been asking awkward questions. He's getting quite anxious and suggests we branch out – look at a different type of cargo for the time being.'

'What sort of questions – and who is it that's doing the asking?' Stefan said, edging forward on his seat. 'Are you sure he's not just punishing us for losing that damned woman?'

'He wouldn't divulge exactly what he'd heard, but he's obviously worried and doesn't want to take any more risks at present. You're wrong in assuming we are being penalised.'

'If we're not transporting women, what exactly is he expecting us to do? I assume it won't be entirely legal.'

'My contact has a colleague in Batavia who is willing to sell us guns at a very reasonable price. There's a good market for such items with one of the Malay sultans. The Siamese invaded and occupied his territory about a decade ago and he's decided to retaliate, at last.'

'Guns! My contact! Who is this man who knows so much?

Even though I've been present on a couple of occasions, you've never introduced us. You've never so much as told me his name.'

'Let's call him Smith, shall we? I believe the English use it all the time to cover a multitude of sins,' Victor said, shifting about uncomfortably. 'I met him when we went to Malacca, that's when he invited me to join in with some of his business interests.'

'Smith, Brown, it doesn't really matter,' Stefan said, knowing that he was in no position to criticise people who decided to conceal their identity by using a false name. 'The thing is, this man determines what he wants us to collect and where from. We have no control over the decisions he makes and yet it's you and me who take all the risks.'

'We get well paid for what we do, and I was under the impression you were content with the arrangement,' Victor said. 'It's much better than sitting behind a desk in Market Street all day long, surely? Besides, it's Smith who is privy to this information about whoever is asking too many questions. You could say he's protecting us.'

'Protecting his own interests more like,' Stefan snapped.

'I don't know what's got into you,' Victor retaliated. 'I thought you'd be happy to return to the place you've told me so much about – the place where you grew up.'

It was true. At any other time, Stefan would have been overjoyed at the prospect of returning to Batavia, especially with someone else paying for him to do so. Why did he and Victor have to leave so soon, he asked himself; the timing couldn't be more inconvenient.

He'd now watched the three people he blamed along with Raffles for his arrest and imprisonment long enough. His constant trekking up and down to Bukit Selegie for the past few months had at last paid off. He'd noted their lifestyle and ferreted out all the information he needed; he'd identified their vulnerability. His opportunity to gain revenge was imminent.

A similar prospect might not present itself again; by the time he returned from Java, it might be too late.

'Fine,' Stefan said. 'No need to get upset. I'm happy to go to Batavia, just as long as we don't have to leave immediately. There's some other business I need to deal with first!'

'Well, you'd better be quick about it,' Victor replied. 'Smith has begun to make arrangements to hire a boat. Once he's got a crew together and purchased supplies, he'll be wanting us to get underway. I think you should plan to tie up whatever it is that's bothering you soon. If everything goes according to plan, I imagine we'll be leaving in a week, two at the most.'

*****

Over the next few days, Stefan busied himself making enquiries. He knew where the bitch lived, he now knew where she worked. What he didn't know was exactly how the clinic operated. He could hardly pretend to be someone in need of medical advice. He couldn't risk the chance of her recognising him but he needed to know what she was using to make her herbal concoctions and where it was all stored. He'd already decided it would be wise to obtain some sort of sedative in case his plan to lure the brat away failed. If that happened, he would need some way of keeping her quiet.

A week later, he was no further forward. He decided his only hope was to go to Cross Street and fix his eyes upon the elaborately-carved door of the clinic until he saw someone emerge who he recognised. Someone who would be able to provide the answers he needed. He settled himself under the shade of a tembusu tree, pretending to read a newspaper he'd purchased from a vendor in Commercial Square. Whenever he raised his head, his gaze travelled straight towards the same spot. Nearly an hour had passed when his patience was rewarded. The door opened, revealing none other than Victor himself. Stefan smiled. Now I have you, my friend, he thought.

That evening, after they had eaten, Stefan pushed back his chair and gazed across the table with a lopsided smile on his face. The two of them were alone. 'I trust you've not caught the pox,' he said.

'What do you mean?' Victor countered, looking startled.

'I've seen you emerge from a certain lady's dwelling before anyone else has risen,' Stefan said, 'before her husband returns from his fishing trips.'

All the colour drained from Victor's face.

'And this afternoon, you visited the clinic in Cross Street. I thought there might be a connection or was it your favourite whore who ...'

'Have you been following me?' Victor shouted at the top of his voice. The blood had returned to his veins and his cheeks had turned to a deep crimson. 'I thought you had urgent business of your own to attend to.'

'I was there merely by chance,' Stefan said. 'But I must admit the place intrigues me. What is she like – the woman who runs it? I've heard she makes all her own medicines, is that correct? Does she keep stocks of them at the clinic?'

Victor spent the remainder of the evening telling Stefan something about Wing Yee and her young helper. He said he'd heard about her special healing powers from Madam Ho – and no, he didn't have the pox, merely an open cut on his leg that refused to mend. He saw no reason why Stefan shouldn't know that Madam Ho was employing Wing Yee to check on the physical well-being of the women they had brought from Sumatra but he was less specific about providing answers to Stefan's further demands for information. He wondered why his illusive colleague was interested in knowing where Wing Yee prepared her remedies and where they were stored. If Stefan was thinking of breaking away from their business arrangement and setting up on his own, Victor was determined not to make it easy for him. Some things were best kept to himself.

So, when Stefan returned to his own quarters, the only

useful information he had gleaned was that the bitch was helping Madam Ho and the young girl was helping her. He still had no idea where the medicines were stored. It also occurred to him that he had no real knowledge of sedatives, let alone how to use them. He enjoyed the occasional opium pipe, but that was entirely different. He was beginning to think he had set himself an impossible task.

*****

Being totally unaware that she and Tijah had been the centre of conversation between Victor and Stefan the previous evening, Wing Yee awoke full of energy. Baba Tan had informed her that a large consignment of herbs had arrived from China. Her stocks had depleted considerably during the weeks she had been treating the Sumatran women, so she was eager to get everything unpacked, labelled, and stored in the various containers set aside for the purpose.

Tijah was excited too. She was now familiar with everything Wing Yee used, but she had yet to experience the thrill of opening boxes and unfolding layers of sacking to discover what lay beneath.

Dick decided to postpone his visit to Baba Tan. He wanted to be able to speak to him in confidence and not cause Wing Yee and Tijah any unnecessary alarm. He arrived at the Beaumonts' house earlier than usual; Wing Yee was pleased as she was keen to get to work. Today, they all travelled to Mr Johnston's warehouse together. Several ships had arrived in the harbour yesterday and Boat Quay was already buzzing with activity. Wing Yee led the way, dodging between coils of rope, crates of vegetables, and gangs of coolies shifting heavy loads from the bumboats to one of the vast number of warehouses that now lined the wharf.

Tijah was finding it difficult to keep up with Wing Yee's long strides. She held her sarong away from her ankles to help increase her pace, but she had much shorter legs than the older woman and she was less familiar with the route. Wing Yee was well ahead when Tijah found herself sliding along at a strange angle; a piece of overripe fruit had been carelessly dropped and she hadn't seen it. Unable to regain her balance, she found herself moving rapidly towards Choo Keng's coffee stall where she crashed unceremoniously onto the hard surface of the pavement.

The two men sitting there enjoying their drinks looked down to see what had jostled their stools. They both laughed and offered no help. Tijah, full of embarrassment, scrambled to her feet, and as she regained her composure, she found herself looking straight into the eyes of one of the men. It was the same man who had followed Wing Yee to the clinic.

Tijah grabbed at the hem of her sarong and hurried away from the scene before Wing Yee had even noticed she was lagging behind; it had all happened so quickly. She kept twisting her bangle around her arm as if she was securing the lid of a jar, making sure that nothing escaped. She was too embarrassed to say anything and she knew Wing Yee was in a hurry. It was more important to help with the unpacking than to recount the embarrassing incident right now. That could wait until later.

＊＊＊＊

Stefan leapt to his feet. 'I've just remembered something,' he said and rushed off along the quay, leaving Victor both bemused and annoyed.

Tijah had just caught up with Wing Yee when he saw them both. Wing Yee opened the door to Baba Tan's warehouse, she ushered Tijah to go in ahead of her. He hurried to catch up. It occurred to him that this might be where the bitch kept her store of plants, roots, and the other materials she used to make her salves and potions. It couldn't be a coincidence, he thought, that they had come here today rather than going to the clinic. Several vessels had arrived in the last few days; it was highly likely that she would come here to deal with a fresh consignment. Perhaps, if he could get inside, he would have time to find something of use as a sedative after all.

He paced around for almost half an hour, completely absorbed with his own thoughts. It was by sheer chance that he caught sight of Mukesh, the moneylender, heading straight towards him. Stefan was wearing European clothes today rather than a kurta and the traditional Indian trousers that he'd worn when they had worked alongside each other. Nevertheless, he couldn't risk being recognised. He dodged into a narrow alleyway and moved along it quickly until he reached North Bridge Road. He would have to find some other means of keeping the brat quiet.

*****

That same evening, after supper had been cleared away and baby Tomas was sleeping, Tijah tip-toed onto the veranda where Dick and Sujana were sitting quietly together, gazing at the deep night sky and enjoying the nightly concert provided by the cicadas. She was hesitant to intrude upon the couple as she knew such moments were precious, and since Dick had taken up his office in Mr Johnston's warehouse, this was their only opportunity to spend time together. However, she had too many concerns buzzing around in her head; they wouldn't go away no matter how hard she tried to dismiss them. She needed their advice.

It was Sujana who was the first to become aware of her presence. 'Is something the matter, Tijah?'

'Can I ask you a question?' she said.

'Would you like to speak to Sujana alone?' Dick asked, being aware that it was unusual to see Tijah without Fakina in tow. He thought that whatever the young girl needed to say, it might be easier if he absented himself, leaving her to confide in another woman.

'Please,' Tijah said, 'it's something I'd like to ask both of you.'

They invited her to sit on a chair right next to them and handed her a glass of pineapple juice.

'If you were me,' Tijah said, trying to look grown-up so they would take her seriously, 'and you were hoping to find your father, where would you begin?' She lowered her head and took a deep breath before continuing. 'When I first had the idea to come to Singapore to see if I could find my father, I hadn't really thought about how to go about looking for him. I rather assumed he would be easy to recognise.'

Sujana moved to the edge of her chair and took hold of Tijah's hands. 'We have been very remiss,' she said, 'please forgive us. We should have been more supportive. It's been so good to have you here, to see you and Fakina become good friends, I almost forgot ...'

'We've all been busy of late,' said Dick before his wife could finish. 'I've been distracted by people who break the law, Sujana and Fakina are always busy running the house and looking after Tomas, and you have been busy working with Wing Yee. But we shouldn't have neglected you. However, the truth is, with such little information to go on, it's not going to be easy.'

Tijah slumped further down in her chair. She pulled back from Sujana's gentle hold and began to rub her hands together. She avoided looking at either Dick or Sujana.

'Let's see what facts we do have to work with,' Dick said, trying to focus. 'What did the people in your kampong back home in Malacca say, exactly? What did they tell you about the man who visited your grandfather during Ramadan? Has your aunt ever described the man your mother married?'

'You're bombarding the poor child with too many questions,' Sujana said, chiding her impatient husband.

'They would never tell me my father's name,' she said. 'Wing Yee says that lots of Europeans came here from Malacca around the time I was born. She said that's where Baba Tan came from; she says she'll ask him if there was anyone he remembers.'

'It's true Baba Tan came here along with other Peranakan and Chinese traders just after the Settlement was first established. He might well remember others who came from Malacca around that time.'

Tijah's eyes brightened and she sat up straight in the chair.

'Has anything happened that made you want to talk to us this evening?' Dick said.

'There's a man,' Tijah said in a voice hardly more than a whisper. 'I've seen him twice now. The first time was across the street from the clinic and then again this morning.' She lowered her eyes to cover her embarrassment. 'I slipped and almost collided with his stool.'

'Have you mentioned this to Wing Yee?' Dick said.

'I did the first time because I thought he'd been following her. Today, we've been so busy, there was no opportunity. Both times, there was something odd about the way he looked at me ...I just wondered ...'

'Looked at you in what sort of way?' Sujana asked, trying to keep her voice calm whilst casting a sidelong glance at Dick.

Dick knew what his wife was thinking, that having seen Tijah, the man in question might have it in mind to recruit her into Madam Ho's employment. And in fact, it was highly probable.

He became aware of Sujana's soothing tones. She had a gift for offering comfort which provided a blend of optimism laced with caution. He was grateful that his opinion was not specifically called for at this moment, there were too many random thoughts racing through his mind. Tijah stood up. The expression on her face was far more relaxed than when she appeared before them a short time ago. She returned to join Fakina, thanking them both for their promise of help.

'Something is troubling you,' Sujana said as soon as Tijah was out of earshot. 'Do you think it's safe for Tijah to continue working alongside Wing Yee?'

'I wasn't too worried when Wing Yee told me about the first incident,' he said, 'It was the day she had to leave Tijah alone at the clinic while she visited Madam Ho, but now I'm not so sure.'

'But there's something else, isn't there?' Sujana said.

'How well you know me,' Dick said, with a wan smile. They continued to talk about all the issues causing Dick concern for the remainder of the evening. By the time the flames in the lamps illuminating the veranda had burned low and begun to extinguish, they were both exhausted.

CHAPTER 23
Late July

Dick had hardly slept, despite his feeling of fatigue. When he did drift off, it was only to dream of Wing Yee and Tijah with grey shadows of male figures lurking in the background. He confused what Wing Yee had told him with the things Tijah had said and woke abruptly, his body hot and clammy. It occurred to him that the men Tijah had crashed into yesterday might be the same pair he'd been keeping an eye on at the coffee stall. This raised his anxiety level another notch as he was sure those men were involved with the smuggling business. It didn't take much imagination to see how they might want to include Tijah in their plans. It was all so muddled.

At first light, he dragged himself out of bed and went in search of pen and paper. A cockerel crowed a long way off; the only other sounds came intermittently when the house timbers stretched and creaked. The notes he'd accumulated over the past few months were safely locked in the drawer of his desk in the office. He contemplated going down to the warehouse and letting himself in so that he could extract them but he didn't want Sujana to worry when she woke and found him absent. Instead, he went to his studio, the faint odour of linseed and walnut oils still hanging in the air, even though he hadn't picked up a brush for well over two weeks.

He found a large sheet of paper and divided it into three columns. Under each one, he recorded what he knew of his three main suspects, the date they had been seen, and by whom. He added notes about their physique and the way they dressed, anything he could think of to help identify them in future.

The third man was the unknown factor with no hint of his name, let alone his nationality. Dick had made notes about his garments when he'd seen him drinking Choo Keng's coffee, but the sketch he'd done was hasty and captured only a side-view; it recorded nothing tangible apart from the moustache. Even when he'd witnessed the argument between the three of them, there was very little to add. The man had headed towards Commercial Square, but that alone didn't convey any-thing meaningful about his place of work or where he might live.

The other two had headed towards Monkey Bridge. Might they be heading towards the Malay kampong? Who had told him the kampong might be relevant? The more he looked into it, the more complicated it seemed to become.

Dick held his head between his hands and rubbed away at his temples. Something was niggling inside his brain; it was a comment Wing Yee had made, or could it have been Tijah? He got up from his chair and paced around, still unable to tease out any detail that might provide the evidence he needed. He walked into a cobweb, its delicate gossamer threads tickled his mouth and chin. He was wiping away the fine strands when he remembered Wing Yee's description of this unknown man. She had been adamant that he was not the same one who had barged into her when she opened Madam Ho's front door last week. She'd said the mystery man had a fat face and what she'd described as whiskers. The first man he'd sketched, sitting near to him at the coffee stall, certainly had an ample moustache, but was his face particularly chubby? Dick still suspected he was the ringleader but there was no way of establishing his identity. He decided to call him moustache-man from now on to distinguish from the other two.

Dick searched his brain for anything else that might help; an alarm bell rang in his head. He remembered Choo Keng mentioning moneylenders and Market Street. He'd meant to follow up the reference at the time, but something had happened to distract him; had he missed a clue along the way? There was also another person to consider, the Indian who had vanished. Choo Keng had said that this man used to meet one of the others for coffee earlier in the year but hadn't been seen for months. Perhaps this is where he should begin, try to find this man, discover anything he could about his relationship with the trio – and why he no longer visited the coffee house. Alexander had suggested speaking to Baba Tan in case he was still in touch with his friend Chanda Khan; he'd said the Indian merchant might know who to talk to in Market Street.

That had been almost a week ago. He'd postponed the idea because he didn't want to discuss his misgivings in front of Wing Yee and Tijah and then for one reason or another, he'd not got around to it. He cursed himself for the oversight and vowed to make it a priority later that morning.

*****

Dick ate his breakfast quickly, finishing just as Sujana arrived on the veranda.

'How long have you been up? I hope you're not intending to do anything dangerous. I've got a strange feeling about all this.'

He reassured her before making his excuses and telling her that he needed to check something in his office. He spent an hour there scrutinising all the notes he'd locked away in his desk and compared them with the chart he'd drafted during the early hours. He re-examined names he'd identified after visiting all the merchants along Boat Quay, six men he'd thought worthy of further investigation. He checked his notes again to see if there was anything that might connect one of them with the man he suspected of being the ringleader of the smuggling gang, but nothing was obvious.

He was now certain that the best place to proceed with his investigations was to track down the missing Indian. Possibly, the reason he no longer frequented the coffee stall was that he'd quarrelled with the other man. If that was the case, he might be feeling aggrieved and willing to talk. Dick gathered his notes together and left the office, heading towards Boat Quay.

'Welcome, welcome!' Baba Tan said, chuckling with delight. 'It's too long since you visited me. Sit. We must share some tea together.'

Dick was accustomed to being greeted in this way and he was happy to observe the usual courtesies. He seated himself opposite his friend, waited for the tea to be served. This ritual, together with the familiarity of Baba Tan's warehouse, helped him to settle down. From his first visit here, nearly ten years ago, he had always been enthralled by the rich kaleidoscope of silks from China and the brightly-patterned cottons from India; the place had a magic all its own.

Baba Tan listened patiently while Dick told him everything he'd discovered about the men who had been smuggling women into the Settlement, then he voiced his concerns about the mysterious Indian moneylender.

'I do know one or two of the people in Market Street,' Baba Tan said, 'and I could certainly make some introductions, but I think we would be better off consulting my old friend Chanda Khan.'

'How is he these days?' Dick said. Although he'd hoped this would be Baba Tan's response, he was aware that he hadn't seen Chanda Khan since the humiliation caused by his so-called nephew over five years ago.

'It took a long while for him to get over that business, but he's been much more like his old self of late. I think, nowadays, he's just glad that his sister wasn't alive to witness the behaviour of her wayward son. I will visit my friend this evening and ask for his advice about your missing Indian moneylender.'

When he'd finished talking to Baba Tan, Dick felt exhausted. His lack of sleep was catching up with him, and his failure to pull the different strands of the puzzle together was draining all his resolve.

✱✱✱✱✱

Three days later, Baba Tan reported back to Dick. His friend's advice had been to go to Market Street themselves and talk to some of the moneylenders. 'Several rumours have been circulating about a man who arrived from Calcutta to work there. Chanda Khan thinks this man might be worthy of further investigation. One moment he'd been working away at his desk, the next he suddenly disappeared. Someone had apparently come looking for him - a European merchant from Calcutta it was believed - but he'd gone away and never returned. Maybe he'd caught up with the person he was seeking, maybe not.'

Dick had a sinking feeling in the pit of his stomach; this suggestion merely reinforced his regret that he'd not visited Market Street sooner. He asked Baba Tan to accompany him.

'Now is a good time to go,' Baba Tan said. 'The men who are desperate for money arrive very early and those able to pay back any of their loan arrive in the late afternoon when they have finished their labours, there will be a lull in trade at this time.'

Baba Tan made enquiries amongst the first group of moneylenders, but they all shook their heads and continued to record details of the morning's transactions in their huge ledgers. The air was oppressive between these closely-packed wooden desks. Each was occupied by a man intent on keep-

246

ing accurate records and being available to offer a reason-able rate to any poor soul whose situation forced them to seek out the services of the Chetty community. Baba Tan contin-ued along the periphery where it was easier to see where he was going and who he was approaching. Dick ventured a lit-tle further into the overcrowded rows of moneylending estab-lishments, asking the same question again and again. No one was able – or willing – to give an answer. The atmosphere inside was stuffy, everything was packed together so tightly; he needed to get out onto the street again. He'd decided not to waste any more time when a furtive-looking man lifted his head and peered at him through rheumy eyes. He paused for a long time, then Dick asked if he knew anything of a man from Calcutta who was reputed to have worked alongside the other moneylenders earlier in the year.

The man looked as if he was weighing up his response. He sighed heavily before turning his body away. Dick repeated the question and shifted his own position so that he could address the man head-on. He thought the man would make an inter-esting subject to draw, had some other motive brought him here today. His hard, distinctive jawline and pinched mouth suggested he had not had an easy life. The man had scrawny hands and when he picked up a pile of coins, dropping them one by one into his other hand, it reminded Dick of some-one counting beads on a rosary. He repeated his question one more time and then added, 'You're not in any trouble, please don't worry.'

'The one you look for is Anglo-Indian,' the man grunted. He stopped fiddling with the coins and pulled his kurta tight around his neck as if to control what he said next. 'His name is Kasim. He glad of job when he first arrive but then he show no respect for us. He look down on us. He leave here with a man from kampong just before Ramadan.'

'Do you know where this Kasim lives?'

'He had boat, small Malay *prahu*. I think he live on boat

but I not know where.'

Dick thanked the man, whose name he found out was Mukesh, and turned to leave. Then Dick asked Mukesh if he had a scrap of paper upon which he could write a note. He carefully wrote down the address of Johnston & Co., gazed into Mukesh's eyes, and asked him to get in touch if he thought of anything else about the man called Kasim.

Baba Tan was waiting on the pavement, examining everything around him. They had almost reached the end of Market Street when Dick began to feel giddy. He had a name but he still lacked detail. Was there any connection between all these people? How was he to begin making sense of it all?

'My head is spinning,' he said. 'Can we go to your warehouse now? I need to sort out what we actually know for certain from all the conjecture.'

After the usual courtesies with tea being served at a leisurely pace, Baba Tan was happy to help Dick clear his head. There were two European men who regularly met to drink coffee at Choo Keng's; they disappeared for weeks at a time and their return always coincided with the arrival of Madam Ho seeking Wing Yee's assistance to examine new arrivals. There was a third man, also European, who occasionally joined the other pair. It was possible he was the organiser, but Dick had no real proof. Did the man who kept staring at Tijah belong to this trio? What was his fascination with Tijah? Could it be that she too was destined for the brothel? They had established an Anglo-Indian had worked alongside the moneylenders in Market Street until just before Ramadan; it was likely that this was the same man who Choo Keng had seen earlier in the year, but what had happened to him?

The mention of Ramadan made Dick think about Tijah and her reason for leaving Malacca, but she'd said her father was European. Dick told himself not to get side-tracked. He must stay focused on what he knew, and one sure thing was the information revealed by Sanjay: Pieter Steffens had returned to Singapore.

*****

In the next street, unknown to Dick and Baba Tan, Pieter Steffens, in the guise of Stefan, was walking along with a puzzled expression on his face. He was returning from a visit to his *prahu* where he'd taken a coil of rope, some basic provisions, and a small blanket. It was nearing lunchtime and he still hadn't worked out what he might use as a sedative, let alone how he could obtain a sufficient quantity without any questions being asked. He was getting desperate.

His attention was diverted by a man lurching towards him with his hand covering the side of his face; he looked in pain. An idea sprang into Stefan's mind; why hadn't he thought of it before? He cursed himself and quickened his step, turning in the direction of the kampong to seek out Victor. As soon as he entered the vicinity of Victor's house, he held the side of his jaw and adopted a pained expression.

'What's wrong with you?' Victor said. 'Have you been in a fight?'

'Toothache,' Stefan said. 'It's driving me mad. I need something to take the pain away before we set off for Java.'

'Opium will do the trick,' Victor said. 'I've got some hidden – left over from when we brought those women ashore. Couldn't take any risks after that one got away. You can have all of it providing you keep quiet about my little early-morning visits.'

'That sounds reasonable,' Stefan said, smiling to himself. His little ploy had made it easier to obtain some means of sedating the brat than he'd envisaged.

*****

Dick parted company with Baba Tan and headed back towards Johnston's warehouse. He was relieved to find Alexander at his desk. They spent the next hour discussing everything that was known about the men who came and went from the wharf and the likelihood that Pieter Steffens might be one of them but they had to admit they had no real proof and the evidence was flimsy.

'Don't look so defeated, my friend,' Alexander said. 'He's bound to step over the mark sometime or other, we just need to be vigilant. In my experience, even the cleverest of rogues usually gets caught in the end; they get careless and take one risk too many. We must believe that justice will prevail, and in the meantime, we must be patient.'

Dick continued to look downcast; he couldn't see any way of solving the problem before Kenneth Murchison's next visit to Singapore.

'Let me see that chart you've compiled,' Johnston said. 'Perhaps we've missed something.'

They scrutinised all the columns, cross-checking all the information they had.

'I think there should be a fourth column,' Dick said, 'to add what we know about the missing Indian called Kasim.'

Alexander furrowed his brow.

'Choo Keng told me, earlier in the year, he'd served coffee to two men, one of whom was Indian.'

'But that man hasn't been seen for several months. It has always been the two Europeans who meet there these days – plus the third man, but you say he's also European.'

'Mukesh said the man that worked with him was Anglo-Indian. Sanjay told me Pieter Steffens had worked outside in the hot sun in Calcutta. He said he had to look twice when he saw him in High Street; he wore European clothes but his skin was deeply bronzed.'

'And Sanjay is sure it was the man he knew in Calcutta?'

'No doubt about it.'

'So, you think it's the same person? How these people dress might be the clue we've overlooked,' Alexander said. 'Criminals will go to any lengths to achieve their goals. Remember Pieter Steffens was calling himself Sidney Percy when you first met him.'

'If Pieter Steffens returned to Singapore dressed as an Indian, if he worked in Market Street, and then left with another European just before Ramadan, that would explain why Choo Keng hasn't seen his Indian customer for the last few months.'

Dick scribbled furiously in the new column he'd added to his chart.

CHAPTER 24
8th August 1831

Edmund lifted the sheet and quietly swung his legs onto the floor, hoping not to disturb his wife. He pulled on the clothes that he'd carefully laid aside the previous evening and made his way to the bedroom door.

'What time is it?' Chin Ming asked, heaving herself into a sitting position against the pillows and yawning.

'Just seven,' Edmund said. He walked over to the bed, lifted her face towards him, and kissed the top of her head. 'There is no need for you to get up,' he said. 'Stay there as long as you like. Enjoy the peace before the children come to find you.'

'But what about you? Why are you up so early?'

'The *Charles Grant* was due to drop anchor at dawn. It should have brought a package for me, something I need to collect personally.'

'Oh, that sounds exciting. Something from the university or your publisher? I wish I could come with you.'

'Now you know that's not a good idea, my love. I'll have some coffee and some bread before I go and I'll come to see you as soon as I'm back from town. Shall I have some break-fast sent in to you or would you prefer to rest?'

'Don't trouble anyone. I'll have something later. Maybe I will stay here a little while longer.' She pulled the cover around her shoulders, slid back down the bed, and closed her eyes.

*****

Chin Ming awoke about an hour later, feeling restless. She still had another five weeks before the baby was due, but the high humidity at this time of year and her inability to do all the things she wanted to do was beginning to make her irritable. She had been short-tempered with Charlotte a few days ago when the little girl had marched in from the garden covered in dust and leaves. Normally, she would have told her to shake her clothes and wipe her feet before she entered the house; there had been no reason to raise her voice. Charlotte had burst into tears and run off to find comfort in May Lin, who had cleaned her up as usual and ignored the upset.

This pregnancy had been more problematic than the others right from the start – nausea, headaches, lethargy, and now frustration. She hoped it wasn't a sign that this child would be contrary; both Charlotte and William – born in temperate a climate - had been such happy babies. But it wasn't just the hot, still air that was making her restless, it was knowing that Edmund, Dick, Wing Yee – all her friends - could come and go as they pleased. Even Sujana, who seemed content to stay at home with Tomas or spend time producing intricate lengths of woven cloth, had a better idea of what had been happening in the town of late than she had herself. Whenever she made an enquiry about either the clinic or Dick's investigations, all she got was some sort of vague response or a change of subject. Did they really believe she was too delicate to deal with whatever they had to say? And why had Edmund had to rush off this morning? Why couldn't he have waited and then she could have accompanied him?

A thought sprang into her head. She seized her robe and went in search of Wing Yee. 'How long before Dick arrives to pick you up?' Chin Ming asked in English.

'Any time now,' Wing Yee replied. 'Why you ask? You want speak with him?'

'Yes, I do,' Chin Ming replied, 'I most definitely do. Don't let him go without - without seeing me.'

Wing Yee was left wrinkling her nose as her gaze followed the departing image of her friend. What was all that about, she wondered.

Chin Ming appeared on the veranda just as Dick was turning the carriage into the driveway. She had dressed hastily, and instead of piling her hair on top of her head as she usually did these days, she had left it to hang loose. She held a small, paper fan in one hand and a rattan basket in the other.

'Where you go?' Wing Yee said. Then, to make herself quite clear, she reverted to Cantonese. 'I hope you're not planning to spend time in the garden, it will be far too hot in no time at all.'

'I'm coming into town with the three of you,' Chin Ming said, continuing to speak in English. 'It's been ages since I walked along the quay, took a good look at the harbour, visited Baba Tan. Very soon, all my time will be taken up with the new baby. I want to take advantage of what freedom I have left before it's too late.'

Wing Yee turned to Dick. Her expression conveyed a plea, a silent wish that he would be able to persuade Chin Ming to stay at home. The two of them spent the next ten minutes trying to convince Chin Ming that her idea was foolish, but she would hear nothing of the sort. In the end, Dick shrugged his shoulders, he remained worried, but he knew it was no use and that Chin Ming would only get suspicions if he and Wing Yee continued with trying to persuade her otherwise.

'If Edmund is already in town,' he said, 'perhaps we can meet up with him, and when you feel tired, he can hire a gharry to bring you home.'

*****

Wing Yee remained silent for the whole of the journey down the hill. Even when Dick had to manoeuvre the carriage to avoid a series of ruts in the road, she didn't utter a sound. The inside of her head was in turmoil. First and foremost, she was concerned about the risk Chin Ming was taking. Secondly, she was annoyed with herself for not being able to convince her stubborn friend that this journey was unnecessary and could even be hazardous.

Dick drew the carriage to a halt just short of the bridge and turned into the yard where he left it while he was working. He was unhitching the horse when Chin Ming announced that she intended to visit Baba Tan first. 'Do you think that's wise?' he said, giving Wing Yee a cue to intervene, which she immediately seized.

'I need to replenish my stock of ginger and turmeric,' Wing Yee said. 'If you insist on going there before coming to the clinic, then Tijah can come with you; she can collect what I need.'

Chin Ming was all too aware of the worry she had caused her friends, but it was so good to be doing something other than resting, reading, or writing letters. She was happy to consent to Wing Yee's suggestion. 'I will enjoy that,' she said, 'Tijah and I haven't spent much time together since she moved in with Dick and Sujana.'

Wing Yee watched the pair stroll across Monkey Bridge until they disappeared into the crowd. 'I hope they'll be alright,' she said.

'Tijah is very sensible,' Dick responded. 'She has matured a great deal since she began to work alongside you. Having you teach her about the herbs and roots you use has provided her with a useful occupation. It's something she enjoys and is something at which she intends to succeed. I suspect she's still hoping to find her father but I think she has resigned herself to the fact that it might not be possible.'

Wing Yee put on a brave smile once she and Dick had also crossed the bridge, she walking in the direction of the clinic, he towards Johnston's warehouse.

*****

When Chin Ming and Tijah reached the beginning of Boat Quay, they stopped for a moment to watch some young boys playing with a rattan ball. The smallest of the three was remarkably skilful, running around and between the legs of the other two with the ball just ahead of him all the time. Before they could continue their walk, Tijah gripped Chin Ming's arm. Standing just ahead of them beside the tables set out in front of Choo Keng's coffee stall were two men. They nodded to each other as if agreeing about something or other, then one turned in the direction of the harbour master's office, the other turned to face the two women.

Chin Ming couldn't think why Tijah was clutching her arm so tightly; it was beginning to feel uncomfortable. 'What's the matter?' she said.

Tijah stared straight ahead; she kept swallowing hard, but she couldn't speak. Chin Ming followed her gaze. Looking straight at her was a tall, swarthy man. He was dressed in European clothes, but there was something about him that made her feel uneasy. Was she picking up on whatever was upsetting Tijah, or was it something else?

'I've seen him before,' Tijah managed to whisper. 'He always wears a red cravat. One day, he followed Wing Yee and ...'

'And?' Chin Ming said.

'He always looks at me in a strange way.'

Chin Ming forced herself to take another look at the man. He too was standing perfectly still, staring in their direction; he had made no attempt to continue along the quay. She found herself focusing on his cold, dark eyes; a shiver rippled down her spine. 'I think perhaps we should go straight to the clinic, after all,' she said. Tijah turned around immediately and hurried ahead.

They had almost reached the ornately-carved doorway

that opened into the clinic when Chin Ming cradled her distended abdomen and let out a piercing cry. She dropped the basket she was carrying. Tijah turned back instantly. Despite her small frame, she managed to support Chin Ming for the last few paces, helping her over the threshold and holding on until she was able to collapse onto the nearest chair.

Wing Yee became aware of all the commotion and came running through from a room at the rear of the building. Even without Chin Ming speaking, she knew what was happening. There was a puddle of water around her friend's feet. 'Help me move her to somewhere more comfortable,' she said to Tijah. 'I want you to find me some sheeting, lots of clean towels, and then I need you to heat some water. Can you manage all that?'

Tijah nodded her agreement, but the colour drained from her face. Between the two of them, they guided Chin Ming into the room where Wing Yee examined the women who came to see her from Madam Ho's emporium. 'It's too soon!' Chin Ming managed to say between spasms of pain. 'I don't understand why this is happening.'

Wing Yee pressed her lips together to avoid having to remind her friend that her insistence to come into town today had been reckless, to say the least. The jolting of the carriage alone was enough to encourage the baby to want to escape from its watery surroundings.

'My back and stomach ache, but that is all,' Chin Ming said, 'I'm sure you're overreacting.' She attempted to sit up but collapsed back onto the mattress as she experienced an early contraction. This level of pain stopped and started, varying in frequency, strength, and the length of time it lasted.

Wing Yee put her hand on Chin Ming's abdomen; it felt hard.

'You have delivered two babies already,' Wing Yee said, 'you must know that you are already in labour. This baby wants to be born. The thing I need you to tell me is what position you prefer to adopt?' She spoke in Cantonese to be sure that she perfectly understood what Chin Ming might want to tell her; she would have to translate for Tijah when necessary.

Another contraction gripped Chin Ming, forcing her to grip Wing Yee's arm. She took a deep breath before asking, 'What do you mean?'

'Chinese custom advocates squatting as the perfect position for labour.'

'Why would I want to do that, it sounds most uncomfortable?' Chin Ming said. She was gripped by another contraction before she could add anything further.

'If you lie on your back, it's believed that the baby won't have enough energy to come out.'

'What nonsense!' Chin Ming said. 'Both Charlotte and William were born when I was lying on my back; neither of them has shown any sign of reluctance - then, or since.'

*****

Another hour passed, during which time the contractions increased both in frequency and the level of discomfort. Just before noon, there was a searing pain much more severe than anything else she had suffered. Finally, the baby slithered onto the towel that Wing Yee had ready. She took the child to the shelf where Tijah had hot water waiting. Gently, she wiped away all the mucus and the blood the baby had brought along, but the infant failed to make a sound of any kind. Wing Yee wondered if she should have encouraged Chin Ming to take up the squatting position after all.

'Why so quiet?' Chin Ming said, turning her head in their direction. 'What's wrong?'

Wing Yee pinched the baby's chest, then she began to caress his buttocks. A loud, piercing yell penetrated the whole room and the sigh of relief uttered by Chin Ming was almost as intense.

'He's a survivor,' Wing Yee said with a broad grin covering her entire face.

'Just like his grandfather,' Chin Ming managed to whisper, just before she passed into unconsciousness.

*****

Wing Yee was almost at her wits' end when she became aware of someone pounding on the outside door. She gave Tijah a brief nod. 'Stay beside Chin Ming. I won't be long, but I need to you to watch her. Shout out loud if you need me.'

Tijah looked apprehensive. The responsibility of looking after the baby had been difficult enough, but the additional burden of the exhausted mother made her uneasy.

Wing Yee pulled back the bolt and started to open the door, but the person on the other side pushed against it and nearly knocked her over. It was Dick; his face was a picture of alarm. 'I needed to visit Baba Tan,' he spluttered between agitated breaths. 'He says he has seen nothing of Chin Ming or Tijah all day! I've searched the quay in case she'd decided to look for Edmund, but there's no sign ...'

'They're here. Come in quickly, bolt the door behind you. I need to get back to her.'

Dick did as he was bidden and followed Wing Yee in the direction of the treatment room. Just as he entered, he heard the baby start to cry.

'She's lost a lot of blood,' Wing Yee said, 'and she has a high fever. I've used her fan to cool her face, and I've tried to reduce her body temperature with a sheet soaked in water, but I only had one to spare; I needed all the rags I had available to stop the bleeding.'

'What can I do to help?' Dick said.

'We need more sheets,' Tijah said.

'We need a wet nurse,' said Wing Yee, 'she isn't strong enough to feed the baby.'

259

'We need to find Edmund,' Dick said.

'That will have to wait. Chin Ming and the baby are more important. Do you – or Sujana - know how to locate a wet nurse?'

'What about the kampong?' Tijah said. 'At home, there was always someone who could feed the babies who needed help.'

'Good idea,' said Wing Yee. 'Leave the baby with me. You go with Dick, he'll look after you, but it must be you who explains what is needed. If they have any bed linen that can be spared, all the better.'

'Will you be able to care for Chin Ming and the baby on your own?' Dick said.

'I will have to, won't I? But hurry, Chin Ming is very weak and the baby is hungry.'

Alone with Chin Ming and the baby, she remembered what Dick had told her about the fever suffered by Raffles' wife following the birth of their last child. That baby had died and Sophia had been ill for several months. Wing Yee was determined such a catastrophe would not happen here today. She picked up the fan and returned to Chin Ming's side.

CHAPTER 25
8th August 1831

Stefan turned away from Victor. A moment ago, he'd agreed to discuss the final arrangements for their Java trip after supper this evening. Now, he needed to leave. Not more than a stone's throw away from him was the young girl who worked with the bitch. Today, she was with the Chinese woman he'd once lusted after, the one who had outwitted him, escaped from his house, and provided Raffles with evidence that had contributed to his downfall. He knew she was now married to that botanist fellow, the one he'd seen waiting beside the wharf only half an hour ago. She was obviously very pregnant. He wondered what she was doing in town without her husband or any of her close friends. The young girl had recognised him, he was sure of that from the expression on her face. But on previous occasions when their paths had crossed, he'd never made any attempt to speak to her. There was nothing she could complain about.

He watched as they hurried away from him in the opposite direction. He followed at a discreet distance. When they arrived in Amoy Street, he congratulated himself; it confirmed his theory that they were on their way to the clinic. The moment they stepped over the threshold, the Chinese woman seemed to collapse. His position limited his view, but he thought the younger one was trying to support her. He moved a little closer to get a better picture, but already they were disappearing away from the door to a place that was invisible to him. What was happening? Was it a temporary condition or might she be indisposed for some time? Her husband was bound to be sent for so that he could fuss over her, and all that could take some considerable time. The husband would probably insist she rested for a while whether she needed to or not.

What an opportunity. It couldn't be better even if he'd planned it this way. It meant the house would be empty apart from the servants – the amah, the cook, and the gardener– and they didn't count as far as he was concerned. What mattered to him, right now, was the brat, and he was about to make it his business to entertain her. This was his chance and he must seize it. Remembering the gardener had sparked an idea; he must hurry back to the kampong. He needed to change into different clothes.

*****

Half an hour later, dressed in a kurta that matched the colour of banana fronds and trousers the same shade as the soil beneath his feet, Stefan rushed away from the kampong. The path, winding up the hillside from Serengoon Road was still rough and hardly used by anyone other than himself. He arrived in front of the Beaumonts' house out of breath, he wiped away beads of sweat that glistened on his forehead. He took a moment to recover as he surveyed the scene; there was no sign of anyone either in the garden or on the veranda of the house. The brat had not been with her mother, neither was the husband. Could the child be with her father? Could he have taken her into town? Maybe she was only allowed into the garden when her father was present. He had no way of finding out other than to skirt around the side of the property, creep through the hole in the perimeter fence and investigate further. Stefan felt deep into his pocket to make sure the opium was still there wrapped inside his handkerchief.

He was almost through the gap, but something was pulling at his clothing. When he looked behind, he could see the hem of his kurta had caught on something sharp. It took him a while to disentangle the material from what turned out to be a vicious-looking spike, but he was pleased to accomplish the task without tearing the fabric.

The satisfaction disappeared, however, as soon as he stood up straight. He came face-to-face with Sanjay. The moment he'd left his shed, the gardener had become aware of a disturbance near to the fence He thought it might be a trapped animal and decided to investigate in case it resulted in either a corpse or an injured creature, both of which would upset Miss Charlotte. He'd gasped when he recognised the person standing in front of him. The intruder was wearing Indian clothing now, but there was no doubt about his identity.

'Why you come here?' Sanjay shouted. He thought Pieter Steffens had somehow found out about the conversation he'd had with Mr Beaumont and his friend when he told them what he knew about Steffens' behaviour in Calcutta. But how could that be? 'You bad man,' Sanjay said, 'you go now!'

Sanjay was totally unprepared for the punch that landed in the middle of his chest. He doubled up and stumbled towards his aggressor. The next blow was aimed at the side of his head; he reeled, howled in agony, and then collapsed on the floor as he lost consciousness.

'Damn you,' Stefan said, 'why couldn't you just keep out of it. I don't need any additional problems, what am I going to do with you?' He continued to curse as he checked to see if anyone had witnessed the encounter. He examined the scene more thoroughly than before; the garden was empty. He dragged Sanjay by his shoulders and pulled him to the shed. Inside, he found garden tools, a pile of sacking, and a short length of rope. He tied the man's wrists together, then looped the restraint around the leg of a workbench. He considered using some of the opium he had in his pocket to prevent the gardener from waking but then he noticed a length of blue silk, the sash usually dragged around by the brat. It was lying on the floor. The man was still out cold. Stefan decided he didn't need to be sedated after all. He picked up the sash, wound it around and between the Indian's flaccid jaw several times before tying it tightly behind his head.

Stefan peered out of the door. Scampering along a path at the side of the house, and now heading in his direction, was the brat. 'Got you,' he murmured to himself.

*****

Charlotte trotted purposefully in his direction; she waved as she got closer. 'Hello, San–jay. Have you seen my sash?'

Stefan kept his head down as she approached. They met halfway between the house and the shed. Charlotte didn't understand why her friend hadn't answered her; she looked up at him.

'You're not San-jay,' she said, full of indignation.

Stefan coughed. 'No,' he said, 'I'm a friend of his. He had to go on an errand. What is it that's gone missing?'

'I've lost my sash. It's blue and very pretty, have you seen it? My name is Charlotte, what's yours?'

'I'll help you to look for it if you like,' he said, hoping to divert her from asking any more questions. 'Perhaps it's blown behind that shed.'

Charlotte nodded and set off in small, purposeful strides towards the hut. Stefan caught up with her and steered her towards the rear; he didn't want her to consider looking inside. He let her search through the weeds and rotting leaves for a while, and when she finally gave up, he offered a distraction. He pulled out his handkerchief, which was also blue, waving it close to her face.

'It's a magic handkerchief,' he said. 'Can you smell the magic?'

'Will it help me find my sash?'

'Perhaps. Shall we give it a try?'

He sat next to her on the ground and tipped the contents of a phial onto the cloth. Then he pretended to say magic words and invoke the spirits to show them where the sash lay hidden. He offered the headkerchief to Charlotte. 'Take a deep breath,' he said, 'then we'll see if the magic is working.'

* * * * *

As soon as Charlotte's body became limp, he rammed the opium-soaked cloth into her mouth. Her hand reached out as her knees gave way and she slithered down onto Stefan's feet. She looked small and vulnerable, but he knew at once that he would not be able to carry her all the way back to Telok Blangah. He cursed himself for not taking this into consideration and he knew time must be running out. He eased his feet out from under her and peeped round the side of the shed; all was quiet. He opened the door to check on the Indian; he still appeared to be out cold and showing no sign of recovery.

When he closed the door again, he noticed a small cart, the sort used to transport goods to market. It had been left at the side of the plot. He checked briefly to see if it was in working order, then manoeuvred it to the other side of the garden. He lifted Charlotte's body into it and then returned to the shed to collect some sacking to throw on top of her. He made sure the door was firmly closed behind him, paying no particular attention to Sanjay.

The wheels of the cart had been recently oiled and it moved easily. Once he was clear of the property, he moved swiftly. He couldn't return the way he'd come; the track was too rough for the cart. He didn't want to risk a bumpy ride that might cause her to wake up. His head was buzzing, he was trying hard not to panic. I can't take the brat back to the kampong. I'll have to get the cart down the hill and somehow get it to Telok Blangah without being seen! If I do meet anyone along the road, I'll just have to hide in the nearest driveway.

Stefan had almost reached the point where Selegie Road joined Bras Basah Road when a gharry turned the corner. There was no place for him to hide, but the driver of the small carriage ignored him and its two passengers were so deeply involved in conversation they appeared not to notice him or the cart.

He ducked and dived for most of the latter part of the journey, avoiding anyone coming in his direction. When he eventually reached his *prahu* at Telok Blangah, he glanced along the wharf to make sure he was unobserved. The two fishing boats adjacent to his own vessel displayed nets drying on their decks, but there was no hint of human activity in the vicinity. He was sweating all over. The small mound under the sacking in the cart was motionless.

As he carried Charlotte onto the boat, she began to come around. She squirmed and wriggled in his arms; she could make no sound because the gag remained firmly in place but her body stiffened and he felt a sharp pain as she kicked into his ribs. He hurried down to the cabin and set her on the floor. As soon as she was free of his grasp, she tried to run. She got as far as the bottom of the steps when he lunged towards her. 'Oh no, you don't,' he shouted.

She kicked and struggled free. She was heading towards the steps when he grabbed at her again. She strained to make some sort of noise and tried to wriggle away from him; she didn't like this man. He tried to tighten his grasp, but his hands slipped on her clammy skin. She lost her balance. She fell. She hit her head against the side of the stairwell. Her eyelids fluttered and then closed.

Stefan swore loudly in Dutch, he hadn't time for histrionics. Part of him was glad she'd been knocked out, it meant that she wouldn't give him any trouble for a while, but he could already see a large bump beginning to form on the side of her head. He snatched her up, placed her onto the bunk, and watched. Her body was completely still, her skin felt cool, and her eyes remained firmly closed. He gasped, then he put his hand in front of her nostrils – not even the slightest hint of breath. Oh god! This wasn't supposed to happen. He swore again and kicked the bunk. It had all gone wrong. He rushed from one side of the cabin to the other, knocking over anything that stood in his path. What to do? How long before they came looking for her? He swore again. He struggled with his inner thoughts as he continued to crash around the cabin. He thought he heard a noise on deck, but when he reached the top step, it remained completely empty. It must have been a gust of wind.

He gazed out to sea. Maybe he should throw her body overboard and let the tide take it away? But what if the current wasn't strong enough and her body washed up further along the shore? None of the ploys that came to mind was feasible and time was running out. He certainly couldn't demand a ransom for a dead body. He would have to abandon his original plan. He would leave her here and return to the kampong. Victor would help him escape. It would take some time for her to be found. He turned towards the wharf, scanning it for any sign of activity. When he was satisfied it was still deserted, he leapt along the plank. He cast his eyes around once more before striding off towards the road without a backward glance. Once he was clear of the wharf, he increased his pace. Walking turned into trotting, trotting gave way to running, and running evolved into sprinting whenever he had sufficient breath.

*****

Edmund was overjoyed, everything had worked out exactly as planned. When he'd received the letter from Li Soong Heng almost two months ago he'd been most uncomfortable about what was being suggested. He hated keeping secrets from Chin Ming, but her father had insisted she should not be informed about his intention to return to Singapore. He wanted it kept confidential to prevent disappointment should his plan go awry. It had been fortunate that on the day Soong Heng's letter arrived, Chin Ming had been feeling exhausted by the heat and had gone to lie down. Edmund had read the letter alone and since then had been counting the days until the *Charles Grant* was due to drop anchor.

When Chin Ming awoke this morning and asked why he needed to go into town so early, he had hated not being able to tell her the truth. He was relieved that they were almost home and in a matter of minutes the burden of deception would be over. He was sure she would be so happy to see her dear papa, that he would be forgiven his part in the duplicity.

The gharry turned into their drive and stopped in front of the veranda. No one emerged to meet them, but Edmund assumed the household was resting, away from the noonday heat. He helped Soong Heng climb down and escorted him to a seat in the shade. The driver followed behind with Soong Heng's meagre luggage, then he turned the gharry around and left them to sort themselves out. He would be back down the hill and waiting for his next passengers almost as soon as they had drawn breath.

Edmund went in search of Chin Ming; he hoped she wasn't sleeping. His plan was to guide her towards the veranda, then put his hands over her eyes, telling her that he had a surprise waiting there. There was no sign of her in the bedroom or anywhere else that he looked. Perhaps she was feeling energetic enough to spend the afternoon with the children? He hurried to the nursery where he found May Lin telling William a story.

'Good afternoon, May Lin. Can you tell me where I can find my wife?'

'She go to town with others,' May Lin said.

'You mean she went with Wing Yee, Tijah, and Dick? What was she thinking about?'

May Lin nodded. She hoped she wasn't about to be blamed for the absence of her mistress. 'They tell her ride in carriage not good, but she say no worry.'

'Did Charlotte go into town too?'

'No, Miss Charlotte go to play- to help – Sanjay, in garden.'

'Don't be alarmed, May Lin. You're not in any trouble. My father-in-law has just arrived from Calcutta. His visit is a surprise for my wife, but I think he might be weary from his journey. Can you find him some food?'

Edmund hastily told Soong Heng what had happened. He said May Lin would bring some soup and then show him the guest room. 'I'm surprised Charlotte hasn't appeared though; she is usually so inquisitive. Perhaps she's tired herself out by now. Sanjay is very patient with her, but she's probably covered herself in garden debris and doesn't want to get into trouble. Either that or she's fallen asleep under one of the trees. I'll take a look and then I'll walk down the hill. Chin Ming has probably gone to visit Wing Yee at the clinic. Why don't you take a rest while I sort everything out?'

*****

Edmund made his way around the side of the house; the garden was completely deserted. It was incredibly hot today and the air was completely still; that might explain everything. Maybe Sanjay had suggested Charlotte should rest in his shed when she became tired. Perhaps he had gone there, too, to keep an eye on her? Perhaps he too was taking a nap? Edmund made his way to the familiar brown hut.

The door was closed – that was odd, especially in this heat. Edmund called out; no response. He pushed against the door.

*****

Edmund was all fingers and thumbs as he struggled to release Sanjay from his restraints. The material stuffed into his mouth was sodden with saliva and the way it had been secured behind his head was complicated in the extreme. Edmund, concentrating on the task in hand, had no inkling that the damp material he was trying to unravel was his daughter's treasured sash. He pulled and tugged at the knot until it had loosened, allowing him to get his fingers through the folds and then slacken it enough to allow Sanjay to speak.

'What happened? Who did this to you?' Edmund said.

Sanjay was unable to make himself heard, even after Edmund had unwound the whole length of sodden material from inside his mouth. He swallowed hard after each attempt to speak, but he was so parched that all he could manage was a high-pitched croak followed by a fit of coughing.

Edmund cast his eyes around to locate anything sharp he might use to cut through the ropes binding Sanjay's wrists together. A small file kept in the shed for sharpening spades was all he could see. He grabbed it and worked away at the twisted fibres until they eventually gave way. As soon as his hands were free, Sanjay thrust them into a watering can that he'd brought inside earlier in the day to keep the liquid cool. He continued to drink until his thirst was quenched and he was able to tell Edmund what he needed to know. He told him that he recognised the intruder and what Pieter Steffens had done. When Edmund asked Sanjay how he knew about Charlotte, he said he'd felt groggy when he'd regained consciousness, but was sure he'd heard Steffens talking to the little girl. 'Then everything go quiet. Steffens open door, but I pretend still asleep. He take sack and throw it over small bundle on cart, the one we use for moving things around. I not see well, but I think cart contain Miss Charlotte.'

*****

Edmund was well-known for his calm and steady nature, but the news about his daughter's abduction, following on the heels of discovering his wife had ventured into town turned him into a whirling dervish. He turned first one way and then the other, he took two steps forwards and one step back; he couldn't keep still. His instinct was to run back down the hill, to inform the authorities, to find Dick or Alexander or Baba Tan. Then he remembered Soong Heng was in the house expecting to be reunited with his daughter. 'His daughter!' Edmund screeched. 'Where is Chin Ming? What shall I tell her?'

'Sahib, I come to help,' Sanjay said. 'I help you find Miss Charlotte. My fault he take her, sahib. Please not send me back to building site.'

'I think you should rest awhile,' Edmund said. 'You've had a bad shock and your mouth looks terribly bruised. And Sanjay, there's no question of you going back to the building site, it's not your fault. The man who took Charlotte is a bad man. Come with me to the house; I need to tell my father-in-law what's happened. I'd be grateful if you and May Lin could look after him while I go in search of my daughter.'

Sanjay hurried along behind Edmund as fast as his aching limbs would carry him.

They had just climbed the steps leading onto the veranda when a horse galloped into the drive, creating clouds of dust as it came to a halt in front of them. Dick jumped down from the saddle and leapt up the steps.

'Thank goodness I've found you,' he said. 'We need to speak, but first can you find May Lin. I must have fresh bed linen, towels, and a clean gown.'

'Have they found her?' Edmund said. 'Has she been harmed? She's so young, she must have been very frightened; what did he do to her?'

'What on earth are you talking about?' Dick said. 'I need fresh linen for Chin Ming. She's had the baby. She lost a lot of blood and was quite weak at first, but she will be alright. I went to the kampong with Tijah to find a wet nurse. I dropped them off before coming here. Wing Yee is looking after every-thing - both mother and the baby will be fine.'

CHAPTER 26
8th August

Edmund started to shake all over. His face turned ashen and he felt cold, very cold despite the tropical heat.

'She's well, please believe me,' Dick said. 'She gave everyone a fright, and Wing Yee says she needs a lot of rest. That's why I've come. I'm to collect more sheets and a clean nightgown. We all said she shouldn't come into town with us this morning, but perhaps it was for the best. At least she was close to the clinic and could be attended to by Wing Yee.'

'I shouldn't have left her,' Edmund struggled to say. 'I should have told her about Soong Heng coming to visit. If I hadn't gone to the harbour, they would both be safe.'

'But they are alright,' Dick said. 'That's what I keep trying to tell you. You have another son, a fine baby boy – and Chin Ming will be her old self again before you know it.'

Edmund glanced to see if Sanjay was still present. 'But you don't understand,' he said. 'It's not just Chin Ming, it's Charlotte too!' He fixed his over-bright eyes on Dick, looking almost feverish.

In halted English, Sanjay told Dick about the incident in the garden.

*****

Dick insisted Edmund drink some tea to calm his nerves. When he'd finished, he was a little more rational. Dick tried to persuade him it was imperative not to tell Chin Ming anything about Charlotte's disappearance for the time being.

'But how are we going to manage that?' Edmund asked in a high-pitched voice. 'It's bad enough that I haven't told her about her papa's arrival. At least that is good news, but this............' He trailed off and the room became hushed. Somewhere close by, the piercing notes of a bird cut through the silence. Edmund's heart hammered inside his chest, a relentless pulse of fear. Each successive call made by the bird was like a bolt of lightning, nudging him further into a dark place filled with dread.

'I want to see Chin Ming, I want to see my new son, but I need to find Charlotte. I need to find out what that miscreant has done with my little girl.' He paced around the room, pushing his hands through his hair, pacing again, and finally slumping into a chair.

'I've got an idea,' said Dick. 'I know you intended to let Soong Heng rest while you went to meet Chin Ming, but now that the situation has changed, why not take him into your confidence? He can come with us to visit her and the baby. You should stay for a while too, of course, but then you can join me in the search for Steffens and Charlotte.'

The blood was beginning to return to Edmund's cheeks. He agreed that Dick's suggestion would create a diversion - and hopefully prevent Chin Ming from wondering why he hadn't brought Charlotte and William to visit their new brother – at least for the time being.

*****

Towards the end of the afternoon, Dick turned the carriage around and conveyed Edmund and Soong Heng back into town. He made sure they had all the things Wing Yee had asked for before he drove off.

'Where will I know how to find you?' Edmund said.

'Don't worry about that now. As soon as I have any news, I'll come back to the clinic; your job is to keep Chin Ming distracted.'

He left the carriage in its usual place and returned on foot to the Malay kampong. Years ago, he'd visited the place often but he'd had no reason to come here of late. Apart from a group of small children playing with a kite, the compound appeared to be empty. The only sound, in addition to the children, was made by a monkey perched on the overhanging branch of a tree. It was chattering away to itself, picking at its fur, and dispensing clouds of boisterous fleas into the surrounding air.

Dick made his way to the headman's house, performing the usual *salam* when he reached the door. The two men shook hands and touched their hearts as a gesture of sincerity. They spoke in Malay.

'So many visitors today,' the headman said. 'I'm told you came earlier with a young girl who was asking about a wet nurse. I believe one of our women went back to town with you. I hope she has been able to help.'

Dick thanked him, told him about the situation, and said that the woman had fed the child, which had been a huge relief to everyone concerned. 'However, I do have another favour to ask,' he said. He apologised for his haste in posing questions, but when the reason was explained, the usual courtesies were dismissed.

The headman knew nothing of a man named Pieter Steffens. 'But a friend of a fellow called Victor has been living here on and off for the last few months,' he said. 'I know him merely as Stefan, it sounds very similar. Could he be the man you are looking for?'

Dick was escorted to Victor's house. He was found lounging on the veranda with his eyes closed and attempting to waft the insects away from his face with a dilapidated rattan fan.

He sat bolt upright when his visitors approached. Although Dick had only seen partial views of this man before today, he was sure he was one of the pair he'd seen outside Choo Keng's coffee shop. Victor wore a serious expression from the start of the encounter, but when the headman explained the purpose of Dick's visit. his eyes rolled from side to side and he rubbed one hand over the other as if washing away at a deep stain. Victor continued to fidget all the while he was being questioned and was guarded about his responses.

'It would be in your best interests to tell me everything you know about your friend,' Dick said. 'I am aware that you have both been making visits to various parts of Sumatra within the last few months and your return always coincides with the arrival of groups of young women at Madam Ho's emporium.'

Victor bit his lower lip, then continued to rub his knees with his hands, moving them in opposing circular directions. There was a silence. He began to rock backwards and forwards, his eyes flared, and he swallowed hard.

'Well? What have you to say for yourself?' the headman said. 'We were happy for you to stay in this village when your mother returned to her family in Malacca. I felt sorry for you. We gave you shelter - and this is how you choose to repay us!' He turned to Dick, telling him in a tone of obvious disapproval that when Victor's so-called uncle, Colonel Farquhar, returned to Scotland, no provision had been made for his Malay family.

All this was news to Dick, but he tried not to let his surprise show. He thought it ironic that Victor and Pieter Steffens had become business associates, both men with some sort of chip on their shoulder. He pressed his questions even harder.

'He has a boat,' Victor said at last. 'He stays here most of the time but sometimes he returns to the *prahu*. It's anchored at Telok Blangah.'

Dick thanked the headman for his help. He left without acknowledging Victor, making a mental note of the house where he lived and promising himself that he would return to deal with the matter of smuggling women on another occasion.

*****

The streets were still crowded. Dick moved as fast as he could, running for part of the way and dodging in and out as briskly as possible when the pavement became too crowded. He remembered previous occasions when he'd had to run hard; once when he and Raffles had found Chin Ming collapsed on the beach and he'd been sent ahead to find help, another when Raffles had sent him to tell Sophia to expect the arrival of Chin Ming and Wing Yee as their guests, and the last time when he'd chased the Frenchman along the quay ...

He beat his fist against the entrance to the clinic before bending over to recover his breath. He'd hardly regained his composure when Tijah opened the door to him. He followed her to the room at the rear. It had been cleaned and tidied now and Chin Ming was sitting in a chair. She still looked pale, but there was joy in her eyes. She was holding the baby and gazing affectionately at her father, still not quite believing he was sitting beside her.

Dick smiled and offered his congratulations.

'Isn't it wonderful,' Chin Ming said, 'my family is now complete. We are going to call him Soong Heng, after my dear Papa.'

Dick smiled and then looked straight towards Edmund. 'Well done, both of you.'

Edmund took the hint and rose from the stool where he'd been perching. 'I think I should leave you for a while, my love. Wing Yee has made you as comfortable as she can, but there is no proper bed here and you need to rest. I'll ask Alexander if we can borrow his landau to take you home, it will be far more comfortable than Dick's carriage.'

Chin Ming made no attempt to protest. Wing Yee had

given her tea that contained a mild sedative; she was relaxed and contented. If she could return home soon and introduce the baby to Charlotte and William, then her happiness would be complete.

*****

Dick and Edmund left together. Dick hurried along the coast road which led to the fishing village at Tanjong Passar; the silhouettes of wooden fishing traps in the shallows made the place easy to identify.

'Where are we going? What have you found out?' Edmund was struggling to keep up with the pace that Dick had set. They had hardly spoken since leaving the clinic and he was desperate for news.

'Steffens has a boat,' Dick said. 'I think that's where we'll find Charlotte.'

'Where is this boat? How did you find out about it? I thought you said he was living in the Malay kampong.'

'It's at Telok Blangah - not far to go now. I'll tell you all the details later. Come on, we need to find it before it gets dark.'

They skirted past the kampong, which occupied the land allocated to the old Temenggong and his followers by Raffles, and headed for the jetty. Next month, this place would be congested with sailing vessels belonging to the Bugis traders, bringing nutmeg, cloves, and pepper to Singapore, and wanting to buy Indian cotton goods in exchange. Now, there were just three vessels tied up along the wharf. Dick and Edmund stopped in their tracks to survey the scene. All three craft were local sailing boats with one mast and a low sail made from matting. Each had its sail furled around its boom, no one was apparently preparing to depart. Dick hoped they had arrived in time, that no other vessel had already left for the off-shore islands. One of the *prahus* was larger than the other two and showed no hint of being used for fishing. The tide was already out, revealing dry reefs.

'Can you see anything? Is there any sign of activity?' Edmund said.

'Nothing at all.'

Before Dick could say anything further, Edmund was striding out ahead. Dick managed to grab the hem of his coat. 'Hold on,' he said. 'If Steffens is on board one of those boats, we don't want to alert him to our presence. If we approach the wrong vessel and he hears us making enquiries, we could put Charlotte in danger.'

'But we must do something. I can't just stand here; there must be some way of finding out if he's there and what he's done with Charlotte.'

'I suggest we keep watch for a little while longer,' Dick said. 'I'm almost sure this is where he will have taken her, but we need to be certain. We should watch to see if anyone approaches or if anyone attempts to leave.'

'But what if we see no one, what are we going to do then?'

Edmund's agitation was becoming obvious. It was quite natural that he was anxious about Charlotte's safety, but Dick was concerned his friend might do something rash and spoil their chances of taking Steffens by surprise.

The next ten minutes felt like ten hours. The wharf remained completely empty. The shadows became darker and longer, the only sound coming from the gulls soaring and screeching over their heads. Dick had already decided that the larger of the three vessels was the one most likely to belong to Steffens.

'I can't stand this any longer,' Edmund said. He was about to make a move towards the larger of the three vessels when a figure stepped out of the shadows onto its deck. Whoever it was moved without making a sound, paused for several moments on the gangplank, and then dropped silently onto the quay. Dick could distinguish some sort of tunic worn over loose-fitting trousers which made him think it was a man, but there was no way of identifying the person.

The figure was heading straight towards them now. Dick grabbed Edmund's arm and pulled him back behind a ramshackle building. They didn't have to wait long before the figure, dressed in kurta and baggy trousers, brushed close to where they stood. They remained perfectly still until the man disappeared along the same road that had brought them here.

'That's him,' Dick said. 'That's Steffens. He dresses in Indian garments when he comes here to check his boat; his friend Victor confirmed that fact when he told me about his boat being anchored here.'

'Well, let's go,' Edmund said. 'We need to see if he has Charlotte ...'

'You stay here and keep watch,' Dick said, grabbing his friend by the coat tails once again. 'You need to stay safe; Chin Ming and your family need you. I'll go. I'll be as quick as I can.'

Edmund started to protest, but Dick insisted. He ran silently to the edge of the wharf, leapt onto the boat, and crept along the deck. He hoped Steffens hadn't left anyone guarding Charlotte, but thought it was unlikely. He found his way to the steps that led down to the cabin. The door was locked. Dick rattled the door and listened; no sound was heard. There was no way of telling whether Charlotte was in the cabin, but he needed to find out. He looked around frantically to see what he could use to break the door down; nothing was obvious, and the light had faded, making it difficult to see anything beyond the stairwell. He climbed back up the steps and almost tripped over a bucket; that would have to do.

He called Charlotte's name and announced his own, but there was no response. He used both hands to lift the bucket high above his head and brought it crashing down onto the padlock. It took two more attempts before the metal gave way. He pushed the door open and searched in the gloom for any sign of the little girl. He called her name again, but again there was no reply. He was just beginning to think he might have made a mistake when he thought he heard a faint noise. He stepped further into the cabin and found her lying on a bunk; there was no sign of movement. He pulled the gag out of her mouth, releasing the all too distinctive floral smell of opium. He put his hand in front of her nostrils; was it his imagination or was there a hint of warmth on his hand? He held her small, fragile wrist between his fingers – nothing. Then he changed to the other wrist and was relieved to find a faint pulse; she was still alive. He scooped her up into his arms and returned to the stairwell. He listened hard; the only sound he could hear was the water lapping against the side of the boat. He hoisted Charlotte onto his shoulder and began to climb.

It was completely dark when Dick stepped off the *prahu* and headed towards the place where he'd left Edmund waiting. He'd taken only a couple of strides when he almost collided with his frantic friend. Charlotte moaned quietly as Dick placed her in Edmund's arms.

'What's wrong with her?' Edmund said.

'She had a lump of cloth stuffed in her mouth; it stank of opium. He must have used it to sedate her. You can still smell it on her breath,' Dick said. 'I looked her over in the lamplight on deck and there was no obvious sign of a struggle. But now I can see she has a bruise just there,' he said pointing to the side of Charlotte's head, 'and I think there's a small swelling beginning to develop. You'd better get Wing Yee to look her over.'

Edmund began to rush away. He cradled Charlotte in his arms, carrying her in the same way he'd done when she was a small baby. He was whispering soothing words to her when he realised Dick was no longer by his side. He swung round to see what had happened.

'We should hurry,' he said.

'You go,' Dick said. 'I think she'll be fine, but make sure Wing Yee takes a look just to be on the safe side.'

'What are you going to do?'

'I shall wait for him to return. Once you've got Charlotte

settled, can you go to the authorities; ask them to send a policeman here as soon as they possibly can.'

*****

Edmund stumbled a couple of times in the darkness, nearly dropping his precious daughter. She whimpered occasionally but still hadn't fully regained consciousness. He decided his best option was to go straight to Alexander's house on Beach Road rather than take Charlotte to the clinic. It was a longer route and despite her small frame he struggled to carry her. When he reached Tanjong Passar, he met some men preparing to take their boats out on the evening tide. One of them offered to help, another offered a fishing net, and between them they made some sort of hammock in which to carry her.

They took it in turns and each time they stopped Edmund checked on her breathing, heaving a sigh of relief when he felt her warm breath, and encouraged the fishermen to hurry. Sweat poured down his face, mingled with tears of relief. Occasionally, the clouds parted and moonlight flooded his path, making his progress easier. He hoped Pieter Steffens wouldn't return to his boat via this coastal route, but nevertheless, he needed to be vigilant.

With all the stopping and checking on Charlotte, it took almost an hour to reach the well-illuminated house on Beach Road. Alexander was horrified when he saw Edmund and the fishermen staggering towards him, carrying a bundle containing goodness knows what.

'What on earth has happened,' he called out as he rushed to help. Charlotte was lowered gently onto a sofa, refreshments were sent for, and then the questions began in earnest whilst the men who had helped returned to their boats.

Alexander listened patiently, waiting for Edmund to recover whenever his emotions got the better of him.

'I suggest you take the carriage and get Charlotte back

home straightaway. May Lin will know what to do, but it won't do any harm for Wing Yee to check on her too once she returns to the house.'

'But what about Chin Ming? She's still at the clinic and I promised to ask to borrow your landau so that I could take her home.'

'And so, you will, but first things first,' Alexander said. 'It's already evening. May Lin will have put William to bed and she can do the same with Charlotte once she is satisfied that no real harm has been done. Look, a little colour is returning to her face and I do believe I saw her eyelids flutter just then. I suggest you collect extra bedding to make Chin Ming comfortable at the clinic for tonight. If she's lost a lot of blood, she won't be strong enough to walk to a point where you can collect her in the carriage. Hopefully, Charlotte will be feeling much better by the time Chin Ming sees her tomorrow.'

Edmund hated all this deception, but he knew Alexander's advice made sense and he would be glad to concentrate on his family. Alexander had promised to help Dick. He would contact the authorities and take a policeman along with him to Telok Blangah. The landau was brought around by the groom and Edmund climbed into the carriage. Alexander carried Charlotte's sleeping body, now wrapped in blankets, and placed her gently into Edmund's arms. They both heard her whimper softly and she settled against her father.

'Walk on,' Edmund heard Alexander say and his groom guided the carriage out into the road. Their pace was kept slow and steady. Edmund hoped Charlotte would remain asleep when they reached home and he handed her over to May Lin's capable care.

CHAPTER 27
8th August, evening

Stefan had never moved so fast in his life. He'd hurried away from the wharf, following dark paths and alleyways to avoid any witnesses. By the time he reached Commercial Road, he was almost sprinting. Although the business establishments had closed and the whole area was largely empty at this time of day, he was desperate not to be seen. He dragged himself along the last section of the journey, arriving at Victor's house wheezing and gasping for breath.

Victor had never seen Stefan looking so dishevelled, what on earth had he been up to this time? Victor was still furious following the interrogation he'd endured from Dick and the castigation he'd received from the village chief; his mood was far from affable.

'What the hell have you been up to? You look dreadful.'

'It was an old score. I had it all planned out, but a problem arose – someone got in my way. You don't need to know the details, but it could be serious if I don't get away from here immediately.'

'Is it anything to do with the fellow who came looking for you earlier?'

Stefan stared straight ahead. He looked like a mouse-deer caught in the light given out by braziers; an animal wanting to run away into the jungle but unable to move.

'Well,' Victor said, 'I'm waiting.' His tone was impatient and threatening.

'Something happened that shouldn't have. They'll blame me when they find her …'

'Find who? What the devil have you done man?'

Reluctantly, Stefan told Victor the whole story. 'So, we have to leave tonight,' he said.

'No, you fool, it's all arranged for tomorrow,' Victor replied, scowling at Stefan. 'When we parted this morning, I made it quite clear that we'd finalise the details this evening. Smith has already sent a message saying we need to be on the Rochor beach at first light. The boat will be waiting in the lanes; a lighter will be sent to collect us.'

'But my life is in danger. If she's dead, they'll hang me!'

'That's not my problem. I'm already in trouble because of you. The headman blamed me for bringing you here, he said I'd brought disgrace to the village.'

'So, what did you say to this so-called visitor?'

'I told him about your boat.'

'What! Why on earth did you do that?'

'I merely said I thought it was moored at Telok Blangah. It will take him ages to find it amongst all the other boats.'

'You idiot! There are only a handful of boats anchored there at present. The Bugis traders won't arrive for another month. I can't go back there now even if I wanted to.' Stefan paced up and down, pulling at his kurta, and glaring at Victor.

'How dare you call me an idiot,' Victor yelled. 'It's you and your stupid plotting and scheming that has caused all the problems. Now we're both in trouble because I was foolish enough to involve you in my business arrangements. That young fellow knows about the smuggling; he threatened to come back and deal with that too.'

'So, he's the one who's been asking all the questions, the man Smith told us about. I might have known – just like the wretched idealist who adopted him! I should have focused on him rather than the brat. I could have dealt with him in some dark alley easily and no one would have been any the wiser.'

'Enough!' Victor shouted. 'It's time to stop all this childish revenge nonsense, we are both in deep trouble and all you do is whine. Given another twenty-four hours, we would be well-away from here; we would be on the boat and heading towards Java.'

'Wait,' Stefan said, looking sheepish. 'You said we'll be picked up from the beach near the entrance to the Rochor River at dawn, is that correct?'

'Those were Smith's instructions. But we need somewhere to hide until then. If that child is dead as you suspect, they'll send a search party out and the first place they'll look for you is here.'

Stefan leapt from his seat. 'The Rochor River? The place where it empties into the sea?' He grinned at Victor. 'I've got an idea,' he said.

Victor let out a long breath. 'What now?'

Stefan told him about the house he once owned along the river. He failed to mention any of the history associated with it. 'It was boarded up when I left and I've no idea what's happened to it since but it might be our only chance. We can lie low until morning and be ready to depart on the early tide.'

Victor turned away. He had an important decision to make. The Java trip was all arranged, but how dangerous was it likely to be? Maybe he could somehow get rid of Stefan, return to Malacca, seek out his old contacts, and join forces with them until the Dutchman had been locked up. In the end, the prospect of making a lucrative profit in Java outweighed the risk. He would take his chances with Stefan.

'Meet me outside in ten minutes,' he said.

*****

Dick pulled out the pocket watch that he'd inherited from Raffles. He examined it in the mooring light of the *prahu* and saw that nearly two hours had passed since Edmund had left with Charlotte; there had been no sign of Pieter Steffens nor any other visitors during that time. Every fibre of his body wanted to move, to pace around on the deck, but it was important to remain still so that he could surprise Steffens when he did show up. Another quarter of an hour ticked slowly by and then he thought he heard someone shout his name. He listened hard; there it was again.

He made his way up the steps without responding, but as soon as he reached the deck, he could see Alexander charging along the wharf. In his wake and noticeably out of breath was a policeman. Dick stood upright and waved.

'So, this is where the Dutchman has been disappearing to,' Alexander said.

'Here and the Malay kampong,' Dick replied. 'This must be the place they told me about when I visited the moneylenders in Market Street. It's where he lived when he first arrived back in Singapore; he must have kept it as a hideaway. Do you think he was planning to abduct Charlotte all along?'

'Who knows how his mind works? I imagine he holds some sort of grudge against the people he believes responsible for his imprisonment: Chin Ming, Wing Yee, possibly you – and Raffles, of course.'

'But that's absurd. Chin Ming and Wing Yee were his victims and Raffles is ...'

'Raffles is no longer with us, but you are associated with him. Why else would he decide to return to Singapore if it's not for some twisted form of revenge. I daresay, he saw Charlotte as a convenient negotiating tool.'

'So why, having gone to all the trouble to abduct her, has he abandoned her? Why hasn't he returned to the boat?'

'From the way she looked when Edmund arrived at my house, I imagine he panicked. He left because he knows he'll be blamed for that bump on her head – especially if he thinks there is any chance that she won't survive.'

'But she will live, won't she?' Dick said, looking alarmed.

'She was very groggy, but Edmund has taken her back home. May Lin will look after her and Wing Yee, too, when she returns to the house tomorrow. Bruises, cuts, and even headaches are easily dealt with. The memory of being kidnapped might not be so easy to overcome.'

The policeman, who had now regained his breath, coughed.

'We're wasting time here,' Dick said. 'If everything you've said is correct, Steffens won't come back here. I think we should head off to the kampong, I imagine that's where he's gone to hide himself away.'

'Very well,' Alexander said. 'But I suggest we leave this man here to keep a lookout. We can collect two more of his colleagues on the way back through the town.'

*****

Victor tossed together a variety of garments, enough to ring the changes between leaving Singapore and arriving in Java. Within them, he hid a bundle of notes and the last dregs of his opium supply. At the last minute, he slipped his gun into the pocket of his trousers. Meanwhile, Stefan returned to his own house, changed into European clothes, packed the rest of his belongings into a seaman's bag, and took a swig of *arak* from his flask. He scooped up his kurta, along with the other Indian garments that had served him so well, and threw them into an old wooden crate, left abandoned in the far corner of the room. He used the steps at the rear to leave the house. Victor was waiting in the shadows.

Stefan was surprised how easy it was to locate the clearing where the path leading towards Rochor began. He'd last used the track when he'd come to this very kampong looking for the brat's mother. He'd been on horseback then and it had taken no time at all, but now the path was little used and the jungle had taken over; the ground was uneven, vines hung down to ensnare their progress, and their hands were cut by the tall *lalang* grass as they attempted to force their way through.

'How much further?' Victor complained. 'Are you sure this is the right way?'

It was already dark when the path came to an end, but the moon appeared from behind a cloud to illuminate what had once been Pieter Steffens' residence. The roof had completely collapsed at one end and the house was no longer boarded up. Stefan lifted his index finger in front of his face, then he pointed towards the steps. Victor hovered in the background, allowing Stefan to creep forward. He tested each of the treads before adding his full weight; they were soft and springy but otherwise sound. He beckoned Victor to follow.

The door gave way effortlessly. It was obvious that the place had been used by bandits or some other type of outlaw since the day Raffles hauled Pieter Steffens away all those years ago. The air was dank and sour. He could see the remains of a hammock dangling from the rafters, some tin plates scattered across the floor, and a battered flagon that might once have contained rum. He kicked the detritus out of his way, causing the animal population that had taken up residence to scatter.

'Not exactly a palace, is it,' Victor said. He cast his eyes around to examine the remains of the furniture and chose a chair that looked more substantial than some of the others; a cloud of dust filled the air as he collapsed onto the cushions. 'I'm exhausted!'

'It's better than sleeping on the beach, I can assure you. You ought to have seen it a few years ago. There were finely -woven rugs from Arabia, vibrant silks and porcelain from China, beautiful pieces of furniture ... I lost it all; Stamford Raffles saw to that. Damn that Englishman and his principles, he ruined everything!'

'And now you're on the run again! You're ridiculous Stefan, or whatever your real name is. And I'm a fool for getting involved with you.' Victor felt the shape of the gun in his pocket. He toyed with the idea of using it, but it was no use. Their argument had frightened the moon away and he could no longer be sure where Stefan was standing; they were enveloped in darkness.

'Shut up, Victor. You need to hold your nerve,' Stefan bellowed. 'Not long now. In a few short hours, we'll be able to breakfast in style and wave goodbye to this godforsaken place.'

*****

The two policemen who had been cajoled into accompanying Dick and Alexander had to run to keep up with them. Alexander, a tall, lithe Scot, and Dick, now measuring almost six feet, easily outpaced the pair who had been rudely awakened from their slumbers when summoned. The sampan that conveyed them across the river had been infuriatingly slow and now the light was fading fast.

When they reached the kampong, Dick asked the first young boy they came across to show them to Victor's house. He vaguely remembered the place the headman had shown him earlier, but it had been daylight then and he didn't want to waste any more time by taking a wrong turning. Several other children joined them, and by the time they reached their destination, a small crowd had gathered. In turn, this attracted the attention of a group of men playing *congkak*. They put aside the cowrie shells and abandoned their game to find out what all the fuss was about. A youngster was dispatched to find the village chief.

By the time the headman arrived, Dick had already searched Victor's house. It was completely empty apart from a few sticks of furniture. The headman led the way to Stefan's abode. It was in a similar state. The only difference was a small wooden crate lying abandoned in a corner of the room Stefan had used for sleeping. The old man strode towards it and raised the lid. He lifted out a dark brown kurta reeking of sweat. He noticed a loose thread that had been pulled near to the hem, spoiling the regular pattern of embroidery. A pair of matching trousers, also smelling unpleasant, appeared next, followed by some brown, leather sandals.

'What does this mean?' he said, addressing Dick in Malay. But rather than wait for answers, he continued to bombard both his guests with questions, insisting that he knew nothing of any illegal goings-on. 'I had my suspicions, of course,' he added, 'but there was nothing I could put my finger on.'

'Nothing to cause you to question them?'

'Not really,' he said, shaking his head. 'However, after you left this afternoon, I began to think. I've been trying to make a connection between the incidents you told me about and anything I'd noticed and thought was odd.'

'And did you find anything?' Alexander asked.

'I didn't even know about the curious clothing Victor's friend left hidden. Presumably, he must have worn those garments himself?'

'Which probably means he's now wearing European clothes,' Dick said. 'We know he always wears European clothing when he goes on an expedition. I'm not a betting man but I'd be willing to wager they're both planning to leave Singapore very soon.'

'Now that I can verify,' the headman said. 'Victor informed me last Tuesday. He said they would be leaving in exactly a week and might be away for several months.'

'I don't suppose he mentioned where they intended to go?' Alexander said.

'Oh, but he did. He seemed quite excited. He said they would be visiting the place where his friend grew up …'

'Java!' Dick and Alexander chorused before the old man could finish, 'and it's Tuesday tomorrow!'

'That means they've gone somewhere to hide overnight,' Dick said. 'It can't be Pieter Steffens' boat – he would have returned there before we left to come here, and there was no sign of him or his friend as we came along the road. Neither will they go to the harbour where their departure would be easy for everyone to witness.'

'I'm told that much of the illegal trade is currently centred around the Rochor River,' Alexander said, rubbing his chin, 'but where on earth would they hide between dusk and dawn?'

'I can't imagine either of them spending the night on the beach,' Dick said. 'Mind you, they must be feeling pretty desperate, perhaps that's where we should begin the search.'

*****

The two policemen had no experience of combing the shoreline; it had never been required before; not by day nor by night. For the first half hour, the party carried torches, but after a little while, Alexander gave the order to extinguish them. With little light to guide them, the policemen could be heard cursing every time they lost their footing in the sand.

'It's imperative we make no noise,' Alexander explained. 'If the men we seek have the faintest idea we are looking for them, they will run, and there is no guarantee we'll be able to catch them.'

Moments later, they reached the banks of the river. They had seen no sign of anything untoward, let alone any fugitives since leaving the lights of the town far behind. Dick was beginning to despair when the heavy clouds parted, revealing a watery moon. It gave out just enough light to confirm the fact that the beach was empty; so too was the ocean. Far away, in the harbour, craft from all over the region jostled for space, but at this point the bay was deserted and the incoming tide brought with it only small piles of shingle. A shiver ran down Dick's spine. It was not far from this spot where he and Raffles had found the exhausted body of Chin Ming all those years ago. It was the morning after she had escaped from Pieter Steffens' house. He took a deep breath. Every sinew in his body tightened. Surely not? The idea's absurd!

'What's wrong?' Alexander whispered. 'Have you seen something?'

'I was just thinking,' Dick said, 'do you know whether the house that Pieter Steffens owned is still standing?'

'I've no idea. It was all boarded up after his arrest. As far as I know, it hasn't been touched since. You're not suggesting …?'

'Why not? Where else is he going to hide? You said yourself that they are most likely to board a ship from around here. It would be very convenient.'

'But how could we find it?'

'There used to be a path along the side of the river,' Dick said. 'That's how Chin Ming got away from him. When he chased her, he assumed she'd followed the road that led back into town, but she chose the route beside the river; this is where we found her.'

For the next few minutes, Dick and Alexander discussed the logistics of finding and following the path. The policemen wanted to turn and run when the plan was explained to them. Neither had any experience of tracking in the jungle, both had been born in the town, and both had an unhealthy fear of wild animals. Alexander gave them no choice in the matter. He explained exactly how they would move along the path, taking advantage of the moonlight, remaining perfectly quiet, and staying close together.

They found the beginning of the path relatively easily. The track was rough and narrowed to almost nothing in places but was not entirely overgrown.

'If this area is frequented by pirates,' Alexander said, 'it's reasonable to assume that they might use the path as a refuge occasionally.'

'Let's hope we don't come across any of them tonight,' Dick said.

*****

They experienced a few mishaps along the way. One of the policemen slipped when he walked too close to the edge and would have plunged into the water had not Dick and the other policeman grabbed him in time.

Eventually, they reached a place where the foliage was less dense.

'There's something dark over there,' Alexander said. 'Could that be the house?'

The moon disappeared behind a cloud. It continued to tease them for a long time. No one moved, they all strained their eyes to search the murky shadows, but they could detect nothing. Dick was about to suggest he creep forward to take a closer look when the moon broke through and brushed the whole landscape with a silvery glow. What remained of Pieter Steffens' house loomed large and sinister against a backdrop of thick undergrowth. The light remained just long enough for them to see that parts of the roof were missing, lianas had penetrated the walls and windows, and the timbers that had once held the door secure were missing.

'I'm pretty sure I saw someone pass in front of one of the windows,' Alexander said. 'I think your hunch was right, this is where they're hiding.'

'How long until it gets light?' Dick asked.

'A couple of hours, three at the most,' Alexander said.

'We know they're expecting to leave for Java tomorrow. It makes sense to leave on the morning tide, just after first light. We don't have long to wait. Accosting them as they are about to leave will be easier than breaking in and risking them getting away,' Dick said. 'And it will provide better quality evidence of their wrongdoing. We'll catch them unawares. I suggest we wait here quietly until we see any sign of activity. We can take it in turns to keep watch.'

*****

Dick and the two policemen were half asleep when Alexander prodded them awake. 'Look,' he said, 'the sky is beginning to change colour, dawn isn't far off.'

They spent the next quarter of an hour discussing tactics. The policemen positioned themselves where they could take hold of anyone trying to escape into the jungle; Dick and Alexander bent low on either side of the path.

Footsteps could be heard approaching long before the blurred outlines of the two men came into focus, their indistinct voices whispering in an agitated fashion. Foliage snapped as it was trodden underfoot; their arrival was imminent.

Dick leapt to his feet and stood astride the sandy path. 'The game's up, Steffens. The ship will leave without you. I'm taking you into custody for....'

The blow hit Dick on the side of his face. He could feel the warmth as blood streamed from his nose and filled his mouth with coppery-tasting liquid. He reeled. Alexander seized Victor to prevent any additional trouble. Victor groaned.

'I knew you were bad news,' he yelled at Steffens. 'I should have got rid of you when I discovered you'd lied to me in Malacca.'

Alexander told the policemen to hold on to Victor and be sure he didn't get away. He tried to grab Steffens, but he was out of reach and hurling insults into the air. Dick ran headlong at Steffens. Steffens kicked. The fight descended into chaos with both men lashing out at each other. Another blow aimed at Dick's torso this time. He stumbled forward. He lay gasping on the ground. He felt as if he'd never breathe again, but he knew he had to try. He had to fight back. He grabbed a handful of sand, used all his remaining strength, and hurled it at his assailant.

Pieter Steffens was blinded. He felt as if his eyes were on fire; he couldn't stop rubbing them, trying to rid himself of whatever was causing the stinging sensation. His vocabulary was ripe, peppered with Dutch expletives which he reiterated over and over again.

Dick struggled to his feet and ran straight at Steffens for a second time. The two of them fell to the ground; Dick jumped on top of Steffens and struck him on his chest. 'You're evil!' he shouted. 'You took innocent young girls'... another swipe... 'from their villages.' He gasped, pounding Steffens on the shoulder whilst continuing to shout. He landed a final blow, this time aimed at Steffens' jaw. 'You seized a small child, and ...'

Alexander stepped between them. He pulled Dick away. 'Stop,' he said. 'We've got what we came for and now we need to take these men into custody. Dust yourself down, and then you can help me.' He produced a length of rope which he instructed the policemen to use to constrain both Victor and Steffens. The two men were cautioned.

It took until the middle of the morning, the men struggling along the jungle path, before they reached a proper road. Alexander gave the order to stop as they approached Bras Basah Road; he recognised his carriage as it turned the corner on its way to Bukit Selegie. Inside, oblivious to all that was going on around them, were Edmund, Wing Yee, Chin Ming, and the baby.

A few people began to take notice of the strange tableau: two men linked together by a rope and being hauled along by two policemen. Some stared, others pointed, but mainly they hurried away. Eventually, Dick led Steffens and Victor through the doors of the jailhouse. There, they were handed over. Each man heard the loud clang of the key as it turned in the lock.

CHAPTER 28

Exactly one week later, the formal investigation into Pieter Steffens' conduct had begun. Dick had accumulated a significant amount of evidence citing Steffens and Victor as partners in crime. He'd talked with Sanjay again and this time made detailed notes of everything the gardener said. Sanjay willingly volunteered to appear in court to speak about Steffens' behaviour in the Calcutta jail and the assault he'd experienced in the Beaumonts' garden. This was the strongest piece of evidence Dick held.

'Feel very bad, sahib,' Sanjay said. 'I should guard Miss Charlotte better.'

'It was not your fault, Sanjay,' Dick assured him. 'Mr Edmund says the same. But if you still feel able to repeat in court the things you've said to me, that would be extremely useful. We can't risk upsetting Charlotte again by asking her to identify him, so your testimony is doubly valuable.'

Sanjay grinned. 'I happy to say same words again, sahib.'

*****

When Dick returned to his office, he went over all the other statements he'd collected. There was a strong case to answer, but did he have enough evidence to convict Steffens once and for all? He wanted to make sure not only that Steffens was found guilty but the sentence handed down to him would be harsh. Transportation to Australia would be ideal with no possibility of him bribing his way out of it this time.

There was a light tap on the office door. When Dick looked up, he saw Alexander standing in the doorway. 'We've got a little more time than we thought,' he said, waving a piece of paper in the air.

Dick stopped shuffling his various notes and charts and raised his eyebrows. He waited for Alexander to continue.

'Murchison has some sort of fever. He's postponing his visit.'

'For how long, does he say?'

'At least another month. He says he now plans to visit Singapore towards the end of September.'

*****

After a week's rest, Chin Ming was feeling much stronger and able to feed the baby herself. Both Charlotte and William had been brought in to see the new addition to their family, but neither child had been as impressed by their sibling as she'd expected. William, at a mere eighteen months, was totally bemused. May Lin lifted him up and he watched as the wriggling bundle, wrapped in a pale-green sheet was introduced to him as his new brother. William pouted, grabbed a handful of May Lin's blouse, and nuzzled his head into the side of her neck. Charlotte's reaction was even more puzzling. After all her earlier protests and pleading for a sister rather than another brother, Chin Ming had been surprised when the little girl came forward, dutifully kissed her sibling, looked up to her papa as if for reassurance, and then ran out of the room.

'Is she upset because the baby has all the attention and we hardly acknowledged her birthday last week?' Chin Ming said, looking concerned. 'I've never known her to be so reserved; she always has something to say.'

'She's tired,' Edmund said, 'she hasn't been sleeping well.'

'Why not? What's wrong with her? Why did no one tell me?'

'She had a headache, but she'll be alright in a day or two. Wing Yee has been looking after her. You mustn't worry yourself; you need to get strong again for all the children – and for me.' Edmund prayed a silent prayer, hoping his wife would not continue with her interrogation. He hated lying, but he was determined to protect Chin Ming from the truth for as long as possible. He searched his mind for something with which to distract her, to take her attention elsewhere.

'Sujana was asking about you yesterday. She was wondering if you felt up to having a visitor,' he said.

'I'm not an invalid,' Chin Ming said indignantly. 'That would be lovely. She could bring Tomas and at least he and William could play together. Or do you think bringing yet another male into the house would upset Charlotte even more?'

'I've told you, my dear, Charlotte is just a little bit under the weather. I don't think she minds that she has another brother rather than a sister, I really don't.'

Chin Ming wasn't convinced, and when Charlotte put her head around the edge of the door a couple of hours later, she beckoned for her to come in.

'What's upsetting you, darling? You don't look like my happy little girl anymore. Can I do anything to help?'

Charlotte hung her head and refused to look at her mother.

Chin Ming waited but there was no sound other than the baby gurgling in the corner of the room. 'Come and sit on the bed,' she said, 'tell me all about it.'

Charlotte climbed onto the bed but remained silent. She twisted the hem of her dress between her hands and kept swallowing hard.

'Is it the new baby?' Chin Ming almost whispered. 'Don't you ...'

Charlotte gulped again. 'Papa said not to ...'

'Not to what? What is it that's troubling you so much?'

'I lost my lovely blue sash, and...' Charlotte began to sob. Her body heaved up and down. She kept muttering something inaudible and tears poured down both cheeks.

Chin Ming pulled herself into a position where she could enfold Charlotte in her arms. She stroked her daughter's hair, becoming aware of the faint aroma of jasmine as she did so; she whispered soft reassurances into her ear. 'It's alright, my darling girl, you are not in trouble. It's alright, my love, it doesn't matter. It's alright Charlotte, we'll get you another sash, even prettier than the last one.'

At that moment, May Lin entered the room and scooped up the baby. Chin Ming was anxious not to upset Charlotte any further, but the promise of a new sash seemed to have appeased her daughter for the time being.

'Time for feed,' May Lin said, making no excuse for the interruption.

'Would you like to watch?' Chin Ming said.

Charlotte nodded. She moved to a small chair at the side of the bed and sat enthralled as her mother took the baby and held him to her breast. She wriggled to the edge of the chair and watched intently. 'Did you feed me like that?' she said.

'Both you and William,' Chin Ming said. 'I've fed each of my babies; I treat you all the same.'

'But this baby has a Chinese name,' Charlotte said, looking puzzled.

'We've called him Soong Heng because he was born in Singapore where most of the population is Chinese,' Chin Ming said. 'He is named after my papa, your grandpapa who arrived back in Singapore the day the baby was born.'

Charlotte screwed up her face while she tried to work out what her mother had said. 'So, William and I have English names because we were born in England?'

'Well, yes, but you have a Chinese name too, can you remember what it is?'

Charlotte squeezed her eyes tight shut but couldn't answer.

She opened her eyelids and looked appealingly at her mother.

'Your Chinese name is Ming Yue, William's is Li Jun,' she said. 'Your name means Bright Moon – just like the silver strands of moonlight you see sparkling on the water in the bay when we allow you stay up late.'

Charlotte's eyes lit up. 'Can I please use my Chinese name now we live in Singapore,' she said.

*****

By the middle of September, Alexander was satisfied that Dick was up to speed with his preparation and ready to take on his role as magistrate, but Dick thought otherwise. 'I'm determined to bring Pieter Steffens to justice,' he said. 'The evidence I've been collecting against him is almost enough to make sure his punishment is severe.'

'So, what's the problem? You could sit with Napier and myself when Kenneth Murchison arrives; your first real hearing.'

'I'm sure that's not ethical as I'm the one who assembled the evidence. When Murchison finds out, he won't allow me to sit on the bench, and I'd hate to do anything that might jeopardise the case; it could even provide a reason to go easy on Steffens. Besides, I've got a better idea; I want to be the person who points the finger at Steffens in the courtroom. I want to present the evidence myself, call the witnesses to support that evidence, and prove to Murchison that Steffens deserves a harsh sentence.'

Alexander smiled to himself. What would Raffles think if he could hear Dick now? How proud he would be of this young man, so different from the shy, insecure boy he'd rescued from slavery in Bali.

'Well, perhaps we'd better have a look at the testimonies you've gathered. If there are any gaps or weaknesses, you still have time to seek out additional proof of Steffens' guilt.'

They sat side by side and began to order the material.

'What's that noise?' Dick said. Through the open door, they could hear raised voices. It was followed by the scurrying of feet across the floor below and then the sound of someone bounding up the staircase. Alexander stood alert, ready to deal with whatever problem was about to be delivered.

A young Indian policeman, fighting for breath, appeared in the doorway. 'The sergeant ..,' he said, gulping in more air, 'say come quick! Prisoner ..., prisoner trying to knock door down!'

Alexander and Dick looked at each other for a moment only. 'You go ahead,' Alexander said. 'I'll assemble a few of the stevedores. If Steffens is trying to escape, which I suspect, we might need some strong men to help us restrain him. I'll be right behind you.'

Dick needed no further encouragement. He leapt down the stairs two at a time, flung open the outer door and was halfway to the jail-house before the policeman, who was out of condition, had reached the bottom step. He was greeted by the sergeant who told him that Steffens had been banging on the cell door, – shouting, blaspheming, and cursing Raffles for over an hour. The noise was intolerable and the sergeant was afraid the wooden boards might shatter at any moment.

*****

Dick approached the cell with caution; the sergeant and two other policemen stood close by.

'You need to stop this noise immediately; what's wrong with you?' Dick yelled above the deafening blows Steffens was inflicting on the timbers. He repeated his command twice more before the dull thudding ceased.

'Why am I still here?' Steffens shouted. 'I know Murchison was due at the end of the month, why have you prevented me seeing him? I'm entitled to have my say!'

Dick asked the sergeant to open the door to the cell, but he was reluctant to do so. Dick insisted. 'I can't conduct a conversation through a wooden barrier. We will both go inside and your colleagues should remain on guard out here.'

The sergeant unhooked his keys from his belt. 'Stand away from the door,' he bellowed. There was a loud click as the key turned in the lock; he pushed the door open slowly. 'Go back to the far side and sit on the bench,' he instructed. Dick and the sergeant entered the cell together; they left the door slightly ajar to allow ready access should the constables need to come to their assistance.

'Kenneth Murchison was unwell, so his visit has been delayed,' Dick said. 'Your case will be heard as soon as he has recovered.'

'I might have known they'd send for you,' Steffens glared at Dick. 'Though what gives you any authority over me I fail to understand. You're no more than a peasant who Raffles took pity on, a bastard I shouldn't wonder! It doesn't give you the right to judge me.'

'You will be judged in the courtroom,' Dick said, 'but I'm afraid your crimes will speak for you, so stop all this hullaballoo. It's your own fault you're in here.'

'How dare you!' Steffens screamed. He launched himself from the far side of the room and took a swipe at Dick; Dick dodged the blow, but it landed right in the middle of the sergeant's stomach.

'Seize him!' the sergeant yelled at his two colleagues. They rushed into the room and pinned Steffens to the floor.

Steffens continued to fling insults at Dick, accusing him of being a spoiled nobody, holding privileges that he should have enjoyed himself. 'I was born to it, but Raffles denied me my birthright!'

Dick noticed a vein throbbing at the side of Steffens's forehead. 'And your animosity has made you a nasty, corrupt man. *You* are responsible for your own downfall, no one else. But even that gives you no right to take out your anger, your bitterness, your resentment on an innocent child. There is no excuse for your behaviour,' Dick said, 'you're pathetic!'

Alexander arrived with a couple of labourers strong enough to keep anyone quiet, but he was impressed with the way Dick was dealing with the situation and decided to remain in the background until he was needed. It took another hour before Steffens finally quietened down. The sergeant delighted in turning the key in the lock once more, but he left one of the constables keeping guard outside as a precaution.

As they moved away from Steffens' cell, they heard Victor call out to them. He'd heard all the commotion and was anxious to distance himself from Pieter Steffens once and for all. He made it clear to Dick and Alexander that he'd had nothing to do with the abduction, and apart from the smuggling business, he had no knowledge of any other crimes Steffens may have committed.

'There's a lot I could tell you,' he said with an emphasis on the word 'could.' A lopsided grin spread across his face; he looked expectant, but neither Dick nor Alexander responded. 'Things I know about him, things about the smuggling business, but I'd want to know you'd show me some clemency before I impart such information.'

'Let's see what you have to say first,' Dick said.

Victor scowled. He considered his options, then he told them about the man known as Smith, naming him as the main contact for smuggling the women. He revealed as much as he knew about the Java trip, and, finally, he verified that Stefan, also known as Kasim, had come to Singapore just over a year ago. He confirmed they met on the wharf sometime in January; they had drunk coffee at Choo Keng's stall, the place where he discovered Kasim wanted to escape from his job with the moneylenders. They had travelled together to Malacca during Ramadan and that's when he began to suspect Kasim was leading a double life.

'Nevertheless, you involved him in your business,' Alexander said.

'At the time, I thought it worth the risk. It wasn't as if someone like yourself - he cast a glance at Dick - was going to be interested in bending the rules a little.'

'So why have you changed your mind?' Dick said. 'By your own admission you are guilty of illegal activity ...'

'But I would never hurt a child!' Victor snapped.

*****

A note awaited them on their return to the office. It informed them that Kenneth Murchison had recovered from his fever and would arrive in Singapore the following week; he would attend to the court cases on the third morning of his visit.

Dick spent the intervening days going over his evidence time and again. He visited his witnesses and prepared them for questioning. Those willing to speak against Pieter Steffens included Mukesh, Sanjay, Choo Keng, Melati, and, finally, Victor. Edmund wanted to appear on behalf of his daughter, but as he still hadn't told Chin Ming about the kidnapping, he secretly hoped he wouldn't be needed. Li Soong Heng had no such misgivings; he was more than happy to tell the court about Pieter Steffens and the part he'd played in his own abduction ten years ago.

*****

The morning of the hearing finally arrived. Alexander Johnston and David Napier took their seats either side of Kenneth Murchison; the rest of the court was hushed. An announcement of the case was read out and Pieter Steffens was led into the dock. His hands were tied behind his back. Chatter arose amongst those who had come to watch the proceedings. The clerk slammed down his hammer onto an old wooden desk, motes of dust filled the air, then all was silent.

Murchison shuffled his papers, Johnston whispered something in his ear. Murchison nodded to the clerk, who read out the charges. Steffens' answer to the question posed was muffled; he was asked to speak up. 'I've done nothing others aren't guilty of,' was all that he was willing to say. Murchison shrugged his shoulders and sighed noisily. He turned towards Dick, blinked, removed his spectacles from the end of his nose, and gave them a polish. When he replaced them, he turned back to Alexander and muttered something inaudible. Alexander merely nodded. Murchison raised his eyebrows; he had recognised Dick from their previous meeting. 'Mr Dick Raf ...,' He coughed before continuing. 'Mr Dick Raffles, you have accused the prisoner of false identity, bringing women into the Settlement for illegal purposes, and the abduction of a child. We have read all the documentation provided. Will you now call the first witness listed in your portfolio?'

Dick got to his feet and paused briefly before looking straight at Pieter Steffens. He braced himself; this was his chance. He was not only keen to uphold the attitudes that Raffles had set store by, values and beliefs he was now proud to call his own, but he wanted to lay down a foundation for the future. It was essential for him to succeed in showing Pieter Steffens to be a villain of the worst sort; a criminal whose behaviour merited transportation to a penal colony. In so doing, he would demonstrate that he was able to do as well as any of the Europeans who now governed the Settlement. One day, he wasn't sure how long it would take, but the local people – Chinese, Malays, Indians – people born here and committed to its success, would take charge.

Determined to ensure Pieter Steffens would be given a hefty sentence and never be able to set foot in Singapore again, he took a deep breath. 'I call Li Soong Heng.'

GLOSSARY

Amah: a girl or woman employed to look after children and some other domestic tasks.

Ang Moh: a phrase used to refer to white people. It literally means "red haired" and is used mainly in Singapore and Malaysia.

Arak: rice spirit.

Ayam kalio: Chicken in spiced coconut gravy.

Bao: A steamed bun stuffed with minced pork, red bean paste, or various other fillings. In Singapore and Malaysia today, the dish is popular among the Hokkien community where it is known as kong bak pau.

Beef rendang: Originally a Sumatran dish. It is a rich curry made with coconut milk and tender beef and served with jasmine rice and steamed greens.

Chetty: Tamils from Southern India who settled in the Malay peninsula in the 18th and 19th centuries.

Eid-al-Fitr: an Islamic festival and general celebration with friends and family to mark the end of the fasting month of Ramadan.

Gambier: a climbing shrub native to tropical Southeast Asia. Local Chinese used it to tan hides.

Indiaman: shortened form of East Indiaman which was a general name for any sailing ship operating under charter or licence to any of the East India trading companies of the major European trading powers of the 17th through the 19th centuries. Vessels carried both passengers and goods and were armed to defend themselves against pirates.

Jamu: herbal medicine made of natural resources such as roots, bark, flowers, seeds, leaves and fruits, honey, royal jelly and eggs.

Jangan takut, anda selamat: Don't be afraid, you are safe.

Kabaya: an open-front blouse secured with buttons, pins, or brooches and adorned with embroidery. It is usually made of a light-weight fabric, such as cotton, brocade, lace, or voile.

Keramat: a shrine or grave that is a pilgrimage site, sacred to Muslims.

Kinta weed: a species of orchid native to the swamps of Malaysia, Thailand, and Vietnam.

Kopi O Kosong: Black coffee [no milk, no sugar].

Kris: a Javanese asymmetrical dagger famous for its distinctive wavy blade.

Kurta: a loose, collarless shirt or tunic worn in many regions of South Asia.

Lalang grass: a species of grass native to tropical and sub-tropical Asia. It can grow to 3m, with narrow leaves which have very sharp tips.

Lily feet: feet altered in shape and size by binding.

Munshi: a Persian word that originally meant writer or secretary but was later used to describe teachers.

Nasi lemak: a dish that consists of fragrant rice cooked in coconut milk and pandan leaf, served with side dishes such as vegetables and egg.

Pelacur: prostitute.

Peranakan: a Malay word that means "local born" and is unique to Southeast Asia. It has its origins in the inter-racial marriages that took place between immigrant Chinese men and non-Muslim women.

Prahu: a fast, sharp-ended rowing or sailing boat that is widely used in Malayan waters and was once popular with Malayan pirates.

Quipao: a loosely-fitted garment that hung in an A-line. Most were made of silk and embroidered.

Ramadan: the ninth month of the Islamic calendar observed by Muslims as a month of fasting [from dawn until dusk], prayer, reflection, and community. It commemorates Muhammad's first revelation, and the annual observance of Ramadan is regarded as one of the Five Pillars of Islam. It lasts twenty-nine to thirty days, from one sighting of the crescent moon to the next.

Yin and Yang: is a concept that originated in Chinese philosophy, describing an opposite but interconnected, self-perpetuating cycle. Knowledge of yin and yang is the basis upon which a diagnosis of disease and illnesses within Confucian-influenced traditional Chinese medicine is developed.

AUTHOR'S NOTE

We now leave Dick, Chin Ming, and Wing Yee to get on with their lives. As readers, you might want to let your imagination take flight; what did each of them do in the years following 1831, and within the constantly evolving culture that would eventually result in present-day Singapore. To help you on this journey, I thought it might be useful to share with you some of the historical facts that occurred in the period immediately after *Living the Legacy* ends.

- In the 1830s, about 200 Bugis craft came to Singapore every season, each crewed by about thirty men. The influx of such numbers often threatened the peace, and although they were forbidden to bring arms ashore, they often ended up in brawls with Chinese middlemen.

- 1832 – Singapore becomes the administrative capital of the Straits Settlements.

- 1832 – A French missionary was granted a site on Bras Basah Road where he established the Cathedral of the Good Shepherd [consecrated 1842], the Convent of the Holy Infant Jesus [1851], and St Joseph's Institution [opened 1852].

- 1833 – Males outnumbered females considerably, almost three to one.

- 1833 – South Bridge Road, built by convict labour, is completed. It became one of the main thoroughfares and was lined with shophouses. The Jamae Mosque [1826] and the Sri Mariamman Temple [1843] were also built here.

- 1833 – Kenneth Murchison [Resident, based in Penang in *Legacy*] becomes Governor of the Straits Settlements and, as such, resides in Singapore.

- 1835 – The poorly-constructed buildings of the Singapore Institution fell into disrepair and were renovated by George Coleman with two new wings added to the original design.

- 1836 – The Armenian Church [first Christian church in Singapore, designed by Coleman] is completed.

- 1836 – George Coleman replaced the market that had been established in Telok Ayer Street [1825]. His version stood until 1876 and has been redesigned/rebuilt many times until it was converted into a hawker food centre in 1973.

- 1837 – St Andrew's Church was built by Coleman, but it was subsequently struck by lightning and demolished. The foundation stone for the new church was laid in 1856.

- In the 1840s, regular steamship services from India, China, and Britain were introduced, but most cargoes continued to be carried in sailing ships for another thirty years.

- 1842 – Mrs Dyers of the London Missionary Society opened a Christian orphanage for girls of all races in North Bridge Road. In 1861, they moved to Sophia Road, and after World War II, it was renamed St Margaret's School.

- 1843 – Munshi Abdullah published his Hikayat Abdullah [the Story of Abdullah, referred to in Chapter 5 of *Legacy*].

- 1845 – The first edition of the Straits Times newspaper is published.

- 1846 - Presentment Bridge [referred to as Monkey Bridge and renamed Thompson's Bridge] was widened to accommodate horses and carriages. Prior to then it had been a footbridge only.

- 1859 – Singapore's Botanic Gardens were established off Cluny Road.

- By the 1860s, many Chinese towkays who had begun as commercial middlemen had diversified into a host of other business ventures that included property, plantations, speculation on commodity prices, and drug peddling.

- 1867 – Straits Settlements becomes a Crown Colony of the British Empire.

- 1867 – Seven Chinese merchants got together to set up Singapore's first traditional Chinese medical institution for the poor.

- 1880 – The first rickshaws are imported from Shanghai.

- 1882 – A new building was commissioned for the National Museum [originally established in 1849 within the library at the Singapore Institution]. It was opened in 1887.

- 1887 – Raffles Hotel is built.

*****

- 1942 – British surrender to the Japanese Imperial Army. During the Occupation, Singapore is known as Syonan.

- 1945 – Japanese surrender; the British return to Singapore.

- 1959 – Lee Kuan Yew becomes first Prime Minister of Singapore.

- 1963 – Singapore declares unilateral independence from Britain and joins the Federation of Malaysia.

- 1965 – Singapore breaks away from Malaysia to establish the Republic of Singapore.

ACKNOWLEDGMENTS

First and foremost, I want to thank a group of writers for the constant feedback and encouragement I have received throughout drafting the whole trilogy and during the writing and editing of Legacy in particular. They are: Carol Cole, Sandra Horn, Valerie Bird, Penny Langford, and Jan Carr. Also to my Beta readers Catherine Avery Jones, Tracy Burge, & Mary Daniel.

My gratitude to the team at Atmosphere Press, especially Asata Radcliff, Ronaldo Alves, and Alex Kale.

Detailed research on the history of the period has been conducted using documents, maps, and historical materials held at the National Library Board, Singapore, and the British Library, London. My thanks go to all the staff at these institutions, people who have patiently searched for – and identified - odd but relevant snippets of information, sketches, lists, and records.

I thank the people who have enjoyed reading *A Strand of Gold* and *Hope Dares to Blossom* and tell me they want to know what happens next. I am grateful, also, to others who have urged me to continue writing and, last but not least, my fantastic husband who is always ready to listen, question, and encourage.

ABOUT ATMOSPHERE PRESS

Founded in 2015, Atmosphere Press was built on the principles of Honesty, Transparency, Professionalism, Kindness, and Making Your Book Awesome. As an ethical and author-friendly hybrid press, we stay true to that founding mission today.

If you're a reader, enter our giveaway for a free book here:

SCAN TO ENTER
BOOK GIVEAWAY

If you're a writer, submit your manuscript for consideration here:

SCAN TO SUBMIT
MANUSCRIPT

And always feel free to visit Atmosphere Press and our authors online at atmospherepress.com. See you there soon

ABOUT THE AUTHOR

ELISABETH CONWAY is the author of an historical trilogy set in Southeast Asia in the early nineteenth century. *A Strand of Gold* was published by Atmosphere Press in 2021 and *Hope Dares to Blossom* in 2022. *Living the Legacy* concludes the story of three young people influenced by the ideals and values of Stamford Raffles, the founder of modern Singapore.

Elisabeth grew up in the Worcestershire countryside but has spent a considerable part of her life in Southeast Asia, which she first encountered as a student of social anthropology.

Her career has included documentary filmmaking and working in the voluntary sector. She now lives in Wiltshire with her husband but returns to Malaysia and Singapore whenever an opportunity presents itself. Her very thorough research takes her to museums, libraries, and a variety of other avenues of knowledge that help with her writing.

Printed in Great Britain
by Amazon

48956096R00189